QUINN

ALSO BY IRIS JOHANSEN

Eve
Chasing the Night
Shadow Zone (with Roy Johansen)
Eight Days to Live
Blood Game
Deadlock
Dark Summer
Quicksand
Silent Thunder (with Roy Johansen)
Pandora's Daughter
Stalemate
An Unexpected Song
Killer Dreams
On the Run
Countdown
Blind Alley
Firestorm
Fatal Tide
Dead Aim
No One to Trust
Body of Lies
Final Target
The Search
The Killing Game
The Face of Deception
And Then You Die
Long After Midnight
The Ugly Duckling
Lion's Bride
Dark Rider
Midnight Warrior
The Beloved Scoundrel
The Magnificent Rogue
The Tiger Prince
Last Bridge Home
The Golden Barbarian
Reap the Wind
Storm Winds
Wind Dancer

QUINN

IRIS JOHANSEN

ST. MARTIN'S PRESS NEW YORK

This is a work of fiction. All of the characters, organizations, and events portrayed in this novel are either products of the author's imagination or are used fictitiously.

Printed in the United States of America. For information, address St. Martin's Press, 175 Fifth Avenue, New York, N.Y. 10010.

www.stmartins.com

Library of Congress Cataloging-in-Publication Data

Johansen, Iris.
Quinn / Iris Johansen.—1st ed.
p. cm.
ISBN 978-0-312-65121-3
1. Police—Fiction. 2. Duncan, Eve (Fictitious character)—Fiction. 3. Women intelligence officers—Fiction. 4. Missing persons—Fiction. I. Title.
PS3560.O275Q56 2011
813'.54—dc22

2011005978

First Edition: July 2011

10 9 8 7 6 5 4 3 2 1

QUINN

CHAPTER 1

STOP ME. FIND ME. KILL ME.

Agony tore through him as John Gallo pushed through the brush, the branches scratching his face as he ran.

How long had he been on the run?

Hours? Days?

And why couldn't he stop?

Why couldn't he let the sheriff's men find him, shoot him? He knew these woods so well that it was easy to avoid capture. Whenever they had come near, instinct and self-preservation had kicked into high gear, and he had fled.

And those instincts were so good, he thought bitterly. They had been honed by all the battles, all the killings, all the ugliness of his life. Save yourself so that you can kill again.

But at least he had not stayed to kill his hunters. That was part of the reason why he had not exposed himself. He couldn't trust himself not to kill them. He was too well trained, too expert in the ways of destruction.

And then there was the madness.

There was no telling where that sickness would take him.

He was climbing, he realized. He was climbing the high hill where he'd done his last kill.

Paul Black. He'd broken his neck.

And Joe Quinn. If he was dead, that, too, could be laid at his door.

He broke free of the shrubs and trees and was standing on the edge of the cliff over the lake.

What was he doing there?

One step, and he would plunge over the precipice.

Why not?

Maybe that damnable instinct would not kick in when he hit the lake below.

"It will, you know."

He stiffened, afraid to turn around to see who had spoken.

Madness. It was back, taunting him, torturing him.

"Look at me."

He slowly looked over his shoulder.

A little seven-year-old girl, with curly red-brown hair wearing a Bugs Bunny T-shirt.

The same T-shirt she had worn the day she had died.

The day he might have killed her.

The agony was overwhelming, searing through him, blocking everything but the sight of her and his own guilt.

His daughter, Bonnie . . .

Milwaukee Airport

Milwaukee, Wisconsin

"YOU'RE JANE MACGUIRE?"

Jane turned away from the baggage claim carousel to see the woman who had spoken walking toward her. It had to be Catherine Ling, she thought. Her adoptive mother, Eve, had described the CIA agent in detail, but the reality was even more stunning. Catherine Ling was part Asian, part Caucasian, and more exotic and magnetic than any woman Jane had seen except on the movie screen. She appeared be in her late twenties, tall, graceful, with high cheekbones, huge dark eyes slightly tilted at the corners, olive-gold skin, long dark hair pulled back in a chignon. But it was the aura of power and vitality that surrounded her that was the most impressive. As an artist, Jane's first impulse was to ask her to pose for her. The second was to squeeze every bit of information she could from her. "I'm Jane. You're Catherine Ling? How is Joe?"

"Is that your bag?" Catherine lifted Jane's suitcase off the carousel with easy strength. "Joe was no better when I left the hospital. But as far as I know, he's no worse. Eve doesn't want to leave him, so she asked me to pick you up. I've made reservations for you at a Hyatt near the hospital. We'll check you in, then I'll take you to the hospital."

Jane shook her head. "To hell with that. I'm going to the hospital to be with Eve. I should have been with her ever since Joe was admitted. It's been almost two days. Why the hell didn't she call me before this?"

"You were in London, and there wasn't much you could do. Joe was in surgery for a long time. Eve said she didn't want to talk to you until she could give you good news." She headed toward the exit. "That didn't happen, so she called you anyway. She thought you should be here."

Jane nodded jerkily. "That's what she said. She was so upset that she didn't realize how that sounded. I felt like I was flying to a deathbed." She took her suitcase from Catherine. "She didn't even tell me what happened with Joe, only about his wound. A knife thrust to the back that did serious organ damage." Her lips tightened. "A knife. Whose knife? I don't want to stress Eve out by asking questions. That means you're on the hot seat, Catherine. I want to know everything before I walk into that hospital."

Catherine nodded. "I thought that would be my job." She stopped before a silver Toyota. "Get in. I'll fill you in while I drive you to the hospital." She slipped into the driver's seat. "But I'm going to go through a drive-through McDonald's and get you a cup of coffee."

"You think I'll need the caffeine to get through this?"

Catherine gave her an appraising glance as she started the car. "I think you're probably a cool customer. But you love Eve and Joe. They raised you from the time you were ten. You have a right to be upset and need a little bolstering." She pulled out of the airport parking lot. "And if you don't, I do. You're going to be pissed at me."

"Am I?" Jane stiffened. "Why?"

"I'm partly the reason Joe was hurt."

"Then yes, I'll be pissed at you. I'll want to break your neck. Is Eve angry with you?"

"No, she says no one could have stopped Joe."

Jane slowly nodded. "She's right. No one could ever stop Joe from doing what he wanted to do. I knew that the first time I saw him. But it relieved me. I knew if Joe ever became my friend, it wouldn't be because Eve wanted him to do it. It would be because he wanted it himself. That was important to me. I was a ten-year-old Eve had picked up from the streets because we'd known the moment we'd come together that it was right we stay together. But Joe was a big part of her life even then. I didn't want to have to walk away."

"And you didn't have to do it," Catherine said. "You became a family." She smiled faintly. "A very strange family. Eve Duncan, a famous forensic sculptor, Joe Quinn, a police detective, and you, a kid from the streets."

"We learned to mesh," Jane said. "Eve was no problem. Joe was slower. But we both loved Eve, so we worked at it." She smiled. "And then as we got to know each other, it wasn't work any longer. Funny how love makes everything easier."

"Yeah, funny." Catherine pulled into the McDonald's drive-through. "Do you want anything besides coffee?"

"No."

"Black?"

"Yes."

She studied Catherine as she gave the coffee order. How much love had Catherine had in her life, she wondered. Eve had told her she'd been a street kid like Jane but had grown up in Hong Kong. She'd married a much older man, then been widowed. She had come into Eve's life when she'd asked Eve to help her find her son, who had been kidnapped by a Russian criminal wanting revenge on Catherine. Eve had helped her rescue him, and they had become close friends. There was no doubt in Eve's mind that Catherine adored her son, Luke. But Jane had gotten the impression that, other than Luke, Catherine's life had been her job as a CIA agent.

"You're looking at me as if you're trying to take me apart." Catherine's look was quizzical as she handed Jane her coffee. "Is it your artist's eye, or are you taking aim?"

"Maybe a little of both." Jane met her gaze. "I admit the first thing I thought when I saw you was that I'd like to paint you. But you'll definitely be on my list for extermination if you had anything to do with Joe lying in that hospital. Tell me what happened to him." She looked away, and added, "Let me start you on the path. It was about Bonnie, wasn't it?"

Catherine nodded. "It's not surprising that was your first guess. I imagine you've lived with Eve's obsession for finding Bonnie since you came to her."

"Guess?" Jane took a drink of her coffee. "Finding her daughter's murderer and her daughter's body has guided her life. It's guided all our lives. She's tried for many, many years to bring her Bonnie home." She looked out the window at the passing scene. "And Joe's been with her, trying desperately to understand, to help, to find Bonnie, so that Eve could be at peace. I can't tell you how many times she's come to what she thought was that final resolution and been disappointed. But she never gives up."

Catherine added quietly, "And Joe was getting tired, weary of worrying about her, wanting her to come to terms."

Jane looked back at her. "Yes, how do you know? Joe wouldn't complain."

"Joe and I are a lot alike," Catherine said. "And I had to examine all facets of Eve's problem before I made a move to ask her to help me find my son, Luke. I didn't want to make a mistake."

"Mistake?"

"I promised her I'd pay her back for helping return my son to me," Catherine said. "She wouldn't accept anything, but I couldn't let it go. I knew the only gift she would think worthwhile would be for me to find her daughter's killer." Her lips twisted. "So that was what I had to give her. Whether or not it might destroy the life she had with Joe."

"You found him?" Jane's eyes widened. "You actually found Bonnie's killer?"

"I found two possibilities. Paul Black, who was already on Eve's search list."

"She told me about him."

"But I was betting on a new stallion in the race. One that would be much more troublesome. Naturally, I had to pull him front and center."

"Who?"

Catherine's eyes were fixed on the towers of St. Joseph's Hospital, which had come into view. "John Gallo. He was Bonnie's father."

Jane stiffened. "What? But Eve told me he was dead."

Catherine shook her head. "A cover-up by the military. Eve will explain everything later. I'm just giving you the bare bones. But there was evidence Gallo was in Atlanta the month Bonnie was kidnapped. So I gave Eve all my information and threw in my opinion."

"And she went after John Gallo," Jane whispered.

"And Paul Black," Catherine said. "But she felt terribly guilty about risking Joe again. So she tried to leave him out of it."

"She should have known that wouldn't work," Jane said. She knew how guilty Eve felt about involving Joe, but she could no more stop hunting for Bonnie's killer than Joe could abandon Eve and stop protecting her. Both were facts of life. "Gallo hurt Joe?"

Catherine shook her head. "Paul Black. And Gallo killed Black."

"Good."

"Not so good. Before he died, Black told Eve that Gallo had killed Bonnie."

"And she actually believed the bastard?"

"She told me that she would swear Black was telling the truth. And Gallo took off and disappeared. Neither the police nor I have been able to find him."

"But what would make him kill his own little girl?"

"He was suffering from bouts of schizophrenia and violent delusions caused by years of mistreatment in a prison in North Korea."

"My God." Jane shook her head. "That must have been a terrible nightmare for Eve. How can you imagine a man who gave you a child could kill it?"

Catherine's lips tightened. "Well, I handed Gallo to her and made her imagine it." She pulled into a parking spot in the lot of St. Joseph's Hospital. "And then I helped Joe try to find him whether Eve wanted him along or not." She turned off the ignition. "Are you still blaming Joe and not me?"

Jane gazed at her a moment. "You're blaming yourself enough. You don't need any help." She got out of the car. "Where can I find her?"

"ICU. The visiting hours are very short, but Eve can watch him through the glass. If she's not in the waiting room, she'll probably be in the hall at ICU."

"Are you coming with me?"

Catherine shook her head. "Eve needs family. I'll check you in at the Hyatt and take your suitcase up to your room. Give me a call when you're ready to leave the hospital."

"Thanks." Jane turned to walk away.

"How did you feel about Bonnie?" Catherine asked suddenly. "I know it's none of my business, but I'm curious. You said that the search for her killer ruled your lives. That must have been difficult for an adopted kid to accept."

Jane shook her head. "I knew what was important to Eve when I came to her. I wasn't her child, I was her friend. That was enough for me. How could I ask for more?"

"Some kids would have been more demanding."

Jane lifted her brows. "You?"

Catherine shook her head. "But then I probably wouldn't have accepted any relationship when I was your age. I was an independent young demon. I suppose I still am."

"Eve is always the exception," Jane said. "You obviously have a close relationship with her now."

Catherine smiled as she started to back out of the parking place. "You're right. You and I are more alike than I would have believed. Eve is the sun we all revolve around."

Jane watched her drive out of the parking lot before she started to walk across the parking lot toward the front entrance. She could feel the tension increase with every step. She was going to Joe, who might well be dying. She was going to Eve, who could lose the man who made her life worth living.

How did she feel about the search for Bonnie? Jane had said all the right things, and they had all been true. What she hadn't told Catherine was the agony she felt when Eve and Joe were put in danger by that search. She could accept it. But she couldn't stop wishing that the search would end.

And she couldn't stop wishing that Eve would release Bonnie.

Or, dear God, that Bonnie would release Eve.

EVE WALKED SLOWLY DOWN the corridor toward the ICU.

Soon she would be able to see Joe again. He'd be pale and drawn, his features appearing as cleanly carved and beautiful as the visage on a tomb. It would scare her to death as it always did.

But it scared her more not to see him and to imagine him slipping away with her not by his side.

That was where she should always be. Next to Joe.

If God would let him stay with her. And if Joe still wanted her if he did come back. The memory of that last day at the lake house was suddenly before her. His eyes looking down at her as she sat in the swing.

"I can't be easy. It's not my nature. But it's my nature to love you."

And it was her nature to love Joe.

Please be better, Joe. Be awake. At least, have more color.

"Good afternoon, Ms. Duncan." The ICU nurse was coming out of the unit. "May I get you anything?"

"Yes, permission to go sit with him."

She shook her head. "Not yet." She hesitated. "But the doctor said that maybe we should let you go to him soon."

She stiffened, her heart leaping. "He's better."

The nurse shook her head. "I shouldn't have said anything," she said quickly. "Dr. Jarlin will talk to you."

Fear surged through her. "You talk to me, dammit. He's worse?"

The nurse was looking at Eve with that same sympathy and kindness that had struck terror in her heart since she'd brought Joe to the hospital. "Dr. Jarlin will talk to you. I'll call him and tell him that you're concerned." She hurried back toward the nurses' station.

Concerned? She was sick with fear.

Joe was dying, and they weren't going to be able to save him. That was why they were going to let Eve go to him. To say good-bye.

She couldn't say good-bye. He had to stay with her.

She leaned her head on the plate-glass window and closed her eyes. She felt the tears running down her cheeks as the agony flowed through her.

Look at him. Surely she'd be able to know, to sense some change. Maybe they were wrong. Doctors didn't know everything.

She took a deep breath and opened her eyes. She stiffened in shock.

Bonnie.

Through the years she had often had visions and dreams of her daughter. Then she had come to believe they weren't visions at all. It didn't matter. Real or not, having Bonnie come to her had made life worth living and let her come alive in so many ways.

But now something was different.

Bonnie, in her Bugs Bunny T-shirt, her red-brown hair shining in the lights of the ICU, as she stood by Joe's bed, looking down at him.

Her expression . . . Love. Perfect love.

Why was she here?

The fear became terror.

To take him away, to ease the transition from this life to the next?

"No, Bonnie!"

Her daughter looked across the room at Eve standing behind the glass.

She smiled luminously. But then turned back again to gaze down at Joe with that same expression of love.

What did that smile mean? Could she help him to live?

Or could she only help him to die?

Eve's palms pressed against the cold glass as tension and sorrow tore through her.

"Joe!"

SWIRLING darkness.

Someone calling.

"Joe!"

Calling him . . .

But he didn't want to leave the darkness. There was comfort here and yet also a strange excitement and anticipation.

Was this death?

He had never been afraid of it. He wasn't now.

But that voice calling . . .

Eve.

She was hurting, needing him. He should go back.

And there was someone else . . .

Bonnie.

She was there in the darkness. Always before she had been the stranger, the one apart; but now she was close, as familiar to him as Eve, and much of the comfort was coming from her. Did she want him to stay in the darkness?

But he could feel Eve's terror and sadness.

He had to stop them both and try to make Eve happy.

As she made him happy . . .

He had known from the first moment he had seen her all those years ago that he could not be happy if he was not with her.

Strange . . . He had not believed that love could come out of nowhere and stay forever. He had been such a cynical son of a bitch. Smart, young FBI agent, sure of himself and everything around him, ready to take on the world.

He'd been certain the Bonnie Duncan kidnapping wasn't going to be a problem. The local Atlanta police were sure that she was the victim of a serial killer, and the little girl would never show up alive. Sad story, but Joe had worked on other serial killings and had experience in profiling as well. He was well qualified to take on the case. He'd go down to Atlanta and dive in and show the locals how the FBI could handle a case like Bonnie's.

But he wouldn't get involved with the family of the victim no matter how sympathetic he was toward them. That was always a mistake. It was better to stand apart so that he could work without emotion. That would be far more efficient.

Yes, after all, it was just one more case. A few months in Atlanta, and he'd be coming back to start another job. There was nothing about this Duncan case in Atlanta to interfere with his career, certainly nothing to interfere with his life . . .

CHAPTER 2

The Past

Federal Bureau of Investigation

Quantico, Virginia

"I HEAR PACKER GAVE you the Duncan case." Jenny Rudler smiled as she stopped by Joe's desk. "I was hoping to get it. There's been a lot of media attention since the kid was taken. I could use a high-profile case. It would help me break through the glass ceiling. But, no, the fair-haired boy was the chosen one."

"Does the FBI have a glass ceiling?"

"You're damn right it does." She perched on the corner of his desk. "Why not tell Packer you need a partner?"

And Jenny would be stepping all over him trying to break that ceiling. He didn't need that. "Maybe next time."

Her smile faded. "Bastard. Damn, you're cocky. You have it all, don't you? Rich kid, Harvard grad, hero in the SEALs. Then you decide you want to be an FBI agent. So everyone is supposed to bow down and give you anything you want."

He held on to his temper. "That's right. But I'll make an exception in your case. I'll settle for you just staying out of my way. I worked for everything I've gotten here at the Bureau. Back off, Jenny."

She hesitated, and suddenly the belligerence was gone. "I'm sorry. You're right." Her smile was dazzling. "I was really upset. It seems as if I'm not getting anywhere, and I'm frustrated as hell. Forgive me?"

He shrugged.

"No, I mean it. Let me make it up to you. When do you leave for Atlanta?"

"Tomorrow."

"Then come over tonight, and we'll have a few drinks."

Which meant that they'd end up in bed as they had a few times before. For a moment, he was tempted. She wasn't bad in bed, and he required sex often and varied.

"You were real good," Jenny murmured. "Maybe the best. We had a good time, didn't we?"

But he didn't need the strings that Jenny would attach to any relationship, even the most casual. He didn't mind paying for sex, but not in the workplace. That could be a big-time headache.

"I'm busy. Sorry."

Her smile disappeared. "I'm not. Who needs you?" She turned on her heel. "There are a lot of people here who resent you and are just waiting to stab you in the back. You'd be smart to keep the friends you have. Have a good time in Atlanta."

Translated that meant go to hell, Joe thought, as he watched her walk away. She had a nice ass. Should he change his mind and go after her? He was always more attracted when there was a challenge involved. That was why he had come to work at the FBI. Life had been too flat after his service in the SEALs.

No, curb that recklessness for once. He'd find enough of a challenge in Atlanta. Probably not physical, but definitely mental.

He turned back to the folder on his desk and flipped it open.

Bonnie Duncan.

230 Morningside Drive
Atlanta, Georgia

IT WAS A NICE LITTLE HOUSE in a nice little neighborhood, Joe thought as he got out of the rental car. Inexpensive, but clean and freshly painted. It had a wide front porch, and red-orange geraniums were overflowing from a hanging straw basket.

A car was in the driveway, a gray Ford at least seven or eight years old. It appeared as clean and well taken care of as the house. Every detail of the house and automobile spoke of meager funds but a determination by the occupants to make the best of what they had.

But in Joe's experience, the obvious didn't always end up to be the truth.

He rang the doorbell.

No answer.

He waited and rang it again.

No answer.

There were reasons why Eve Duncan would not answer the bell, but he still felt a little annoyed. How the hell could he help her if she shut herself away from him like this? Overcome it. Do your job, he told himself. He had to do the interview before he could dismiss Eve Duncan from his mind and get down to the business of finding her daughter's killer.

He went around the house to the steps leading to the kitchen screen door. Through the screen, he could see a woman at the stove with her back to him. He wanted to pound impatiently but instead knocked discreetly.

"Ms. Duncan. FBI. I rang the front doorbell, but no one answered. May I come in?"

She looked at him and turned back to the stove. "Yes, I suppose you may."

He opened the door and entered the kitchen. "I can understand why you wouldn't want to answer the door. I hear the media has been harassing you. I'm Special Agent Joe Quinn. FBI. I wonder if I could have a few words with you."

She glanced over her shoulder at him. "Questions? I've answered millions of questions. It's all in the ATLPD records. Go ask them."

He stiffened as he gazed at her. She wasn't what he had expected. Eve Duncan was tall and slim, with shoulder-length red-brown hair and hazel eyes. The high cheekbones of her face made it more fascinating than pretty. His report said she was only twenty-three, but she could have been any age. She was . . . extraordinary.

Usually when meeting a woman, his first impression was of beauty or ugliness, not intelligence and personality. That came later, along with an evaluation of whether he wanted to go to bed with her. But gazing at Eve Duncan, he couldn't think of single aspects but the woman as a whole being. He was only aware of the tension, the painful restraint, the burning vitality of her. Why couldn't he look away from her?

Get a grip. What had she said? ATLPD. "I have to make my own report."

"Red tape. Procedures." She scooped up the omelet and put it on a plate. "Why didn't they send someone right after it happened?"

It had only been two weeks, but it had probably seemed a lifetime to her. "We had to wait for a request from the local police."

"You should have been here. Everyone should have come right away." Her hand was shaking as she picked up the plate and put it on a tray. "I suppose I'll have to talk to you. But I have to take this omelet to my mother. She hasn't gotten out of bed since Bonnie disappeared. I can't get her to eat."

"I'll take it," he said impulsively as he reached out and took the tray. "Which room?"

"First door at the top of the stairs."

What was he doing? Joe wondered as he started up the stairs. So much for his philosophy of noninvolvement. He had practically jerked that tray out of her hands. Why?

To help her, ease her, make all that pain go away.

Crazy. He had seen Eve Duncan for only a few minutes. Sympathy, yes. That was natural and right. Not this urgent need to banish the torture she was experiencing in any way possible.

Okay, deliver the omelet to her mother and go back down

and interrogate Eve Duncan. No doubt that temporary aberration concerning the woman would have vanished by that time.

He stopped short as he saw a framed sketch on the wall. It had to be a sketch of Bonnie Duncan, but it was extraordinary. The photograph he had in his file was good, but the little girl in this sketch was drawn with such love and skill that it made her come alive.

Who had drawn it? Eve Duncan?

Stop wondering about her and stick to his job.

He knocked, then opened the door. "Mrs. Duncan? I'm Agent Joe Quinn. Your daughter sent you breakfast. May I come in?"

"I suppose . . ." Sandra Duncan was lying propped up in bed, and her Southern accent was much heavier than her daughter's. "But I'm not hungry, you know. I haven't been hungry since Bonnie . . ." Her eyes filled with tears. "I miss her. Why can't you find her?"

Eve Duncan's mother was in her late thirties and prettier than her daughter, but she had none of her strength or that riveting vitality.

"That's why I'm here." He carried the tray over to her and put it on her lap. "That's my job. But you have a job, too. You have to keep up your strength and help your daughter."

"Eve's so strong," she whispered. "I've never been strong. Except for Bonnie. I took care of her when Eve worked, and I did a fine job. Eve told me that all the time. But then somebody took her away."

"But your daughter is still here. She needs you."

She frowned. "Does she?"

"Yes. I want you to eat that omelet and take a shower, then go downstairs and help her. Will you do that?"

"I'd rather go to sleep."

"It doesn't matter. She needs you." He handed her the fork. "We all have our jobs." He turned and headed for the door. "It's time that you did yours, Mrs. Duncan."

"Sandra. Everyone calls me Sandra."

He smiled at her over his shoulder. "Pretty name for a pretty lady. My name is Joe. I hope to see you downstairs next time I visit here."

Sandra smiled tentatively. "You're strong. I like a strong man. But are you strong enough to help Eve to find our Bonnie?"

"If you'll all help me." He closed the door and paused a moment before he went downstairs. Involvement. He should have let Eve Duncan handle her own personal problems. His only duty was to find her daughter's killer. Yet he hadn't been able to resist pushing Sandra Duncan to help her. According to his report, Eve Duncan's mother was a former drug addict who had been rehabilitated at the time of her grandchild's birth. It wouldn't take much for Sandra Duncan to slip back into addiction at a traumatic period like this, and that burden would be all Eve Duncan would need on her shoulders.

Protecting Eve Duncan again. What the hell? The woman hadn't even said a kind word to him.

It didn't matter.

And that was more disturbing than anything about this encounter.

Go down and face her, talk to her, and that weird fascination would probably disappear.

He paused in the kitchen doorway. She was standing at the sink, washing the pan. He inhaled sharply. Impact. Strong. Stronger than before.

Ignore it. It will go away.

"She started to eat," he said as he came back into the room. "Maybe it was the shock of seeing a stranger."

"Maybe."

"And how are you eating, Ms. Duncan?"

"I eat enough. I know I can't afford to lose strength." She started drying the pan. "What do you want to know, Agent Quinn?"

Yes, she was strong. He could see it, feel it. Like a fragile tree that would bend but never break. It hurt him, somehow. He quickly looked down at his notes. "Your daughter, Bonnie, disappeared at the park over two weeks ago. She went to the refreshment stand to get an ice cream and didn't return. She was wearing a Bugs Bunny T-shirt, jeans, and tennis shoes."

"Yes."

"And you didn't see anyone suspicious loitering anywhere nearby?"

"No one. It was crowded. I wasn't expecting anyone to be—" She drew a deep breath. "No one suspicious. I told the police that I wondered if maybe someone had seen what a sweet kid my Bonnie was and taken her away." She stared at his face. "And they only looked at me the way you're doing and made soothing noises. It could have happened that way."

"Yes, it could." He paused. "But the odds are against it. I'm not going to lie to you."

"I knew that. I'm not a fool. I grew up on the streets, and I know all about the scum who are out there." She looked wonderingly up at him. "But I have to hope. She's my baby. I have to bring her home. How can I live if I don't hope?"

He felt as if he were breaking apart inside. He could feel her pain, and it was becoming his pain. "Then hope." His voice was hoarse. "And I'll hope with you. We'll explore every way we can to find her safe and alive. There's nothing I won't do. Just stick with me and give me a little help."

She hesitated, gazing up at him.

Believe me, he urged her silently. Put your hand in mine, trust me, let me guide you. Something strange is happening here, but it's not anything bad. I won't let it hurt you.

She moistened her lips. "Of course I'll help." She stood staring at him for a moment. She could feel it, sense what he couldn't say, he realized. In her pain, she couldn't define the nature of what she was sensing, but perhaps it would become clear to her later.

As, God help him, it was becoming clear to him.

She glanced away from him as she put the pan in the cupboard. "I'm afraid, you know," she said unevenly. "I'm afraid all the time. My mother gave up and just went to bed, but I can't do that. I have to keep fighting. As long as I'm fighting, I have a chance to find Bonnie."

Tentative trust. It was the first step. Come closer. Let me hold you safe from the storm.

But he could only nod, and say, "Then we'll fight together. I'll stay with you until we get through this." He paused. "If you'll let me."

Together. The concept was strange on his lips. He had always been a loner, totally self-ruled, shunning the dependence implied in the word. But he offered it to her.

And Eve didn't even realize how much it meant.

Or maybe she did. There was something in her expression . . .

She slowly nodded. "I think that would be very kind." Her words were oddly formal. "Thank you, Agent Quinn."

AFTER HE'D LEFT THE HOUSE, Joe sat in the driver's seat of his car, staring at the sunny front porch of Eve Duncan's home. There was nothing sunny about anything inside that house, he thought. There was pain and trouble and a woman who was battling just to stay alive after her reason for living had been taken from her. The short time he'd spent with Eve had been full of disturbing images and emotions. Emotions he hadn't expected and had wanted to reject. His responses had been completely foreign to who he thought himself to be.

What the hell had happened to him?

He had felt like Sir Galahad wanting to fight dragons and lay them at her feet. She had moved him, possessed him, and made him see himself in a different light.

It was insane. She was only a woman and one who would bring him only trouble. Dammit, he couldn't even think of sex in connection with her. She was wounded and might remain that way for a long time. Sir Galahad? There was nothing pure about Joe. He was earthy and sexual, and he had always leaned toward being more like wicked Mordred, or maybe Lancelot, who enjoyed toying with a married Guinevere.

Okay, it was temporary insanity. If he couldn't have her,

then what he was feeling would surely pass. That was his nature where women were concerned.

But sex hadn't been the force that drove him toward Eve Duncan. It might have been a light shimmering in the background, but he hadn't been aware of wanting her sexually. And that was a first for him. Maybe it had been there, and he hadn't wanted to admit it.

No, it was something else, powerful, protective, completely without precedent in his experience.

And he wouldn't put a name to it.

If he didn't recognize it, then it might go away. Much better for him. Much better for her. Because he wasn't a man who could let go. Even now he was thinking, planning, how he would keep his promise to her. Yeah, try to walk away from her. Find her kid's killer. Help her to come to terms with reality when she learned her little girl was never coming back.

But don't put a name to this strange feeling that was beginning to disturb him.

Time to stop thinking about Eve Duncan on this level and begin working constructively on her daughter's case.

He drove to the nearest drugstore and placed a call to his contact with the ATLPD, Detective Ralph Slindak. He was glad they'd given him Slindak. He was a good man, and he and Joe had a history. They'd been in the SEALs together though Slindak had left the service two years earlier than Joe. "Joe Quinn. I'm in Atlanta."

"I heard they were sending a hotshot down to shape us up," Slindak said. "The other detectives in the squad were a little pissed. But I told them they had nothing to worry about.

Nothing hot about Joe Quinn I told them. He's cold as ice unless he gets annoyed. They didn't like that either."

"I can always count on your support," he said dryly. "I've just interviewed Eve Duncan. You've been handling the case?"

"Or it's been handling us," Slindak said sourly. "The media thinks that we're blowing it. That's why the captain asked for help. We need to share the blame."

"Great attitude," Joe said. "Suppose we forget the media and just try to find the kid's killer?" He paused. "If there is a killer. You're sure that she won't be found alive?"

"I wish I didn't think that Bonnie Duncan was a victim. Sweet kid. Did you see her photo?"

"Yes." It was in the file, and he could see why the photo was one of the reasons the media were being so tenacious. The child's smile seemed to light up the world, and it had completely touched and captivated the public. "I know that cases like this almost always end with a corpse. But do you have anything concrete?"

"No. Except that there have been several similar disappearances over the last few years in this area. We found one child's body six months ago, a little boy. Butchered."

"Oh, shit."

"Yeah. That's what we thought. And the killings have gotten enough media attention so that Eve Duncan must know about them. She has to be trying to close her eyes and block them out."

"Wouldn't you?"

"No question. I have a four-year-old boy myself, and I nearly threw up when we found that murdered kid."

"You have a boy? Are you married?"

"No, you know me and commitment. But it may end up

that way. She's a nice woman, and we all get lonely." He added, "Except you, Joe. You never needed anyone, did you?"

Not until now. Not until I walked into that house and saw her.

He didn't answer the question. "No clues? No info? He didn't leave any evidence?"

"Oh, we have evidencc. Hc was pretty careless with the disposal of the body, or we wouldn't have found it. But we can't connect it to anyone to make it work for us. We think he's a local since he's been working exclusively in the Atlanta area. We've checked nearby cities, and they have no similar cases during the time span of the Atlanta kidnappings."

"But a big city is better hunting grounds for predators. If he lived in a small town, he wouldn't necessarily do his killing there. Not if he was smart."

"You think he commuted to do his kills?"

"I'm just not ruling it out. I'm not ruling anything out. What about a killer close to the family? Bonnie's father?"

"She was illegitimate, and Eve Duncan never put his name on the birth certificate. She said the father was a John Gallo, who was killed while he was in the Army. It all checked out. Her mother was a possibility since she was into drugs for years, but she was with Bonnie's mother when the little girl was taken."

Think like a professional. Stop trying to protect her. "That doesn't mean anything. Maybe they were in it together and protecting each other. Neither one of them has to be a monster. It could have happened in a moment of anger, when the child was struck, and it ended in death. Then they had to scurry to make up a story to keep themselves from being charged."

Slindak was silent. "You think that's likely?"

Hell, no, everything within him was rejecting the scenario he had put forward. "I'm just saying nothing should be ruled out."

"I think you'd have ruled it out if you'd seen Eve Duncan after the kid was taken. I was one of the detectives who came to the park where the kid disappeared that day. Eve Duncan was terrified. And angry. And ready to take on the world to get her daughter back."

"Then maybe we'll be able to erase her name from the suspect list after we investigate a little further. You've made inquiries of neighbors and teachers?"

"The kid was bright and friendly and loved the whole damn world. Everyone said that Eve Duncan was totally dedicated to Bonnie. She was respected, even admired, by everyone we questioned. She worked two jobs, was finishing college with a 4.0 average, and still managed to be a great mother." He paused. "I like her, Joe. Though she's given our department nothing but grief since her daughter was kidnapped. Who could blame her? I'd do the same. Don't give her a hard time."

"I'm not trying to hurt her. I generally don't like to become involved with the families of victims." That was the truth. "And I can see why you'd admire her and want to protect her." And God knows that was the truth. "If everything checks out, we'll assume that we have a serial killer. I'll check into a hotel, then come down to the precinct and go over the case files on the missing children."

"I'll be here," Slindak said. "We're all working extra hours on this case." He hung up.

Joe stood there for an instant longer after he'd replaced the receiver, thinking about what Slindak had said. Everything that Slindak had recounted about Eve had been exactly what his own senses had told him. She was a victim who refused to be a victim. How could you help but want to come to her rescue? Slindak had obviously had that same response to her.

No, it hadn't been the same for him. No one but Joe could have had this crazy, wild reaction when he'd seen Eve Duncan. It was too bizarre. He remembered what Slindak had said about him.

Cold as ice?

Never in this world. Not where Eve Duncan was concerned.

Two Weeks Later

"YOU SAID YOU'D HELP me," Eve said, when Joe picked up the phone. "All those fine words, and you're not doing a damn thing. Why haven't I heard from you?"

Because he'd been trying to forget that first interview, divorce himself from his reaction to Eve herself, and concentrate on the case. He wasn't about to tell her that concentration had been centered on going through all the files of known child molesters in the Southeast. "I haven't had anything to report to you."

"Well, I have something to report to you. Come and see me."

He stared at the phone after she'd hung up. He could send Slindak.

But he knew he wasn't going to do it.

He pushed back from the desk and stood up. He was feeling alive, eagerness mixed with a low, simmering excitement. This was what he had been waiting for no matter what he had been telling himself.

It was starting . . .

EVE THREW OPEN THE DOOR before he could ring the bell. "You took your time. Come in." She turned her back and strode toward the kitchen. "I have something to show you."

She was the same and yet not the same, he thought as he followed her. She was dressed in khaki slacks and a loose white shirt. The fragile restraint that was so difficult to watch was still there, but she was more forceful. The vitality that had so drawn him was burning high. She was not even quite as pale.

"What are you looking at?" She had turned at the kitchen table.

"You," he said quietly. "You look better. You're still too thin, but you appear to have been eating. That's good."

"I told you that I wouldn't neglect myself. And I'm always thin." She raised her brows. "You probably don't like skinny women. Most men don't. They like boobs and ass."

He was surprised at her bluntness. "I find that thin women usually have a grace and elegance that's appealing."

"Very tactful. Very polite. But I understand that your tastes are definitely on the voluptuous side. So don't be tactful. All I want is the truth from you."

"About boobs and ass?" His brows rose. "And just how do you understand anything that intimate about me?"

"I called your office at Quantico. I told them I wanted to know everything there was to know about you. They tried to put me off and sidetrack me, but I kept at them. I called five times and got different agents. I finally found one who gave me what I wanted."

"And why did you do that?"

"Because you made me believe you." She stared him in the eye. "And I had to be sure there was something to believe in."

"I see. And what did they tell you?"

"More than I thought they would. The person I talked to didn't give me much of an argument. He seemed to be taking a kind of malicious enjoyment from telling me about you. I don't think he was your friend."

"That doesn't surprise me. Who was it?"

"An Agent Rick Donald." She saw his expression. "He doesn't like you?"

"We've been in competition a few times." And Donald had not come out on top. "No one can please everyone. What did he tell you?"

"Part of it was okay. That you've only been with the Bureau for a few years and have already solved three difficult cases. That you were a SEAL and decorated twice. Harvard graduate. Rich boy. Parents dead. You inherited a potload of money and don't need to work." She paused. "I didn't like that. I have no use for a dabbler. But they said when you were on a case that you were totally dedicated. So I guess that's all right."

"I'm glad I don't have to divest myself of all worldly goods," he said mockingly.

"This isn't funny," she said. "I have to have someone who

will take Bonnie seriously. You talk the talk, but I have to know."

"And you evidently had to know about my private life as well. I'm not surprised he told you everything you wanted to know about me. He was probably as amused as hell. I'm just surprised you thought it important."

"It's important. You're good-looking, you're tough, you have a sort of virile magnetism that would be appealing to women. If you liked them too much, then they'd distract you." Her lips tightened. "I grew up in the projects, and I know all about vices. Sex can be as addictive and distracting as any drug. I don't want you screwing around when I need you. When Bonnie needs you."

He looked at her in disbelief. "My God, I feel as if I'm applying for a Secret Service job."

"And you're probably pissed. I can't help that. I have to do whatever needs doing. If you don't like it, go back to Quantico and have them send me someone else."

"I don't like it," he said coolly. "But I'm not pissed. I'm considering the source. But stay out of my private business, or I'll start delving into yours."

She looked surprised. "Really?" Then she shrugged. "But my private business couldn't be more boring. Delve away."

"I'll do that. So I assume I've passed muster if you called me here to chew me out."

"That's not why I wanted you here. I just had to be honest with you." She moistened her lips. "And I had to be sure you'll be honest with me. The police won't tell me the truth. They just make soothing noises and look away. And you said you'd help, but then you disappeared and pretended I wasn't there."

"Oh, I knew you were there." Every minute. Though he'd tried his best to block her out. Now he realized there would be no blocking her out, and they would just have to learn to deal with each other. But this bolder, blunter Eve Duncan was easier to accept than the woman who had touched him so deeply that he'd wanted to scoop her up and heal every wound. He could handle this woman, and it was better for him to keep this aspect of her in the forefront. "I was busy." He added with deliberate rudeness, "I didn't know I was supposed to be here to hold your hand."

She instantly flared. "I never asked you to—I don't want pity. I want help."

"Then tell me how you want me to start. Isn't that why I'm here?"

She nodded. "Yes." She drew a deep breath, obviously struggling to control herself. She looked down at the box of papers and envelopes on the table. "I need you to look at these. I want every one of them to be investigated."

"What are they?"

"Letters. I've received a lot of letters since Bonnie was taken." She tapped one pile. "These are the ones that are from people who say they've seen her alive and well in different locations." She tapped the next pile. "These are the sick ones. Some of them say I'm to blame and should go to hell for letting Bonnie be taken." She moistened her lips. "Some of them are from people who say they took Bonnie and describe what they did to her before they killed her. There are only three of those. Two of them I got the first week, and I turned them over to the police. They checked them out and said that they were nutcases and actually had alibis for the day that Bonnie was kidnapped. The last one I received yesterday. I held it to give to you. I was careful about fingerprints." She gestured to the box. "Take them all."

"You said that you'd told the police about them? The ones where Bonnie had been sighted?"

"Of course, I did," she said harshly. "They said that they'd checked those out, too. I don't trust them. I want you to do it again."

He carefully opened the last letter she had received yesterday and was scanning it. Incredibly ugly. Sickeningly explicit. It must have been pure torture for Eve to read it. "Didn't Detective Slindak tell you to just give the unopened letters to him?"

"Yes. I couldn't do it. They were addressed to me. She's my daughter. I had to be part of what happened to her."

"These aren't part of what happened to her. These are just a bunch of hyenas crawling out of the woodwork and trying to tear you apart. I've seen it before in these cases."

"Have you? Well, I haven't. It's all new to me. So I have to treat everything that comes my way as if it had never happened to anyone else before. Maybe you and the police are taking it too much for granted because you don't have the same perspective as I do. Maybe you're not careful enough."

"I'm careful." He carefully put the letter back in the box. "I'll check these out again for you."

"Particularly the ones where Bonnie was seen alive."

"Particularly those," he said gently.

"I want to go with you."

"That's not procedure."

"To hell with procedure. You said we'd search for Bonnie together. Was that bullshit?"

"No, but I didn't think you'd be this proactive."

"I was supposed to sit here and wait for you all to do everything according to 'procedure'?" Her eyes were glittering fiercely, her hands clenched. "I can't do that. I've waited for her to come home. I've waited for you to tell me you've found her." Her voice was uneven. "I've waited for you to tell me my baby is . . . dead. I can't wait any longer. I have to find out for myself." She took a step closer to him. "Can't you see that? I won't behave like some hysterical female. I won't get in the way. But I have to help bring her home."

She was tearing him apart. What she was asking was strictly against the rules and procedures. He'd be handed a reprimand and could even be taken off the case.

To hell with it. He couldn't deny her the chance she wanted.

He turned away. "I'll drop this last letter off at ATLPD for processing. Then I'll come back and pick you up, and we'll go interview those four people who say they've actually seen your Bonnie."

"I could go with you now," she said eagerly. "I'll just get my—" She slowly nodded. "You don't want to be seen with me while you're investigating. You'll get in trouble. I don't want you to lose your job."

"I won't lose my job. I just want to avoid difficulties." He smiled faintly. "But what would you do if you thought that I would?"

"You've got plenty of money. It wouldn't hurt you like it would some people. Still, it wouldn't be good." She hesitated. "But it wouldn't change what I had to do. I'd just call your boss and tell him that I'd go to the media and tell them how uncooperative the FBI was being with a bereaved mother. I don't think they'd like that."

He chuckled. "Lord, you're tough."

"I told you, I grew up in the projects. I had to fight every day of my life in one battle or another." She turned away. "Go to the precinct and see if they can start the process of finding out anything from that poison-pen letter. I can wait." She sat down at the table and opened one of the envelopes. "I've gone over these letters dozens of times to see if I could find anything in them that would offer me any hope or insight as to where Bonnie might be." Her hands were shaking as she spread out the first letter. "It won't hurt me to go over them again. Maybe I'll notice something more this time. Then I'll phone the people who wrote the letters and ask them for permission to come to see them."

She was sitting very straight, her lips tight, and her gaze fixed on the letter. Her concentration reminded Joe of a painting he'd once seen of Anne Boleyn in a London museum, staring at the sword that was going to take her head. The same fascination, the same resolution, the same tortured bewilderment. It was incredibly painful for him to stand there and watch her. He wanted to reach out and touch her, ease that terrible tension.

She glanced up at him. "What are you waiting for? Go on. We need to get started checking these right away."

And the chances that they'd come up with anything new were poor at best. The sad thing about that knowledge was that in her heart, Eve knew it as well. But he'd be damned if he'd voice it. He turned away. "I'll be back as soon as I can. I'll call you if I get delayed."

CHAPTER 3

7:15 P.M.

Stone Mountain, Georgia

"MRS. NEDRA TILDEN. IT'S THE last name on your list," Joe said quietly. "Are you sure you want to talk to her?"

"You mean because the other so-called witnesses were such disasters? I can see why the police didn't want me involved," Eve said. "Facing the mother of a victim must be difficult for anyone. Two of them were embarrassed about their mistake when I pinned them down to a description of her. The other man was belligerent and just wanted me to go away and leave him alone." Eve was gazing at the cedar-shingled gray house at the end of the block. "At least you haven't said I told you so."

"I'll never say that to you."

"I'll hold you to that." She opened the passenger door. "Let's go see, Mrs. Tilden."

"Eve," he said hesitantly. "According to the police report, she's not quite rational."

"You mean she's nuts?" She shrugged. "That doesn't mean

that I should ignore the chance that she may have seen something. Maybe the police didn't question her thoroughly because she seemed unbalanced." She glanced at him before she stopped at the front door. "I'll go in alone if you think you're wasting your time."

"I didn't mean that," he said. "I just don't want you to be punished unnecessarily." He punched the doorbell. "By all means let's talk to the lady."

It was opened immediately by a small, plump woman somewhere in her seventies or eighties whose eyes were bright as an inquisitive squirrel's. "You're Eve Duncan." Her dark eyes were fixed eagerly on Eve's face. "Come in. Come in. I've been waiting for you. It's about time you came to see me. If I'd wanted the police to come knocking, I would have called them." She glanced at Joe. "You police?"

"FBI." He put his hand on Eve's elbow. "Thank you for seeing us, Mrs. Tilden. We'll try not to take too much of your time."

"I'm seeing her, not you." She gazed back at Eve. "You'd think you didn't want that little girl back. You should have come sooner."

"I'm here now," Eve said. "You said you saw my daughter the night after she was taken? Where?"

"Right in front of my house," the woman said. "It was a full moon, and I saw her walking down the street beside a man. She was wearing that Bugs Bunny T-shirt that the newspapers said she was last seen in."

"What did the man look like?" Joe asked.

"I couldn't make him out. Sort of dark. Tall. The little girl was skipping to keep up with him. She looked like she was trying to tell him something."

"She didn't seem frightened?" Eve asked.

"No. She seemed kind of . . . worried. But not scared." Nedra Tilden nodded. "Why should she?"

Eve gazed at her in disbelief. "She was kidnapped, Mrs. Tilden. Of course, she would be frightened. Perhaps it was another little girl you saw."

Her lips tightened. "Don't you tell me who I saw. It was that Bonnie Duncan. I may be getting a little up there in years, but that only makes me see things clearer. I'm closer to the other side."

"Other side?" Eve repeated.

"Do you think your daughter is still alive?" She shook her head. "It was a spirit I saw. You might as well stop looking for her. It was her ghost that I saw running beside that man and trying to get his attention."

Eve inhaled sharply as if the breath had been taken out of her. "A spirit?"

"I see them all the time. The first one was my first cousin, Edgar, about ten years ago. Then there was my neighbor, Josh Billiak, who was killed in an automobile accident in the next block. After that they just seemed to keep coming. It made me nervous at first, but then I got used to it." She lifted her chin proudly. "I decided that I must be special or something. That's why it didn't surprise me to look out my window and see your Bonnie. No sirree, you're not going to find her alive. She's dead as a doornail."

Joe wanted to strangle the woman. "Thanks for your time." He nudged Eve toward the door. "We have to go now."

"No thanks?" Nedra Tilden stepped forward and grabbed Eve's arm, her dark eyes greedily searching Eve's face. "You didn't want to hear what I had to say, did you? But I did you a favor. You have to come to terms with the grim reaper."

"You come to terms." Joe opened the door. "We'll wait until we have more evidence."

"Wait." Eve pulled away from him and looked at the woman. "You hurt me. Why did you want to hurt me?"

"I only did my duty," Nedra Tilden said righteously. "You have all these cops and FBI people running around and spending taxpayers' money. I barely manage to get by on Social Security, and they're pouring out cash trying to find a lost kid. You should accept that your Bonnie has been butchered and let everybody go about their business."

Eve turned pale. "But I can't accept that." She turned away and walked out of the house. "Any more than I can believe that if she was dead, she'd make an appearance to someone who is as vicious as you."

Joe followed, but stopped to bite out to the woman who was starting to scurry after Eve out on the porch, "Say one more word and I'll have you taken in for a psychiatric evaluation." He slammed the door in her face and ran down the steps after Eve. "Vicious is right." He opened the car door for her. "I told you she wasn't stable."

"That's very close to saying I told you so, Joe," she said dully.

"No, it isn't. I'm just reminding you that you shouldn't pay any attention to anything the bitch said." He ran around and got in the driver's seat. "None of that bullshit was in the police report. Evidently she was saving it for you."

"How kind." She was rigid, staring straight ahead. "I wanted to hit her." Her hands were clenching on her lap. "No, I wanted to kill her. I've seen cruelty before, but not like that. I couldn't understand why she'd do it. I'd never done anything to her, and yet she was drinking in my pain . . . she liked it."

Joe nodded. "That's why I wanted to get you out of there."

"Thank you." She looked back at the porch, and Joe could see her start to shake. She was sitting so straight, struggling desperately for control, but her body was betraying her. "I couldn't understand . . ."

And Joe couldn't take it any longer. He reached over and pulled her into his arms.

She stiffened. "No."

"Shut up," he said hoarsely. "You're hurting, and I'm offering comfort. That's all this is about." It was a lie. But God, he hoped she believed him. He had to find some way to help her, or it would kill him.

She was still, frozen. Then she slowly, tentatively, relaxed against him. "She said 'butchered.'" Her words were muffled against him. "She said my Bonnie was butchered."

"Because she's a crazy woman." His hand was in her hair. He loved the feel of her, the textures of her. Ignore them, help her. "And you handled her; you told her the way it is. I was proud of you."

"I couldn't let her words hurt me, hurt my Bonnie." She gave a long, shaky sigh. "I wouldn't believe the police or you. I had to talk to them myself. And now look at me. I'm acting like a child." She started to push him away.

Not yet. Another minute. Another hour.

Another lifetime.

His arms tightened, then he slowly released her. "You're no child. You're very brave. And I feel honored you let me be here to help you. That's what friends are for."

She met his gaze. "Are you my friend, Joe?"

"I think we're on our way." He pushed back a strand of red-brown hair that had fallen across her forehead. "Don't you?"

She didn't answer for a moment, then nodded. "I believe we may be. It feels very strange for me. I haven't had time for friends. First, I was fighting my way out of the slums, then there was Bonnie."

"I was fighting, too, but not in the same arena." He started the car. "Come on, let's find a restaurant and get some dinner. You haven't eaten all day."

"You don't have to do this," she said quickly. "I've taken enough of your day. You can take me home."

"Yes, I could," he said. "But I'm not. You're going to eat and we'll talk, and by the time you go home, you'll have forgotten that bitch." He grimaced. "Well, not forgotten, but you'll have a different perspective on her. Now, where do you want to go to eat?"

"I don't care."

"I'll pick someplace close to your place so that you can dump me and walk home if I bore you."

She smiled slightly. "That's a good idea."

One step at a time. Just don't let her close herself away from you, he thought.

She was looking out the window. "What if that woman was right? Bonnie could be dead. We both know it, Joe."

"Yes, but we knew it before we went to see that witch. It was no revelation."

"She said Bonnie wasn't frightened. That was a revelation. I pray every night that Bonnie will be safe and not frightened."

"Eve, back away from what happened tonight. She's crazy. And you're crazy to let anything she said linger with you."

"Am I?" She glanced back at his face. "Is it a sign of our budding friendship to call me insane?"

"Damned right. I'm being honest. You said that was important to you. It's important to me, too. Only the best of friends have the guts to tell you the truth."

"I can see that," she said quietly. "But no pity, Joe."

"I wouldn't be honest if I didn't tell you there will be moments that I won't be able to help myself from pitying you. You can only feel what the situation dictates, and this situation pretty much sucks." He smiled. "But I'm a callous bastard. I'll have no trouble keeping it to a minimum."

"Are you callous, Joe Quinn?" She tilted her head. "You don't impress me as being . . . but we don't know each other. All I know is that you've been kind to me."

"Plus all the stuff you managed to squeeze out of the Quantico office," he said. "I'll let you judge for yourself after I tell you the story of my wicked life over dinner."

She smiled. "That will be interesting. It will be good for both of us to think of something besides me and my problems. Are you promising to be honest about that wicked past, too, Joe?"

He nodded. "Every detail."

Being honest about the past would be no problem.

It was the present that would have giant lapses of truth.

One step at a time. Protect her. Help her. Never let her see anything beyond what she wanted from him.

Damn, it was going to be hard.

"I LIKE THIS PLACE." Eve gazed out the window at the Chattahoochee River flowing lazily only yards from the restaurant. "It's peaceful."

"Slindak recommended it." Joe handed the menus back to the white-jacketed waiter. "You've never been here before? He said it was popular, and you're a native."

"I've heard of it." Her gaze shifted back to him. "But it's not cheap, and I'm a single mom with a daughter to support. A night out for me is a visit to McDonald's."

"Then you should have ordered something besides salad and a sandwich. No wonder you're thin."

"I'm not hungry." She looked out the window at the river again. "Atlanta has so many creeks and rivers. I worried about them after Bonnie was taken. I thought what if she wandered away and slipped off a bank and— But then I worried about everything. You never realize how many dangers there are in the world until you have a child." She leaned back as the waiter came and set their salads in front of them. "Growing up, I was totally fearless about anything happening to me. I thought I was immortal—like all kids. Then I had Bonnie, and I found out a pinprick could cause tetanus, a tiny germ could give her pneumonia. So many things to fear . . ."

"Stop looking at your salad and eat it." Joe picked up his

own fork. "And I don't believe you were the kind of mother to hover over her child. You probably made sure that she enjoyed life."

She smiled and nodded. "That was easy. She loved every single minute of the day." Her smile faded. "Past tense. I keep falling into that trap. I mustn't do that."

No, ease her away from it. "You were sixteen when you had her?"

"Yes." She picked up her fork and began to eat. "You know all that from the reports. She's illegitimate, but I made sure she didn't miss having a father."

"I'm sure you did. But you must have missed the emotional support yourself."

"Why? I had Bonnie, I didn't need anyone else." She shrugged. "Stop thinking of me as some heartbroken victim. Sex was the only thing that bound me to Bonnie's father. I made a mistake. Our time together happened like a lightning flash, then it was gone. But I had my daughter and that was all that mattered." A luminous smile suddenly lit her face. "Anyone who has never had a child like Bonnie is the victim, not me."

"I can see that." He had been watching with fascination the play of expressions that flitted across her face. Every now and then he could capture the Eve she had been before she had been forced to face the horror that now dominated her life. "It just surprised me that it happened when you were so young."

"It surprised me, too. I assure you I wasn't prepared to be a mother. All I wanted to do was get out of the projects and build a decent life for myself."

"But you decided to keep her."

"She was mine," she said simply. "I couldn't give her up. You'd understand if you had a child." She tilted her head. "Or do you?"

He chuckled. "You mean you don't know? Rick Donald must have slipped up."

"He said you weren't married, but that doesn't mean you don't have a child." She finished her salad and put down her fork. "I can't tell you how many unwed mothers lived in the projects where I grew up. Men don't have a great sense of responsibility where their children are concerned."

"I'd take care of my own." He smiled faintly. "And, no, I don't have any kids. I've been too busy to make that kind of commitment. And for me, it would be a commitment. I know what it's like to feel like an orphan."

"Oh, yes, your parents are dead. Were you very young?"

"No, it was after I went into the service. A yachting accident. Just the way they would have liked it."

"Weren't you a little old to feel like an orphan? I was feeling sorry for you. I don't know why. You have as much money as Richie Rich."

"Richie Rich? He was a comic book character, wasn't he? Lord, I admit I haven't had anyone compare me to him."

"Bonnie liked those comic books. She thought all the gadgets and toys Richie owned sounded fun."

"I'm surprised you encouraged such blatant materialism."

"Why not? It was a world full of fun and adventure. Bonnie never wanted to own any of the toys. She just liked to learn about them." She smiled. "And they were so outrageous that I doubt even you owned anything like them. Did you?"

"I received a few fairly 'outrageous' gifts from my parents from time to time. Usually, they were sent as a substitute for some trip they'd promised me. Or when I'd been unusually good for a time and not gotten tossed out of the current school of choice where they'd sent me." He grimaced. "That didn't happen often."

"You weren't a good boy?"

"I was a bastard," he said flatly. "My parents didn't care as long as I didn't get in their way. I did that a lot. I was willful and reckless and willing to fight to get what I wanted. It was no wonder that I wasn't welcome in their orderly lives. My father was a stockbroker and my mother was a socialite who did nothing but look pretty and act as my father's hostess, companion, and mistress. They lived smooth, pleasant lives, parties and trips to the Hamptons, journeys on my father's yacht. That's all they wanted, and I disturbed the flow." He lifted his shoulders in a half shrug. "So most of the time, when I wasn't being a son of a bitch, I just stayed away from them. It was better for both of us."

"I can see that it might be. Poor little rich boy."

He chuckled. "Are you mocking me?"

"Yes." She met his gaze. "Because whatever hurt you, you've managed to put it behind you. You can take a little mockery now, can't you? I feel sorry for the boy whose parents didn't want him, but I'm familiar with a lot of those kinds of stories. Most of them didn't include the soothing clink of coins to ease the pain. Sorry if you think that I'm not suitably sympathetic."

"But you're trying to be honest."

She nodded. "I think you were as tough a person then as

you are now. We're alike in that. We've both learned to look ahead, not behind us."

"And you're not impressed by my wicked past?"

"Not as a kid. You'll have to do better than that." She frowned. "If you were kicked out of all those schools, how did you get into Harvard?"

"I cheated?" He shook his head. "No, I'm too damn smart. Things are easy for me. That's why I was so frustrating for everyone. My parents swore I'd never get into Harvard, so I set out to do it. And I made it through."

"Brilliantly?"

"Of course, it wouldn't have given me any satisfaction if I hadn't done it well." He waited for the waiter to change out their salads for the sandwich plates. "My parents wanted me to go into politics. They thought a senator would be a nice addition to their circle. I took a look at Congress and decided that I'd probably be a zombie by the time I was thirty. So I joined the SEALs instead."

"From what I've heard, they definitely don't develop zombies."

"No, I've never felt more alive in my life. They made me into the quintessential warrior, with all the skills and opportunities for battle. I'd found my niche in life."

"Then why did you get out?"

"I liked it too much," he said simply. "And I was too good at it. At first, I considered myself a patriot, and that was okay. Then there comes a point when you know you're coming too close to the line between fighting for a reason and doing battle for the sheer heady love it. If you don't stop before you cross that line, then you become what you're fighting. I was tottering on the brink because I knew I was good enough to let loose all that violence and skill and probably never have to account to anyone. It was a hard decision for me to make."

She studied him. "I can understand how it would be."

Yes, she could sense that streak of wildness and violence in him, and he wouldn't try to hide it from her. She wasn't afraid of those qualities in him. If she was, then he'd have to handle that as it came to the forefront. He wasn't going to lie to her about that side of his character. He hated deceit, and he was having to practice too much of it with her.

"Why the FBI?" she asked.

"It offered a certain amount of action, the technology interested me. I'd always been good at search and destroy. I'm insatiably curious, and I liked puzzles." He nodded at the waiter, who was filling their coffee cups. "And it forced me to be the good guy." He smiled. "You wanted frankness. Did I give you too much?"

She shook her head. "Because you're no saint? I admire the fact that you know yourself and are setting up barricades to be the person you want to be. I don't believe I've ever met anyone who had the discipline to do that."

"Necessity. Everyone has a choice to make about the path they take." He lifted his cup to his lips. "And I noticed that you have a great deal of discipline."

"I thought I did." She took a sip of her coffee. "I'm a mother and a daughter, and I worked two jobs and went to college. That kind of responsibility forces you to develop discipline, or you end up a basket case." She looked down. "Particularly in this situation."

He acted quickly to distract her. "You're a student. What are you studying?"

"Electrical engineering."

"I wouldn't have thought that would be your forte."

"Why not? I'll be good at it."

"I don't doubt it. No offense. But you don't impress me as . . ." He half shrugged. "I saw that sketch of your daughter in the upper hall of your house. It was very good. I can see you as an artist or a designer. But, then, I could be wrong. Am I?"

"You're very perceptive. I've dabbled at drawing in my spare time. When I'm not waiting tables at Mac's Diner, I work for a photographer part-time doing sketches of kids and dogs. Some parents prefer sketches to the realism of the camera. I like it, but I've never been tempted to try to earn a living at it. Engineering is more practical and secure. I have to support my Bonnie." She looked him in the eyes. "If I still have my daughter. That woman tonight . . ."

"Has nothing to do with reality."

"I keep telling myself that. But the reality is that hope might not be enough. Sometimes I wake in the middle of the night screaming." Her hand tightened on her cup. "I don't have to tell you what I'm dreaming. There are monsters out there."

"Yes, there are."

"And you know about them, you've dealt with them. These last two weeks, you've been looking for the monster that might have killed my little girl." She moistened her lips. "I knew that, but I didn't want to admit it. I wanted to close my eyes."

"That's understandable."

"Stop being so damn understanding. I can't close my eyes

after today. I can't rely on hope." She was beginning to tremble. "I have to accept that she might have been taken by one of those monsters. But maybe he didn't kill her. Maybe she's a prisoner somewhere. That could happen." She shook her head and said through her teeth. "Stop *looking* at me like that. I know what the odds are that if she was taken by someone like that she's probably dead. I made Slindak tell me, and he said that almost all children who were kidnapped by those kinds of monsters are killed within the first twenty-four hours. But there's a chance you're wrong." She whispered, "There's a chance I'm wrong."

"Not a very good chance, Eve," he said gently.

"It doesn't have to be a good chance. I'll take what I can get." She drew a shaky breath. "But I didn't bring this up because I wanted you to tell me it was likely that I'd get Bonnie back. I'll follow every clue, every path that could lead me to my daughter alive and well. But I have go down that other ugly path, too. The one you and the police are almost sure that she's taken. Maybe I'll find her there." She smiled with an effort. "But maybe I won't, and then I'll still be able to hope."

"What are you saying, Eve?" he asked quietly.

"You've been searching for the man they think killed those other missing children, haven't you?"

He nodded. "Among other leads. I'm not closing the door on anyone or anything."

"What does that mean?"

He didn't answer for a moment. "I'm looking through records on child molesters." She flinched, and he swore softly. "It's just routine."

"Because the routine has proved valid."

"Yes."

"I want to help you." She held up her hand. "No, not doing that. I'd do it if I had to, but I'll skip that punishment if I can be useful somewhere else. And, I *can* be useful. I want you to give me copies of the cases of those children who have disappeared. I want to study them and see if I can see similarities or anything that might pop up in the way of a lead."

"That's my job, Eve."

"No, it's my job, too. My daughter may have been taken by the same man who killed that little boy who was found by the freeway. If I find him, I may find her." Her jaw squared. "I have to try. If you don't give me a copy, then I'll go to the morgue or the newspaper and ask them to let me study past issues. It will be slower, but I'll still be able to do it. But the police report would give me a head start. Will you do it?"

"I'll think about it."

"I'm putting you on the spot again, aren't I?" She added wearily, "I don't want to do that, Joe. I like you. Maybe I should go check out the newspapers."

"Screw that. I'm not worried about being put on the spot. I'll do what I want to do." He said roughly, "I've gotten to know you. You're going to get attached to those kids in the reports. You're going to identify with the parents. It's going to hurt you big-time."

She just looked at him.

Yeah, what's a snowball going to matter when it's thrown at an avalanche, he thought.

"I can help, Joe," she whispered. "No one would work

harder or concentrate more on doing this than I would. Let me help find my daughter."

"I'll think about it," he repeated. He signaled the waiter for the bill. "No promises."

"And if I don't find Bonnie by doing this, I may discover something that will help those other parents," she said urgently.

"You don't have enough on your plate? See, you're already beginning to worry, and you haven't even started." He reached into his wallet and drew out some bills and threw them on the tray. "Finished?"

"I'd better be," she said dryly. "I have an idea you're about to scoop me up and throw me into the car."

"It's a possibility." He stood up. "You're backing me into a corner, and I have to get some space between us. You're not going to stop. You'll keep coming at me, won't you?"

She nodded as she got to her feet. "I don't give up easily." She preceded him out of the restaurant and paused beside the car, gazing at the river. "You've been very kind to me tonight, Joe. You're right, I'll never forget what that woman said to me. But you made some of the sting go away. I'm very grateful to you." She glanced at him as she got into the car. "And I'm sorry that I'm going to keep on giving you headaches. You don't deserve it."

He smiled. "I can take it. It's nice of you to apologize in advance." He ran around and slipped into the driver's seat. "And this place is only fifteen minutes from your house. I can ward you off for that long."

"I'm done for the night." She added, "I'll call you tomorrow."

And she would, he realized, and keep on calling until she had the answer she wanted. He was only beginning to realize the ruthless determination that existed behind that fragile exterior. "I'll make my own decision, Eve," he said. "I won't let you push me."

"I won't push. I'll just remind you that there's a decision to be made. And I have to keep you on track in case I have to take that other route." She leaned back on the seat and wearily closed her eyes. "I'm so tired. But I learned a lot about you tonight. I know how strong you are. I know you have a balance of values that few people possess. I know there's bitterness and independence and recklessness. You've told me that you could be violent, but you're very protective of me. I feel as if I'm coming close to understanding you."

"That doesn't mean you can control me, Eve."

"No, but it means I can argue and try to persuade." She opened her eyes to look at him. "As friend to friend."

But not as lover to lover.

Get used to it. Accept it. There was no telling how long it would be before she could even contemplate a relationship that held anything beyond the comfort of friendship. But he had made strides in understanding himself tonight. And he was beginning to know Eve as well. Eve, the person, not the object of this crazy fixation that had struck him the first time he had seen her. It was a relief that he actually liked Eve. He appreciated her courage, her discipline, her honesty, her lack of vanity.

What the hell would he have done if he'd found her a complete bitch? Would it have negated that instant powerful attraction? Or had he somehow sensed who and what she was, and that was the reason she had drawn him to her? Who knows? Love at first sight was all very well, but it was confusing as hell and out of his realm of comprehension.

"Love." It was the first time that he had used that word even to himself. It was too sentimental and too much of a commitment. He didn't know anything about it. But what other word could he use for an emotion that made him feel like a cross between a knight in shining armor and a kid with his first crush. Perhaps he'd get lucky and it would go away as fast as it had come.

"Friend to friend?" Eve repeated.

He smiled and nodded slowly. "As long as you realize that it's always a friend's privilege to say no."

"Of course." She closed her eyes again. "It would be unfair to think anything else."

But it would be hard to say no to Eve. Even if he thought that to refuse her might be the best thing for her. "I'm glad that you have such a keen appreciation for justice."

"I do. But I'll still phone you tomorrow . . ."

"YOU'VE HAD THREE CALLS." Sergeant Castro looked up as Joe came into the squad room the next afternoon. "Two from Washington, one from Eve Duncan. They all want you to call them back." He made a face as he handed Joe a slip with numbers on it. "I have other things to do than act as your secretary, Quinn. Where have you been?"

"I was at that park where Bonnie Duncan disappeared. Sorry."

The calls from the Washington office were from Jenny Rudler and Rick Donald. He had no need to return them. It would be Jenny making contact and trying to inveigle her way into the investigation. Rick Donald would have been sly and a little gloating to discuss what he'd told Eve about Joe.

The call from Eve?

He knew what that was about, too.

And he'd been weighing his decision for the greater part of the day.

He stared at the message for a long moment.

Then he turned on his heel and strode out of the squad room.

CHAPTER 4

"CASTRO SAID YOU WANTED to see me." Slindak gazed curiously at the huge pile of reports on the table beside the copy machine. "What are you photocopying? I could have had someone do it for you."

"I wanted to do it myself." Joe turned to face him. "I'm glad you're here. I wanted to talk to you."

"Yeah?" Slindak had picked up one of the sheets. "Kenny Lemwick's missing person's report."

Joe nodded. "And I have the other reports on the other children. I'm making copies of all of them." He paused. "I'm going to give them to Eve Duncan to do a comparison check."

Slindak stiffened. "What the hell?"

"You heard me. I'm going to have her assist in the investigation."

"Are you crazy?"

It was no more than Joe expected. "She's smart, dedicated. I believe she could give valuable input."

"Her kid could be one of those victims. You're asking for trouble. I don't know how your superiors at the FBI feel about family involvement in an investigation, but I could get fired for it if I got caught doing anything that nutty."

"They wouldn't like it either. That's why I'm being up-front with you." He stared him in the eye. "If you want to report me to protect your ass, do it now."

"I'd rather talk you out of it." Slindak scowled. "But I'm not going to be able to do that, am I?"

"No way."

"Dammit, *why*?"

"Eve Duncan has the best reason in the world to find the man who caused those kids to disappear. She'll do a good job."

"But that's not the real reason, is it?" Slindak's eyes were narrowed on Joe's face. "You're not the man I knew in the service. You've always been a loner. There's no way you'd have taken on a partner, not even me. And breaking the rules and involving the mother of a victim? Not in a thousand years."

"People change."

"I can see how she'd arouse your sympathy, but there's a reason for those rules against fraternizing with family members. There are not only the legal ramifications, but their emotional state leads them to act irrationally, and the department might—" He stopped and gave a low whistle. "But you're not just sorry for her, are you? You've got a thing for her. You're doing this to get her into bed."

Joe wished it was that simple. "No." He ran another report

through the copier. "I'd be very stupid to think that she'd hop into bed with me because I'm letting her help with the investigation. You've met her. You know what kind of person she is."

"I know she's desperate. I think she'd do anything to find that kid."

So did Joe. He was trying not to think about it. "I may be a son of a bitch, but I wouldn't try to make that kind of deal with her."

"But she'd be grateful," Slindak said softly. "One thing could lead to another. You like women too much to go the platonic route. Are you fooling yourself, Joe?"

Maybe. He didn't know where this path was taking him. He just knew that he had to follow it. "I'm going to work Eve Duncan and myself to the bone to solve those disappearances. I promise I'll find who is responsible and hand him over to you." He added curtly, "Now are you going to file a report on my making these copies? I'd like to know so that I can be prepared."

Slindak hesitated. Then he slowly shook his head. "I may be sorry, but I'll trust you not to make an ass of yourself and me. Keep her under control." He turned on his heel. "Hell, keep yourself under control."

Joe watched him walk out of the copy room.

Keep yourself under control.

He was trying. It was getting harder by the hour.

EVE THREW OPEN THE DOOR to his ring. "You didn't return my call. Why—"

"I was busy." He pushed past her and strode into the kitchen. He opened his briefcase and pulled out the pile of files and loose papers and dumped them on the table. "The missing children. You wanted them. They're yours." He met her gaze. "And mine. We work on them together."

She stood looking at him, then slowly moved across the room. "I wasn't sure you'd do it." She touched one of the files with a tentative finger. "You didn't want to let me help. Why did you decide to do it?"

"Impulse?" He smiled recklessly. "How the hell do I know? Neither would anyone else at the precinct. My old buddy, Ralph Slindak, had an interesting thought. He said that he believed you were desperate enough to go to bed with anyone who'd give you a chance to find your daughter."

She looked up at him. "He's right," she said quietly. "I wouldn't think twice. Not with Bonnie in the balance. It wouldn't matter at all." She met his eyes. "Is that what you want? I wouldn't think that I'd be your type, but all you have to do is ask."

Oh, shit.

Not his type? If he was going to feel this overwhelming emotional response for her, why couldn't it have been confined to compassion? But even while he felt that pity, he wanted to touch her, put his hands on her, take her to bed, and make her forget everything but him. He couldn't separate the mental from the physical. And the physical was burning hot and trying to submerge everything else.

It didn't help that now when he looked at her that he'd remember what she'd said, that he could have her if that was the price he demanded to help her. Another thought to block, another image to try to forget.

Look away from her. Don't let her see what you're thinking.

"I didn't want to hurt your feelings, but I'm afraid you're right. You're not my type. You look so fragile that I'd be afraid I'd break you." He snapped his briefcase shut. "Besides, I can get a lay anytime." He smiled at her. "I have a lot more trouble keeping friends." He could see relief lessen the tension in her face. "So, if you don't mind, we'll skip the roll in the hay."

"I just wanted to make my position clear. I know I'm asking you to do things that are a little outside the boundaries."

"You're being very clear." Too damn clear.

"I just want you to know that I value you. I felt very much alone before you came. It's better now."

"Then suppose you give me a cup of coffee. Then we'll get down to going over those reports."

"I'll give you the coffee." She went to the cabinet and got down a tin of coffee. "But I'm going to ask another favor. Would you leave me and let me look through these reports by myself tonight?"

"Why?"

"Because I can concentrate better if—" She shook her head as she put on the coffee. "No, I won't lie and protect myself. You were right when you said that I'd be upset when I read about these kids. I can be tough about some things, but not about children. After I get through the reports once, I think that I'll be okay." She smiled with an effort. "I guess I don't want you to see how weak I can be."

"Then by all means read them by yourself. I'm just a guy, and I have trouble coping with tears. I'll come back in the morning, and we'll talk."

"That would be good." She glanced at the files. "There seem to be quite a few. I didn't realize that there were that many cases." She frowned. "I thought I read . . . six? And that included the little boy they found in the grave by the freeway."

"That was all the ATLPD and the media had on their list. But they were all local and within the last five years. They checked nearby cities and came up with nothing. But I found cases in more distant cities in Georgia and Tennessee that I thought were worth looking at. And I dug down another ten years. I ran across a story about the body of a child found in a swamp near the Florida border twelve years ago."

"Fifteen years. You think he's been killing that long?"

"Or longer. It might not be the same man, but it could be. Serial killers like what they do. They tend to make it a life's vocation." He took the coffee she handed him. "You'll find enough there to keep you busy tonight. There are eight or nine that I thought close enough to run a comparison."

"And only two bodies found?" She shivered. "Those poor parents. In agony all these years, not knowing . . ."

"After a certain amount of time passes, just the lack of knowledge is a sort of proof that the child is never coming home. That must be a kind of comfort."

"The hell it is. There's nothing worse than a child who's lost or thrown away like some piece of garbage. A child has value, she should be cared for and brought in from every storm." Her voice shook with passion. "Dead or alive, I'd have to bring my child home."

"Then maybe we can help some of those parents in the reports." He poured her a cup of coffee. "But you need to calm down and get a breath of air before you start. Walk me to the porch."

She took the cup and followed him out onto the porch. "I get too . . . upset. I didn't used to be like this. You're being very patient with me." She leaned against the porch rail and lifted her gaze to the night sky. "Everything reminds me of her. We'd sit here on the steps and look up at the stars and I'd tell her stories about all the constellations and we'd try to identify the Big Dipper and Orion and . . ." She took a sip of coffee. "Sorry. I'll shut up."

"Not for me. She's part of you. And memories can save, not destroy, if you accept them."

"Can they? I only know I wouldn't give up a single memory of her no matter how much it hurt." She added, "My mother doesn't feel that way. She loves Bonnie, but she's trying to block the thought of her. I guess everyone handles grief differently."

"I haven't seen your mother the last two times I've been here. Is she still staying in her room?"

Eve shook her head. "She's been going to church. She was never religious, but a local pastor came to visit and invited her to come to services. I think the congregation has taken her on as a project. They keep her busy. That's fine, Sandra needs people. It may keep her off the drugs. She quit when Bonnie was born, but this is a dangerous time for her."

"What about you? She's the only family you have. She should stay with you and give—"

"Stop being so protective." She smiled and finished her coffee. "The last thing I need is Sandra hovering over me. We're both surviving in the best way we can. She has her congregation, and I have Joe Quinn." She took Joe's empty cup and turned toward the door. "I'll see you tomorrow, Joe. It's time I got to work."

"Good night. Lock your door."

"Why? I'm not worried about being in any kind of danger."

"I know. But I'm worried for you. It's a violent world. Lock your door."

"Whatever."

He watched her as she entered the house and waited until he heard the click of the lock.

No, she wasn't worried. She couldn't care less about her own physical safety. It had no meaning for her in comparison to her loss of her child. He realized that he was the one who was going to have to care for her.

Another duty for him to assume in the emotional storm that had come to him.

Protecting Eve.

Watching over Eve.

Loving Eve.

That word was coming easier to him now. He was beginning to understand the elements that comprised it. Perhaps the fact that he had to block sexual desire made him more aware of what else he was feeling.

But it also made him aware that the storm of feeling was

growing stronger. He was no longer rejecting it. He wanted to go back inside the house and stay with her, be with her . . .

Tomorrow.

He turned and went down the porch steps and strode toward his car.

"COME IN," EVE CALLED, when Joe rang the bell the next afternoon. She looked up impatiently from the papers she was working on as he opened the door. "For heaven's sake, why are you still acting like a visitor? Just walk in."

"I'll keep that in mind. Have you gone to bed yet?"

"For a couple hours. I had to get away from them." She grimaced. "But they followed me. I decided I'd rather deal with them than dream about them. There's coffee on the stove."

"Have you had any?"

"Too much." She nodded at the two piles of files that were in front of her. "I've divided the children into two categories. Male and female. Whoever took these children obviously preferred girls. There are nine cases here, and six of them were girls. But evidently he doesn't entirely rule out little boys." She leaned back in the straight chair. "I had questions. I wanted you here."

"I wanted to be here." He poured a glass of orange juice and brought it to her. "What questions?"

"You know about profiling and all that stuff. You were studying records of sexual molesters." She moistened her lips. "Are these killings all about sex? Is that why he likes little girls? Does he rape them?"

"Probably." He looked away as she flinched. "But it's not about the sexual act as much as it is about power. Most serial killers are addicted to power. Sexual domination is a form of power. Perhaps little boys don't give him the same rush as little girls." He sat down across from her. Look at her. Ignore the fact that every word was hurting her. "Perhaps that's why he butchered that little boy so terribly. He was angry with him for not being what he wanted him to be. But we can't be sure because we've never found any of the little girls' bodies." He stared her in the eyes. "Any more questions?"

"Not for the moment." She swallowed hard. "But thank you for not trying to sugarcoat your answer. I had to know. Then it's all about power?"

"And ego. If a killer has murdered successfully for a long time, then he begins to think he's impervious to capture. He usually develops a pattern according to how often he needs his fix."

"Fix," she repeated. "It's truly an addiction?"

He nodded. "And he'll be as reckless as a heroin addict to get what he needs. More, because he believes no one can touch him."

"A pattern." She looked down at the sheet of paper in front of her. "The dates of the disappearances of the first three girls are approximately five months apart. Janey Bristol, six years, disappeared from Dunwoody three years ago on August 10. Linda Cantrell, eight years, was reported missing on January 30 from her home in Marietta. Natalie Kirk got off the bus but never made it home on June 5." She glanced up. "But the other disappearances were less predictable. The next disappearance didn't happen for another eighteen months. And the next two followed almost immediately. Within a few weeks of each other." She tapped the third pile of files. "And none of these out-of-town disappearances took place during those eighteen months. They were all before the local Atlanta killings started. And there was over a year between those kidnappings. If he's what you say he is, I don't think he was taking a vacation. Where was he? What was he doing?" She added unsteadily, "Who was he killing?"

"That's what we're going to find out. He could have been away from the area. Or he might have been in jail." His gaze narrowed thoughtfully. "First a year, then five months. He's getting hungrier."

"Bonnie would have been three months. So maybe she wasn't one of— I'm trying not to think of Bonnie." She took another sip of orange juice. "That was one of the nightmares I was having last night."

"And my nightmare is your having a nervous breakdown and leaving me without someone to help me find this bastard." He took a pile of files from her. "So we'll both go over these files and make notes and talk about them for another two hours. Then I'll keep on, and you'll take a nap on the couch."

"I won't be able to sleep."

"Then I'll call a doctor and get him to give you a shot. Take your choice."

"We'll talk about it later." She went back to the file in front of her. "What are we looking for?"

"Circumstances surrounding the disappearance. Similarities, indications of any common traits in the victims or family members."

"Family members?"

"It's possible revenge was taken against the child for a perceived slight by the parents."

"Why wouldn't he just kill the parents?"

"It could still be on his agenda. He might want them to suffer first."

"Yes, that would do it." She opened the first file. "That's a lot of things to look for, Joe."

"And better done with a clear head."

She ignored the jab. "How can you continue to work on cases like this? Doesn't it make you sick?"

"Sometimes. But it makes me sicker to know that some arrogant son of a bitch is out there killing whoever he pleases and thinking no one is going to catch him." He was scanning the files in front of him. "Seasons don't seem to make any difference to him. In some instances, killers only murder in certain seasons or time of the month. Here we have victims in summer, fall, winter . . ."

"Maybe they're not all dead," Eve said. "We keep talking about killings. Maybe some of them were runaways or taken by relatives. Maybe they're not— But I have to think of them as victims, don't I? I have to look at these damn reports and think that a monster grabbed them and how and why he did it."

"You don't have to do it. Let me bundle up all these reports and take them away. No one is forcing you but yourself."

"I know that." She focused her gaze on the report in front of her. "Linda Cantrell." The picture of the girl showed a child with dark hair and eyes and a wide white smile. "She was Hispanic, but that didn't seem to have anything to do with her being chosen. The other children were black, white . . . no Asian . . ."

* * *

"I DON'T WANT TO DO THIS." Eve glared up at him even as she lay down on the couch three hours later. "I can keep on going. I don't want to sleep. You have no right to threaten me with your damn doctor."

"No, I don't. But might is always right, and I have the advantage." The sun had gone down an hour ago, and he turned off the lights in the living room. "So go to sleep." He sat down in a chair across the room. "Four hours at least. Then I'll let you work a little longer before I leave and go back to my place."

"Go now. I don't want you sitting there in the dark like a guard at an asylum."

"Asylum. Strange choice of words. Why not a guard at a jail?"

She didn't answer.

"Unless you're worried because you might have a nervous breakdown. Do you think about it?"

"No, I don't think about myself at all. I don't matter. That just came out. Now stop trying to dig into my psyche."

"Naturally, you're distraught, and all kinds of crazy ideas are going through your mind. You're walking a fine line, but we'll get through it."

"We? I'm the one who is walking that line. You're strong and sane, and everything is in control in your world."

"I'll walk the line with you. If you think you're going to fall, reach out, and I'll be there."

She was silent. "Why are you being so kind to me? You're tough and cynical and . . . I don't think that you're one of those do-gooders who want to save the world."

"The world is too big a project. You're damn right I'm not a do-gooder. I usually run the other way. But every now and then, I run across someone who it bothers me to see struggling. I want to see you come out on top of this. It will make me feel good. It's purely selfish."

"Well, that relieves me," she said dryly. "I'd hate being someone's project."

He chuckled. "No chance. You'd toss me out on my ear."

"Maybe not," she said. "I told you that I didn't feel as alone when I was with you."

"Then I may be safe for a while. Until the situation turns around, and you don't need me any longer. Now why don't you stop talking and try to nap."

"I don't want to sleep. You can force me to lie here, but you can't make me sleep."

"Are you paraphrasing that proverb about leading a horse to water?"

"I guess so." She was silent again, and the next words came haltingly in the darkness. "Three months. The pattern is wrong for Bonnie. She has a chance that it wasn't that monster, doesn't she?"

"She has a chance."

"You're so damn encouraging. Give me a break."

"I'd like to give you anything that you want from me. But I won't give you lies . . . or false hope."

"Damn you." She said a moment later, "No, bless you."

"Go to sleep, Eve."

"If I do, the nightmares will come."

"No, they won't. I'm here for you. After you go to sleep, I'll turn on that little stained-glass lamp by the door. If you show any signs of distress, I'll wake you."

"You'll keep them away?"

"I'll guard you through the night."

"I shouldn't be this weak. I hate it. I should be able to handle . . . I *hate* it."

"I know you do. But it's my turn now. When I'm walking my fine line someday, I'll expect you to guard me from the night monsters."

"I'll do it. I promise . . ."

She was still, but Joe didn't hear her breathing even and steady for another five minutes. Then he got to his feet and turned on the stained-glass lamp. He tucked a worn red cotton throw over Eve before he went back to his chair across the room.

He leaned back and watched the play of the soft, colored light on her face. Her cheekbones were more prominent than he had noticed before. She had lost weight in the short time since he had first met her. She couldn't afford to lose it. He had to get her to eat more, dammit.

Eat and sleep so that she could survive.

So that he could survive.

HE DIDN'T HAVE TO WAKE Eve until almost three hours later.

She jerked upright when he put his hand on her shoulder. "No!"

"It's okay," Joe said. "You were starting to breathe hard. I figured that you were being ambushed."

"I was." She pushed the hair back from her forehead. "But you showed up with the cavalry just in time." She swung her feet to the floor. "I need to get a glass of water and wash my face." She glanced at the clock. "I assume I'm being permitted to get back to work?"

"For a little while." He headed for the kitchen. "I'll put on a fresh pot of coffee while you—"

Eve's phone rang, and she picked up the receiver on the chest by the door and answered it. "Just a minute." She frowned as she handed the receiver to Joe. "Detective Slindak. He said you told him you'd be here."

He nodded. "I had to give him a contact number. I was planning on calling him anyway." He spoke into the phone, "Quinn."

"I tried to get you at your hotel first," Slindak said sourly. "You must be burning the midnight oil."

"You might say that. Problems, Slindak?"

"Big-time. Some hunters found a child's remains in a cave in Gwinnett County."

"Girl or boy?"

He could see Eve tense.

"Girl. There wasn't much left of the kid, but the scraps of clothing that remained coincided with the description of what Janey Bristol was wearing when she disappeared. I'm heading out to the crime scene. I thought you'd want to go, too."

"I'll meet you there." He pulled out his notebook and pen. "Give me the directions." He scrawled rapidly. "Is forensics already there?"

"Yes. And the officers who were called secured the area as best they could. There were three hunters who made the discovery, and they ducked into the cave to shelter from the rain. It's still raining cats and dogs up there. They pretty well messed up the crime scene."

"Great," Joe said sarcastically. "Not that it would probably have done much good anyway. The kid has to have been subjected to animal and environmental exposure for all these months. But there might have been something. I'm on my way." He hung up.

"Who?" Eve asked.

"Not Bonnie. We can't be sure. The body is in poor condition, but the clothing would point toward Janey Bristol."

Eve crossed her arms across her chest as if to keep them from shaking. "Six years old . . ."

He turned toward the door. "I'll call you when I know more."

"I'm going with you."

He had been half-expecting it. "This is going way beyond just looking at records, Eve."

"Yes, it's looking at the remains of that poor kid. It makes me sick to think of it. But I have to be there." Her hands clenched into fists at her sides. "I know nonprofessionals aren't welcome at crime scenes. But you've stuck your neck out for me before. Do it now. I won't get in your way. Look, I won't even go to the crime scene itself. I'll stay in the car."

"And you'll still see things you don't want to see."

"So I'm supposed to bury my head in the sand? No, I don't want to see it. But that little girl didn't want to be killed, either. It could have been Bonnie." Her lips tightened in a mirthless smile. "Why not let me go? Slindak should be expecting it. You said he thought we might be sleeping together. He'll just think that I'm getting what I paid for."

"And what if I don't want him to think that?" Joe asked grimly.

She ignored the question. "Take me, Joe," she said urgently. "You knew I wouldn't be satisfied with studying those reports. You knew where this would lead."

Yes, he had known. Why was he even arguing? When he had copied the reports, he had made the ultimate commitment.

One more attempt.

"What would you do if I said no?"

"Follow you."

He turned back toward the door. "Grab a raincoat. It's raining up in Gwinnett County."

THE MEDICAL EXAMINER'S VAN was parked on the side of the road, and Joe drew in several yards behind it. "Stay here."

Eve nodded. "You don't have to remind me. I promised I wouldn't get in your way. I just want to be here in case you find out anything."

"Which will probably be nothing until we get the forensic reports." He jumped out of the car and was immediately soaked by the pouring rain. He followed the glow of lanterns carried by shadowy figures that turned out to be officers moving behind the yellow tape several yards from the road.

"Quinn."

He turned to see Slindak coming toward him. He was

wearing a yellow slicker, but his head was bare, and his hair was as wet as Joe's. "Where's the cave, Slindak?"

Slindak nodded to the left. "Around that bend. It's only a football field's distance from the road. And it's only two miles from a ritzy subdivision. The son of a bitch who killed her has balls of steel."

"He thinks that he's too smart to be caught. Not unusual." But the degree of boldness was not common, Joe thought. "And he buried that other kid beside the freeway. How the hell could he be sure not to be seen by a driver while he was disposing of the body?"

Slindak shrugged. "Nuts." He was sloshing through the mud toward the cave. "But he'd have to be crazy to do what he did to that little girl. She doesn't have a head. At first, we thought an animal had taken it, but we found it on a shelf of the cave. He cut it off and put it on display."

Joe felt the anger tear through him. "Bastard."

"Did you and your lady find anything in those reports?"

Joe gave him an icy glance. "Ms. Duncan worked very hard, but didn't come up with anything yet. And you will speak of her with respect, or you'll find yourself facedown in this mud while I wash out your mouth."

"Hold it," Slindak said quickly. "No offense. I do respect her. I just called it the way I saw it."

And Slindak hadn't been really insulting. It had been Joe's anger at the killing that had become mixed with his annoyance with Slindak. Joe couldn't blame him for reading sexual overtones into his connection with Eve. On Joe's part, those overtones were definitely there, and it wouldn't take a psychic to see them. He just hoped they weren't as clear to Eve. "You saw wrong," he said curtly. "There's no payoff. No matter what I'm feeling, I'm not that much of an asshole."

Slindak shook his head. "You poor bastard," he murmured. "I'll be damned. I never thought I'd live to see it."

"You may not if you keep on talking," Joe said grimly.

"My lips are sealed." They had come close to the cave, and Slindak gestured to the opening. "I think they're ready to bring out the body. Do you want to go inside?"

Joe nodded and moved carefully to enter the cave. Two techs were carefully transferring the body parts to the tarp on the stretcher. The parts were mostly skeleton. The little girl was hardly recognizable as a human being. The anger was searing again, and he took a moment to overcome it before he glanced around the cave. It was a small area, and evidently the child hadn't been buried or hidden in any way. It was a wonder that the body hadn't been discovered sooner.

Again, the killer's boundless arrogance was staring Joe in the face.

"We're ready to go." A young forensic tech kneeling beside the body was looking up at Joe. "Do you need anything else, sir?"

"The skull was on that ledge?" he asked.

"Yep, it nearly scared those hunters shitless," Slindak said. "The field rats had gotten to it."

"Can we zip her up?" the tech asked again.

"Yeah, go ahead." Joe turned away as they zipped up the body bag. "Did we get any footprints besides those of the hunters?"

"A possible near the ledge, but it's badly eroded," Slindak said. "He didn't even try to erase his footprint. It's like the other case. If we could catch the bastard, we could nail him in court."

"He doesn't think we're going to catch him. That couldn't be more obvious." Joe watched the techs pick up the stretcher and carry it out into the rain. They were going to take it to the M.E. van.

And Eve was going to see them put that pitiful sack of bones into the van.

"Is there anything else I should see?" he asked Slindak.

Slindak shook his head. "I just thought you'd want to be here."

"You were right." He turned toward the cave entrance. "Let me know when we get a definite ID."

"That may not be easy. I can't bring in the parents to ID that skeleton. No prints. I can only try to get dental records."

"Damn," Joe said in frustration. "We just had a lecture at the Bureau about the potential for using DNA in identifying victims. But that's still down the road a bit. I want it *now.*"

"I'm satisfied with the old tried-and-true methods," Slindak said. "We get along just fine without your fancy scientific bullshit."

"Except when all you have to work with is a skeleton." Joe walked out of the cave. The rain felt good on his face after the stench and closeness of death inside the cave. He moved quickly through the stand of trees toward the road.

The techs were closing the back doors of the M.E. van as he came out of the woods.

And Eve was standing beside the car, watching them.

"Shit." His pace quickened. He reached her in seconds.

"Dammit, why did you get out of the car?" He opened the passenger door and gently pushed her onto the seat. "You're wet as a drowned rat."

"I had to see her," she whispered. "But there was nothing to see, was there? It looked like a bag full of . . . nothing."

Joe ran around the car and got into the driver's seat. "It wasn't nothing. It was a skeleton, but the bones were . . . not together." He started the car and drove past the M.E. van as quickly as he could.

"Animals?"

"Partly."

Her hands clenched together on her lap. "And what's the other part? Tell me."

"So you can hurt more?"

"So I can know what he is."

She wasn't going to give up. He said curtly, "He cut off her head and put it on a ledge over her body."

She inhaled as if he'd struck her.

"And now you know what the bastard is. Does it make you any happier?"

"No. Poor little girl . . . It's Janey Bristol?"

"We're not sure. There's not much to ID."

"It's going to kill her parents. I want to help them."

"You can't do anything."

"I guess not. I'll think about it. Is there any evidence?"

"A possible footprint. He didn't try to hide what he'd done. He's bold as brass."

"You said that before. Then we should be able to find him."

"We'll find him. Stop thinking about him for a while."

"We may find other bodies. He's being careless."

"That's a possibility."

She was silent for a long time, watching the rain hit the windshield. "I'm glad she was found. She was alone so long in that cave. When we find out who she is, she'll be able to go home to people who love her."

She was identifying the child with her Bonnie, Joe knew. His heart was aching for her, but there was nothing he could do. "I'm glad she was found, too."

"I keep thinking that . . . it might have been Bonnie. I have a chance that she's still alive. But if he did take her, then I have to find him to be sure either way."

And she was beginning to accept that her daughter could be dead, a victim of the monster who had killed the little girl in the cave.

He pulled the car to a stop in front of her house. "Come on. Let's get you inside. You need a hot shower and some rest."

"Go home, Joe." She got out of the car. "I wouldn't put it past you to strip me down and throw me in the shower."

"It's an interesting idea."

"Not really. I'm too skinny for you, remember?" She shook her head. "I have some thinking to do. I don't want you here."

He didn't want her to be alone, dammit. Should he push it?

She started up the steps. "I'll be fine. Stop worrying. I got along before you dropped into my life."

"But not as well."

She turned as she unlocked the door. "No, not as well." She smiled slightly. "Though I hate to cater to your ego. I'll see you tomorrow, Joe."

"I'll call you first thing in the morning. I want you to tell me that you slept a little."

"I'll work on it."

"But you're going back to those reports."

"He's a monster, Joe," she said quietly. "He might be *my* monster. We have to stop him." She disappeared into the house.

Joe waited until the lights went on inside before he pulled away from the curb. He couldn't force her to let him help her. He'd already invaded her space and compromised her independence. It was a wonder that she hadn't rebelled against him before. He'd go back to the precinct and see if any of the forensic reports were completed yet.

Whether the man who killed that little girl in the cave was Eve's monster or not, he was definitely a monster. Joe could feel the anger tear through him as he remembered the hideously macabre scene in the cave.

Get to work. Show the bastard he wasn't as invulnerable as he thought he was. Joe felt a familiar exhilaration mix with the rage. The warrior instinct that had been a part of his life for years was starting to simmer.

Yes, he was in the mood for hunting monsters.

CHAPTER 5

JOE THREW A FOLDED NEWSPAPER on the table in front of Eve the next morning. "The media got hold of the story. Interviews with the hunters. Descriptions of what they saw in the cave. *Damn* them. We hadn't yet notified the Bristols that it might be their daughter. We were waiting to check with her dentist. The phones have been ringing off the hook from parents of those kidnapped kids, and we can't even tell them yes or no."

Eve opened the newspaper and shook her head. "Why didn't they wait? This is cruel."

"It's a scoop. The reporter wanted to get ahead of the competition. The bastard will do anything for a story."

"Brian McVey," Eve read the byline. "I hope he's happy about this ugliness." She looked up at him. "How long before you get a confirmation on the dental records?"

"This afternoon." His lips tightened grimly. "And the information will not go to Brian McVey. We'll leave him so far out in the cold, he'll freeze to death." He looked at the files in front of her. "Did you find anything?"

"All the children were in the age brackets from four to eight, all of them were from middle- to high-income families, all of them lived in homes in nice subdivisions." She looked up. "Except Bonnie. I'm poor as dirt, and this is a rental property. It's nicer than anywhere I've lived before, but it doesn't compare with one of those houses in Towne Lake or Chestnut Hill subdivisions. I was very happy when I saw that she didn't make the A-list. That's two things that are different: three months between the kidnappings, and the kind of place where she lived. It may not seem a lot to you, but to me it's gigantic."

"It's gigantic to me, too," he said gently. "Anything else?"

"Not yet." She leaned back in the chair. "What about the footprint in the cave?"

"We're working on it. It's not the usual shoe. It's rubberized . . ."

"A tennis shoe?"

"Not exactly. The pattern is different . . . We're working on it. We'll get there. I'm going to go to a shoe manufacturer downtown when I leave here and see if he can identify it." He was glancing through the reports. "But first, why don't we go and take a look at these houses."

"Why?"

"These are the kids' home bases. Children stay close to their home at this age. It's where they may have been kidnapped."

"But according to the reports, only two of the parents think their child was taken from the neighborhood."

"We'll still take a look." He turned. "If you want to go with me."

"Of course, I do." She was beside him in a moment. "And to the shoe factory, too."

He shrugged. "Just routine investigation. I could just as well phone you after I finish."

"Nothing is routine." She got into the car. "I've forgotten what the word means."

So had Joe. Since the moment he had met her, nothing had been routine or commonplace in his life. "Where, first?"

"Chestnut Hills. Linda Cantrell. It's in Kennesaw."

His brows lifted. "You rattled that off. I'm surprised you haven't memorized the address."

"I have. I've memorized all of them. I'll tell you when we're closer."

"THE HOUSES ARE ALL DIFFERENT styles," Eve said. "Tudors, modern, cottage . . ." Her gaze wandered over the neat lush lawn and clipped bushes that surrounded Nita Teller's home. "Small, medium, large . . . As home bases, they have very little in common. They're just pleasant houses in suburban neighborhoods. I think we struck out."

"Maybe. Maybe not." Joe was staring thoughtfully at the house. "I can't put my finger on it right now, but something may strike me later. What's next?"

"Janey Bristol. She's the last one in Atlanta. The others are from your list of outside the city. She's about five miles from here, in Roswell. Do we have time before we go downtown to that shoe company?"

Joe nodded. "We got through these neighborhoods quickly. You had them organized very efficiently."

She handed him the address. "I put her last. I guess I wasn't very eager to imagine Janey where she was happiest. It hurts after last night." She tilted her head. "You're very thoughtful. You do think this was helpful?"

"As I said, sometime something sticks in your mind, then it comes together later."

"You're very good at this, aren't you?"

He smiled. "Hell, yes."

"And so modest."

"I've never lacked an appreciation for my own worth. I see nothing wrong in confidence as long as it's not misplaced."

"Neither do I. It was the first thing I noticed about you," she said quietly. "I wanted the FBI to send an older agent. Someone who had worlds of experience and could use it to find Bonnie. I was angry that instead they sent me a young man who acted as if he knew how to shape the world to suit himself. You were good-looking, tough, smart, and oozed assurance. I wanted to kick you."

"I appreciate your restraint."

"And then I saw something in you. And I thought that maybe it would be okay between us."

"And it is." He glanced at the address again. "The Bristol subdivision should be just ahead."

She tensed. "Last night I kept thinking of that skeleton and the skull. I couldn't get it out of my mind. I kept thinking how I'd feel if that was all I had left of Bonnie."

"And it tore you to pieces."

"Yes, that goes without saying. But I wanted to help the Bristols. And there was nothing that I could do." Her smile was bittersweet. "I almost feel as if we're all a family who have been visited by some catastrophic disease and have to nurse each other through it."

Joe turned into the subdivision. "I think you have enough on your plate without trying to cure all those other victims."

"There is no cure except catching that monster. I believe we have to— What on earth!"

Joe muttered a curse as he stomped on the brakes. The street before the Bristol house was full of cars and media vans. Three ATLPD squad cars were in the driveway. "Son of a bitch, someone must have leaked the information about Janey Bristol to the media. We weren't even supposed to have a dental confirmation until later today."

"It looks like those reporters are on the family like locusts," Eve said. "Can't you keep them away from them? It nearly killed me to have to deal with them after I first lost Bonnie."

"I can knock a couple of heads together and end up in court. I may do it. But you can't interfere with the freedom of the press." He stiffened as he saw someone get out of one of the squad cars. "There's Slindak. What the hell is he doing here?" He rolled down the window. "Slindak!"

Slindak turned at his call and strode over to the car. "How did you hear about this mess, Quinn?"

"What are you talking about? Did someone leak the results on the Bristol dental records?"

Slindak shook his head. "We haven't heard anything yet." He glanced at Eve. "She shouldn't be here. Those reporters are going to recognize her, and they'll surround her like sharks. I'll get someone to take her home. I need you inside, Quinn."

He nodded as he jumped out of the car. "Why? What's going on?"

"Ellen Bristol answered the phone this morning. It was a phone call from a man who claimed he was the one who killed her daughter. He told her that Janey was the victim that they found in the cave." His lips tightened grimly. "And then he gave her details about exactly what he did to her child."

"Oh, my God," Eve whispered.

"She collapsed, and her husband grabbed the phone. But the man had hung up. Ellen Bristol is hysterical, and her husband isn't much better." Slindak muttered a curse as he heard an outcry from the reporters, who were running across the lawn toward them. "Get her out of that car and inside the house! They've recognized me."

Joe was already around the car and jerking open Eve's door. "Come on, move."

Eve was out of the car and running toward the front door.

But she was too late. They'd recognized Eve as well. She was surrounded by reporters and photographers. Bulbs were flashing in her face. Questions were being hammered at her.

"What are you doing here, Ms. Duncan?"

"Did you receive a similar call?"

"Has your daughter's body been found?"

"No comment." Joe muscled his way through the mob and took her wrist and pulled her toward the front door. "She's just here as a gesture of sympathy toward the Bristols. Now give her space, dammit."

"Inside." Slindak was throwing open the front door.

Joe pushed Eve over the threshold, then followed her and turned to the reporters. "You'll get a story when we have one to give." He slammed the door.

Eve was pressed against the wall of the foyer. She shuddered. "I felt as if they were going to devour me."

"No wonder you were so wary of the media when I first came down here." He turned to a tall, dark-haired officer who was standing attention just inside the living room. "Where is Mrs. Bristol?"

"Upstairs with the doctor and her husband, Agent Quinn." The officer shook his head. "She's in a bad way."

"What a surprise." Eve drew a ragged breath. "I'm surprised she's not in the hospital. But what I want to know is how all those reporters knew about that call. Surely the Bristols didn't phone them."

"You'll have to ask Detective Slindak."

"I intend to do that," Joe said. "Do you know when the Bristols received the call?"

"About nine forty this morning. We were called in about ten. The media started arriving about ten fifty-five. It was all happening pretty—"

"Shit." Slindak barreled through the door and slammed it behind him. "I feel like a damned rock star. They were practically tearing me apart." He looked at Eve. "Are you all right?"

She nodded. "I should be used to it. But I'm not."

"I'll have an officer drive you home as soon as I can."

"No, you won't," Joe said. "They'll follow and camp out. I'll find someplace else for her."

"That doesn't matter," Eve said impatiently. "What happened here? How did those reporters know that Ellen Bristol got that call?"

"They got calls themselves. At least CNN and the *Atlanta Constitution* received calls from the killer. The other stations were tipped off when they started moving."

"What kind of calls?" Joe asked.

"Similar to the one Ellen Bristol received." Slindak paused. "And they were told that Ellen Bristol had been phoned. I suppose just to make sure that she was roasted over the flames a little more."

"How vindictive can you be?" Eve asked.

"Evidently there aren't any bounds," Joe said. "What was the content of the call? Are we sure it wasn't just some weirdo wanting to take credit for the murder? He could have read the newspaper account the hunters had given."

Slindak shook his head. "He knew other details. The placement of the body. The fact that one of her tennis shoes was thrown in the far corner." He paused. "I think that he killed her, Joe."

"Then why don't you catch him?" The man who had spoken was coming down the stairs. George Bristol was a man in his early forties, with a high forehead and blue eyes that were glittering with moisture. "Why did you let him do this to us? Why did you let him do this to Janey?"

"I'm sorry, Mr. Bristol," Slindak said quietly. "I don't wish to intrude on your grief, but I wonder if I could speak to you regarding the call? It would help us to track him."

"I didn't talk to him. Ellen was the only one—and she can't talk to anyone right now. It nearly drove her into hysterics telling me what he said. You'll have to make do with my report." He had reached the bottom of the stairs, and his glance fell on Eve leaning against the wall. "You're Eve Duncan."

"Yes."

"Last night, when I heard they'd found a little girl in that cave, I hoped it was your daughter. Terrible, isn't it? But I hoped it was anyone's daughter but mine. Anyone but Janey."

"I understand," Eve said unsteadily.

"Yes, you would understand." He closed his eyes for an instant, then opened them. "What are you doing here?"

"I wanted to help. I didn't know about—I wanted to help."

"Thank you. But you can't help us. No one can. You can't bring my baby back. You can't stop those foul things that monster did to her. Do you know what he said when Ellen asked for his name? He said to call him Zeus because he was as powerful as a god. He could reach out and take and destroy and no one could ever stop him. And then he started to tell my wife what he meant. Ellen said he sounded as if he liked it, that he was proud." He shook his head in wonder. "He'd have to be Satan to enjoy hurting a sweet little girl like Janey. Maybe he is Satan. Do you think that could be true?"

"I don't know," Eve said. "Whoever he is, I hope we can catch and punish him."

"I want him punished. I'd like to kill him myself. But it's

too late for Janey." He turned back to Slindak. "If you'll send someone, I'll give a statement, but I can't leave my wife."

"That won't be necessary," Slindak said gently. "I'll have someone here later today if you think you won't be too tired to do it."

"I can do it." He started back up the stairs. "It doesn't matter if I'm tired. It has to be done."

"One question, Mr. Bristol," Joe said. "Was there any accent, any indication of where the caller might be from? Southern accent? Midwest? New York? Did he sound like anyone to whom she might previously have spoken?"

"I think Ellen would have told me if she'd recognized the voice. And she wasn't concerned with accents. She was listening to what he was saying." He was going slowly up the stairs. "I believe that's all she'll ever remember."

"If you get the opportunity, would you ask her?" Joe asked.

"Don't expect anything anytime soon. The doctor is going to keep her unconscious for a while, then bring her back very slowly. He's hoping to keep her from having a complete breakdown." He looked back over his shoulder at Eve. "I'll pray for you. I can afford to do it now. But I don't think it will do any good."

"If I can help you . . ." Eve broke off as George Bristol turned the corner of the stairs and was lost to view. She turned to Joe, her eyes swimming with tears. "Why? Why would he call and taunt them?"

Joe didn't answer. He turned to Slindak. "Did the newspaper or TV station he called manage to tape or trace the call?"

"No, the calls were made one after the other with no advance notice. They weren't expecting it. He asked for the program director at CNN. At the newspaper he asked for Brian McVey, who wrote the article in this morning's paper. McVey tried to put him on hold and stall, but he hung up."

"Damn. But at least we can talk to them and ask the questions we can't ask Ellen Bristol."

"If they'll answer," Slindak said sourly. "They may want to protect their story."

"They'll answer," Joe said grimly. "They'll tell me everything I want to know." He turned back to Eve. "Come on. I'll check you into my hotel. Those reporters may be camped out in front of your house."

He took out his car keys and tossed them to Slindak. "Get one of your officers to drive my car outside the subdivision to the gas station on the corner and leave it there. Eve and I will go out the back door, cut across the yard, and try to lose ourselves in the subdivision."

Slindak nodded. "It's your best shot. You'll probably be seen, but we've ordered the media not to trespass on the Bristols' property." He made a face. "Not that they don't break the rules when the stakes seem high enough. But it will give you a little time." He gave the keys to the officer guarding the door. "You heard him, Dunigan. See if you can't lose them if they follow you. Then report back here." As the door closed behind him, he turned back to Joe. "This is nasty. But it may be a break for us. At least we're not dealing with a phantom any longer."

"No, I think that the Bristols would agree that it wasn't a phantom that savaged them today," Joe said.

"I'll go out in front and give a statement," Slindak said. "That should distract them until you get out of here."

"Thanks." He took Eve's arm. "Let's see if we can find that back door."

She nodded. "The kitchen." She was already moving down the hall. "There it is to the right."

A moment later, they were on the deck outside the kitchen door. A chain-link fence. No back gate.

"We go over the fence," he said. "Then cross the backyard next door and keep on moving. At the end of the block, we turn north one block and double back toward the subdivision entrance. Okay?"

She nodded and ran down the steps. "Stop planning and start moving."

He glanced around, but couldn't spot any media. That didn't mean they weren't under observation. But Slindak might have drawn them away. They might get lucky. He followed Eve, who was already across the yard and had entered the bed of daffodils bordering the fence.

She slipped and almost fell. "Be careful. Mud."

He nodded. "Irrigation. There's a price for these nice lawns and landscapes." He helped her across the fence and climbed after her. "Run!"

JOE GLANCED OVER HIS shoulder as he opened the car door for Eve at the gas station. "I think we made it. I'll drive around for five or ten minutes to make sure that we're not being followed."

"I feel as if I'm in some Alfred Hitchcock movie. Jumping over fences, dodging from yard to yard," she said as she got into the car. "This isn't right. It's not the media that we should be afraid of."

"We're not afraid." He drove out of the gas station onto the street. "We're just avoiding an unnecessary annoyance. And getting you to a place where you'll not be hurt by their questions. You looked like a butterfly being stabbed by a dozen pins when they surrounded you."

"You got me away from them." She was gazing out the window. "I'm used to the reporters now. I was more shocked by what had happened to the Bristols than I was about being attacked by them. I was just too stunned to react. It was the last thing I expected." She looked at him. "You didn't answer me. He called those poor people and the media. He hadn't done anything like that before. Do you have any idea why he would do it now?"

"Maybe. Ellen Bristol said that he sounded proud when he told her about killing Janey."

Eve shuddered. "Horrible."

"Yes, but it may be the key to why he made the call. He's proud of his cleverness, he's proud that he's managed to kill and never been close to being caught."

"Then why would he be this reckless and risk everything?"

"But you see, no one knows how clever he is. No one knows what power he has. It may have been enough for him to have this delicious secret for all these years. But now that his confidence has grown, and he thinks that no one can touch him, he's ready to be admired by one and all. He even gave himself a name, Zeus, so that there's no question of anonymity."

"Power," she murmured. "Who has more power than a god?"

"And Zeus was far from virtuous and completely absorbed in his power. The choice was logical."

"Is that hunger for fame common in serial killers?"

"It's not uncommon. Some are satisfied to stay beneath the radar for their entire career. Others get restless and want to thumb their noses at authority and show their power. My guess is that maybe when they found the remains of that little boy by the freeway, he got a taste of notoriety and liked it. Then when the news story appeared in the paper this morning, he was primed to exploit it and show everyone what a truly superior fiend he was. That call to the media wasn't only to twist the knife in the Bristol family. He was hungry for more attention, more fame." He shrugged. "But often that need for public attention only lasts for a limited amount of time, and they go underground again."

"So he may not make any other calls?"

"As I said, it's not predictable."

"But if he did call again, you'd have a chance of catching him. The newspapers wouldn't be caught off guard again, they'd be prepared. You could set up ways to trace him."

"If."

"But Slindak said this may be a break in the case. Dammit, stop being negative."

"I told you I'd never lie to you. Any change in the status quo offers opportunities, but it's not a sure thing. I've briefed you on all the theories and my experience with them, and that's all I can do."

"So what are you going to do? Are we still going to that shoe factory downtown?"

"No, I'll give that job to one of Slindak's men. I have to go and question Brian McVey and that program director from CNN." He added emphatically, "And you are not going with me. I want answers, and all I'd get would be questions from them if you were within viewing distance."

"I'm not arguing. I realize I'd be a distraction."

Since the moment he'd seen her. "As I said, you can check into the Hyatt. The media may still track you down, but we won't make it easy for them."

She shook her head. "Too expensive. I'll be fine at the house."

"I'll put you on my expense account."

"You wouldn't do that. You're too honest. Which means you'd probably be paying for it out of your own pocket."

"One night. Just enough time to take the heat off," he coaxed. "Otherwise, I'd feel obligated to camp out in front of the house. It's worth paying for your room just to make sure I get a good night's sleep."

"It's not worth it to me." She paused. "There's a cheap motel about two miles from the house. I'll check in there with my mother for tonight. I don't need the Hyatt." She made a face. "I'm no fancy Easterner who has to have room service and a concierge."

"Yeah, guys like me need a lot of care and nurturing. Otherwise, we just wither away. Where is this motel? I'll take you there, then go to your house and pick up your mother and have her choose some clothes to pack for you."

"I can call her."

"Where is the hotel?" he repeated.

"It's the Rainbow Inn on Piedmont."

"Sounds very whimsical."

"Not very. You'll turn up your nose at it." She leaned wearily back in the seat. "Ask me if I care."

"After my stint in the Middle East, it takes a lot to make me turn up my nose. If it has a shower, I'm good with it."

"It has a shower." She was silent for a moment. "Mr. Bristol said he'd pray for me. I'd rather he prayed for Bonnie. But he doesn't think she's alive. When he was talking, I was having trouble . . . I still have a chance. Things were different in her pattern from the other children who— I have a chance."

"George Bristol is a man in pain. He probably doesn't realize what he's saying."

"He knows." She was silent again. "We've got to find that monster, Joe. For all those children, their parents. For Bonnie. He mustn't be allowed to be proud of killing any more children. He's got to be stopped."

For Bonnie.

She was getting closer and closer to accepting that her daughter could be dead.

"That's what we're trying to do."

"Not 'trying.' We've got to do it."

She didn't speak again until they arrived at the Rainbow Inn.

He gazed at the small one-story economy motel skeptically. It appeared in fair repair but had probably been built at least thirty years before. "Definitely no whimsy. You're sure it has a shower?"

"I'm sure." She got out of the car. "And telephones. Will you call me after you talk to CNN and Brian McVey?"

He nodded. "Or I'll tell you in person after I've finished with them, and I bring your mother here."

"I'll call her and tell her to come in my car. I might need it."

"No, she might be followed, and all this would be for nothing. I'll make sure we're not tailed. Do you need anything besides a change of clothes?"

"Tell her to bring my notebook and that box of missing person's reports. I have to go over everything again. There has to be something there that we missed." She moved toward the office, and there was a touch of despair mixed with the frustration in her voice. "He's being so damn reckless. He has to have done something that will give us a lead."

Joe backed the car out of the lot after the door shut behind her.

He couldn't blame Eve for the exasperation that been founded on fear. Today had been a bad day for her, a complete roller-coaster ride. She had identified with the Bristols, and George Bristol's certainty that Bonnie was dead had come as a shock. No matter how often she told herself that was a possibility, she couldn't accept that it might be true.

How the hell would he handle it when she could no longer deny that the distant horror was a reality? And he could see that nightmare hovering on the horizon. Eve was taking comfort in the exceptions, the differences. He was seeing the similarities, and his experience and instincts were scaring him. He could try to prepare her, but at some point she would block him out and stop listening. It would be a purely self-defensive device.

Stop worrying about something he couldn't change. He'd

face that problem when he had to. He checked the address and phone for the *Atlanta Constitution*.

Now his problem was Brian McVey.

"I DON'T HAVE TO ANSWER your questions, you know." McVey leaned back in his chair. "I gave Detective Slindak a statement, so I'm not impeding the progress of the investigation. I could send you back to him."

"You could," Joe said. "But you're a young reporter on your way up. You don't want to antagonize anyone if you don't have to. You're going to have enough enemies."

"You think so?" McVey chuckled. "That's what journalism is all about. A lot of people don't like the truth."

"Particularly in stories like the one you wrote about the hunters finding Janey Bristol's body. It was pretty grisly."

"But all true." His smile was cocky. "I was the first one to get the story, and I ran with it. And the public loves a little blood with their morning coffee."

"You'd know that better than I."

McVey's smile faded. "Don't be so patronizing. I've done my research on you. I may write about it, but I don't kill. While I understand you were absolutely terrific at it. Who stinks the most, Quinn?"

"I suppose it's a matter of perception."

McVey nodded. "And I'll win a Pulitzer before I'm thirty, and you'll still be hunting crazies for the next twenty years."

"Entirely possible. But you'll not win a Pulitzer by publishing crime-scene details just to appeal to the masses."

"Why not? I gave everyone what they wanted, and I didn't hurt anyone." He met Joe's eyes. "I could have described the bits of clothing that would have tipped the ID in Janey Bristol's direction. I didn't go that far. I decided to let the police get a firm ID before I laid that on the Bristols."

It was a restraint Joe hadn't expected. "It was still a shock to every one of the parents of those missing children."

"Give me a break. I'm no angel. But I do have a few scruples."

"As long as they don't get in the way of your Pulitzer."

"You're laughing, but I meant it. You have to have a goal, and I'm aiming at the big prize." He sat forward, his eyes sparkling with enthusiasm. "And I'm on my way. How would I know that first story on the hunters would get me an interview with the killer himself? It was fate."

"No, it was your byline on a story that stroked the monster's ego," Joe said dryly.

"Whatever. It happened, and next time he calls, I'll have a tape recorder and—"

"You think he'll call you again?"

"Why not? I listened. I figure he wanted an audience, and I gave him what he wanted." He grimaced. "Though it made me want to puke."

"But anything for the Pulitzer."

"Well, I did try to ask him questions, but he ran right over me. But that could be good. I didn't make him mad, and that could mean he'll call me again. Lots of reporters have formed relationships, even friendships, with killers."

"I wouldn't count on it. He called CNN, too. I don't think you're that special to him."

McVey's face fell with disappointment. "I can hope. In the meantime, I can milk the story for all it's worth. Would you like to comment? I don't have an FBI quote."

"I'd like a few comments from you."

"Exchange?"

It would be easier than using force or threats. Joe nodded. "Did he say anything different to you than what he told Ellen Bristol?"

McVey shook his head. "Not from what I can tell from what Slindak told me. He made a big thing about calling himself Zeus. I think he wanted to make sure I had that for the story. Maybe like the Zodiac Killer or something. All the rest of the details were vague except about the murder itself. He was very explicit about that."

"Would you recognize the voice if you heard it again? Was it distinctive?"

"I'd recognize it. It was deep and smooth."

"No accents?"

He shook his head. "Hard to tell. Not Southern. Just . . . American."

"Well, that helps," Joe said sarcastically.

"Sorry, I'm no elocution expert. I even tried to concentrate while he was talking because I knew it would be important, but I couldn't tell anything." He stopped. "There was one thing. House."

"What?"

"He mentioned watching the Bristol house. He said the word a couple times. House. Only it didn't sound quite the same as we say it."

"What was the difference?"

He shook his head. "It's hard . . . It was almost the same."

"You're sure he was American?"

He nodded. "Everything was the same except for that one word."

"What kind of emotion? What was he feeling?"

McVey thought about it. "Excitement. Eagerness. Pride. He was speaking quickly, with energy."

"Did he mention any other children?"

"No, not specifically." His eyes suddenly narrowed. "You were with Eve Duncan at the Bristol place. Has she been contacted?"

"No."

"Pity. She's interesting. All the other parents are steady, ordinary couples. Boring. A young woman who has an illegitimate child sparks the imagination. Why was she at the Bristols'?"

"You'll have to ask her."

"I can't. I tried, but she wasn't at her house. Did you hide her away?"

"Now why would I do that? Surely you and your colleagues wouldn't bother a grieving woman. You do have some scruples."

"I'll find her," McVey said softly. "It's the story of a lifetime, and she's part of it. I don't know what chapter she's in, but I'll find out."

"Leave her alone, McVey. You don't want to deal with me."

McVey studied him. "No, but I'll do it. It would be worth it." He paused and picked up his pencil. "Now, what's my quote?"

"The FBI is aiding the investigation of the ATLPD and offering the full services of the Bureau. We're making progress and hope to have a break in the case soon."

“Got it.” McVey looked up. “Anything else?”

“Yes.” Joe turned and started down the aisle toward the door. “Go screw yourself.”

"THAT'S ALL?" Eve asked, disappointed.

“It’s more than we had before,” he said. “We’ll have to work with it. But I think you’d better stay away from your house for a few days more. McVey is going to be persistent. He’s a very ambitious man, and he’s got his teeth into this story.”

“I’m not going into hiding. I can’t afford it, and it makes me angry. I’m going home tomorrow.”

He shrugged. “I tried. I didn’t think I’d succeed.” He nodded at the box he’d brought into the motel room and set on the coffee table. “There are the reports. I suppose you’re going to tackle them again?”

“Yes, I’m going to look at Janey Bristol. Did you receive the dental-record confirmation?”

“Yes, it came in right before I stopped to pick up your mother. I’m afraid I failed in my mission. She wouldn’t come with me.”

“I know. She said if she couldn’t spend the night at home that she’d go to stay with Pastor Nambrey and his wife. They are always inviting her,” she said. “It was definitely Janey Bristol?”

“Yes.”

“Poor little girl.” She shook her head. “Do you know I just felt a rush of relief? I’m like George Bristol. I wanted it to be anyone but Bonnie. He said he was terrible. I guess we’re all ruthless when it comes to protecting our children.” She paused. “If I still have a daughter to protect.” She went on haltingly, “But I was thinking about what you said about that skull being hard to ID unless you knew where to find the dental records. What if you didn't have any idea who that victim was? She might be lost forever, maybe buried by the county in a nameless grave with her parents never knowing. It breaks my heart to think about it. There are a lot of victims like that, aren't there, Joe?"

He nodded. "Too many."

"It breaks my heart," she repeated. "What if it were—" She drew a deep breath and gestured to the boxes. "Thank you for bringing these."

"That sounds like a dismissal."

"You don't want to go over these records again. Things are moving for you. You have things to do."

"And you don't want me to be here."

She met his gaze. "No, I don't. I have some thinking to do, and I want to be alone to do it. I don't want to be soothed or protected. I've been leaning on you too much."

"I haven't noticed."

"And I don't want to look at you and know that you're wondering how I'll survive when I find out my Bonnie is dead." She added jerkily, "You've been very kind, but I need a break from you, Joe. Get out of my life for a while."

He hadn't realized he was that transparent to her. But Eve was intelligent and more savvy about people than anyone he had run across. Even upset as she had been today, she had managed to pick up on all the signals he had not wanted her to see. Damage control was clearly necessary. "What about throwing me out after dinner? You have to eat, and I'd bet this place doesn't have room service."

She smiled faintly. "I've been rude as hell, and you still try to take care of me."

"It's beginning to be a habit. I like it. I never had a cat or a puppy when I was kid. I was always envious of the kids on TV who had animals. You're supplying a need."

Her smile widened. "You're nuts. I refuse to be a substitute for Lassie."

"Dinner?"

Her smile faded. "No, I meant it. I need to be alone and think. What happened today may . . . it could open a door."

"What door?"

"I don't know. That's why I have to think about it." She added pointedly, "Without you to question me while I'm doing it."

She was determined. Okay, back off before she tossed him out on a permanent basis. "No problem." He turned away. "If I hear anything that might interest you, I'll be in touch. Call me if you need me."

"Thanks, Joe."

"You're welcome." He smiled at her over his shoulder. "But I'll stop at that pizza restaurant across the street and ask them to deliver a pizza and a drink to you in about an hour."

"Joe . . ."

"I'd do the same for Lassie."

His smile vanished as he shut the door and strode toward his car. It was going to be hard as hell to give her space. He wanted to hover, build a wall, keep all the ugliness away from her.

And he didn't like the fact that she was distancing herself from him. She had gone through a tremendously painful experience at the Bristols'. Instead of it drawing her closer to him, she had become quieter, more independent. He had been almost able to see her strengthen as each blow had struck her.

If he hadn't cared before, that courage would have made him love her.

He stopped at the pizza restaurant and sat in the car for a moment. No, he couldn't go back. He would do what he'd told her he'd do.

Be patient. Keep in contact, but give her a moderate amount of space. Do his job and find the bastard who had killed her Bonnie.

And be ready to catch Eve when she was downed by that final horrible blow.

CHAPTER 6

"**WE GOT THE REPORT** on the print on the shoe." Slindak stopped by Joe's desk the next afternoon and handed him a sheet of paper. "He's big. Size thirteen. It's a work shoe, but it's not the usual model built for construction workers. The pattern on the soul is different and deeper. It's not a product of any of the major U.S. companies. Schweitzer, the owner of the shoe company, is going through his catalogs and seeing if he can locate where it was purchased."

"Different and deeper," Joe repeated. "What the hell is that supposed to mean?"

"I suppose we'll know when Schweitzer gets back to us."

"That's not good enough. I'm calling the Bureau and getting them on it." Joe reached for the phone. "I'll make a copy of this before I give it back to you."

"Suit yourself. My feelings won't be hurt. That's why we

called you into the case." Slindak strolled across the room toward his desk.

Joe finished his call and leaned back in his chair. Call Eve and tell her what they'd learned? Which was virtually nothing as yet.

Hell, yes. It was a reason to make contact. She had only been going to spend the one night at the motel. She should be home now. He was about to dial again when the phone rang.

"Mr. Quinn?" It was Sandra Duncan's soft, Southern voice. "I do hope you'll excuse me for phoning you. It's really nothing, but you've been so nice to me I just knew you wouldn't mind me bothering you."

"You're right. I'll be glad to help you. Are you still at Pastor Nambrey's? Do you need a ride home?"

"No, Eve doesn't want me to come home yet. She said I was to stay at the pastor's until she called me."

Joe's hand stiffened on the receiver. "That's . . . strange."

"That's what I thought, but Eve didn't want to talk about it." She hesitated. "Eve's been real upset. You know that. I just wanted to make sure that she wasn't— It was such an odd call."

"You believe she might try to hurt herself?"

"I don't think so. Not when she's so set on finding Bonnie. But she was firing all kinds of orders at me and wouldn't answer questions. Then she just hung up."

"What orders?"

"Not to come home. Not to pay any attention to the afternoon papers or anything else. To stay with the pastor and not go with anyone I don't know. Don't you think that's peculiar?"

"Yes, very peculiar." His heart was pounding, and all he

wanted to do was to get off this damn phone. "But I'm sure she has a reason for everything she said. She'll be fine." God, he hoped he was telling the truth. "And it's probably best to do exactly what she told you."

"Well, I did promise her. But I thought that maybe you knew more, and I could find out what Eve was talking about. I know how much Eve trusts you."

That was more than he knew, Joe thought grimly. "No, she didn't confide in me. I have go now, Mrs. Duncan. I'm sure Eve will be fine. If you have any other concerns, just call me."

"I knew you wouldn't mind me phoning you. I do feel better after talking to you. Sharing always helps, doesn't it?" She didn't wait for an answer but hung up.

Sandra's sharing didn't make him feel better, Joe thought as he jumped to his feet. It was scaring him to death.

He had to get his hands on the afternoon paper. There was a machine downstairs.

Suicide? Yesterday had been a nightmare for her, and he'd known she was coming closer to accepting that her daughter was dead.

But she had been stronger than he had ever seen her last night before he had left her.

Yet she had pushed him away, and he hadn't been able to persuade her otherwise. She would know that he wouldn't let her harm herself.

He didn't wait for the elevator, but ran down the stairs. The newsboy was cutting the cord on the pile of newspapers that had just been delivered. Joe snatched up the top newspaper.

Son of a bitch.

"What the hell is she doing?" Slindak had come up behind him. His expression was tense as he grabbed another newspaper. "The captain just called me from a meeting at the mayor's office. He wants to know if we had anything to do with this. Did we?"

"Hell, no."

There was a photo of Eve on the front page. She looked sober, but her chin was lifted defiantly. That gesture was the theme for the entire story below the photo.

The story was written by Brian McVey.

"I'm going to murder him," Joe muttered as his gaze scanned the interview.

It led off with an emotional introduction to Eve Duncan, who had lost her child. Then it went to the Q&A directly following.

Q. "You've heard about the death of Janey Bristol. Do you believe that your daughter was taken by the same killer?"

A. "It's possible. The man who killed Janey Bristol was obviously a coward who only has the nerve to prey on children. Adult interaction obviously terrifies him. He was so stupid he didn't even hide the child's body but left it in that cave to be discovered."

Q. "Stupid? He's allegedly killed at least nine children without being apprehended."

A. "Children. He's a moron who is only capable of attacking and overcoming little children like Janey. That's why he concentrates only on them. It takes logic and intelligence to attack adults. Someone told me that killers like him are into power. Since he'd be defeated by anyone other than a five-year-old, he'll probably continue to kill helpless children. He won't attempt to attack anyone who might challenge him."

The article continued for another two columns, but it was all in the same insulting vein.

Slindak gave a low whistle. "Ugly. She couldn't be more insulting. Is she trying to get herself killed?"

"Don't ask me," he said through his teeth. "She didn't consult me about this insanity."

"And I thought you were so close," Slindak murmured.

"Not now," Joe said curtly. "I'm very near to blowing, Slindak."

"I can see that." He added, "But I told you that there was the danger of not being able to control her. Now she's going to cause us a hell of—"

"I know what she's doing." He strode over to the lobby telephone booth. "And she would have done this if I'd never shown up here in Atlanta. She'd have found a way to reach out to the bastard."

"Reach out? She bludgeoned him. Are you calling her?"

He was trying. But she wasn't picking up on her home phone. She could be there, but not answering. He hung up. "I'm going to her place and talk to her."

"You may have to stand in line. She could have made Zeus mad enough to want to have his own discussion with her." Slindak added, "The captain isn't going to be happy if Eve Duncan ends up in a cave with her skull on a shelf. We're getting enough heat without that maniac expanding his chosen field."

"Dammit, it won't happen. She *won't* be killed." He tore out of the precinct and down the steps.

Thirty minutes later, he was at the house on Morningside. No answer when he rang. The front door was locked. He went around to the back porch. No answer there.

What the hell? He jimmied the window and climbed into the kitchen.

Five minutes later, he'd searched every room in the house, and Eve was not to be found.

But there was an envelope on the kitchen table.

Joe

He tore it open.

You'll be angry, but I had to do this. It's my chance. You told me that this monster is all ego, and I thought this way I could draw him closer to me.

You wouldn't let me do that, but McVey has no qualms about it. As you said, he's hungry. He doesn't care about anything but getting his story.

Isn't that lucky for me?

Thank you, Joe.

Eve

His hand clenched on the paper.

Lucky.

Yeah, lucky enough to have that bastard zero in on her and slice her to pieces.

Cool down. Panic wouldn't get him anywhere. He had to find her, talk to her, persuade her to step back and away from acting as bait for McVey.

Find her.

She wasn't in the house. Her mother didn't know where she'd gone. But she was working with Brian McVey. He might have thought he was using her, but he'd soon find out differently. Eve would be in control.

He called the *Atlanta Constitution.*

Brian McVey had taken an indefinite leave of absence and could not be contacted.

Strike one.

The hell he couldn't be contacted. He called the ATLPD and had a clerk pull out all the profile information they could gather on McVey.

"What are you doing?" Slindak came on the line. "What does Duncan say?"

"I'd know if I could get hold of her," Joe said. "She's not home. I think that McVey has her stashed somewhere while he runs these stories. Get off the line and let me get the info I need."

"I've got it here. McVey has an apartment in Dunwoody—1321 Ashford."

"That would be too easy. Anything else?"

"Let me see . . . He inherited a house from his mother two years ago. It doesn't say whether he sold it or still has possession."

"Address."

"It's 4961 Rosecreek Drive. It's near Lake Allatoona." He paused. "McVey's story has caused a buzz with the rest of the media. There was lot of talk on the local TV news this evening. Including Eve Duncan's quotes."

"That doesn't surprise me. McVey might have even given them a call."

"And shared his story? Not likely."

"To stir the pot. To add the final irritant that would make an explosion certain. Anything else you can tell me about McVey?"

"I can tell you he's a member of the press, and you should be careful what you do to him. I know you're pissed at the hot spot he's put Eve Duncan on, but he can cause us big-time trouble."

"Ask me if I care." He hung up.

The apartment in Dunwoody or the house near Lake Allatoona?

The Dunwoody apartment was closer, and he didn't know whether McVey still owned the house he'd inherited.

But his instincts were leaning toward Lake Allatoona. He called the telephone company, identified himself, and asked if there was still a telephone connection at 4961 Rosecreek Drive.

Yes.

Private number.

Joe waited for the operator to call Washington on another line and check his authority. Five minutes later he had the number.

Name of party holding the service?

Edna McVey.

Brian McVey had never changed the name and evidently occasionally still used the house.

Okay, phone the number he'd been given?

If Eve was there, then she'd be given time to leave before he could get there.

He strode out of the house and jumped in his car.

THE MCVEY PLACE ON ROSECREEK Drive was a pleasant two-story cottage only a few hundred yards from the edge of Lake Allatoona. Its gray sideboard needed painting, but there was a cane rocking chair on the wide porch that gave the place a comfortable ambience.

There was light gleaming from windows on the first floor.

Joe cursed softly. Nothing like leaving a welcoming beacon.

He parked his car a good distance away from the house and moved silently into the woods.

He was a hundred yards to the rear of the cottage when he knew someone was following him.

He paused, listening.

To the left, in the brush.

He faded into the stand of trees to the right.

A sudden crashing of shrubs to the left.

Definitely following him.

He circled swiftly, silently, to the left to get behind the pursuer.

A male figure in a black Windbreaker was now moving ahead of him.

Now.

He covered the distance between them in seconds and brought him down.

The man started to struggle frantically.

Joe's hand tangled in his hair and jerked back hard as the edge of his knife was pressed to the man's throat. "Don't move, or I'll cut your throat."

The man froze. "For God's sake, Quinn. What are you doing? Let me go."

McVey.

"Why should I, you son of a bitch?" He deliberately pressed the edge of the knife a little harder so that it broke the skin. "I'm a little angry with you. Maybe you can tell."

McVey went rigid. "I can tell. But I don't think you're pissed enough to commit murder."

"But you told me that I was so good at it."

"Let me up, Quinn. You know you're just toying with me."

Joe drew a deep breath. "Toying"? McVey didn't know how close he'd come. All of Joe's training, his instincts, the savagery that had been both his friend and his enemy had come racing back in that moment.

"Let him go. What are you doing, Joe?"

He looked over his shoulder to see Eve standing with a gun pointed at him.

"A gun, Eve? Did McVey give you that gun? He probably thought you'd need it if you were going to have to rely on him."

"I asked him for a weapon," Eve said as she lowered the gun. "But I don't need to use it against you, Joe. Dammit, you scared me. I thought you were going to— Let him go."

Joe shrugged and took the knife from McVey's throat. "It

was a close call for him. I was mad as hell, and the bastard decided to follow me. I thought he was a threat." He got off McVey and stood up. "As much threat as a day-old Chihuahua."

"You cut me." McVey's fingers were on his throat and came away with blood on them. "You knew who I was, and you still cut me."

"I cut you *because* of who you are, you son of a bitch. Maybe I should tie you up on the front porch and see how you like being bait. You've got our killer all primed. He's probably almost as angry with you as with Eve. What do you think he'd do to you if he found you helpless?"

"None of this was McVey's idea," Eve said. "It was all mine, Joe. I called him and sketched it out to him."

"And he jumped at it."

"Of course, I did," McVey said as he got to his feet. "Do you think I'd turn my back on a chance like this? I told you that I'd do whatever I had to do." He glared defiantly at Joe. "I didn't go out of my way to cause a killer to go after her. That wasn't my fault. But I wasn't going to say no if she wanted to run the risk. Hell, if we catch Zeus, it might mean that we'd save some other kids. What's wrong with that?"

"You sound almost noble, McVey."

"Stop this, Joe." Eve turned to McVey. "Come back to the house and I'll try to find something to put on that cut." She glanced at Joe. "You're not going away, are you? I can't convince you."

"You can't convince me."

"Then I suppose you'll have to come with us, and we'll

talk." She turned and strode toward the house, with McVey at her heels.

Joe watched them until they reached the porch, then faded back into the brush.

"WHERE HAVE YOU BEEN?" Eve was standing waiting on the porch when Joe came toward her twenty minutes later. "I didn't know what had happened to you."

"Were you worried? Good. I was worried about you, too. And with a hell of a lot more reason."

"Where have you been?" she repeated.

"You decided to declare war on Zeus. This evidently was going to be your first battle site. I know about war. First, you familiarize yourself with the terrain and the places that lend themselves to ambush. While you're doing it, you make sure the enemy isn't already within the gates."

"That's what McVey was trying to do."

"Not well. He'd have had his throat cut, and the way to you would have been open. Where is he?"

"Inside. He's calling in tomorrow's story."

Joe muttered a curse.

"Do you want to go in and cut him again?" she asked sarcastically.

"It's tempting."

She shook her head in exasperation. "For God's sake, be civilized. This isn't his fault."

"But there's a wide streak in me that isn't at all civilized. I think you've always sensed that. If you'll be honest, you'll admit that's one of the reasons that you thought that I could help you find Bonnie. You didn't want some slick, dutiful cop who would make all the right moves. You wanted *me.* Because you knew I'd break any rule I had to break to get what I wanted. Isn't that the truth? Well, you can't have it both ways. You wanted me. You've got me. And there's no way I'll let you turn your back on me."

She stared at him, her expression a mixture of frustration, anger, and something else that he couldn't define. "Damn you, Joe. Okay, come in and talk. But don't you dare hurt McVey." She turned on her heel and opened the front door.

"I'll try to resist." He followed her and glanced around the living room. Nothing fancy. The furniture was contemporary, but there were doilies on the arms of the blue denim couch. Probably another legacy from McVey's mother. It surprised him that McVey hadn't stored them away. He wouldn't have thought the reporter would be that sentimental. "McVey must not use this house much."

"Only an occasional weekend. He told me he has a boat that's stored at the marina a few miles away." Eve led him down the hall to the kitchen. "But it was convenient for our purpose. Private. Out of the way. And he still had the phone service connected. Since he's a reporter, he has to be reachable even on his time off."

"Yeah, very convenient. It wouldn't do to invite a killer to a place that wasn't isolated. He might not accept the invitation."

"That's right." She poured him a cup of coffee. "You might as well sit down. Though you can cut the sarcasm. I got the point. You don't have to belabor it."

"I'll try." He dropped down in a white chair at the kitchen table. "I'm having trouble with control at the moment."

"That couldn't be clearer." She poured herself a cup of coffee. "I think you scared McVey."

"He should have been scared."

She sat down opposite him. "I never saw you like that before."

"But you always knew it was there, didn't you?" He stared directly into her eyes. "You said you grew up with violence all around you. Well, violence isn't confined to the housing projects. It can exist anywhere. It may be a breeding ground, but you have to have someone to throw out the seeds."

"And you're a regular Johnny Appleseed," she said dryly. "I didn't expect you to get so angry. And I didn't think you'd track me down so quickly. I thought I'd have time."

"It wasn't that difficult. I just had to stretch a little. Time for what? It's obvious to anyone that you're trying to set yourself up as bait. Would you like to tell me how you expect to do it without getting yourself killed?"

She glanced away from him. "I expect him to call me. McVey has set up a tracer on the phone. If I can keep him on the phone long enough, I can find out where he is."

"And you don't think he won't suspect that's what you're doing? If he has any brains at all, he'll know why you were so insulting in that interview."

"He'll suspect it. But if he's as egotistical as you think, then he'll still come after me. It would be a feather in his cap to be able to get to me in spite of a trap." She moistened her lips. "And I'm counting on rage. He has to be full of rage if he could do what he did to those children. That's why I was so insulting during the interview. I wanted to trigger that rage."

"I don't believe you'll be disappointed."

"I hope not," she said quietly.

His hand clenched on his cup. "Look, he's crazy. Nothing could be more evident. Crazy people don't react as normal people do. Even when they know that there's danger, they just keep on coming."

"Maybe he won't come after me. We may be able to trace his call and have the police pick him up before it gets that far."

"Eve . . . Dammit."

"Joe . . . Dammit." She smiled unsteadily. "I had to do this. He can't be allowed to go on. I know that the chances aren't wonderful of everything coming out the way I want them. That's why I didn't want you involved. I knew you would try to stop me."

"Damn right, I am."

"Too late, Joe. If he's as crazy as you think, he'll already have his sights on me."

"I could knock you out and have Slindak stuff you in a cell as a material witness."

"And when he let me out, the problem would still be out here waiting for me."

"Not if I find Zeus first."

"What are the chances of that?" She shook her head. "My way is better."

"Your way is as crazy as he is." But he could see that he wasn't budging her. "So what are you doing? Just camping out here and waiting for him to call you?"

"Yes."

"And what if he comes instead of call? That's what I did."

"That's why I had McVey get me a gun. But if I made him angry enough, he won't want to just kill me. He'll want to connect with me, tell me how wrong I am and what he's going to do to me."

"Maybe."

"Am I supposed to argue with you? None of this is written in stone. I'm guessing, based on what you told me about the mind-set of serial killers."

"I should have kept my mouth shut."

She shook her head. "You were trying to help me. You did help me."

"Enough to put you squarely behind the eight ball with the help of Brian McVey."

"Am I hearing my name taken in vain?" McVey strolled into the kitchen, his gaze fixed warily on Joe. "Has Eve convinced you that you shouldn't take my scalp?"

"We hadn't gotten around to discussing you yet," Joe said coolly. "But I doubt if she'd be able to tell me anything about you that would tip the scales."

"I went to him," Eve said. "He only agreed to what I wanted from him. It's entirely my doing."

"I'm insulted," McVey said. "I contributed. I wrote a damn good article. Maybe not Pulitzer quality, but it's the quantity of work that counts in this case. And I furnished the house and the telephone, not to speak of the equipment and technician who's going to trace the dreaded call." He grimaced. "Though it's not really dreaded. It's much anticipated. I admit I want to get this over with as soon as possible. I wasn't expecting you to appear and offer me bodily harm."

"I only offered. If you'd been following the one you'd set this bullshit trap for, you'd be missing a larynx." He paused. "And you've convinced me that you're just as much to blame as I thought. So maybe we should take it outside and start over."

"You will not," Eve said. "Since you won't go away, you'll stop trying to vent your temper on McVey."

"Eve to the rescue," McVey murmured. "I know it's supposed to be the other way around, but I've always believed in women's liberation. It's much more comfortable."

Joe ignored him and stared at Eve. "This is sloppy as hell. It would be a miracle if it worked."

"But our killer isn't neat or tidy. He's sloppy, too. Or should I use the word 'reckless'? Either way, he might take a chance if it suited him."

"I can see that happening and that's why I'm going to call Slindak and have him surround this place," Joe said.

"No, Joe."

"Why the hell not?"

"We may not get the trace. If we don't, then he'll come after me. A police presence would scare him off."

"Exactly."

She shook her head. "He's a monster. He's killed all those children. He may have killed Bonnie. I can't let him get away."

Joe's hands clenched into fists at his sides. It was the one argument for which he had no response. There would be no persuading her because Bonnie and those other children were the only thing that mattered to Eve. She did not care about the possible danger. It didn't matter to her.

"What would you do if I said I was going to do it anyway?"

"I'd go away somewhere you couldn't find me and set up the trap all over again," she said quietly. "I'd have no choice. I don't know how long I can stand feeling this helpless before I break. It has to end."

How could he argue when he was aware of the terrible strain that she was enduring? He had watched her fight it with every bit of her strength and been unable to help her with anything but silent support. Now she had taken the only path she thought she could and still survive. Hell, maybe she was right. Perhaps they were just down to a question of survival.

"Lock the doors and windows." He turned to McVey. "Show me where you've set up the equipment for the trace. I want to check it out. If we're going to do this, we might as well do it right."

"It's in the dining room," McVey said. "But it should be okay. I had a geek who's done stuff like this for me before to set it up. I was going to use it in the newsroom, but then Eve called."

"I'll still look at it." He glanced at Eve. "He may not call tonight. It may take some time for him to search out where you are. And this is a private number. They wouldn't have given it to me if I hadn't been FBI."

"He won't have that much trouble."

"Why not?"

"I figured that he'd try my house and McVey's apartment first. He won't find anything at my house, but I asked McVey to leave a scrawl on a notepad in the office with my name on it and the word 'Allatoona.' "

"And?"

"There's a Rolodex on the other side of the desk. It would

be natural for him to scan through it. This is the only address and phone number in the Rolodex in Allatoona."

"You had it all planned."

"But it all depends on whether he taps McVey's apartment." She smiled faintly. "I tried not to be too 'sloppy.'" She got to her feet. "I'll go lock those doors."

They watched her leave the kitchen.

"Smart lady." McVey looked at Joe. "I expected her to be different. I tried to get an interview with her right after her kid was kidnapped. She was a basket case. She's changed. She took over from the minute she called me on the phone. She trumped me every time."

"And you didn't harass or try to manipulate her? What a surprise."

"Knock it off, Quinn." McVey gave him a sour glance. "Look, I'm still pissed about what you did with that damn knife. Sure I'd have tried to manipulate her. But she wasn't having it. If anyone was manipulated, it was me. And that was fine. I couldn't be happier. All I want is my story. I'm not going to get in your way as long as you know my priorities. You're better at this than I am. Take over."

"I intend to do that."

McVey's brows lifted. "Then you'd better watch out for Eve. She may cause you problems."

He'd had nothing but trouble from Eve since the moment he'd walked into that house on Morningside. Those problems had been escalating lately from hills to mountains. He started down the hall. "I'll worry about that when I have to. Just show me that equipment."

* * *

HE PHONED SLINDAK TWO HOURS later. "Just thought I'd check in. I've located Eve and McVey and I've been trying to persuade them to call off this craziness. No luck so far."

"Do you know McVey has another story running tomorrow? I talked to his editor, and it's almost as inflammatory as the one today. Is the bastard trying to get her killed?"

"It's all Eve. I can't blame McVey this time. Though I'm doing my damnedest. Anything else new?"

"The shoes may have been manufactured either in Buffalo, New York, or Toronto, Canada."

"You said they were different. Did you find out what was different about them?"

"Heavy rubber content in the soles . . . and maybe the uppers. I'll call you back when I contact the manufacturer and find out who would buy a shoe like that."

"Toronto . . ." He remembered something McVey had said. "Check the Canadian connection first. McVey said he thought the man on the phone was American, but that he pronounced the word 'house' a little oddly. I knew several Canadians when I was in the service, and you'd swear they were raised in the U.S. except for tiny differences in pronunciation."

"Toronto, first," Slindak said. "I'll get back to you as soon as I can. Are you at your hotel?"

"No, I'll check back in with you."

A silence. "And you're not going to tell me where you are?"

"I'm with Eve Duncan. You can make what you like of that. You did before."

"I'm not about to make any insinuations. I don't give a damn if you're going to bed with her any longer. In fact, I hope that's what you are doing. It's safer than anything else she might draw you into." He paused. "You're putting a lot on the line for her. Is it worth it?"

Strength, exquisite fragility, intelligence, a smile that was a luminous rainbow in the darkness, the feeling that he was complete only when he was with her.

"She's worth it." He hung up.

He glanced at the clock on kitchen wall.

Eleven forty.

It's close to midnight. Do you believe in the witching hour? Many murderers stage their kills based on superstition or the time of day.

He left the kitchen and strode down the hall to the living room. Eve was sitting in an easy chair beside the fireplace. Her back was straight, and her muscles appeared as tight as her expression.

She smiled with an effort. "Well, is everything satisfactory? I haven't seen you for a couple hours."

"It's as good as it can be." He turned out the overhead lights and dropped down on the couch. "Let's keep this one off. Now it's dim but not dark. There's still light streaming in from the foyer."

She was silent. "You don't want us to be targeted from outside."

"A precaution. I don't think it would happen. He's angry, and he'll prefer a knife to a bullet. If he comes tonight at all. Where's McVey?"

"In the dining room playing with that equipment again. He appears besotted with gadgets."

"They can be interesting." He leaned back in his chair. "I like them, too."

"You spent enough time with McVey examining it. Will we be able to get a trace?"

"Good chance. It's hooked up correctly, and it's fairly sophisticated. Why don't you lean back and try to relax? You look as if you're so stiff you'd break if I touched you."

"I can't relax." She made a face. "But you look as if you're having no problem. This kind of situation doesn't bother you?"

"It bothers me." But only because of the danger to Eve. "But I like it. This is why I joined the Bureau. Moments like this are as close to what I felt as a SEAL as I can get."

"Living on the edge?" She was studying his face. "Yes, I can see that you like it. I've never seen you more alive. You're relaxed, but you look as if you're ready to jump up and go for the kill." She smiled faintly. "Aren't you lucky that I furnished you with a reason to resurrect old times?"

"I'm lucky as long as you stay out of it and let me—"

The phone on the table beside her rang.

McVey was in the room in a heartbeat. "I switched on the machine. Let me take the call." He picked up the receiver. "McVey." He listened, then shook his head at Eve. "Thanks, Pauley." He hung up. "Pauley Williams. He's in the next apartment and has a key to my place. I asked him to listen for any disturbance and check if he heard anything." He added quickly as Eve made an exclamation, "I told him to be careful. Don't worry, Pauley isn't that self-sacrificing. He wouldn't go in if he didn't think it was safe."

"And did he hear anything?"

McVey nodded. "And he found the lock was broken. I left the desk neat as a pin, and the pad was on the floor and the Rolodex had cards missing from it." He grinned jubilantly. "I think we've got him, Eve."

"It seems you're right." Her hands were clenching the arms of the chair. "When did this Pauley first hear an intruder?"

"About fifty minutes ago. Like I said, he wouldn't take a risk. He waited to go into the apartment until after he thought he heard the front door close."

"Less than fifty minutes," Joe said. "And he has this phone number and address." He looked at Eve. "Now he only has to choose which one to use."

"He'll phone." She moistened her lips. "I think."

"Fifty minutes. If you guess wrong, he could be here from that apartment in Dunwoody in another ten minutes."

"He'd want to be sure."

"Maybe. Or maybe he's furious enough to kill anyone here he can get his hands on."

"Why are you trying to scare me?"

"I want you to get the hell out of here and leave this to me."

"After all the preparations we've made?" McVey interceded. "It's not going to hurt her to take a phone call, then I could—"

"Be quiet, McVey," Joe said. "Eve?"

She shook her head.

Joe had known that she'd refuse, but he'd had to make one

last attempt. He turned on his heel. "Then get back to the dining room and make sure that we can trace any call, McVey. I'm going to scout around outside and make sure the area is secure." He unlocked and opened the door. "In case you're wrong, and he wants immediate and lethal contact."

CHAPTER 7

JOE RETURNED THIRTY MINUTES later. "No bogeyman is lurking at the moment," he told Eve. "That doesn't mean the situation might not change in another five minutes." He headed toward the room. "I'm going to go to the kitchen and listen on the extension if there's a call."

"Okay."

It was only a breath of sound, and he glanced over his shoulder at her. Then he muttered a curse and turned and strode over to her. He took her face in his two hands and stared fiercely down into her face. "Don't be afraid. It's going to be fine. Whatever happens, I'll make sure you're safe. I won't let that son of a bitch touch you. Do you hear me?"

"I hear you," she whispered. "But there's no way this can turn out fine. Unless there's a miracle, and Bonnie is alive and not been thrown into some hole by this monster. I'm not afraid for myself, Joe. I'm afraid of what I'll find out if we do catch him. That's terrifying me so much I'm sick to my stomach."

And there was no way he could take away that fear. All he could do was share her pain and let her know she wasn't alone. "We'll get through it together." He brushed his lips gently across her forehead. "We've not done so badly so far."

She laughed shakily. "When you're not yelling at me and trying to cut McVey's throat."

"That's only a sign of closeness. I only abuse the people I care about." He kissed her forehead again and let her go. "If he does call, he'll try to hurt you. Don't let him. Assume he's lying until we find out otherwise." He turned and walked away from her. "If you want me, just call."

"Joe."

He looked over his shoulder.

"I'm not afraid for myself, but I'm afraid for you. Take care of yourself. I don't have that many friends. I can't afford to lose you."

"You don't have to have that many friends if you have me. I fulfill all needs." He smiled and walked out of the room.

THE PHONE RANG FORTY MINUTES later.

Joe stiffened, then picked up the phone at the same time as Eve did in the living room.

"Have you been expecting me, Eve?" A deep voice, but it wasn't smooth, as McVey had described; it was rough with ugliness and fury. "I think you have. I know what you're doing. I'm not the moron you called me. I suppose the cops are right there recording everything I say. I don't care what they do. They're not going to catch me, so it doesn't matter."

"They'll catch you," Eve said. "You've already left so many clues around the crime scenes that the detectives are stumbling over them, Zeus." She stopped. "And that ridiculous name you've given yourself. That's as stupid as everything else you've done. Pretensions of grandeur. You probably picked it because Zeus was supposed to be all-powerful. There's nothing godlike about a child killer. You're just a vicious, ludicrous comic-book character, and you don't even know it."

"Ask the Bristols if I belong in the comic books," he hissed. "Ask Linda Cantrell's mother if she thinks what I did to her little girl is funny."

"You pick on children because you're afraid to face anyone else. You're a coward."

"And you're a bitch who doesn't even know that she's a dead woman." He paused. "I'm going to send you to join that red-haired brat that I took from you. But I'm going to make it go even slower with you."

Silence.

"That got you, didn't it?" he asked. "Not so brave now. Do you know why I take the kids? Because there's no greater power to be had than when you kill a man's child. It's like throwing a stone into the pond and seeing all the circles that spread and never stop. The death of a kid touches everyone around her."

"You're saying that you killed . . . my Bonnie?"

"She was dead six hours after I took her. I'd tell you how and when, but I'm going to cut this call short. I'll do that before I cut your heart out. I know you're probably tracing this call. I've got to be gone before the cops get here." His voice lowered to malignant softness. "I just wanted to tell you that you're the stupid one to think that you could bring me down, bitch. Look over your shoulder, and I'll be there. Go to bed, and I may be in the closet waiting for you to sleep. Get in a car, and you'll never know if I've rigged a bomb to blow you to hell and back. If you feel as if someone is watching you, then you'll be right. I'll be right behind you until the day I decide to send you to hell." He hung up.

Joe crashed down the receiver and ran into the dining room, where McVey was looking up from the machine. "Where?"

"2030 Cobb Parkway. It's a pay phone at a convenience store."

Joe grabbed a phone and called Slindak.

"You woke me up. Don't you ever—"

"Send a patrol car to a convenience store at 2030 Cobb Parkway. He's probably already taken off, but we might be able to get a description."

"He?" He paused. "Zeus?"

"Yes. Get someone out there fast." He hung up and turned to McVey. "None of this gets into print. Do you understand?"

"Not unless we get lucky and catch the bastard," McVey said. "I can wait for the big story." His eyes were shining with excitement. "But we're close. I could hardly breathe while Eve was talking to him. She did a good job, didn't she?"

"He tore her apart," he said savagely. "Couldn't you tell?"

He didn't wait for an answer. He was striding down the hall to the living room.

Eve's was sitting frozen, her face paper white. "Did we . . . get a location?"

"Yes, a convenience store on Cobb Parkway."

"So he could jump in his car and get away. So it was all for nothing."

"We could get a description."

She reached up a shaking hand to her forehead. "And there's something else . . . I'm having trouble thinking. He hates me. I think he was telling the truth about shadowing me until he finds a way to kill me. We've got that advantage."

The desire to reach out, to comfort, was an ache inside him. But he couldn't touch her right now. He didn't have the control, and she would realize the truth.

And that realization would rob her of what little comfort he could give her.

"Some advantage," he said tersely. "Did it occur to you that your logic is a little twisted?"

She nodded. "I guess it is. It's all I've got." She looked up at him. "You heard what he said about Bonnie?"

"Yes."

"I'm trying to remember what you told me. That he'd probably say anything to hurt me. He could be lying."

"Yes, he could."

"But what if he's not?" she whispered. "What if she's . . . gone?" She swallowed. "What if he did the same things to her that he did to Janey Bristol? I can't stand the thought of . . ." She stopped to steady her voice. "But I don't know that, and I can't let him break me and keep me from going after him. I have to hold on, don't I?"

He nodded. "You have to hold on with all your strength."

She got to her feet. "Then I can't just sit here. I want to go to that convenience store and talk to the clerk. I want to know what a monster looks like."

"Slindak will be taking care of that. And don't expect Zeus to look like a monster. Most of the serial killers I've seen have looked like your next-door neighbor."

"I still want to go. I need to go."

He hesitated. "Why not? Stay here a minute and let me look around outside." He grabbed his flashlight, left the house, made a quick tour of the perimeter, then came back. "Let's go."

"I told McVey what we were doing. He wants to stay here and transcribe his notes from the phone call."

"Good. He's not invited. I can take only small doses of McVey." He held the door for her, and his hand cupped her elbow as they walked down the driveway to the car. "And he probably couldn't resist getting in the way while we're questioning the clerk."

"You're too hard on him. McVey is just doing his job."

"It surprises me that you defend him considering what a beating you took from the media. He'd probably be after you like a vulture if he—"

"What's that?" Eve was standing next to the car, staring at the windshield wipers.

Joe froze, his gaze following hers. A piece of paper was folded beneath one windshield wiper. "I don't know. I didn't notice it when I came by the car when I was out checking the perimeter. But then I wasn't looking for it. I was hunting bigger—" Eve was reaching for the piece of paper. "No, let me get it."

She already had it and was cautiously unfolding it. "Give me some light, Joe."

He reached into his pocket and pulled out his flashlight.

She inhaled sharply as the beam illuminated the message on the paper. It was printed in large letters with a black pencil.

Stupid Bitch.
Do you think anyone can keep you safe?

"He was here," she said. "He was outside all the time."

"He was here. But not all the time. He wasn't here the last time I checked the perimeter before you got the phone call. I don't make mistakes like that. But he came very soon after, checked out the house, and decided that he didn't want to chance an attack on you with me and McVey on the premises. Then he took off for the convenience store to make his call." He carefully took the paper from her. "I'll put this in the glove box and give it to Slindak to check for prints and analyze the handwriting." He shrugged. "If there are any prints. He may be arrogant, but he was very savvy about the trace. He was probably wearing gloves. But he may have screwed up on the note."

"Yet he was so reckless about leaving evidence at those crime sites."

"Maybe he's recognizing that it's not the same ball game. He's willing to play, but he knows the rules may be different." He opened the passenger door and put the note in the glove box. "You've taught him that, Eve."

"Have I?" Eve got into the car. "That supersize ego was one of our best weapons against him. I just hope that he won't become cautious and take off. That would ruin everything."

"I don't think you have to worry about that," Joe said grimly as he started the car. "You've seen to it that Zeus is wholeheartedly committed to do at least one more kill before he goes to a different hunting ground."

TWO PATROL CARS AND SLINDAK'S gray Honda were parked in the lot of the convenience store when Joe arrived.

Slindak strolled over to the car as Joe opened the door. "Pretty much a waste of time. The store manager said someone used the outside phone booth to make a call, but he was busy and only got a quick glimpse of him."

"Model of his car?"

"He was parked down the street, and the manager didn't notice the model. You're sure it was Zeus?"

"I'm sure. Did you dust the phone booth for fingerprints?"

"We've taped off the booth, and the forensic team will be here soon." He glanced at Eve. "Hello, Ms. Duncan. You don't look too well. Could I have someone see you home?"

"I'm fine." She got out of the car. "It's . . . been a difficult night."

"I can imagine," Slindak said dryly. "I'm sorry, but you brought it on yourself."

"I know that." She watched another patrol car pull into the parking lot. "Forensics?"

"Yes, and I had them roust a sketch artist we use occasionally out of his bed. Kim isn't going to be pleased."

"Artist?" Eve nodded. "I've heard that you can sometimes get an accurate facsimile from a description."

"Sometimes. In this case it's important that we try to do it right away since the manager said he only got a fleeting glimpse. Memory tends to fade quickly, and we need him fresh."

"May I go and watch him?"

Slindak shrugged. "Why not?"

"And I sketch a little myself. Could I have a pad and see what I can do?"

"I'll ask Kim Chen." He gestured to the small, spare man of Asian descent who had gotten out of the patrol car. "As long as you don't get in his way, I don't think he'd object."

"Thank you. I'll ask him myself."

Joe and Slindak watched her walk over to the artist.

"I thought she was close to fainting when you pulled in," Slindak said. "She bounced back pretty quickly. Is she always like that?"

"When she has a purpose. I'm glad she found one right now." He was watching the play of intense emotion across Eve's face as she spoke to Kim Chen. "And I'll be interested to see what she does with that sketch. I saw a sketch she'd done of her daughter in her house. It was remarkable."

"It's not the same thing."

Joe knew that, but Eve had a talent that he'd never seen in a police artist. "Her sketch came alive. It was as if Bonnie's personality was leaping from the page. Let's see if she can do the same thing with a description."

"Don't hold your breath."

As Eve and Kim entered the convenience store, Joe turned toward the phone booth. Three techs were already brushing it down for prints. "I have a note that may have Zeus's prints on it that you may be able to match. He left a calling card on my windshield at the cottage." He reached into his car and retrieved the note from the glove box. "Or maybe not. He guessed we were tracing the call and setting him up. He may have worn gloves."

Slindak carefully took the note and handed it to one of the forensic crew. "That close, huh? She must have really pissed him off."

An understatement. He was trying not to remember the bastard's words. He nodded curtly and started to cross the lot. "Let's go down the block where he left his car and see if we have any witnesses."

EVE WAS COMING OUT of the front entrance when Joe and Slindak came back to the convenience store over an hour later.

"Finished?"

She nodded as she came toward them. "I did the best I could. It was hard. The skill isn't really in the sketching. It's the questions that you have to ask the witness. Kim Chen is very good at what he does. And you have to be ready to change every feature as the witness changes their mind. That evidently happens a lot. It's definitely a work in progress all the way through."

"But she did very well for a beginner," Kim Chen said as he came out of the store. He smiled at Eve. "But you should have changed the eyes."

"Why? The manager said he didn't see the eyes from the front, so it's purely a matter of opinion what they looked like. I just went with instinct."

"But I told you that you're supposed to go with generic features in that case. You have a greater chance of coming close to a resemblance."

She shook her head. "It just felt right."

" 'Felt'?" Kim Chen frowned. "You don't rely on feelings. You're not creating, you're duplicating."

"You're probably right. Detective Slindak is lucky he has your sketch to use."

"It was nice meeting you, Ms. Duncan." Kim handed the pad to Slindak. "Here's the best I could do. Not bad. The manager remembered more than he thought."

"Thanks, Kim. Sorry I had to get you out here in the middle of the night."

"So am I." Chen grimaced. "But it's better than trying to pry a description out of someone after they've had a day or two to let it blur." He waved and strolled toward the patrol car.

Slindak glanced at the sketch. "He's not a handsome specimen and looks pretty ordinary." He handed the sketch to Joe. "What do you think? Those cheekbones a little Slavic?"

"Maybe." Joe studied the sketch. High, broad cheekbones, a wide, full mouth. Dark curly hair, cut close to the head. Ordinary-shaped dark eyes and brows. "Let me see your sketch, Eve."

"You heard Kim. I injected too much into the eyes in the sketch." She handed him her pad. "I did okay with the rest, though. I came pretty close."

Joe gave a low whistle. "I can see what Kim meant."

The dark eyes looking up at him almost jumped off the sketch. They were large, close-set, and seemed to glitter with ferocity. The brows above them were straight slashes as dark as the eyes they framed.

Slindak was glancing over his shoulder. "Nothing ordinary about that face."

"He's not ordinary," Eve said. "He's a monster. I don't care if you tell me monsters seldom look like what they are. I think the soul must reveal itself in some way. This felt right to me." She turned to Joe. "Use it or not. I don't care. But I think that I have an idea now what he looks like. I may need it."

"We'll use it," Slindak said. "We'll use both of them. It may be the only thing useful to come out of this. Joe and I found two witnesses who saw Zeus, but not close enough for a description other than he appeared big and muscular. Neither of them agreed with the other about the car. One said it was a brown Ford, the other a dark blue Honda."

"Maybe you should get Kim back to draw the car for them," Eve said dryly.

"Maybe I should. But I don't think it would do much good." He turned and walked over to the forensic crew, who had just finished with the phone booth.

"Are you ready to leave?" Joe asked Eve. "I don't think there's much more we can learn here."

She nodded wearily and got into the car. "I guess you're right. I just wanted to do something that would get us closer. Something concrete."

"The sketch will help."

"If that store manager gave us the right information." Her lips firmed. "But I have to think positive, don't I? I can't think we're just going down a blind alley, or I'll go crazy."

"I'm taking you back to my hotel, okay? No Rainbow Inn."

"No Rainbow Inn." She leaned her head back against the rest. "Take me home, Joe."

His hands tightened on the steering wheel. "No way."

"Take me home." She looked at him. "You heard him. He's coming after me. He has to be able to find me."

"So you're making it easy for him."

"No, I'm sure that you'll make it a challenge," she said. "You're not going to let me be there alone."

"And you're not arguing with me about it?"

"I tried that, and it didn't work." She smiled with an effort. "You just keep on coming."

"You're damn right I do." He paused. "That second newspaper article McVey wrote will be coming out in a few hours from now. It's going to cause Zeus to blow sky-high again."

"Then maybe he'll make his move sooner. Or he'll get so angry, he'll make a mistake. Either way, it won't be bad for us. Nothing will be bad as long as he doesn't get discouraged and disappear. I figure we can hold him here if he knows I'm there in that house, and all he has to do is worry about how to get to me."

"We probably can," Joe said. "But I'm not going to be your only protection, Eve. That's bullshit after we saw how close he came. I'd like to surround you with an army, but I'll limit it to pulling in one of Slindak's men to watch the house." He held up his hand as she started to speak. "Don't worry; Zeus will be expecting it. One man will be a challenge, not a deterrent. I just want the extra insurance."

"You may be right." She was silent, thinking about it. Then

she slowly nodded. "If you promise he won't interfere. I don't want him in the way."

"It would take a lot to discourage Zeus. Having you within his sights will be like putting a steak just outside the cage of a hungry wolf. It will only be a question of time before he finds a way to break out and get it."

"You're calling me a piece of meat? Not at all flattering, Joe."

"I'm not in the mood to be flattering. The only thing I can see good about this is that I'll be with you in that house."

She was silent a moment. "That's the only good thing I can see good about it, too, Joe. You help keep away the darkness."

Forever. Let me hold the darkness at bay for you. Let me help you find the dawn.

Don't say it. Keep it on an even keel.

"I'm glad we're in agreement on something at last. It's about time. But I've decided that it's your house that's dark. I think that we'll paint a couple rooms while I'm staying there."

She stared at him in bewilderment. "What?"

"It will make the time pass. I thought the living room could use brightening. What color do you think?"

She said blankly, "I have no idea."

"Maybe a gold-beige?" he suggested. "Think about it while I stop at my hotel and pick up a bag. It shouldn't take long . . ."

Two Days Later

"WHAT IS THIS STUFF?" Eve asked as she tentatively tasted the salad. "Exotic. You know I'm just a simple Southern woman with down-home tastes, Joe. Are you trying to educate my palate?"

"It's not 'stuff.'" Joe sat down across from her. "I got the recipe from an Indian woman in Bombay. And you're about as simple as an Einstein equation. Try it. You'll like it."

She took another bite. "It's good. Where did you learn to cook?"

"When I was in the service. I was young, with a tremendous hunger, and food was only part of it. I was all over the world tasting and experiencing everything. The good things I wanted to take home with me."

"And the bad things?"

He shrugged. "I learned from them, too, then tried to let them go."

"Not easy."

"No, but that's life." He smiled. "I'm glad you let me loose in your kitchen. Cooking relaxes me."

"And it bores me. I had to put wholesome meals on the table for Bonnie, but I assure you that they lacked inspiration. And definitely nothing exotic." She finished the last bite. "I doubt that I would have picked up any exotic recipes even if I'd gone to India. Which I most certainly didn't. I've never been out of Georgia."

"You've missed a lot. I'd like to show you some of the parts of the world I've visited. It would be great seeing them through your eyes."

"I don't feel as if I've missed much. I had everything I wanted or needed here. It would have been nice to take Bonnie to those places when I could afford it, but it wasn't important to me." Her face clouded. "But maybe it would have been important to Bonnie. She enjoyed every minute, every new experience."

He quickly changed the subject. "I'm glad you like the salad. The main course is much more ordinary." He got to his feet. "Steak and mushrooms. I'll let you take the dishes into the kitchen while I serve it up. Get to work."

"Right." She picked up the salad plates and followed him into the kitchen. She put the dishes in the sink and stood watching him as he served up the steak and mushrooms on a plate. She said quietly, "Thank you, Joe."

"Wait until you're sure I'm not going to give you indigestion before you thank me."

"No, thank you for making these days bearable for me. I would have gone crazy without you," she added with frustration, "Where *is* he? I thought that he'd contact me long before this. Not one word after that second news interview came out."

"He's biding his time. He's probably enjoying the hell out of thinking about you on pins and needles, waiting for him to strike."

"But you don't think he's given up and gone away?" she asked anxiously.

"No." He looked up and met her eyes. "I think that he's close, waiting for his chance."

She breathed a sigh of relief. "That's good."

"Do you know how sick that sounds?"

She nodded, then asked immediately, "And that policeman outside hasn't seen anything?"

He shook his head. "Bramwell says that there's been no suspicious activity since he took over the duty day before yesterday."

He handed her a plate. "Now go sit down and try my steak. I made it medium well-done. Okay?"

"Fine." She didn't move. "I meant it, Joe. You kept me so busy painting that damn room that I had no time to think."

"Oh, you were thinking. I just tried to keep everything troubling on the edge of your consciousness." He headed for the dining room. "Now let's finish dinner, and we'll have coffee on the front porch. I made Turkish coffee with a few interesting spices."

"Coffee with spices?" she repeated warily. "I'm not so sure about that. Coffee should be black, strong, and hot, and not subject to all your fancy exotic tinkering."

"I realize that I'm taking a chance in fooling with your holy of holies." He smiled as he glanced over his shoulder. "But trust me one more time. Try it, you'll like it."

"HERE YOU GO." HE HANDED Eve the small demitasse cup and sat down in the cane chair next to her. "I guarantee it's black and strong and a small enough quantity that you won't have to sample much. I heard the phone ring when I was in the kitchen. I gather it wasn't Zeus."

She shook her head. "My mother. She wants to know when she can come home. Evidently, she's bored. I thought it might be McVey again."

"He called you this morning, didn't he?"

She nodded. "He won't give up. He wants to come here and become part of the action." She made a face. "When and if there is any action. I told him that he can't do it."

"I'm sure he didn't like that."

"He's being very persistent. I said we'd give him an exclusive as soon as the story broke."

"That's more than he deserves."

"You're still angry with him."

"He took you to that house on the lake and let you stake yourself out for that nutcase."

"It was my call."

"And he grabbed at the chance to help you to do it. No trying to talk you out of it. Just set up a house in an isolated area and let the bad times roll. Anything to get his story." He took a sip of his coffee. "Yes, I'm still angry."

"Then I'll try to keep you away from him. He was scared of you, but he's so ambitious that he'll keep pushing." She took a sip of the coffee. "I don't want him to—" She gasped. "Good Lord, what are you doing to me? It's *nasty.*" She made a face as she thrust the cup and saucer at him. "It's like cinnamon-flavored tar."

"Maybe it's an acquired taste."

"If you ever give me anything but the real thing when I ask for coffee, I'll murder you."

He chuckled. "I knew it was taking a chance."

"You knew I'd hate it. It's some kind of sick joke."

"You malign me. Would I do that to you?"

"I'm beginning to think that you have a wicked sense of humor. You just haven't let me see it before."

"I had to wait to show that side of my personality. You weren't ready for it." He got to his feet. "I'll take your cup inside." He stood from a moment, looking out into the darkness of the quiet street, the well-kept yards, the lamplight streaming out of the windows. "So peaceful. It's a nice neighborhood. Bramwell said that it was a hell of a lot easier watching your house than the usual neighborhoods he's been accustomed to monitoring." He moved toward the door. "Stay here. I'll get you a real cup of coffee."

"Don't bother." She got to her feet. "All that painting has worn me out. I think I'll shower, then go to bed." She moved toward the door. "I'll do better without coffee."

"You're sure?" He held the door open for her. "My duty is to please."

"Tell that to McVey."

"There's always an exception to prove a rule." He turned on the light in the living room and watched her walk up the steps. She did look tired, but it had been a fair day. He had worked her at painting, making sure the physical exertion would be enough to block out the mental torment that was always with her. He checked his watch. It was near ten in the evening. He'd check in with Slindak and go to bed himself.

He hoped he could sleep. Eve wasn't the only one who was on edge from all this waiting.

Where are you, bastard?

THE PHONE RANG IN THE middle of the night.

He reached over to the pick up the receiver of the phone on the end table beside the couch on which he was sleeping.

Eve was already on the line.

And so was Zeus.

"You have such a pretty house there, bitch. Does it make

you feel safe to be with the FBI man? Are you sleeping with him?"

"No. And, yes, I do feel safe. All your threats, and you weren't able to touch me. You're a coward. I was right in all things I told the world about you."

Oh, shit, Joe thought. That's right, wave the red flag at the bull.

But Zeus didn't seem angry. When he spoke again, his voice was calm and honey-smooth. "You're trying to make me mad. Are you trying to trace the call again? You'll be disappointed. I have only one thing to say to you and then I'm gone . . . for a little while."

"What?"

"You didn't say 'thank you' when I complimented you on your house. That was rude, but I'll forgive you. Do you know what I like about your house? It's that lovely porch, with the hanging basket of flowers. I like plants and flowers far better than I like people. They have no ugliness about them unless I choose to make them ugly. Flowers make a statement, don't they? You should pay attention to that statement." He hung up.

He heard Eve's exclamation before he crashed down the phone.

He threw on his clothes and ran out to the hall to see Eve at the top of the stairs.

"The porch," she said as she ran down the stairs. She flipped on the light in the foyer. "He was talking about the porch. Why would he—"

"Don't go out there." He passed her and drew his gun as he carefully opened the front door. "Let me take a look. I just hope

Bramwell doesn't mistake me for Zeus and decide to take a shot at me."

"Be careful, dammit."

"Always." His gaze was darting over the porch, street, and neighboring houses. It was still and dark except for the streetlight on the corner. "I don't see anything."

"That doesn't mean he's not there." Eve pushed closer to him, following his gaze. "And where's Bramwell? Shouldn't he have come running when the lights went on?"

"Yes, he must be in back doing his hourly tour." His gaze again wandered over the same area. "I don't see anything. Maybe it was a bluff." He took a step out onto the porch. "He might have wanted to keep you—" He broke off, stiffening.

She was right behind him. "What is it?"

"Go back inside."

"The hell I will. What's—" She inhaled sharply as she saw where he was looking.

A group of dark liquid drops was spattered on the floor of the porch.

As he watched, another drop fell from the hanging basket to the floor.

"Blood?" she whispered.

"Go back inside," he repeated. He was remembering the details of Janey Bristol's crime scene. He took a step closer and took out his flashlight. "You may not want to see this." He shined the beam up to the bottom of the basket.

The earth at the bottom of the basket was soaked with blood that dripped steadily downward.

His beam traveled upward.

"Hair!" Eve's eyes were focused on the patches of blood-soaked hair clinging to the head that had been shoved into the basket. "Oh, my God."

"Easy."

"Who is it? Another child?"

"I can't tell. It could be Bramwell. I'll have to move around to the other side to see the face." He said through his teeth, "Have you had enough? Or do you want to see that, too?"

"No, but I'm not going to leave you out here to do it alone." She braced herself, and said unevenly, "And it could be Bonnie. He told me he killed her right after he took her."

"There wouldn't be all this blood." He moved around to get another view of the skull. "This is a fresh kill."

"You said it might be Bramwell?"

"Maybe." He was now shining the beam directly into the face. "No, it's not Bramwell."

She was suddenly beside him. "Then who is—" Her back arched as if struck. "McVey!"

Sandy hair soaked in blood, blue eyes staring at them, lips open in a silent scream.

"Dear God . . ." Eve ran to the rail of the porch, bent over, and threw up. "Brian . . ."

"I told you to go inside." Joe was beside her, his hands on her shoulders. "Will you do it now? Lock the door. I need you to call Slindak and get him out here. I have to find Bramwell."

"Yes . . ." She staggered toward the door, then, clinging to the jam, she turned to face him. "No. You can't go without me. What if it's some kind of trap? What if he kills you like he did Brian? I can't—"

"What's going on?" Bramwell was running up the porch steps. "Why are the lights—" He stopped short as he saw the bloody head. "What the hell?"

"That's what I want to know," Joe said grimly. "I have a lot of questions to ask you, Bramwell." He turned back to Eve. "I evidently don't have to go hunting him down. Now will you call Slindak?"

She nodded jerkily and disappeared into the house.

"Who is it?" Bramwell was looking up at the basket. "Pretty gory, huh?"

"Brian McVey."

"The reporter? He doesn't look much like the photo that runs with his byline." He grimaced. "That was stupid. Of course he doesn't. Poor guy."

"How did he get here without you seeing it?"

"It wasn't here before I made my rounds thirty minutes ago."

"And why did it take you thirty minutes to make those rounds?"

"I saw something funny. The flowers in the border were all crushed, and the back gate was open. I was looking around to see if I could find the reason."

A red herring, Joe thought, to give Zeus enough time to deposit McVey's head in the hanging basket, get away, and make his phone call to Eve.

"And you saw nothing suspicious before you started your rounds. A car? A pedestrian?"

"The Simmonses, that young couple who live in that duplex down the street, drove in and went into their house, but that's all. I was on the job and watching close, Agent Quinn."

He looked again at McVey's head. "But evidently not close enough. Slindak is going to kick my ass."

"Probably. I may help him." He turned and went down the porch stairs. "Stay here and guard Eve Duncan. If you screw up, I'll put your head in that basket with McVey's."

Five minutes later, Joe was looking down at the broken lock on the trunk of the Simmonses' Saturn. It would have had to be held shut from inside so that it wouldn't fly open as the car was driven. He carefully lifted the lid of the trunk.

Drops of dark blood on the black plastic interior.

He tensed as the smell wafted up to him.

And something else . . .

CHAPTER 8

"SLINDAK SHOULD BE HERE ANYTIME," Eve said, when Joe walked into the house. "He said to tell you that he can't wait until you go back to Washington, so that he can sleep through the night." Her lips were trembling, as she added, "Of course, he had a few words for me as well. He holds me to blame for all of this."

"Did he say that?"

"No, don't go on the attack. He didn't have to say it. It couldn't be clearer, could it?"

"He's lucky to have your help. At least, we have a chance of bringing Zeus down now. They were running around in circles a few weeks ago. He can stuff his damn blame where the sun doesn't shine."

"Lucky?" Her lips tightened. "And was McVey lucky to have my help, too?" She shuddered. "I must go out on the porch and tell him how lucky he is."

"I knew this was coming." He pulled her to her feet. "We're going into the kitchen. I'll make you a cup of coffee, and we'll talk." He pushed her down at the kitchen table. "Sit there and block out everything." He turned to the cabinet and got down the coffeepot. "That shouldn't be hard. You have plenty of practice."

"I do, don't I?" Her smile was bitter. "Only I think that the blocks are beginning to crumble. What do I do when the flood rushes in and overwhelms me?"

"No problem. I'll be there to pull you out." He heard the sirens. "You'll have to finish making this. I have to go out and report in to Slindak. It's probably better for you to be busy anyway."

"Yes." She got to her feet and reached for the tin of coffee. "Go on. I don't need you to coddle me."

The coffee was ready, and Eve was sitting at the table with a cup cradled in her hands when he came into the kitchen thirty minutes later. "Is he . . . gone?"

He knew she didn't mean Slindak. "Yes, they took him a few minutes ago." He poured a cup of coffee. "But forensics is still working on the porch and the backyard and the Simmonses' car."

"The car?"

He nodded. "Zeus hid in the trunk of the car of the young couple down the block. He couldn't just walk down the street carrying a bloody head under his arm. He was watching and knew that you were guarded. He waited in the trunk until he saw Bramwell go toward the backyard, then got out and placed the head in the basket. He'd already gone around back and arranged a suspicious scenario for Bramwell to investigate to keep him from coming back too soon."

"And then he made the call to me." She shook her head. "Zeus had it all planned." Her lips twisted. "I thought he'd go after me. But I should have known that I wouldn't be enough. He couldn't get to me easily, so he went after Brian." She shook her head. "And I called him stupid."

"He's cunning." Joe sat down across from her. "But he took a big chance. It's clear he's still as arrogant as he ever was. McVey was no fool. He wouldn't have been an easy mark."

"But Brian wasn't expecting to be targeted. Maybe if I hadn't set myself up in the aggressive role, he might have suspected. But we both thought that the setup would lead Zeus straight to me."

"It did."

"And I dragged Brian along with me."

"Bullshit. He wouldn't have had it any other way." He held up his hand as she opened her lips. "Yes, I know that you think that I'm biased. You're right. I wouldn't have wanted McVey killed, but I did blame him for letting you set up that scenario at the lake house. I can't deny it. But I'm not letting you think that anyone but Zeus is to blame for McVey's head being in that basket."

Eve was silent. "He was only twenty-six, Joe. He told me he was going to have a Pulitzer by the time he was thirty."

"He told me the same thing. Too bad. He was smart and had enough drive to make it. But you have to remember, he was nagging you to let him come here and make another try at Zeus as late as yesterday morning. If you want to blame something besides Zeus for McVey's death, then hang it on McVey's ambition."

"It was horrible." She closed her eyes. "Brian's eyes . . . I'll never forget his face."

"Then you'll be giving Zeus exactly what he wants. Don't do it, Eve."

"I'll do my best." Her lids opened to reveal eyes shining with tears. "Because you're right. You're pretty damn smart, Joe. How did you get that way?"

"I'm a natural. Me and Solomon and a few other gifted guys out there. We could run the world if you gave us a chance."

"I believe Solomon tried." Her voice was steady, but her hand was shaking as she lifted her cup to her lips. "Okay, I'll stop blaming myself because of McVey and see if I can help find that bastard who murdered him. Zeus must be feeling very triumphant right now."

"Yes, smug and self-satisfied as a Cheshire cat. But he may have tripped up."

She went still, her eyes locking with his. "What are you talking about?"

"Ego. He's always been careless because he thought no one could touch him. I thought I'd seen signs that he was changing but maybe not. Maybe that arrogance is just too ingrained to overcome."

"And why do you think he may have tripped up? How was he careless?"

He shook his head. "I'm not discussing it with you yet. I have to check on some things, then think about it. I know you, Eve. You'll grab hold and try to run with it. I'm not ready to do that."

"Tell me."

He shook his head. "When I'm sure." He finished his coffee

and stood up. "Now get to bed and try to sleep. I'm going out on the porch and see what I can help wrap up. And I want to make sure that they clean it, so that it's not going to hurt you every time you go out there."

She was glaring at him. "You're not being fair."

"No, but I'm making it easier on myself. It won't hurt you to wait. I'm not having you disappointed if my theory doesn't pan out." He headed for the door. "And thinking about how angry you are at me will keep you from dwelling on what happened tonight."

"Your decision, your opinion. Tell me, dammit."

He paused at the door to look back at her. Her eyes were glittering, and her cheeks flushed with color. Much better than when he'd walked into the house earlier. Good.

He turned and went out onto the porch. "When I'm ready."

THE LAB TECH HANDED JOE the report the next morning. "Here it is. No wonder you didn't send it up to the Bureau for analysis. A first-year intern could have done this one."

"Thanks." Joe scanned the report before turning away. It was what he'd expected, but he still felt a flare of excitement at the confirmation. "I appreciate your making it a priority."

The tech shrugged. "No problem. Literally."

Joe moved quickly down the hall toward the elevator.

One down.

A moment later, he was at Slindak's desk in the squad room. "Did you check out that shoe factory in Toronto?"

"Yes, we haven't got the report yet."

"Give me the name and phone number. I'll follow up."

"Sure." Slindak studied Joe's face as he searched the papers on his desk for the information. "You're wired. What's happening?"

"Nothing yet." He took the report Slindak handed him. "But maybe soon." He turned and went to his desk across the room.

A moment later, he was dialing the number in Toronto.

Fifteen minutes later, he leaned back in his chair and looked down at his scrawled notes. It was all coming together.

But there were still a few pieces to fit into the puzzle. Get to work and make it happen.

He reached for the telephone again.

EVE MET HIM AT THE FRONT DOOR when he came back to the house that afternoon. "Well?"

"You're barring the door. Does that mean you're not going to let me in the house unless I divulge everything I know?"

"You've got it." She grimaced and stepped aside. "I'd do it if I thought I could get away with it. I'm frustrated as hell, Joe. I didn't think you'd—" She stopped, staring at his expression. "You look . . . Joe?"

"How do I look?" He passed her and went into the living room. "Slindak said 'wired.' Yeah, that's what I feel." More than that, he thought, as he turned to face her. He had the bastard in his sights and was aching to pull the trigger. "I think I've got him."

She inhaled sharply. "What?"

"Or at least I know how to get him."

She dropped down on the couch. "Talk to me. Who is he?"

"Zeus could be either Donald Novak or Ralph Fraser."

"You don't know which one?"

"I will by the end of the day." He paused. "I'm going to go pay him a visit."

"You know where he is?"

He nodded. "It was easy to trace him. He's not trying to hide. He doesn't think it's necessary."

She shook her head. "My mind is spinning. Start at the beginning."

"The beginning." He pulled her up and toward the back door. "We'll start here." He threw open the door. "What do you see?"

She looked at him in confusion. "Fence, flowers, lawn."

"A nice lawn. Pretty flowers. Did you put in the landscaping after you moved in?"

"No, I wouldn't have been able to afford it. It was already established. I just took over the care of it."

"But you were offered a maintenance contract by the landscape company who does most of the rest of the neighborhood."

She nodded. "The price wasn't too bad, but I'm a student and work two jobs. I can cut my own lawn." She frowned. "Where is this leading?"

"It's leading to the fact that there was a landscape-maintenance crew in your neighborhood several times a month. Including five of the homes on this block. That's why all the lawns and gardens look so well kept."

Her eyes widened. "Yes . . ."

"And all the houses of the victims' parents that we visited

had the same nice lawns. They all had that in common if nothing else. Such a little thing . . ."

"The landscape company?" Eve repeated. "Is that what you're saying? He works for the landscape company?"

"It would be the perfect opportunity for him to observe possible victims playing in the neighborhoods where he was working. He could take his pick of the children."

"Are you guessing?"

"Yes, but I'm betting I'm right. In the trunk of the car where he was hiding last night, there was blood, but there was also a scraping of something that looked like dirt. It wasn't dirt; under testing, it proved to be fertilizer. It was a common brand used by most landscapers in the area. I contacted the company in Toronto that manufactured the shoes from which we got that print in the cave. Heavy rubber content. The company said that it sold those shoes almost exclusively to professional gardeners and irrigation specialists."

"And last night on the phone Zeus said something about liking plants and flowers better than he liked people," Eve said. "I didn't think anything about it." She moistened her lips. "But you did."

"Only because it was all coming together for me."

"This landscaping company . . ." She lifted her hand to her cheek. "I know I've seen their truck in the neighborhood, but I can't even remember the name."

"Johnston and Son. They service every one of the subdivisions of the kidnapped children. It's a big company, and they have branches all over the Northeast as well as the South. The operations are extensive in Georgia. It wouldn't have been a stretch for Zeus to have killed those children who disappeared outside Atlanta." He paused. "But the company is based in Toronto, Canada. I checked with Johnston and Son personnel in Toronto, and the only workers they have in Georgia who were hired in Canada are Novak and Fraser."

"What difference does that make? Zeus is Canadian?"

"I couldn't tell on that first phone call, but on the second he was talking about your house. McVey was right, the pronunciation is different. Novak is Canadian. Fraser is a U.S. citizen, but raised in Toronto."

Her hands clenched as she looked out at yard. "It makes . . . sense."

"Yes."

"And this man could have been working on one of the yards on the block and watching Bonnie. I could have passed him when I went to the bus stop to meet her."

"It's possible," he said gently.

"If he killed her. I can't be certain. I won't be certain."

But it was coming close to the time when the truth would be thrust upon her, Joe thought. "The only thing I have to be certain about right now is catching the son of a bitch."

"You said you were going to pay him a visit. Where is he?"

"The crew Novak and Fraser are on is working at Nottingham Subdivision in Towne Lake today." He turned. "I'm on my way there now. I've changed cars so that Zeus won't recognize it. I just wanted to stop and let you know what was happening."

"You didn't send the police to pick them up?"

"They'll be there outside the subdivision. First, I have to make sure I locate him before he gets spooked by the squad cars pulling into the subdivision. The crew doesn't all work on the same house. He could be anywhere in the area."

"But you'd recognize him. You saw the sketch I drew of him." She paused. "And I'd recognize him."

"Yes, you would," he said quietly. "But he'd also recognize you. I know where this is going, Eve."

"Of course he'd recognize me. But that's no argument. We both know while he was doing surveillance on this house that he saw you. If he spots you, he'll take off."

"You want to go with me."

She met his gaze. "And you want me to go. Why else did you stop here before going after him? You may have told yourself you just wanted to keep me informed, but that's bullshit. You knew I had to go. You know I deserve to go."

"I don't want you hurt," he said roughly. "I don't want him to touch you."

"And that makes it hard to do the right thing. That's why you're lying to yourself. You promised we'd do this together." She threw back her head and stared him in the eye. "Do you want me to make it easier? If you walk out that door without me, I'll be at Nottingham Subdivision before you get there. If you take me, I'll stay in the car. But I have to be there. I have to see him captured. I want to see his face when he knows that he's not Zeus any longer."

She was right. He had known that it would come down to this when he had come here. They had taken this journey together, and he couldn't leave her behind now. He just couldn't admit it to himself because it caused him to break out in a cold sweat at the idea of letting her come that close to Zeus. Yet he had to admit it and drown that fear because he could not cheat her.

"Joe?"

His hand closed on hers. It was a soft, graceful hand belying the strength that lay beneath that fragile surface. His grasp tightened. "You stay in the car," he said hoarsely as he led her toward the door. "Unless you want to drive me crazy, you stay in the car."

NOTTINGHAM SUBDIVISION WAS an upper-middle-class neighborhood that had been built within the last ten years and had all the amenities. Including a homeowners' association that demanded the homeowners pay to keep the verdant lawns and shrubs meticulously maintained.

And Johnston and Son had a truck that was parked close to the clubhouse and swimming pool.

Joe parked across the road from the clubhouse, his gaze raking the surrounding area. "There's a man in the truck, but I don't see any workers." He got out of the car. "I'll go ask questions. Lock the door."

"You think the man in the truck is a supervisor?"

"He's not doing hard labor. That's a good sign."

She frowned. "Aren't you going to call the police waiting outside the gate to assist?"

"As soon as I can point the way to Zeus." He crossed the road and drew out the photos of the sketches of Zeus as he approached the truck.

"May I help you?" The man in the truck smiled politely at

Joe. "Les Cavanaugh. I run this crew. I know we're a little late coming to do the maintenance this week, but we got behind because of the rain. We'll get to your yard as soon as we can."

Joe showed his ID. "FBI. You can help me with an identification. You have an employee working for you who we have an interest in questioning."

Cavanaugh stiffened warily. "What for? Look, we got rid of that joker who was planting marijuana in some of the flower beds. We don't stand for anything like that."

"I'm glad to hear it. But the FBI doesn't deal with drugs." He handed him Kim Chen's sketch. "Do you know him?"

Cavanaugh frowned. "He's . . . familiar."

He handed him Eve's sketch. "Is this clearer?"

Cavanaugh's eyes widened. "Hell, yes. Ralph Fraser." He looked at Joe. "But Fraser is a good guy. Been working for us for years and never caused any trouble."

"Where is he working now?"

"In the flower bed behind the clubhouse, next to the pool. But he's not the guy you're looking for. He's real quiet, works hard and—"

"Stay in the truck." Joe started for the clubhouse.

And saw Ralph Fraser come around the corner toward him.

Shit!

Fraser stopped, then whirled and ran into the clubhouse.

Joe tore after him, but instead of going through the front entrance, he ran around back and entered from the pool area.

A bullet splintered the jamb of the door as he dove down and to the left.

"Put down your weapon. You're under arrest."

"The hell I am." Another bullet, closer.

But Joe had the direction now. Fraser was behind the bar across the room. He aimed and got off a shot. "Give it up, Fraser. Last chance. I'll kill you. It's what I want to do anyway. Why waste the taxpayers' money on shit like you?"

"You're not going to kill me. All these years, and you assholes haven't been able to touch me. I'll get out of here and kill you and that whore, too." Another shot. "Just like I did that newspaper reporter."

"But it's really me you want to kill, isn't it, Fraser?"

Oh, my God, Eve.

She was standing in the front doorway. But only for an instant, then she dove to the right behind the couch in front of the huge fireplace.

A bullet embedded itself in the soft cushions.

"You missed," Eve called. "Stupid, Fraser. Incompetent and stupid and—"

Take advantage of Eve's distracting him.

Another bullet struck the coffee table. "Bitch." It was a scream of rage. "I'll blow your—"

The scream was cut off as Joe dove across the bar on top of Fraser, jerking the gun from his hand and tossing it aside.

"No!" Fraser struggled wildly.

God, he was strong. Joe would have to put him out quickly.

But Fraser had rolled over, taking Joe with him. His face was contorted with rage as he looked down at him. There was fierce malice imprinted on every line of his heavy face. "You helped her. You helped the bitch. I'm going to cut your—"

Joe's knee jerked up into Fraser's groin.

Fraser groaned with pain.

Joe bucked him off his body. He moved swiftly to give him a karate chop to the neck.

Fraser went limp as he lost consciousness.

Joe was breathing hard as leaned back against the bar.

Eve was beside him, looking down at Fraser. "It's him. It's Zeus?"

"Ralph Fraser." He reached in his jacket pocket and pulled out handcuffs. "And you were supposed to stay in the car."

"And you were supposed to call in the police when you knew where Fraser was." She was still looking down at him. "And then I saw you run after him. What could I do?"

He cuffed Fraser and sat back on his heels. "And you wouldn't have come running to the rescue anyway? I could have handled it, Eve."

"I had to be sure." Her glance shifted to Joe. "And I had to make certain that you didn't kill him."

"I gave him the usual warning."

"But I think you wanted him dead. Didn't you?"

"He's a son of a bitch. I didn't want some slick lawyer to find a way of getting him off."

"That's not all. You're my friend. I think you wanted it over for me."

"Maybe. And now we have to wait for a jury to pull the plug on him." His lips twisted. "And I have to watch what that does to you. Is that what you want?"

"I have to talk to him. I have to make him tell me if he lied about killing Bonnie."

It was coming as he'd known it would. Joe could almost see the dark shadow looming over her.

"Maybe he lied," she added shakily. "Maybe he'll tell the truth if he thinks it will get him off."

"And maybe he'll lie again." He got to his feet. "Come on, let's get you in the car and away from him."

She didn't move. "I have to ask him, Joe."

"You're not going to get anything from him but curses if he regains consciousness anytime soon." He took her elbow. "We need to call Slindak and get those squad cars up here."

"They should be here any minute. I told that man in the truck to go down to the gates and get them as I ran past him toward the clubhouse."

"Good." He glanced once again at Fraser. He still wasn't stirring. "I don't think he's playing possum, but perhaps I'll stay here until Slindak gets here."

"Because he might be strong enough to walk away from this? I never thought evil could be as strong as good. I hoped it couldn't be that powerful." She shuddered. "But that was before I lost Bonnie."

Joe heard the sirens and gently took her elbow again. "He won't walk away from this." He nudged her toward the door. "I promise you, Eve."

"When can I see him again?" she asked. "I have to see him. He has to tell me about Bonnie."

"We'll talk about that later." A long time later, he thought. When she was stronger, when he could find a way to cushion the blow. As if he could ever cushion that blow. "Let me take you home."

Two Weeks Later

PAPERWORK, JOE THOUGHT SOURLY as he finished the third page of the report. It was the bane of every law-enforcement officer's life, and that went double when you had to make reports to the local police department as well as the Bureau.

"You look pissed." Slindak had stopped by his desk. "You shouldn't mind doing a little bragging on paper. You're a rising star. The Bureau is probably going to give you a promotion."

"Knock it off."

Slindak hesitated. "How is Eve Duncan?"

"Fine."

"Did you see her today?"

"Last night."

"Did she mention Fraser?"

He raised his head. "Every day. She wants to see him. I've been making excuses."

"I think that she saw through them. I just got a call from the jail. She's talking to Fraser now."

"What?" He jerked upright in the chair. "How did she get in to see him?"

"She went to his lawyer, and he arranged it."

Joe was cursing as he jumped to his feet. "Damn him. Do you know what that's going to do to her?"

"I have an idea. I thought you'd want to know. She doesn't need any more . . ."

The last words were lost as Joe ran out of the squad room.

Fifteen minutes later, he was taking the stairs two at a time to the second-floor room where they'd brought Eve for her visit with Fraser.

Shc was coming out of the room when he reached the top of the stairs.

She was stark white and was moving slowly, like an old woman.

"Eve, dammit."

She looked at him as if she didn't recognize him. "Joe?"

"Why did you have to do it?" He put his arm around her waist to support her and pulled her down the stairs. "I knew he'd do this to you."

"Did you?" She almost fell as they started down the next flight. She was walking stiffly, as if her legs weren't be able to function. "I guess I knew he would do it, too. But I had to ask him. It's Bonnie. Do you know what he told me?"

"Shh. Not now. Let me get you home first."

"If that's what you want."

"That's what I want." They were walking out of the station, and he put her into the passenger seat of the car he'd parked at the front entrance.

She stared straight ahead as he drove the twenty minutes to her home, but he doubted if she was seeing anything. Her breathing was shallow and quick.

He brought the car to a screeching halt in front of the

house. The next moment, he was around the car and half lifting her out of the seat. "Come on. Only a little farther."

She was looking at the empty place where the hanging basket had been. "He's a beast," she whispered. "Why did God let him come into the world?"

"Maybe he didn't. I think he's a creation of Satan." He had the door open, and he pushed her over the threshold. "And Satan will take him back soon."

"Not yet. Not until he tells me where to find my Bonnie." She stood straight, frozen, looking straight ahead. "He did it, Joe. He really killed her. I was afraid it was true, but I didn't really believe it. I didn't see how anyone could kill my Bonnie. But he did it. He looked into my eyes, and he smiled. And then he started to tell me what he did to her." Her voice was uneven. "I sat there and I wanted to scream, but I couldn't do it. I wanted to cover my ears, but I was frozen in that chair. So I listened and listened and I—"

"Hush." He couldn't stand any more. It was tearing him apart. "Just give me a minute." He lifted her in his arms and carried her across the room and up the stairs to her bedroom. He placed her on her bed, then followed her down, holding her in his arms. Her skin was cold where he touched her. "I didn't want you to go to see him. God, I didn't want you to go."

"I know. You wouldn't help me. I had to do it myself."

"You should have told me. I would have tried to make it easier for you. I'd never want you to be alone."

"I am alone. I'll always be alone now. He killed her."

He could feel the moisture sting his eyes. "He'd lie anyway, Eve. Are you sure?"

"He gave me details. Details down to the flavor of the ice cream she got from that booth in the park. It was her favorite flavor. Details about how soft and curly her hair was to the touch . . ." Her voice broke. "It was so soft, Joe. I remember her sitting on my lap the night before he took her. I was singing a song to her, and her head was pressed against my cheek . . ."

He could feel the pain in every word, it reverberated within him. He desperately wanted to take it away, but there was no way to do it. All he could do was give her his warmth. His arms tightened around her. "Do you want to talk about her?"

"Not now. All I can think about is Fraser and what he said about her. It hurts, Joe. I can't tell you how it hurts. It keeps twisting inside me. I want it to go away."

He couldn't even tell her the pain would get less. The loss of a child was eternal. "I'll be here to share it with you. Always."

"No . . . not fair. No one should . . . Go away, Joe. Not fair."

"It's fair, if I say it's fair." He was stroking her hair. "What's a friend for?" And what's a lover, a guardian, a warrior to protect you, for? I have to be all things to you, Eve. Something crazy happened, and my whole world changed when you came into my life. "So be quiet and just let me hold you."

"I want it to go away. I don't think I can stand . . ."

That was one of the things he'd feared when he'd known what Eve was going to have to face. "You can stand anything. You're tough." His hand was gentle on her hair. "Give it time. The state's going to kill that bastard, then some of the—"

"They can't kill him. I have to know where he buried Bonnie. I can't let them do it."

"He didn't tell you?"

"He said to come back, and he might tell me."

"And put you through this torture again? No way."

"I can take it. I have to take it."

"I said you were tough. I didn't say you were invincible."

"I'll find a way to block it out. I have to make him tell me."

"Eve . . ."

"You've never had a child, Joe. You don't know how important it is for me to bring her home. I can't leave her out there alone. Every night of her life, I tucked her into her bed, sang to her and kissed her good night. She was safe, she was home, she knew she was surrounded by love. Now I have to tuck her in one final time. I have to surround her with my love. I think wherever she is that she'll know it." Her voice was hoarse. "I have to . . . bring her home."

Oh, God in heaven. What could he say? What could he do?

"We don't have a weapon to use against Fraser, Eve. He knows he's going to be convicted of one of those killings. It's just a choice which case the state is going to choose to prosecute. But the bastard has a weapon he can use to hurt you, and he'll do it."

"I have to try. It's not only Bonnie. It's all those other lost children, too. If I go there often enough, he may get cocky and let something slip. I have to try."

He couldn't make the attempt to talk her out of it. Not right now.

She lay there silent for a long time. "Your cheek is damp, Joe. I feel it." She reached up and touched his lashes. "Are you crying for my Bonnie?"

"Yes, and for you." He cleared his throat. "It wouldn't hurt you to do a little crying yourself. It might help."

"I can't cry. I can feel all the tears in a tight little ball deep inside me, but they won't come out. Maybe later . . . After I've brought Bonnie home."

"Then I'll cry for you."

"Will you do that?" She cuddled closer to him, her cheek in the hollow of his shoulder. "You're so good to me. Maybe Bonnie will know that, too. She was so special, so full of love. I wish she'd known you, Joe . . ."

For an instant, he could almost see how different their lives would have been if tragedy had not entered it. An Eve vital and smiling, the child, Bonnie, who would love Joe as well as her mother. The image was bittersweet, but he would not push it away. That was neither their life nor their future, but he would work with what he had. He'd drain every bit of joy and happiness around them that he could to make it a good life, create a shelter and a haven for them.

His lips gently brushed her forehead. "I wish I'd known your Bonnie, too, Eve."

Diagnostic Classification Facility

Jackson, Georgia

January 27

11:55 P.M.

IT WAS GOING TO HAPPEN.

Oh, God, don't let it happen.

"Lost. She'll be lost. They'll all be lost," Eve said.

"Come away, Eve. You don't want to be here." Joe tried to

hold the huge black umbrella over her. "There's nothing you can do. He's had two stays of execution already. The governor's not going to do it again. There was too much public outcry the last time."

"He's got to do it." Her face was white and strained, her expression frantic. "I want to talk to the warden."

Joe shook his head. "He won't see you."

"He saw me before. He called the governor. I've got to see him. He understood about—"

"Let me take you to your car. It's freezing out here, and you're getting soaked."

She shook her head, her gaze fixed desperately on the prison gate. "You talk to him. You're with the FBI. Maybe he'll listen to you."

"It's too late, Eve." He once more tried to draw her under the umbrella, but she stepped away from him. "You shouldn't have come."

"*You* came." She gestured to the horde of newspaper and media people gathered at the gate. "*They* came. Who has a better right to be here than me." Sobs were choking her, but there were no tears. She hadn't shed one tear all the time that Fraser had gone through his trials and appeals. Joe had prayed that she would cry and gain at least a little release from the terrible tension. But she had never broken down through all the agony. "I have to stop it. I have to make them see that they can't—"

"You crazy bitch." A man jerked Eve around to face him. He was in his early forties, and his features were twisted with pain and tears were running down his cheeks. Bill Verner, Joe realized. His son was one of the lost ones.

"Stay out of it." Verner's hands dug into her shoulders. He shook her. "Let them kill him. You've already caused us too much grief, and now you're trying to get him off again. Damn you, let them burn the son of a bitch."

"I can't do— Can't you see? They're lost. I have to—"

"You stay out of it, or so help me God, I'll make you sorry that you—"

"Leave her alone." Joe stepped forward and knocked Verner's hands away from Eve. "Don't you see she's hurting more than you are?" All those months of torture and torment Fraser had put her through had been enough to drive a less strong woman mad. And still, in the end, Fraser would not tell her where he'd buried Bonnie.

"The hell she is. He killed my boy. I won't let her try to get him off again."

"Do you think I don't want him to die?" she said fiercely. "He's a monster. I want to kill him myself, but I can't let him— There's no time for this argument." She was suddenly frantic again. "There's no time for anything. It must be almost midnight. They're going to kill him. And Bonnie will be lost forever."

She whirled away from Verner and ran toward the gate.

"Eve!" Joe ran after her.

She pounded on the gate with clenched fists. "Let me in! You've got to let me in. Please don't do this."

Flashbulbs.

The prison guards were coming toward them.

Joe was trying to pull her away from the gate.

The gate was opening.

The warden was coming out.

"Stop it," Eve gasped. "You've got to stop—"

The warden gave her a sympathetic glance. "Go home, Ms. Duncan. It's over." He walked past her toward the TV cameras.

"Over. It can't be over."

The warden was looking soberly into the cameras, and his words were brief and to the point. "There was no stay of execution. Ralph Andrew Fraser was executed four minutes ago and pronounced dead at 12:07 A.M."

"No!"

Eve's scream was full of agony and desolation, as broken and forsaken as the wail of a lost child.

Joe caught her as her knees buckled, and she slumped forward in a dead faint.

He turned and carried her quickly toward the parking lot, his eyes never leaving her face. Even unconscious, her features were frozen in agony.

But, as he watched, two tears brimmed and slowly rolled down her cheeks. The tears she had not been able to shed for her Bonnie. Was it the start of healing?

God, he hoped so.

"Sir." A guard had followed him. "Is there something I can do? May I help you?"

"No." He looked down at Eve, and suddenly the love was flowing over him in such a powerful tide that it was spiraling, cresting, filling him with hope. "We'll get along fine. You can't help." His arms tightened around Eve as he started across the dark parking lot. "She's *mine.*"

CHAPTER 9

St. Joseph's Hospital

Milwaukee, Wisconsin

Present Day

MINE . . .

All through the years. Always mine . . .

Even in the glowing soft darkness that was trying to take him away from her, Joe could remember what had been and was feeling a wrenching sadness.

Eve . . .

But Eve was far away, and he could barely feel her now.

"THEN GO BACK TO HER. She needs you."

It was Bonnie. He could not see her, but the vision of her was there before him. A child, curly red hair and a smile that lit the darkness. Bonnie who had dominated his life since he had first known he loved Eve. He was not surprised to see her. What could be more natural than to have Bonnie here with him as he slipped away? It was not the first time he had seen the spirit of Eve's daughter.

When she had first come to him, he had thought he was going crazy, that the constant search had affected his reasoning. It had taken a long time before he had accepted that what he perceived as reality had an exception in the form of the ghost of Bonnie. It had not really affected his life with Eve, which was based on trying to find Bonnie, keeping Eve alive while she searched for her daughter, making life a gift instead of a burden through the long hunt.

"And you did all of that," Bonnie said gently. "But it's not over yet. Mama still needs you. Can't you feel how she's hurting?"

He could feel it. "I don't think I can go back. You can stop it. She loves you."

"But she loves you, too. And I love you, Joe."

"Do you? There were times that I resented you. She wouldn't let you go no matter how much it hurt her."

"How could I not love you when you loved and cared for her? It didn't matter what you felt about me. I knew you only wanted what was best for her. But you can't leave her now, Joe. She's going to need you more than ever soon."

"Is she? Then I have to be there for her. But I don't know if I can make it back."

"You can make it. We're walking together now, and now we have a destination. Can't you see it?"

Eve.

And beyond her something else.

"The . . . end?"

"There's no end in a circle, but there's sometimes the loosening of a knot in the fabric. I guess you could call it the end. But she needs you to help her do it. We all need you, Joe."

"Then I'll be there. I'll find my way."

"No, take my hand. It will be easier for you."

Somehow, she was clasping his hand, and he suddenly felt as if light was streaming through him, around him. "Dear God."

"See, the darkness is going away. You can see her more clearly now. And you're growing stronger, aren't you?"

"Yes."

"We're almost there, Joe. Hold on. I won't let you go. Just as you've never let her go."

Brilliance. Radiance. Love.

His heart pounding with wild eagerness as he saw Eve at the window of the ICU.

I'm coming. Don't be afraid. I'm coming, Eve.

"I'm letting you go, Joe," Bonnie said. "For a little while. I'll be with you again, but you don't need me now, do you?"

"No." He couldn't look away from Eve's face. Why had he thought that he could ever leave her? "It's okay for you to go, Bonnie. I'll take care of her now. After all, she's mine."

"No." Bonnie smiled. "She's ours, Joe."

SHE WAS GONE BUT THE LINGERING golden radiance was still keeping the darkness at bay.

And he couldn't wait to dispel it entirely.

He opened his eyes.

And then he smiled at Eve.

JOE WAS SMILING at her!

Eve could feel the tears running down her cheeks.

Good-bye? Surely not good-bye.

Bonnie had vanished only seconds before, and Eve had feared the worst. But there was a flush of color in Joe's cheeks, and he was smiling.

"Oh, God, thank you." She tore open the ICU door. "And thank you, baby." She was at Joe's bed in seconds. She took a deep breath. "Hi . . . took you long enough," she said unsteadily. "No, don't say anything. I just want to touch you." She pressed the bell for the nurse. "I want to hold your hand."

"So—did—she," Joe whispered.

"Who?" She answered herself as she took his hand in both of hers. It wasn't as warm as it usually was, but she could feel a faint pressure. He was alive and it was a miracle. The only miracle she knew had a name. "Bonnie?"

He nodded. "Bonnie." His eyes closed. "I couldn't—find my way back. She knew . . ."

"Yes, she knew." Her clasp tightened. "Don't talk anymore. I'll let you go, but don't you get lost again. Do you hear me?"

He nodded. "I hear . . ."

He was asleep again.

But the flush was still on his cheeks, and his hand was holding hers.

He was going to live.

The nurse was running into the room, a frown on her face.

They would tell Eve to go, and she would do it. She would put him in their hands to heal.

As Bonnie had surrendered him to Eve's hands.

* * *

EVE SAW JANE GET OFF the elevator as she left the ICU.

"Eve?" Jane was hurrying toward her, her face concerned. "You're crying. You look . . . how's Joe?"

She smiled shakily. "He's going to be fine."

"That's what they told you? But Catherine said he could be dying."

"Could doesn't mean that's going to happen." She wiped the tears from her cheeks. "He's taken a turn for the better. I just talked to him."

"Thank God." She took Eve in her arms and held her. "I was nearly frantic when you told me."

"I thought it was the end." Eve hugged Jane tighter. "He came so close, Jane."

"But he's tough. We both know that." She released Eve and handed her a handkerchief. "You seem to be a little damp. I'm pretty close to a deluge myself. Dammit, you should have told me right away. Do you think I would have let you go through this alone?"

"It was enough for one of us to go through this." Eve dabbed at her cheeks. "I told you when I thought I should."

"Should you leave him? Can you go to the waiting room? I'll buy you a cup of coffee."

Eve looked back at Joe, who now had three nurses and an intern by his bed. "He won't need me. They're not going to let me near him until they figure out which of those brilliant doctors managed to save his life and turn him around."

"And which one did?"

"None of them. They'd written him off. Joe did it on his own." She paused. "With a little help."

Jane stiffened. "Help?"

"He said Bonnie held his hand." She glanced at Jane. "I think she did and showed him the way home."

Jane didn't answer for a moment. "I'm not going to argue with you. You know I have a few problems with the idea that Bonnie pays you visits, but if you tell me it's true, then I accept it." She glanced at her and smiled. "And if you tell me that she helped keep Joe alive, then I'll jump up and down and shout hallelujah."

"Don't jump up and down. This is a hospital." She smiled brilliantly. "But you can do it in the parking lot."

Jane nodded. "Later." She went to the coffee machine and pressed the button. She let her breath out in a long sigh. "I can't tell you how relieved I am. I was so scared riding up in that elevator."

"I've been scared for days. Since the moment Paul Black stabbed him, it's been a nightmare." She took the coffee that Jane handed her. "Catherine told you everything that happened?"

"In broad strokes." She got a cup of coffee for herself and came back and sat down by Eve. "I got the gist of it. I was too on edge to cross-examine her. Though I think she's probably not a good candidate for interrogation. She impressed me as being a very tough cookie."

"She would have let you ask her anything. She's a good friend to both Joe and me." She took out her phone. "Which reminds me; I have to call her and tell her about Joe."

"Even before you get the official news from the doctor?"

She made a face. "You're right. Catherine is very practical. She always wants everything crossed and dotted. She'd run down here and have the doctors backed against a wall demanding guarantees."

Jane's brow rose. "But you still like her very much."

"Very much. She's as close as I've ever had to a woman friend." She reached out and squeezed Jane's arm. "Except you. I'm glad you're here."

"Me, too." She lifted her cup to her lips. "Catherine's at the Hyatt getting me settled."

"You don't have to get settled. You can go back to London if you like. Everything is going to be okay here."

"Stop trying to get rid of me. Do you mind if I stay and be with you? I'll go when Joe is better."

Eve nodded. "I just wanted to give you the option."

"You're rushing me out of here, and you haven't even heard that he's definitely on the mend."

"I've heard." Eve took another sip of coffee. "Joe told me."

"And no one with more authority."

"Well, Bonnie told him, and who has more authority than that?"

"Impossible." Jane chuckled. "But I'm so glad that you're this happy and giddy that I don't give a damn. It was the last thing that I was expecting. You're absolutely certain, aren't you?"

"Yep." Eve leaned back in her chair and felt the happiness flowing through her. She did feel giddy. After the tension of the last days, the relief was overwhelming. "And you will be, too. We'll just sit here and give those doctors time to congratulate themselves, then come out and tell us how clever they are." She lifted her cup in a mock toast to Jane. "And then we'll call Catherine and tell her to come and celebrate with us."

* * *

"I CAN'T BELIEVE IT." Catherine's face was luminous as she came into the waiting room. "The doctors confirmed it? Joe's going to be okay?"

"Believe it," Eve said. "It's true."

"No danger of his slipping back?"

"Oh, they tried to tell me that we had to be cautious. That there was a possibility of a relapse." She shrugged. "That's what they always say when they're confused. But I'm not confused. It's not going to happen."

"She has it on the highest authority," Jane said with a grin.

"I'll take your word for it," Catherine said. "Next question. How long before Joe is on his feet again?"

"It depends on his progress. Joe usually heals quickly."

"Months?"

"Weeks," Eve said. "But I don't know how many weeks. It will take as long as it takes. I don't want him to hurry and injure himself."

"Once he starts to recover, it's going to be hard to keep him down." Catherine frowned. "You know that, Eve."

Eve's smile vanished. "I'll keep him down even if I have to tie him to the bed."

"That may have to be the solution," Catherine said grimly. "Once he finds out that you believed Paul Black when he said it was Gallo who killed Bonnie."

Eve's smile faded. "Black believed what he was saying. I could see it." She paused. "And so did John Gallo. That's why he ran away."

"And Joe will be right after him."

"No." Eve could feel the fear tighten her chest. "We can't let him do that."

"No, we can't," Catherine said. "Which means I have to find Gallo first."

"You've been trying. Everyone's been trying."

"Then I'll try harder. I haven't had a chance to concentrate yet. I've split my time between searching those woods and running back here and checking on Joe." Her lips tightened. "I'll find him."

"He may not even be in those woods," Eve said. "If he got clear of them, he could be anywhere in the world. He has plenty of money, and he worked for Army Intelligence for years as a troubleshooter and assassin. It's not as if he won't know how to slip in and out of the country."

"I know that," Catherine said. "But it wouldn't have been easy for him to escape the sheriff and deputies we called in when Joe was hurt. They had him on the run. He was sighted at least twice."

"And then they lost him, and he hasn't been seen since," Eve said. "You told me yourself that it was as if he dropped off the face of the Earth."

"I think he's still in those woods. He owns the property. He knows it better than anyone hunting him," Catherine said. "I have a feeling."

"Instinct," Jane murmured. "I believe in instinct."

"So do I," Catherine said. "And it's saved my ass too many times for me to ignore it." She met Jane's eyes. "I don't like leaving Eve here alone. Are you staying?"

"I'm staying," Jane said. "I wouldn't leave her."

"Good." She turned back to Eve. "Is there anything I should know about Gallo? Anything that could help me?"

Eve thought for a moment. "He's not . . . When he killed Bonnie, he may not have been aware of doing it. He claimed he loved her, and I believed him at the time. He had blackouts after those years of torture in that North Korean prison."

"And does that mean you think she should be easy on him?" Jane asked in surprise.

"Hell no; if he killed Bonnie, he deserves everything anyone could do to him," Eve said coldly. "I'm just telling Catherine that he's definitely unstable, particularly where Bonnie is concerned. She may be able to use it."

"It's a possibility." Catherine turned to Jane. "And no, I won't be easy on him. It's tough that he went through hell in that prison through no fault of his own. But if that turned him into a child killer, then he deserves to be exterminated."

"No, you can't do that," Eve said quickly. "Not until he talks to me. I have to know where my Bonnie is buried."

"If he remembers. He might not if he's as unstable as you say."

"I have to talk to him," Eve repeated.

Catherine didn't speak for a moment, then shrugged, and said, "Okay, I made you a promise, and I'll keep it." She smiled. "And now I think I'll go to the ICU and see Joe."

"They won't let you visit him," Eve said.

"Then if he's awake, I'll make faces at him through that glass window. He'll get the message." She gave Eve a hug. "Take care. I'll be in touch and tell you how it's going."

"See that you do."

Eve watched her leave the waiting room and walk quickly down the hall. There was purpose in Catherine's steps and determination in her demeanor. She looked like a warrior going into battle.

"I was right. She's tough," Jane said. "Is she as good as she thinks she is?"

"Better, probably." And Eve was feeling a rush of relief about having Catherine moving quickly to find Gallo. Having Gallo out there was a double-edged sword. He'd be both a threat and temptation to Joe once he was in his right senses. And she was still experiencing the pain of that moment when Black had told her that Gallo was guilty. The bond between them as Bonnie's mother and father had turned tight and bitter, but she found that it still existed. It was Eve's job to go after Gallo and bring him to justice, but for the moment, she had a more important job in helping get Joe well. She could rely on Catherine to search in Eve's place until she was able to turn her attention away from Joe.

"I'm going to call the Hyatt and get a room for you, too," Jane said. "We'll probably both be here at the hospital most of the time, but we don't have to live here as you've been doing. It seems the urgency is gone."

"Yes." She again felt that profound rush of thanksgiving she had felt when Joe had opened his eyes. "The urgency has definitely been downgraded. You make your call, and I'll go back to the ICU and try to get the nurses to let me go in and sit with him again."

Jane smiled. "You feeling lucky? You said the rules were pretty stern."

"Yeah." Eve threw her cup in the disposal. "I'm feeling very lucky, right now."

JOE WAS sleeping.

Catherine stood at the window and gazed at him and the nurse moving around the ICU.

His color was good, and the sleep appeared normal.

Catherine let out a sigh of relief. She had believed Eve when she'd told her Joe was on the mend, but she'd had to see for herself. It was too easy for love to paint a false picture.

And the love between Eve and Joe was very strong. Catherine had had moments of envy when she had seen them together. When Catherine had married, she was seventeen, and her husband was sixty-two. They had both been CIA, and it had been more a partnership than a love affair.

Not that she had not loved him. But it was a quiet affection rather than a passion. She would not have done anything any differently. If she had not married Terry, she would not have given birth to her son, Luke. Why would she change anything when she had been given that gift? Her son was everything.

But the love that Eve and Joe possessed appeared to have all the facets missing in Catherine's marriage. Yet she had not even realized that they were missing until she'd met Eve and Joe.

Joe was opening his eyes. Did he see her?

Yes, he was smiling at her.

She blew him a kiss.

He smiled again and closed his eyes.

Yes, rest, my friend. Get well. I'll stand guard over Eve. You can trust me.

She turned and moved down the hall toward the elevator. But first she had her own decks to clear before she went on the hunt.

She took out her phone as soon as she was in the car. She dialed her number at the house she rented in Louisville. It was after midnight, but her son, Luke, probably would still be awake. He read till all hours of the night and still managed to be up early in the morning. She'd tried to tell him it wasn't healthy, but Luke would only look at her and not say a word. It was hard trying to convince him such an act would affect him in any adverse way when it brought him pleasure. Luke had not had much pleasure in his life. He had been kidnapped at the age of two from her home in Boston by Rakovac, a Russian criminal, as an act of vengeance against Catherine for undermining his mafia operation. She tried not to think of the torture and deprivation he had suffered until she and Eve and Joe had managed to free him. Nine long years. He had been two when he'd been kidnapped and eleven when they'd managed to free him.

It was no wonder that, now that he was safe and free, he was gobbling up experiences as if they would be snatched away from him in a heartbeat. He still didn't totally trust her, but he was coming close. She had to handle Luke with the most delicate touch imaginable, so that he wouldn't walk away from her.

She tried to make her tone light when he picked up the phone. "Luke, what the heck are you doing? Didn't that tutor I hired give you a curfew?"

"Yes, Mr. O'Neill said that I had to get to bed before three. I'm in bed."

Thank heaven that Sam O'Neill didn't keep Luke to an ordinary child's schedule. But Sam was too savvy to do that. That was why Catherine had chosen Sam as Luke's tutor. He was not only ex-CIA and fully capable of protecting her son, but he was a wonderful teacher. After what Luke had gone through during his captivity, strictness would have been absurd. He had been stunted in many ways by his isolation, but his childhood had been stolen from him. His independence had to be respected. "But you're reading. What's the book tonight?"

"*Midsummer Night's Dream.* I'm trying to understand it. But it's very odd."

"Yes, it is. But don't give up on it. You might learn something."

"I never give up."

No, he had boundless stamina and determination, or he would never have survived those nine years. "What else are you and Sam doing?"

"Swimming. Tennis. Golf. I don't like golf. It's too slow," he said quickly. "You're going to tell me that golf is like *Midsummer's Night Dream.* I might learn something."

"You might. There are a lot of golf pros out there who don't think it's slow."

He was silent. "Why did you call me in the middle of the night? Are you in trouble?"

"No." She paused. "Can't I call you without being in trouble?"

"Maybe I said it wrong." He didn't speak again, and she

could almost hear the cogs turning. "I meant you think that I might worry about you being in trouble."

"And would you worry, Luke?"

"You're very strong and smart. It wouldn't be reasonable for me to worry. Everyone says that you're very good at what you do."

"I didn't ask if it was reasonable. I asked if you'd worry."

He was silent, then said slowly, "I'd worry."

She felt a warm rush of love and joy. Every admission from him of a growing affection between them was a triumph. When she had rescued him, she'd had to start at the beginning in earning his love. After his emotional deprivation, she could not push him, but slowly he was learning that there was a bond between them.

"I don't mean to insult you," Luke said. "But I'd be willing to come and help you if you need me. I've been taught very well."

Taught the skills of weapons and guerrilla fighting, taught violence and cruelty, taught to bear pain without flinching. All the things a child should never have to face. Lessons that Rakovac had known would torture Catherine when he told her about them. And it had been torture, it had nearly broken her heart. "I know you have. But I'd like you to forget that now."

"But how can I do that?" he asked in wonder.

She had responded instinctively. She wanted to block out all that ugliness, but she knew she had to deal with her own horror and accept what Luke had become through those experiences. "That was stupid of me. Of course, you can't forget it. And thank you for the offer. If I find I need you, I'll be sure to call." She added lightly, "But I'd rather think of you having a good time with Sam. You like him?"

"I think so," he said cautiously. "He knows a lot." Another silence. "He smiles quite a bit. But I don't think he's laughing at me."

"I'm sure he wouldn't dare. Maybe he's just enjoying his job. He always wanted to go back to teaching."

"I guess that could be why."

"Did I tell you that Kelly was coming to visit you this week?"

"No, but she called me," he said shortly. "She told me to get ahead in my studies so that we could have some time together. She's very bossy."

"But you like her." It was true that fourteen-year-old Kelly Winters could be very domineering with Luke and had been from the start of their relationship. But he seemed to accept it from her as he would not have taken it from an adult. They struck sparks from each other, but it didn't stop them from getting along. Kelly was as mature and scarred in her own way as Luke. She had come into Catherine's life because Catherine had been sent to rescue her and her father when they'd been prisoners in the camp of a drug lord in Colombia. Kelly had survived, but her father had been killed before her eyes. She was a genius on the scale of a young Einstein, and that had led her down another rocky path. Perhaps that was why she and Luke understood each other. "I hoped to have her with us before this, but she has to attend that think tank at that college in Virginia."

"I didn't miss her. Well, maybe a little. She's kind of . . . interesting."

"I'm sure she'd appreciate it if you'd tell her."

"No, she wouldn't. She doesn't need me to tell her stuff."

He paused. "She won't like it that you aren't here. She likes you better than anyone. She told me you saved her life."

"We're friends. But she likes you, too. So enjoy yourselves and don't argue too much. Okay?"

"Okay." He added haltingly, "You know, I think I'd like it better if you were here, too." Then he added quickly, "But I'm not like Kelly. I don't need— You go do what you have to do."

He would never say he missed her, but this was so close it brought tears to her eyes. "I want to be there with you, too. You know I wouldn't have left you right now if it hadn't been to help Eve. I can't ever repay her for helping me find you, but maybe this is a start. Do you understand?"

"I think I do. It's like the honor thing in all those Knights of the Round Table books. Sometimes it's hard to connect the ideas in books with real life."

And books were all Luke had had to go by in that barren world Rakovac had made for him. "Yeah, it's like the honor thing. I'll be back as soon as I can." She cleared her throat. "In the meantime get back to *Midsummer Night's Dream.* And talk to Kelly about it. Maybe she'll have an opinion that will make you see something worthwhile in it."

"Nah, she'll only tell me to look for the patterns in the story. That's all she thinks about."

Catherine chuckled. "Probably. Good night, Luke."

"Good night, Catherine." He hung up.

He never called her "Mother," and she would never insist on that intimacy. Perhaps it would never happen. It was enough that he looked upon her as a friend. They were just learning each other, taking small, halting steps.

But this step tonight had been bigger and might lead her closer to him. Lord, she hoped that it would. Sometimes she ached with the need to tell him how much she loved him, how desperately she had loved him all through the years they'd been separated.

Play it cool. Don't blow it. Let him come to you.

She shoved her phone in her jacket pocket and started the car.

But for now put him out of your thoughts and go do your job. One of the big reasons she had her Luke back was the risk Eve and Joe had taken to rescue him. Now, as she'd told Luke, it was payback time and Catherine had an agenda.

Give Eve what she wanted most in the world.

Keep Joe from injuring himself more by trying to get out of that hospital bed and going after Bonnie's killer.

Find Bonnie's body and the man who killed her.

Where are you, John Gallo?

CATHERINE HEADED NORTH TOWARD the vast woodland acreage Gallo owned about seventy miles north of Milwaukee. It wasn't an easy area to search: thick woods and shrubbery, hills to the north that plunged to a huge lake hundreds of feet below. She had told Eve she believed in instinct, and she would go with it until proved mistaken. Gallo knew those woods, they were familiar, almost home to him. He even had a cabin on the property.

Not that he would be at the cabin. With the sheriff and his deputies crawling all over the property, it would be stupid for him to stay anywhere but in the wild. Gallo wasn't stupid. She had only met him face-to-face once, when they'd been on the hunt for Paul Black. It had been a fleeting encounter and barbed with antagonism on her part, but she'd become accustomed to making quick judgments. It had often been necessary to save her neck. She had grown up on the streets of Hong Kong, and that ability had developed in those first years of childhood. Her first impression of John Gallo was of sharp, lethal capability.

Definitely not stupid.

But she had to know more than that about him, dredge her memory of every single inkling she'd had of Gallo in that moment. Not only in that moment, but what she knew of him in general from Eve and her own research. She would take time as soon as she reached the property to go over everything that she knew and felt about John Gallo.

You always had to know your target.

CHAPTER 10

TWO HOURS LATER, SHE DREW up before Gallo's cabin, where two sheriff's cars were already parked.

She was surprised. When she'd been there before, the sheriff had been doing twenty-four-hour searches, but she'd not expected them to set up a command center. She certainly hadn't expected them to be there at this hour of the morning. It was nearly 3:00 A.M.

A young man in a deputy's uniform came out of the cabin as she opened the car door. He was stocky and sandy-haired, and his boyish face was very wary. "Ma'am?"

"Catherine Ling. CIA." She showed him her ID. "Is Sheriff Rupert here?"

"Deputy Rand Johan." The concern in his expression vanished as he grinned. "No, ma'am. He only left a couple of us here overnight in case Gallo showed up. The sheriff will be back in the morning."

"He thought Gallo would show up at his cabin?" She shook her head. "Not likely."

"Well, the search is kind of winding down. Actually, Sheriff Rupert thinks maybe he's left the area. He says we'll continue the search for the next few days, but then we'll gradually start pulling back."

"I see." Evidently the sheriff was getting frustrated and had the same thought as Eve concerning the possibilities that Gallo would try to leave the woods. Catherine had thought he'd give it more than these few days before he'd abandon the hunt.

The deputy saw her expression, and said quickly, "It's not as if Gallo is any real threat. He's only wanted for questioning."

"He killed a man in these woods only a few days ago."

"Paul Black. But we've got the report back on Black as well as Ms. Duncan's statement." His lips tightened. "A serial killer who specialized in murdering kids? Anyone deserves a medal for killing a snake like that. I'd do it myself."

And so would Catherine, but she wouldn't admit it to this youngster. "Black made a statement to Eve Duncan that Gallo was guilty of the same crime, the killing of her daughter, Bonnie."

"Who's to say the scumbag wasn't lying? Like I said, Gallo's wanted for questioning. Don't get me wrong, we're doing our job. But it's not a case of life or death, and we've spent enough of the taxpayers' money." He smiled. "Would you like to come in and have a cup of coffee? The sheriff didn't tell me the CIA was interested in this case. Gallo isn't connected to terrorists or anything, is he?"

"No."

"I didn't think so." He turned toward the cabin.

But Catherine had been caught by that first response. "Why didn't you think Gallo was connected to terrorists?"

"Gallo's not the type. He seemed to be a real nice guy."

She stiffened. "Wait a minute. You've met Gallo?"

"Yeah, he invited us all up here for a barbecue when he took over the place. He said that you never could tell when you needed the law to protect you, and he wanted to make sure that we all knew each other and exactly where the place was located."

"What?"

"It was a real nice barbecue. My wife brought the potato salad."

"How . . . nice."

"He's a local. He was brought up in Wisconsin before he went into the service. He was an Army Ranger, you know."

"Yes, I did know."

"I always wanted to be a Ranger, but then I met Sarah. That put an end to that. I'll be right back." He ducked into the cabin.

She pursed her lips in a silent whistle. A barbecue? Just a local boy trying to protect himself by getting to know the local authorities. Clever and foresighted. Gallo was a man who was accustomed to trouble and trying to minimize the impact.

And he had done just that with the sheriff and his deputies. They would do their job, but they liked Gallo and would give him every benefit of the doubt.

And by tomorrow she would be almost alone in these woods with Gallo.

Under the circumstances, that would not be a bad thing. No one to get in her way. She'd always preferred to work alone. No one for her to worry about when she got on the hunt.

"Come on in." Deputy Johan stood in the doorway. "Andy is putting on the coffee. He's real eager to meet you. He said the sheriff told him about you." He grinned. "The sheriff said you were one of those Lara Croft types. You sure look the part."

"Thank you . . . I think." She moved toward him. "I actually came to take a look around the cabin and see if I could find anything that would be helpful. I don't really know what I'm looking for. Do you think the sheriff would object if I did that?"

"Nah, you're one of us. Though I think you're out of luck. Do you want us to help?"

"No, I know my way around. On the night that Gallo took it on the run, I brought a child here who Paul Black had kidnapped. I had to find a haven for her until we could get her out to safety."

"See, Black was a real scumbag. Not worth bothering about."

"Yes, I see your point." She took a last look at the dark woods before she entered the house.

You're out there. I feel it, Gallo. You felt safe here with all these good old boys looking for you, but that's going to change. I'm going to know you so well that you're not going to be able to breathe without me knowing how deep. Before long, we're going to be close as lovers.

Lovers. Where had that come from? Probably because Gallo had been Eve's lover all those years ago when she was only a sixteen-year-old kid.

"Agent Ling?"

Her smile was dazzling. "Coming. I need that coffee. Then you and Andy can tell me all about the barbecue and everything that you learned about Gallo. Probably a lot of details sank into your mind though you didn't realize it. It's automatic with a good law officer like you . . ."

CATHERINE WATCHED THE TAILLIGHTS of the three sheriff's cars fade in the distance before she turned and went back into the cabin. Sheriff Rupert had been pleasant and firm and as much as told her she was wasting her time, continuing to search for Gallo.

And she had been pleasant and firm and resisted telling him to go to hell. It had been a very satisfactory interchange because she was now rid of them and could run her own show.

Should she get some sleep before she took off into the woods?

Probably. She wouldn't get much rest once she was on the hunt. She'd had breakfast cooked by the accommodating deputies, so that she could dispense with food for a while. She'd have the field rations in her backpack when she needed them. She'd be living with that backpack for the next days or weeks. She'd leave her suitcase in the trunk of her car and take only the necessities of the hunt.

But first she'd go over the Gallo information as she'd meant to do when she'd first driven up to the cabin. She sat down at the kitchen table and opened the folder she'd taken from her knapsack.

She knew most of it by heart, but there might be something she'd missed. Some of the information she'd gathered from various intelligence agencies. Some were notes about details Eve had told her about Gallo during the period she'd known him as a young girl.

Those Eve notes were very short and to the point. She'd lived in a housing project in Atlanta. At sixteen, she'd met John Gallo, who had recently moved down to the neighborhood from Milwaukee so that his uncle could get medical treatment from the local veterans' hospital. She'd become impregnated during the four weeks they were together before he'd left to join the Army. After that time, she had not seen him again and had been told by his uncle, Ted Danner, that he'd been killed on a mission to North Korea. She'd given birth to her daughter, Bonnie, and her life had gone on without John Gallo or contact with his uncle.

All brief, cool, and cut-and-dried. Yet Catherine was sure that there was nothing cool or unemotional about that period between Gallo and Eve. Even as a sixteen-year-old, Eve would have been strong and in control, and for her to be careless and become pregnant would be unlikely. Eve had told her there had been no emotional bond between her and Gallo, and that it had been a purely sexual relationship. But that sexual affair had been enough for Eve to take a chance that would change her life forever.

And Gallo had been the catalyst.

She took out the picture of Gallo taken when he had gone into the Army.

Olive skin, dark eyes, a full sensual mouth, a faint indentation in his chin. Yes, stunning good looks. Mature for his nineteen years. Anyone could see why a woman would be drawn to him.

And the brief glimpse she'd had of the older John Gallo had been even more impressive. A streak of silver in that dark hair, wariness, confidence born of experience . . . and yet still that hint of recklessness. And a personality so strong that he had managed to persuade Eve that he was innocent when she'd found out he was still alive and a suspect in her daughter's murder.

Innocent and able to point the way to a suitable substitute, Paul Black.

"You're quite a spellbinder, John Gallo," she murmured. "Now what can I do to break that spell and bring you down?"

She switched to the intelligence reports on Gallo. He had been a Ranger who had been sent with two other soldiers into North Korea by Army Intelligence officers Nate Queen and Thomas Jacobs on a supposed mission to retrieve a ledger with information regarding North Korea's attempts to acquire nuclear materials. The mission had gone south and he had hidden the ledger before he was captured. He had been thrown into a prison and undergone deprivation and torture for seven years before he escaped. In the hospital in Tokyo he had been diagnosed as mentally unstable, a schizophrenic with frequent blackouts. Yet Queen and Jacobs had taken him out of the hospital and continued to use him in their intelligence missions abroad. Catherine had thought it bizarre the first time she'd learned about it. The action stank of a suicide mission. But Gallo had survived and learned that Queen was dirty, involved in drugs and smuggling. He had retrieved the ledger from Korea.

The ledger.

Catherine flipped back to the statement Eve had given her about the story Gallo had told her about the ledger. It had proved to be evidence of Queen's and Jacobs's involvement in the drug trade and had been held by a North Korean officer who had been their partner. Gallo had used it to blackmail Queen to make them release him from those missions that were becoming increasingly deadly in nature. He had demanded money for his years of incarceration as a prisoner of war and built the fund into a fortune by his ability at card counting, a skill he had taught himself in prison.

Her telephone rang.

Eve.

"How is he?" Catherine asked when she picked up the phone.

"Better. I wanted to let you know Joe asked for you. He wants to see you."

"Did he tell you why?"

"Yes, he said to wait for him."

Catherine chuckled. "Tell him to tend to his job of getting well, and I'll tend to mine. He's afraid he's going to be left out of the action."

"Is he? What are you doing?"

"Not much. I'm at Gallo's cabin." She glanced around the living room and kitchen. "It's nice. Rough, but all the basic comforts. I like it much better than those A-frame luxury cabins I've seen. That's not even like being in the woods. You were here when you were setting a trap for Black, weren't you?"

"Yes." Eve paused. "I can't imagine you lolling around doing nothing."

"I didn't say I'm doing nothing. I'm thinking and trying to get a mental fix on Gallo," she said. "But it's hard without having the most important piece to the puzzle." She paused. "I know that for years Queen had Black in his employ as an assassin who removed everyone who got in Queen's way. I know that Gallo supposedly thought that Paul Black had killed Bonnie as revenge against him and went after him. He searched for him for years."

"So what's the missing piece?"

"Bonnie. John Gallo never had any contact with Bonnie. He couldn't have even known about her until after he got out of that prison. Why did he care enough about her death that he would devote all that time to finding her murderer?"

Eve was silent.

She obviously didn't want to answer, but Catherine couldn't drop it. She had to know. "You told me once that he'd told you that he loved Bonnie, and I said that he couldn't. He never knew her. But he had to have told you something that convinced you. What was it?"

"What difference does it make? I was gullible. He spun me a tale, and I wanted to believe him."

"What tale?"

"It doesn't matter. You don't have to know that to be able to find him."

"You're wrong. I have to know *him.*"

"Then heaven help you. He'll probably dazzle you as he did me."

Dazzle. Yes, it was a good word for the way Gallo was manipulating everyone around him. "You're not going to tell me."

Eve was silent again. "You wouldn't believe me."

"We're friends. I know you."

"You wouldn't believe me. If you catch up with John Gallo, ask him."

"I will. But by that time, the question may be moot."

"I'm going to hang up now and go back to Joe. I'll keep you informed of his progress. He's already making great strides."

"Then I'd better stop thinking and start moving." She chuckled. "I don't want you to have to keep that promise to tie Joe to the bed. How is Jane?"

"Protective, loving. She's with Joe now. Good-bye, Catherine. Take care." She hung up.

Catherine slowly put the phone back in her jacket. Eve had been of little help. Catherine wouldn't believe Eve? They were close friends. Eve should know that she'd trust anything she told her.

But the bond that was between Eve and Gallo was complicated, and Catherine had been aware of the emotion that still lay between them. No longer sex. Not love. Eve loved Joe with her entire being. But that clearly didn't stop her from feeling something for Gallo.

What? If Catherine was forced to kill him, would Eve feel a hidden sense of resentment? She said she'd kill him herself because of Bonnie's murder, and Catherine had believed her.

Eve was not going to talk to her about it, so she might just as well block it out and work it through on her own. That was her usual procedure anyway. Why was this any different?

Because Eve was her friend, and that was a treasure beyond price, and Catherine was trying to bend over backward to keep from hurting her.

Stop fretting about it. She got up from the table and went to the tiny bedroom and lay down. Four hours' sleep. Then she'd be up and leave the cabin.

She pulled up the coverlet and closed her eyes. She was lying in Gallo's bed. It felt . . . strange to have this strong sense of awareness of him. If anything, she should be aware of those deputies who had recently used this bed. Before they left, they had changed the linens and made up the bed in case she wanted to use it, but it wasn't of them that she was thinking.

Gallo.

He was dominating her thoughts, and it was natural she would imagine him lying in this bed in the cabin that belonged to him.

But it was closer to *feeling.* She could almost smell the scent of him. The mattress was hard against her body, and she wondered if that was the way he liked it.

She had promised herself that she was going to be as close to Gallo as a lover.

Was this the way it started . . . ?

St. Joseph's Hospital
Milwaukee, Wisconsin

"I JUST SPOKE TO CATHERINE," Eve said as she sat down beside Joe's bed in ICU. "She said to tend to your business of getting out of this hospital and not to nag her. Or words to that effect."

"She's on Gallo's property?"

Eve nodded. "She's at the cabin." She added quietly, "She'll find him, Joe. I know how you're feeling. I want to be out there hunting Gallo, too. It's my job, not Catherine's. But we have to wait until you're better."

"I am better. They're moving me out of ICU in a few hours," he said impatiently. "What would it hurt to give me a little more time?"

"It would be more than a little. You almost died, Joe."

"Yeah, I know." He was silent. "But I'm going to heal fast. She won't have to wait long."

"Tell that to the doctors. Their most optimistic prediction is four weeks."

"Then they'd better go back to the drawing board. I'm not going to be here that long."

"Joe . . ." Her lips tightened. "Dammit, stop this. Do you want to scare me? You can't jump out of bed just because you want to do it. Let yourself heal."

"You think I'm just being bullheaded." He didn't speak for a moment, looking down at their clasped hands. "And considering the fact that I'm usually the most stubborn ass on the planet, you have a right. But I'm not about to get out of this bed until I'm strong enough to function. I'm just telling you that time is coming very soon."

"That's not what—" There was something in his expression that caused her to stop the protest she was about to make. Her gaze searched his face. "How can you know that?"

"We're coming to the end," Joe said simply. "She says I have to be there for it."

She stiffened. "Catherine?"

He shook his head.

She whispered, "Bonnie?"

"She brought me back. She took my hand and told me it wasn't time for me to go." He looked up and met her gaze. "She said you were going to need me."

"I always need you."

"No, this is different." He paused. "We're coming to the end, Eve."

She laughed shakily. "Does that mean we're going to be called to the great beyond?"

"Maybe. I don't think so." His hand tightened. "But if it did, I wouldn't mind if you were there with me. That was my only regret when I was in that darkness. I didn't want to leave you. I wanted you to live, but I wanted to be there to make sure you were happy."

"Joe, you've spent most of our years together trying to make me happy."

"And that was my privilege." He lifted her hand to his lips. "I don't think that a love like this happens every day. I couldn't believe that it happened to me. And then I realized there had to be a reason that I had to nurture that love and the gifts it was bringing me."

"Yeah, some gifts." She stroked his cheek. "Dealing with my obsession for finding Bonnie, being put on the back burner whenever I was doing a reconstruction."

"And the gift of your honesty . . . and your love."

"Oh, I *do* love you, Joe," she said softly. "It's a wonder you were patient enough to put up with me until I saw it. Talk about gifts." She could feel the tears welling, but she had to get the words out. "When Bonnie was taken from me, I couldn't see any light at the end of the tunnel. Everything was dark. But then you were there, and I knew something was . . . different. I didn't know what it was, but I felt as if I might be able to make it through." She drew a deep shaky breath. "And then later, when I knew how much I loved you, I'm not even sure that you knew it, too. I said the words, I tried to show you, but my love for Bonnie was always there between us."

"I knew it." He smiled. "And how could I blame Bonnie? I wouldn't have known you if it hadn't been for her. As I've been lying here all these hours since I came around, I've been wondering if maybe it was Bonnie who purposely brought us together. You were alone. Did she know you needed someone to love you as much as I do?" He made a face. "Though I'm glad that she didn't make a ghostly appearance on that first day I met you. I was having enough trouble coping with the way I was feeling."

And Joe had begun seeing Bonnie only recently, and it had still shaken him, Eve thought. He had been on edge and uncertain and questioning his own sanity. It had taken him a long time to accept that the spirit Bonnie was no hallucination, and he had never been comfortable with the idea.

But there had been no hint of disturbance in his demeanor now when he was talking about Bonnie bringing him back to Eve. His expression was calm, thoughtful, and yet there was determination and strength in the set of his mouth and chin.

"It's possible, I suppose," she said. "I believe in the power of love, and Bonnie loved me. And she loves you, too, Joe."

He nodded. "I know she does. She told me." He was silent again, thinking. "I got to know her very well while we were traveling in that darkness. All through our years together, Eve,

I could never love her because I never knew her. She was gone before I came to you. But I know her now. She *touched* me. She took my hand, and I experienced everything about her. She's . . . beautiful."

"Yes, she is." The tears were falling now. "Like you, Joe."

"Don't say that too loud. It will destroy my macho image," he said. "But I can love her now. It's so easy . . ."

It had been a long time coming, but the joy Eve knew at those words would have been worth a much longer wait. It formed a bridge that spanned the emotional abyss that had been the only rift between them. "I'm glad that you got to know her," she said unsteadily. "I tried to tell you, but there weren't any words."

"There still aren't." He reached out and touched the tears on her cheeks. "Don't do this. It hurts me."

"It shouldn't. I'm happy." She wiped her eyes. "But next time you talk with Bonnie, tell her that she should bring me into the conversation. I can never count on when she's going to show up, and it's disconcerting when she tells you to disobey doctor's orders."

"She didn't exactly tell me that. I just knew."

"Knew what? That she wanted you to bail out of this hospital?"

"No, that she was going to help me to heal. It should be a cinch for her to offer a little mojo in that direction. After all, she managed to pull me back from the pearly gates." He chuckled. "If that was where I was heading. It felt pretty good, so maybe I might have gotten lucky."

"No, I was the one who got lucky."

"Keep thinking that way." His gaze went to the door, where a nurse and two orderlies were coming into the ICU. "And here's my escort to my new room. It's the first step, Eve. Tell Catherine I'm on my way."

One Week Later

SHE HAD found him!

Catherine wriggled snakelike down the incline that led to the cliff that fell off steeply to the lake below.

She had caught a glimpse of Gallo as he moved through the forest a half mile back. At first she hadn't been certain it was Gallo, but then he had come out of the shadows of the trees, and she had caught a glimpse of his face. Slight indentation at the chin, dark hair . . .

Yes.

She had been concentrating on this area of the property for the last three days, and she'd had a hunch she was getting near.

She propped herself against a boulder, and her gaze narrowed on the thicket of trees on the slope. He should be coming out of those trees any minute, and she'd have him.

Eve wanted him alive. Catherine silently took her dart gun from her backpack and inserted one of Hu Chang's special darts. Not as special as some others her old teacher had made for her. But the mamba venom and a few other lethal poisons weren't applicable in this case. This sedative would put Gallo out for a solid five minutes and give him another fifteen of lethargy.

"Come on, Gallo," she whispered. "Let me give you a little nap."

One minute.

Two.

He didn't come out of the trees.

Five minutes.

Dammit, where was he?

And then she felt the hair rise on the back of her neck in the most primitive of signals.

Someone was watching her.

He was watching her.

She instinctively dove behind the boulder and waited.

Where are you, Gallo?

Her heart was pounding.

She could feel him out there in the darkness.

Or was he behind her?

She wasn't sure. She listened.

She couldn't hear him. God, he was good.

But she couldn't stay there when he knew her location, and she didn't know his. Since she was trying to get him without a lethal commitment, she was at a disadvantage.

Fade away. Disappear. If she caught a glimpse of him, then try to line up the shot.

If not, give up the opportunity and come back another time.

She dove into the bushes that bordered the scraggly line of pines beside the boulders.

No sound.

Move swiftly.

She no longer felt his eyes on her.

But that might only mean he was close but could not see her.

And she couldn't see him, dammit.

Put distance between them.

Damn, she hated to run from Gallo.

She'd almost had the bastard.

She *would* have him.

Only an opening foray, Gallo.

The battle is yet to come . . .

Two Days Later

SHE WAS GETTING CLOSE again, Gallo realized.

He felt a rush of excitement as he caught a fleeting glimpse of Catherine before she disappeared into the pines.

She was probably going to circle and come at him from behind. He was still, listening for a sound.

There was no sound. But he'd bet that she was in motion.

Stay and confront her? Risky. She had almost gotten close enough to take him out twice in the last few days.

Why not stay? What did he care?

But he did care, or he would have plunged off the cliff into the lake in those first hours after he'd gone on the run.

Bonnie had made him care.

And he cared because Catherine Ling's pursuit had pierced the wall of despair and desperation that surrounded him and injected him with a shot of pure adrenaline. The hunt brought back memories of the missions that had been his life for so many years. Memories that enabled him to block out the more recent painful recollections.

The missions had been brutal, fast, deadly. Hunt, find, kill.

But Catherine Ling's pursuit had not been brutal. In the few glimpses he had caught of her, he had thought she was like a black panther, stalking, graceful, beautiful.

But, yes, definitely fast and deadly.

So did he run again?

He started moving. As silent as Catherine. As fast as Catherine. He could feel his heart start to pound, the excitement electrifying every muscle.

Follow me.

Let's play the game a little longer.

Who knows? I may let you win it.

CHAPTER 11

One Week Later

SHE NEEDED A BATH, Catherine thought as she woke in the cave where she'd sheltered for the day. She slept from dawn until late afternoon because the hunt was at night. She'd taken a chance and swum in the cold lake on the property the day before yesterday. She couldn't afford to do it again anytime soon. She had thought she sensed Gallo and had quickly returned to shore.

It could be imagination. It seemed she was always sensing Gallo these days. His presence was all around her, in the trees, the hills, the lake.

He was the last thing she thought of before she went to sleep and the first thing when she woke in the morning. Not that she slept much.

Not since she became aware that Gallo was also stalking her.

The realization had come to her about two weeks after she had found and begun to stalk him. This hunt had been like nothing in her experience. He was like no one she had ever targeted. A phantom, silent, swift, moving all around her and yet only permitting her brief glimpses, the slimmest of opportunities.

After that first encounter he could have chosen to leave the area, but he hadn't done it. He had stayed and let her stalk him. Then, as time passed, she was aware that it had become a duel. He was no longer content to be the prey.

Why?

She didn't care any longer. She had been swept up in the dance, and every minute was charged, every hour was electrified by the knowledge that any minute she might see him again.

And that minute might be her last.

Her phone vibrated, and she pulled it out of her jacket.

Eve.

"You haven't called me in the last two weeks," Eve said.

"I've been busy."

"And you sound funny."

"I just woke up." And she hadn't spoken to anyone for the last two days, when she'd called home and checked on Luke. "How is Joe?"

"Better all the time. He's out of bed and in therapy. He may get released soon." She paused. "I hoped I'd hear something positive from you before that."

"So did I. Nothing yet."

"You still think he's in those woods?"

"Oh, yes." She gazed at the shrubs several yards away. He could be as close to her as those trees. But she didn't think so. She would feel him. These days, every nerve, every muscle of her body seemed attuned to him. "He's here. I may be getting closer."

As close as a lover.

"Well, you may have company soon," Eve said. "I won't be able to keep Joe away from there for long. Then we'll both be up there to reinforce you."

"No!" The rejection was sharp and instinctive, and it had nothing to do with protecting Joe, she realized. This dance with Gallo belonged to her. She didn't want anyone else to cut in before the end. "Do your best to keep him away."

Silence. "Are you all right, Catherine?"

"I'm fine. I'm dirty, I stink of sweat and dirt, and I know this forest better than I ever wanted to know any place. But other than that, I'm doing well." She added, "I'll try to call you more often. Give my best to Joe." She hung up.

She took a protein bar out of the knapsack. Eat. Find a creek to wash her teeth and face, then start out again.

The eagerness was beginning to sing through her as she bit into the bar. It was going to end soon. She would find him and put him down.

Or Gallo would find her.

Either way, it would be the end of the dance.

Eight Days Later

CATHERINE'S BREATH WAS COMING hard and fast as she ran up the hill.

He was no more than a football field ahead of her. She had

caught a brief glimpse of him on the lower slopes, then another a few minutes ago.

He was getting careless. He could have stayed deeper in the brush, and she might not have seen him. Are you getting tired, Gallo? I'm not. I can go on forever.

As long as the adrenaline of the dance kept her moving.

But he'd reached the top of the hill and disappeared into the trees.

She slowed, and her hand closed on her dart gun.

Her catching sight of him could have been a deliberate ploy on his part to lead her into a trap.

She darted into the trees, her gaze searching the darkness.

No Gallo.

She moved carefully toward the opening in the trees near the top of the hill. Where was he?

She stopped short as she reached the edge of the trees.

Gallo. Out in the open. The moonlight revealing him with crystal clarity.

He was on the shale slope of the cliff.

Why the hell had he led her there?

It didn't make sense. He had to realize there was no cover for him until he reached the trees over forty yards away. He had been increasingly reckless for the last two days, and it had bewildered her. Dammit, did he want her to shoot him? For all he knew, it wouldn't be a dart but a bullet that would cut him down.

She was being ridiculous. What difference did it make how reckless he was being? It was her chance to take him down.

She lifted her dart gun.

But if she shot him while he was on that slippery shale slope, he would probably roll down off the cliff to the lake hundreds of feet below them. She would kill him.

He glanced behind him.

She knew he couldn't see her in the trees, but he was aware that she was there. Just as she knew when he was near her. It was part of the dance.

He smiled, and she knew it was at her. He was taunting her. Crazy. Dammit, he knew he was in range.

"Damn you, get off that slope," she whispered.

He moved slowly, deliberately, toward the trees on the other side of the slope.

She breathed a sigh of relief. Now to figure a way that she could cross that barren strip of shale and track him into the trees. Maybe go up toward the top of the hill and work her way—

The edge of the slope broke away from the hill and threw Gallo to the ground. He rolled toward the edge of the cliff!

"No!"

She was out of the trees and crossing the shale slope, her boots sliding on the slippery surface. The slope was still crumbling . . .

Where was Gallo?

Clinging to the edge of the cliff. His fingers white as he gripped the edge.

She stood over him. He was looking up at her, his gaze on the gun in her hand.

"Do it," he said hoarsely. "All it would take would be one shot. Even that dart gun would do the trick."

She hadn't even known she was still holding the gun.

"Do it." His dark eyes were glittering fiercely into hers. "Dammit, one shot."

"Screw you. I'll do what I please." She threw the gun aside and fell to her knees. "Give me your left hand and boost yourself on the edge with the right when I pull."

He didn't move.

"You *listen* to me. I won't have it. It's not going to end like this. Dammit, give me your hand."

"You're not strong enough to bear my weight."

"The hell I'm not." She gripped his left hand and wrist with both of her hands. "Now when I count to three let go. One. Two." She braced herself. "Three!" She pulled, jerking backward with all her strength. Then she lunged forward as the weight of his body unbalanced her. But his right hand was bracing on the ground, lifting his weight as she grabbed him under the arms.

She jerked backward, and he came down on top of her as he scrambled over the edge of the cliff!

The breath was knocked out of her. She struggled to breathe as she fought the darkness. Then Gallo was off her, and she was looking hazily up at him. Dark eyes glittering, lips tight and bitter . . .

There was something in his hand . . .

A gun.

"I told you to shoot me," he said. "I expected it. You should have done it."

He pulled the trigger.

Darkness.

* * *

SHE OPENED HER EYES TO SEE a fire only feet away from her. A campfire, shouldering low . . .

And the shadows of the flames playing on the face of the man sitting cross-legged on the ground across the fire.

Gallo . . .

"Good. You're awake. I didn't know how potent the drug in that little pop pistol was going to turn out to be. You could have set up the dose for me, and I'm a hell of a lot bigger than you. How do you feel?"

She felt fuzzy and lethargic. But that was how she should feel, she realized, as his words sank home. He had turned her own weapon against her. "I'll live . . ." Her tongue felt thick as she tried to speak. "Disappointed?"

"No." He stirred the fire with the stick he was holding. "Aftereffects? Paralysis?"

"I'll be back to normal after fifteen minutes."

"A very efficient drug. What is it?"

"You . . . wouldn't recognize it. Hu Chang made . . . it for me."

"Hu Chang?"

"An old friend." The thick lethargy was starting to clear, and she realized that her wrists were bound in front of her. "You have me tied up like a pig for market. Are you . . . afraid of me, Gallo?"

"Yes. You're formidable, Catherine. I can't tell you how much I've enjoyed our game."

He called it a game. She called it a dance. But the concept was the same. "I saved your neck, you son of a bitch."

"And you would have taken it the minute you had me on safe ground. I'd judge you acted on impulse when you decided to pull me back from the brink. I'd probably have done the same." He glanced at the dart gun on the ground beside him. "Or maybe not. Why the darts? Why not a bullet?"

"Eve wants you alive. She thinks you know where Bonnie is buried. Do you?"

He looked down into the fire. "Maybe. I don't know . . ." He didn't speak for a moment. "Then I'm not the only one who tied your hands. Eve did it, too. It could have been fatal for you."

"Eve didn't tie them. I tied them. I make my own choices."

He glanced at the dart gun again. "I can see that." He reached over and picked up the pan of boiling hot water bubbling over the blaze. "Some of them have unhealthy consequences. I don't—" He stopped as he saw her stiffening, as she gazed at the boiling water. "You thought I was going to use this on you? That would be sacrilege. You have the most beautiful skin I've ever seen." He set the pan on the ground while he got a cup from the knapsack, poured instant coffee into it. "I may be a son of a bitch, but it would make me sick to damage it."

"You are sick. Eve says you're insane. She says you admitted it yourself."

"I did." He poured the hot water into the cup. "But it appears to come and go. Isn't that convenient? But all the more dangerous for anyone who might trust me in my saner moments." His voice was bitter with self-mockery. "I'm like a mad dog that should be put out of his misery. I tried to do it myself. But she wouldn't have it."

"Eve?"

"No, Bonnie." He brought the cup to Catherine and knelt

beside her. "Or maybe that was a delusion, too. Self-preservation is a powerful thing."

"I don't care about your delusions. But your sense of self-preservation doesn't appear to be too well developed. You were skipping around on that slope like the madman you claim to be. You must have known I'd have a clear shot."

"But you didn't take it." He smiled. "I was disappointed. But then providence took a hand." He looked down at her. "Are you strong enough yet to take this coffee cup, or should I help you?"

She was still too weak, but she was tempted to take it anyway. She needed the caffeine in her system. But she would probably spill it all over herself, and that would put her at still greater disadvantages with him. "I don't want it."

"And that means you're not strong enough yet." He put his arm under her shoulders and lifted her to a half-sitting position. "You have a choice of spitting it back in my face or drinking it and getting a bit closer to your usual fighting weight. It's up to you." He brought the cup to her lips. "I think I know which you'll choose. You may be pissed off at me for taking you out, but you're too professional not to prepare for our next battle."

She hesitated only for an instant before opening her lips.

"Ah, that's right." He tilted the cup, and the hot liquid poured into her mouth. "You're being totally intelligent." He took the cup away. "Just what I'd expect of you."

She was cradled in his arm, and he was so close she could smell the earthy scent of him and feel the heat of his body against her own. It was . . . disturbing.

His gaze was narrowed on her face. "What are you thinking?"

She met his gaze. "That you stink as much as I do."

Surprise flickered across his face. Then he chuckled. "I like the way you smell. It's . . . basic. I'm sorry the feeling isn't mutual."

It was mutual, she realized. But it shouldn't have been. Or maybe it was because of the almost barbaric interaction between them of the past days. "I prefer a higher plane to basic."

"I know. You would never have chanced taking that bath in the lake if it wasn't important to you."

Her gaze flew to his face. Dammit, she had *known* he was there.

He nodded. "But I had only a glimpse before you took flight like a frightened swan. Your instincts are too damn good." He lifted the cup to her lips again. "Who is Hu Chang?"

"I told you, my friend."

"A very skilled friend. Was he also your lover?"

"No."

He gave another sip of coffee. "A father figure?"

"No. Hu Chang is old enough to be my grandfather. Not that it would make any difference. Age is nothing."

He held the cup steady as he gave her the last of the coffee. "That's right, I remember that when I was reading the dossier on you that you married your CIA partner and he was sixty-two to your seventeen. Not exactly a marriage of equals."

"No, he was a better agent than I was."

"At first."

She was silent, then said grudgingly, "At first."

"You didn't want to admit that, but you were too honest to

lie." He smiled. "But that wasn't the playing field I was talking about."

How had they come to be talking about her private life when it had started with Hu Chang? "You had a dossier on me?"

"You were asking questions about me. You were pushing Eve in a direction I didn't want her to go." His smile faded. "Or maybe I did and wouldn't admit it. She had been out of my life for so long that I didn't think I had the right to have her know I was still alive. But you changed all that, you told her, and there was all hell to pay."

Yes, all hell, she thought. Black's death, Joe's wounding, Eve's agony. "I thought she had a right to know." She added grimly, "Since you were my first choice for Bonnie's killer. But you managed to convince Eve that I was wrong. You must be very persuasive."

"Yeah, that's me." He met her gaze. "Can't you tell? I can persuade the birds not to sing. I can persuade a wonderful little girl to step into my lair so that I can kill her." He carefully put her down and sat back on his heels. "You're blaming yourself for setting all this in motion."

"Don't you?"

"I don't blame anyone but myself. I don't have the right," he said wearily. "I thought I did once, but that's all gone."

There was something about his words that were reaching her, touching her, she realized incredibly. Dear God, what was happening? "You're right, you're the only one to blame." Move away from the terrible intimacy that was obscuring the facts and the way she should be regarding him.

"I'm glad we agree." He moved back to his former position beside the fire. "Are you feeling any better now?"

"Yes." Almost normal, almost ready to act. "Are you going to kill me?"

"I don't think so." His lips curved bitterly. "But we can't be sure, can we? I'm not stable."

"Then are you going to let me go?"

He shook his head. "I'm in something of a quandary. If I let you go, you'll just go back on the hunt. I couldn't be more sure of that. The next time one of us might die. Probably you, since you're more honorable than I am, and you made a promise to Eve. That would upset me." He tilted his head. "Unless you'd promise me not to try to hunt me down?"

She was silent.

"I didn't think so." He looked down at the fire. "So I don't see any solution but keeping you here with me. It probably won't be for too long. I imagine Eve and Joe will come looking for you if you don't communicate with them."

"No!"

"You're thinking I'm setting you up as bait?" He shook his head. "Maybe I am, but not as you think. I'm the prize, not you. Joe Quinn has the same training and instincts I have. Eve may want to keep me alive to pump me, but Quinn won't be able to resist giving me the coup de grace if I set it up right."

"You want him to kill you," she whispered.

"I can't seem to do it myself. I don't think she'll let me. I don't know why. I thought you would do it." He looked back at her. "That would have been the most divine way to go. The journey was probably the most exciting one I've ever taken, and the destination would have been right. But you failed me, Catherine."

He was telling the truth, and those simple words were shaking her to the core. It was too much. She shook her head. "Screw you. I won't be used by you. You want to commit suicide? Get a couple of hara-kiri swords and go to it."

He shook his head. "She won't let me," he said again. "I don't know why. Maybe she's saving me for Joe and Eve. But it's not like her."

"You're nuts," Catherine said curtly. "Now I do believe you're crazy. You're saying that Bonnie has come back from the grave to keep you from killing yourself? Bullshit."

"Is it? Ask Eve if it's bullshit." He held up his hand as she started to speak. "There's no use continuing on this vein. I know it's bizarre and beyond belief." His lips curved in a faint smile. "Chalk it up to another hallucination."

"I will." She paused. "You intend to keep me here all trussed up like this?"

"Yes."

"Then will you loosen these ropes? They're cutting into my wrists."

He studied her expression. Then he slowly nodded and got to his feet. "I don't like the idea of your being uncomfortable. It bothers me." He knelt beside her. "Hold up your wrists."

She lifted them and held them out to him.

"They don't—"

Now!

Her wrists came down whiplike on the bridge of his nose.

She rolled into his body, and her knee lifted and struck upward into his groin.

He grunted and bent double.

She rolled past him, jumped up, and took off for the trees.

She made it five yards before he tackled her and flipped her over.

She brought her tied wrists up and struck him in the side of his neck.

"No!" He was glaring down at her as he straddled her. His nose was bleeding, and he looked as fierce and barbaric as she felt. "Dammit, it's not going to be that way. I told you that I won't have you—" He stopped, staring down at her, the ferocity slowly faded from his expression. "Even bound and drugged, you managed to almost do it. Wonderful . . . Damn, you're wonderful. That's why it should have been you." His one hand was holding her wrists and with the other he loosened her hair, which was tied back in a chignon. His fingers combed through it until it was tumbling around her face and shoulders. He added softly, "And beautiful. This was the way you were when I saw you in the lake. You were all golden silk and shining ebony. I only got a glimpse of you, but it made me so hard I couldn't think of anything else for hours afterward." He was stroking her hair, slowly, sensuously. "And every time I stopped to sleep, I remembered . . ."

He was hard now. She could feel him against her. Feel the heat he was emitting. His eyes were dark and glittering in his taut face. His lips were half-parted and full and sensual. She stared up at him in helpless fascination. Dammit, her anger was abandoning her. She was having trouble breathing. Her breasts felt full, taut . . .

It was impossible. This mustn't happen. She had to get him away from her. She tore her gaze away from his own. "My hands are tied. Is that the way you like it? Are you going to rape me?"

He stiffened. "It was damn close." He got off her. "But it wouldn't be rape, would it? I'd see that it would just be another road of the journey we're on. And you liked that journey as much as I did."

He jerked her to her feet. "These ropes are loose enough. I'm going to tie you to that oak tree so that we can both get some sleep." He was pulling her toward the oak. "Neither one of us has been getting much of that in the past weeks."

"This doesn't make sense. Kill me or let me go."

"We've discussed that, and those aren't options." He shrugged. "And maybe I don't want them to be options. You've cheated me of what I thought was my way out. I think you should keep me entertained until Quinn shows up as a replacement." He shook his head. "And I don't mean that in the sexual sense. I don't believe you'll let me—but that's up to you. Maybe you'll decide that you should use me to distract yourself. I'm at your disposal."

She wouldn't look at him. She was still feeling the heat that had touched and scorched her only minutes before. "Make up your mind. An hour ago you were ready to kill me."

"Was I? But that game is over." He was roping her to the tree. He took her jacket and put it beneath her head to cushion it against the trunk. "I'll let you lie down full length next time

I'm awake enough to watch you. Do you want me to fasten your hair back up?"

"No!" She didn't want his hands on her. That loosening and threading had been unbearably sensual.

"Good. I like it down anyway." He turned and stretched out before the fire. "But I can see how you'd want it out of your way when you were after me. But that's all over now, isn't it?"

"No, this is just an intermission."

"I believe you're wrong. I think we've entered a new phase."

"And I think that you're fooling yourself."

"It's possible." He rested his cheek on his arm, his gaze focused on her. "But it feels different. You look fantastic with the firelight on you. I'm going to enjoy looking at you until I go to sleep." He made a face. "Well, maybe not enjoy. I'm definitely experiencing some discomfort at the moment. But that goes with the territory. It's worth it."

She was silent. "Why are you saying these things?"

"Because we've reached the end of our game. No subterfuge. No tricks. I can be open with you."

"Because you think Joe is going to kill you?"

"I hope he does. I hope I don't fight back." He added soberly, "But I might. You could take care of that if you chose. I'll keep this dart toy of yours and give you your gun back. We could have one final game."

"And let you use me? Screw you."

"I thought that's what you'd say." He smiled. "So I'll just lie here and accept the pleasure of the moment. Tomorrow I'll take you down to the lake and let you take a bath."

"I don't think so."

"We'll work something out that will cheat me, but give you a sense of security." He paused. "How close are we to getting Quinn out here?"

"I'm not sure. Eve said that he's making an amazing recovery."

"That doesn't surprise me. Bonnie is probably helping things along. I'm glad. It was my fault that Quinn was wounded. He was trying to keep me away from Black when the bastard knifed him."

"Bonnie, again? You appear to be as obsessive about Bonnie as Eve." She added deliberately, "I find that very strange when you told Eve that you believed Black when he claimed you killed her."

He flinched. "It doesn't seem strange to me. I love my daughter. I love her more than anything in this world or the next. But isn't there some saying that you always kill the thing you love?" His lips tightened. "That would be particularly applicable if you're mad."

"And not remember it?"

"I used to have blackouts about the time that Bonnie was killed." He tilted his head. "Are you questioning that I killed her? Eve didn't. She believed Black, too."

"I usually question everything. So far the only sign of insanity I've noticed in you is that you're convinced a dead child is controlling your actions. That's pretty weird. Particularly since you never met the kid." She looked at him curiously, "Or did you?"

"I guess you could say I never formally met her. I saw her once when she got off the school bus, and Eve met her. She was very . . . happy. I knew I couldn't show up in their lives and interfere between her and Eve." He shook his head. "But I knew her, Catherine. I knew her, and I loved her. Eve believed me when I first told her that, but she may not anymore."

"Can you blame her?"

"No, I've never blamed her for anything. I'm the one who left her when she was pregnant to fight her way in life with a child."

"She said you didn't know. She said that she didn't want you to know." She grimaced. "And you couldn't help her when you were in that North Korean prison. So it's idiotic to blame yourself for that."

"You're defending me again."

"No, I'm not." But she had been defending him, she realized with frustration. She kept falling into that trap. Why? It didn't make sense when he had bound her to this damn tree, and she was feeling annoyingly helpless. No, not helpless. He had given her choices. None of them acceptable. "I just don't like inaccuracies."

"I can see that would bother you. You're so sharp and clear-thinking that you always want to cut to the bone. I noticed that when I was tracking you." He smiled. "I'm glad I had that time with you, Catherine. You were a constant pleasure."

She went back to the question that he had only waltzed around. "So why are you fixated on those weird ideas about Bonnie?"

He shook his head. "I don't think I'm prepared to discuss that with you now, Catherine. I like the idea of you defending me even if you're mistaken. I want to enjoy it for a while."

She gazed at him in astonishment. "You're enjoying this?"

"Not nearly as much as I'd like, but I've always believed in taking pleasure wherever I could. I learned that in that Korean prison." He stretched like a cat before once more settling his head on his arm, gazing at her. "So yes, I'm enjoying this moment. I'm enjoying *you,* Catherine."

"Why? Are you into bondage?"

He chuckled. "No, I wish I could release you. You can't imagine the excitement you brought me during the past weeks. Every day, there was the anticipation of catching a glimpse of you. Every trail was one that you might have taken."

And she had known that same excitement, that identical anticipation. She looked away from him. "So now you're gloating because you have me?"

"No, this wasn't how I intended it to be." He said softly, "I'm enjoying it because you're beautiful and strong and honest, and I don't believe I'd ever tire of looking at you."

She glanced back at him and wished she hadn't.

Spellbinder. That was what Catherine had thought when she had been going over Gallo's dossier and trying to learn him. Lying there in the firelight, he was completely sensual. Flat stomach, muscular thighs, and broad shoulders, his intent dark eyes and full lips that held the faintest smile. Everything about Gallo was male, sensual . . . sexual.

And she could feel the beginning of her response to that sexuality. The heat that was moving through her veins, that tautness of her breasts, the pounding of her heart.

"Close your eyes." His voice was suddenly hoarse. "Don't look at me."

Her lids snapped shut. He had noticed, dammit. He was aware of her vulnerability and his effect on her. How could he help it? The emotion was vibrating like raw electricity between them. She had to confront it and bring it down. "It doesn't mean anything, Gallo. I won't let it mean anything."

"Then keep your eyes closed." She heard him moving. "And I believe I'll forgo my pleasure in looking at you for a while. I live in the moment, but you don't. I may not be around to experience regrets, but I hope you will."

"All this sob-story stuff you're putting out is getting redundant." She opened her eyes to see him lying with his back to her. "I don't know if I should believe you."

"Maybe you shouldn't. Call Eve and tell her to get Quinn out here. Then you can bow out."

"Shut up. I'll do what I please."

But what would please her right now had nothing to do with her mission. What was happening between them? A good deal of it had to be because of the weeks they'd spent in these woods on the hunt, getting to know each other in the most intimate and dramatic way possible. Life and death and the hunt. It had dominated both of their minds and bodies. Even after the scenario had changed, it was still present, charging every word, ever look with urgency.

But there was suddenly more, and the hunt had taken on the most basic and earthy of meanings.

Eve had said Gallo had killed her child. How could Catherine feel anything for him but horror? Yes, he had been suffering from a mental breakdown. Yes, he was suffering enough now to want to end his life. But that did not stop the horror.

All Catherine's life, she had relied upon her instincts. How could they have failed her in this crucial moment? She could not respect herself if her mind and emotions were being subjugated by Gallo. She was either completely overwhelmed by Gallo and her own desires and unable to separate those instincts from the truth, or there was something terribly wrong.

And at the moment she couldn't sort anything out. Too much had happened. Too much was hovering on the horizon. She closed her eyes and leaned her head back on the makeshift pillow. She would sleep, and tomorrow she would start to deal with it.

Even though her eyes were closed, she still felt as if she could see Gallo, feel him, sense his every movement.

Spellbinder . . .

CHAPTER 12

"I'LL LET YOU GO INTO THE lake without the rope, but I'll be here with the dart gun. Start to swim away, and you'll take another nap," Gallo said. "And I haven't figured any way to save your modesty. I accept suggestions."

"Don't be absurd." She started to take off her shirt. "Do you think I haven't bathed naked with men before? I'm CIA. I spent years in the jungles of South America."

"Pardon me." He settled himself on the bank. "And it never presented problems?"

"I didn't say that." She took off her boots. "But the problems never occurred more than once." She shed the rest of her clothes and waded into the water. "Pitch me that green bottle in my knapsack."

"What is it?" He picked up the small bottle and lifted it to his nose. "It smells like rotten leaves."

"Soap." She looked at him as she reached water deep enough

to cover her breasts. In spite of her words, she had to block the tension that was a product of her awareness of him. "It was created for me by Hu Chang. You know the scent of products is a dead giveaway when you're on the hunt or being hunted." She caught the bottle as he tossed it to her. "You must have something like it. No matter how close I got to you, I couldn't detect your scent."

He nodded. "But yours is very good. I'd like to meet your Hu Chang."

"He'd be interested to meet you. He appreciates competence." She soaped her hair, then dipped her head to rinse it. "You're very good, Gallo."

"How long have you known this Hu Chang?"

"Since I was fourteen."

"Not a CIA man?"

She chuckled. "No, he was very upset when I decided to join them. He was sure they'd corrupt my free will."

"A valid concern."

She shrugged. "I had to make a decision I could live with. I grew up on the streets of Hong Kong, and I survived by dealing information to whoever would pay the highest fee for it. But I could see where I was going. Then a CIA agent, Venable, offered me a job with the CIA, and I took it. The Agency wasn't always clean, but they were trying to protect something besides themselves. That was unique in my world."

"All of this at seventeen."

"I told you, age doesn't mean anything."

"Hu Chang," he prompted.

"He had a shop that sold unique poisons and drugs. It's very profitable on the street, and he was targeted by a couple thieves on his way home. I helped him discourage them. But he was hurt, and I took him home and took care of him until he was well enough to take care of himself. We became . . . close."

"I suppose I don't have to ask how you discouraged them."

"If I hadn't killed them, they would have come back and targeted me, too," she said simply. "In Hong Kong, you don't take chances like that."

"And Hu Chang was grateful." He smiled. "And made you soap that smells like rotten leaves."

"Among other things." She started to wade back to shore. "I'm done. Give me that shirt on top of my knapsack. I managed to wash that one two days ago."

"Use my sweatshirt to dry off." He handed her a dark green shirt. "It's not that clean, but it will absorb the water."

She dabbed her body quickly and reached for her shirt. She had felt more comfortable in the water. She was too close to him. "I feel better now." She swiftly buttoned up the shirt. "In spite of the rotten leaves."

"I never said I didn't like the smell of rotten leaves." He slipped the looped rope around her waist, then took a step back and gazed at her in the shirt, which hit the top of her thighs. "Pity. But I think you'd better put on something else as soon as possible. I'm feeling a problem coming on. I don't want a demonstration on how you deal with this one."

She stared him in the eye. "You have me on a rope. I'm helpless."

"You're never helpless."

"You don't know me well enough to say that." She started

to dress. "I was helpless when you shot that dart into me. Everyone has moments when they're not totally in control."

"You're right. I don't know you. Why do I feel as if I do?"

Because these last weeks had taught them as much about each other as if they had known each other for years. "I have no idea."

"Yes, you do. We may have some gigantic holes in the structure, but the foundation is there."

"Your foundation is with Eve. That's why I'm here."

"Eve . . ." He was tying her to the tree. "Yes, it all goes back to Eve, doesn't it? She holds all of us. You've gone the limit for her in the name of friendship."

"I've gone after a man who has torn her life in pieces."

"I never meant to do it. We came together like a summer storm. We never realized that it would last for the rest of our lives. I tried to stay away."

"But you didn't do it, did you. Why?"

"Bonnie. I would never have interfered with Eve's life. She was right to put even the thought of me out of her mind. We'd both changed out of all recognition, and she had Quinn." His lips twisted. "And I was a man who couldn't even offer her a sound mind."

Her gaze was probing his expression. "You care about her. She told me that what was between you was only sex."

"It was the truth. But Bonnie changed everything. Passion became something else. We both loved Bonnie, and that meant we had to care about each other." He shook his head. "Oh, nothing like what she had with Quinn. There are all kinds of love and caring. I'll always feel that bond with Eve." He smiled faintly. "Even if she did send her favorite ninja after me."

"She didn't send me. I owed her, and I knew she couldn't come here herself." She added, "If you care about what happens to her, why don't you let me go? Do you think that she'll want Joe to come after you? Let it be me."

"But that's changed, too. The dynamics are different now, aren't they? The hunt wouldn't be the same, and neither would the finale." He met her gaze. "No, it has to be Quinn."

She couldn't breathe. "Let me go."

He shook his head. "You'll have to do it yourself." He began to strip off his clothes. "Because I'm going to take this time for myself." He waded into the water. "Something is happening between us. You may not like it, but it's there. I think that we'll have to ride it out."

She watched him as he moved in the water. Magnificent.

Tight muscular butt, flat stomach, totally male.

Totally.

And that maleness was having an effect on her own body.

"We'll have to ride it out."

The sentence brought to mind an image that was causing her body to ready. Stop it. So he was magnificent physically and fascinating mentally. She couldn't be drawn into the web that was hovering. Enemy. She had to think of him as the enemy.

He was coming out of the water. She should close her eyes. Not from any sense of embarrassment. That did not exist for them. But every step he took was causing a jolt of feeling, a surge of heat.

She would not close her eyes.

She met his gaze with boldness as he stopped before her.

"Me, too," he said quietly. "What do we do about it?"

"Ignore it."

"I've never been known for my restraint. I have a tendency to take what I want." There was a glitter of pure recklessness in his eyes. "And I don't believe I've ever wanted anything as much as I do you, Catherine Ling."

She could see the crystal drops of water beading on his shoulders and tangling in the thatch of dark hair on his chest. He was close enough for her to feel the heat of his body. She wanted to reach out and touch him.

Dizzy. The intensity was overpowering. She felt like a damn virgin. She had been married and had a child. She'd had occasional one-night stands in the years since her husband had been killed. But she'd never felt anything of this intensity before.

"Catherine?"

He wasn't forcing, he was asking. She should say yes, and he would cut the ropes. A man was never so vulnerable as when he was engaged in sex. She would be able to go on the attack.

But would she do it?

Dear God, she was afraid that she wouldn't.

She couldn't afford to take a chance of that self-betrayal.

She shook her head. "There's too much baggage. I won't let you complicate my life, Gallo."

He stared at her for a moment in which she saw emotion after emotion flickering in his expression. "You mean the way I've complicated the lives of everyone else around me? Complicated and destroyed." His smile was bitter. "You're right. And I'd do it, too." He turned away. "Just give me the chance." He was dressing quickly. "And you can bet that I'd take advantage of any chance you gave me. So keep me away from you." He grabbed a knife from his knapsack and came back to her and cut the ropes that bound her to the tree. Then he cut the ropes binding her wrists. "Or take off. That would probably be better."

She stared at him in shock. "You're releasing me."

"I'm not stupid enough to let you have any of your weapons back. Though I'm sure that you could be formidable in hand-to-hand." He looked at her. "But you don't want to be that close to me, do you? It might turn into something else."

She shook her head as she rubbed her wrist. "I won't stop, Gallo. Why did you change your mind?"

"Victims. I'm sick to death of victims. I won't make you one, Catherine."

" 'Victim'? You son of a bitch. You can't make me a victim. Who the hell do you think you are?"

"A son of a bitch who seems to have a talent for bringing down even the strongest and most worthwhile." He turned away. "Why don't you get going? There aren't any guarantees that I won't change my mind."

She didn't move. "And you'll wait for Joe. I'm supposed to run the risk that you'll let him kill you? Hell, you tell me that you're unstable. That there aren't any guarantees, that you can change your mind. You have warrior instincts. So does Joe. That creates a scenario that spells big-time trouble. I'm not going to lose him."

He turned to look at her. "And what are you going to do?"

"I'll stay with you until Joe comes and make sure that he survives." She met his gaze. "And if I get the chance, you'll go down. I made a promise to Eve, and nothing has changed that."

"No, I guess that would be your first priority. She's lucky to have you for a friend."

"Lucky? She helped me find my son. There's nothing that I wouldn't do for her." She paused. "But we can end this now. I'll postpone trying to bring Eve your head for the time being. All you have to do is tell me what happened to Bonnie and where she is."

"All?" His lips were tight with bitterness. "That would be fine, wouldn't it? But I can't help you, Catherine. I told you, I don't remember. I don't even remember taking her life."

She glanced away from the unbearable pain in his expression. She mustn't let him affect her like this. "Then we're at an impasse. I stay."

He gazed at her for a moment, then his expression changed. The recklessness was suddenly there again. "Why not? Go with the flow. Step into my parlor, Catherine."

"Bad phrasing. That would indicate that you were in control. You're not, Gallo. This is my choice. You'll never be in control of me."

"A challenge." He smiled, and the recklessness was even more obvious. "Up or down. The compromise would be for us to take turns. What do you think?"

She ignored the inference. "I think if your memory suddenly returns, we'll both be better off."

"But maybe I'm suppressing it. It's possible. It would hurt me, and I'm a selfish bastard. Maybe I don't give a damn about anything or anyone but myself." He grabbed his knapsack and slung it over his shoulders. "I'm going back to camp. Come along if you like. We'll see what comes of it."

"I want my phone back." She picked up her knapsack. "Keep the weapons. But I want my phone."

"A phone can be a weapon."

"I want to call Eve. She may have been trying to reach me. I won't have her worried. What difference does it make? I'm not going to tell her anything that would bring them here. I don't want Joe on your trail until he's entirely well."

He thought about it. "There are all kinds of ways that you could use that phone to bring havoc down on me. You're probably up on every technical advance that could cause me to be traced or destroyed." He shrugged. "What do I care? It should make the game more interesting." He reached into his knapsack and brought out her phone. He disconnected it from its solar battery charger and handed it to her. "By all means, call Eve."

BUT CATHERINE DIDN'T make the call until later that day. Eve had phoned her during the time that Gallo had possession of her phone and Catherine wasn't sure what excuse she wanted to give her for not answering. She could tell her that she was out of tower range. Eve might accept that because she knew Catherine had had problems before when they were trying to track Paul Black through this forest.

But that would be lying, and she hated to lie to Eve. She would just have to play it by ear.

"You're frowning." Gallo looked up from cooking fish over the fire. "You don't like fish? Or you don't trust me? I promise I won't poison you."

"Why should I trust you? For God's sake, you shot me after I saved your life." She made an impatient gesture. "Yes, I know that you didn't regard that as a favor. You said you were trying to get around your ghostly Bonnie's interference in your doing away with yourself." She scowled. "Which is some of the most complete crap I've ever heard in my life."

"My, my, how bad-tempered you are." He tilted his head. "Not that I blame you. It sounds like crap to me, too." He took the fish from the fire. "I don't expect you to believe me."

"It's ridiculous." She glared at him. "And you're not a man who would imagine that kind of nonsense."

"Hallucinations. Talk to the doctors who examined me after I broke out of that prison in North Korea."

"That was a long time ago, and you're not nuts now, dammit."

"How do you know?"

She didn't have any idea why she was so certain. Instinct, again? Lately, she had been thinking long and hard while she had been with him. Carefully sorting out the basic emotion and what her judgment told her was true. But, dammit, she had known him for such a short time that she had to rely on her faith in herself. Yet when had she ever relied on anything else? From the moment she had started the hunt, she had tried to predict his every move, every thought. At times, she had felt as if she could read his mind.

And that mind was clear and sharp and entirely sane.

But this bullshit about Bonnie was a complete contradiction of what she knew was true about him.

"You didn't even know her. You'd never even talked to your daughter. You admitted that yourself."

"I knew her."

"How?"

"Would you like any of this fish?"

"No. How?"

He didn't look at her as he helped himself to the fish. "She came to see me."

"What? You said that you'd never met her."

"Not formally. She never told me her name. But after a while, I knew who she was." He looked up and met her eyes. "You won't let it alone, will you? Okay. It doesn't matter. It will probably convince you that I'm as crazy as I say I am." He poured coffee into a cup and handed it to her. "But that part of Bonnie I didn't imagine. She was *real.* She did come to me."

"What are you talking about? Came where?"

He picked up his coffee and sat down again before the fire. "In that hellhole of a prison. I was being tortured and starved. I was sure I'd either die or go crazy and after months I didn't care. Then I started to dream of a little girl. She had curly red hair and a smile that could light up the world, much less that stinking hole where I was being held. She was very young when she first came to me, but then she seemed to grow older. She would sing me songs and tell me about going to school. She saved my life and my sanity. She kept me from hanging myself in that cell." He took a drink of coffee. "She never told me about her mother, but I knew it was Eve. And I knew her name was Bonnie."

Catherine stared at him, stunned. She hadn't expected this, and she didn't know how to deal with it.

His lips twisted as he looked up and saw her expression. "I told you that you wouldn't believe me. But that was no hallucination. Bonnie was more real to me than the whip or the knife or all the other little toys they used on me. I thought she was a dream in the beginning, but later I knew she was somehow there. How else could I know . . ." He shook his head. "She was real."

He believed it, Catherine realized. Nothing could be more certain than his belief that Bonnie had visited him in that prison. She was silent, then shook her head. "How can I believe you? Have I heard of tales like that? Of course. Astral projection and all kinds of weird stuff. But I've never encountered it in any plausible form. I think perhaps your mind was distorted by what you were going through."

"My distortion gave me a name—Bonnie. At that time, I didn't even know she existed."

"Then it had to be something else." She moistened her lips. "Bonnie was alive when you were having those visions. Did you have them after she died?"

He nodded. "Not often. And then I did think they were dreams. Until recently." He paused. "When Eve told me that she had them, too, and that they weren't dreams."

"What?"

"I thought that would shake you. Your friend, Eve, who is definitely sane and not prone to imaginary visits from a spirit. Yet she was the one who told me that she had gone through years telling herself that her visits from Bonnie were hallucinations or dreams." He lifted his shoulder in a half shrug. "Until she realized that it wasn't true. She wanted to prepare me for the same painful rejection process."

"She told you that Bonnie—"

"Ask her." He took another sip of coffee. "Or not. She might not want to discuss it with you. It's difficult to admit to believing in spirits when the world around you is so pragmatic." He lifted his cup in a half toast. "Like you, Catherine."

"I've had to be pragmatic. I wouldn't have lived to get out of my teens if I hadn't been practical and rejected things that go bump in the night."

"Bonnie doesn't go bump in the night. She smiles. She lifts the heart."

"And won't let you kill yourself." She shook her head. "Can't you see how weird that sounds, dammit? If you killed her, wouldn't she want you to throw yourself headfirst into a volcano? It's what any sensible ghost would want." She lifted her hand and rubbed her forehead. "What am I saying? I'm actually going along with you on this."

"I thought of that," he said quietly. "Maybe Bonnie wants it to be Quinn and Eve who end it. They've been searching for so long . . ." He added wearily, "I don't know. I just want it over. I don't understand any of it. I don't know how I could love her so much and still take her life. If I could do that, I don't deserve to live one more hour, one more minute."

"If you killed Eve's daughter, I couldn't agree more." She finished her coffee and threw the last drops into the flames. "And I'd be glad to help you along if you could tell me where you buried Bonnie. How can you be so sure that you killed her and not know anything else? Because that slimeball said it was true? I don't understand why both you and Eve believed him."

"If you'd been there, you'd understand. Black believed every word he was saying," he said hoarsely. "I'd swear it."

She gazed at him in frustration. So much pain. So much bewilderment. She couldn't imagine the insecurity that the blackouts had given him. How would it feel to come around and not know what violence you'd committed? He had been an Army Ranger and violence had been inherent in the job and the opportunity was always present. In every other way he was such a confident, complete person, and yet this crack was going to widen until it destroyed him.

But both he and Eve believed Black had been telling the truth. As Gallo had said, Catherine hadn't been there. She could not judge.

But why was it bothering her so much?

Because she didn't want it to be true? Because even at this moment, she was feeling drawn to him and was looking for an excuse to take off her clothes and go to him and—

She wouldn't accept that reason. She wasn't a mindless animal in heat.

Though, God knows, she felt like one right now. Hot and aching and ready. Why couldn't she have picked someone with no baggage before she let herself fall into this trap? But there had been no picking and choosing. It had been Gallo since that first moment of the hunt. She didn't know where it was going to take her, but she had to accept that she had to deal with it.

Was this how Eve had felt all those years ago when Gallo had come into her life? Strange that both Eve and Catherine had fallen under Gallo's spell. But Eve had been little more than a child herself, while Catherine was a woman and should have had more control.

Control. Look away from him. Don't ask him any other questions because you want the answers to lead you where you want to go.

He looked back at her and nodded slowly. "It's becoming difficult for you, isn't it? I think you'd like to believe I didn't kill her. It would be easier if I'd tell you that Black was lying. I can't do that." He got to his feet. "You've probably had enough of me. I'll walk over to the creek and give you some space to make your call to Eve."

"Don't you want to know what I say to her?"

He shook his head. "None of it matters any longer. As I said, anything you do will only make the game more interesting."

And he'd already decided what the end of the game had to be, she thought.

She watched him as he strode toward the creek before she reached for her phone.

"I tried to call you," Eve said when she picked up. "I was worried."

"I'm sorry. I wasn't able to receive any calls." And she was being deceptive even though she'd been trying desperately to think of a way to avoid it. "How is Joe?"

"Good." She paused. "How are you? You sound . . . strange."

"I'm fine."

"Gallo?"

"I'm very close to him." She gazed at Gallo across the short distance separating them. "Very close."

"Be careful."

"You think that he'd hurt me? You were defending him for a long time when I was warning you not to trust him. And you were working with him to hunt down Black."

"I think any man who would kill Bonnie would be capable of any atrocity."

"And you're positive he killed her?"

"Gallo as much as admitted that he thought Black had told the truth."

"Thinking isn't knowing. You told me once he loved her. I couldn't figure out how he could do that if he'd never had any contact with her before her death. But you were very sure. How could you be so sure, then change in the blink of an eye? Why were you so sure?"

"He told me something that made me think we had a bond."

"Something about Bonnie? Something you shared about Bonnie? What was it, Eve?"

Eve was silent. "Why are you asking me these questions, Catherine? I feel as if I'm being interrogated."

Catherine drew a deep breath. "I'm sorry." She hadn't known she was going to ask those questions until they'd come tumbling out. She felt as if she'd been driven to verify what Gallo had told her, to find truth in those strange words about Bonnie. Dear God, she wanted them to be true. She wanted to believe the impossible. Gallo had called her pragmatic, but for that moment she wanted to believe. "There's just so much I don't know. But I'm part of this now. I think I deserve to ask about you and Bonnie."

Silence. "Then go ahead and ask, Catherine."

She hesitated, then asked jerkily, "Did you—ever think that you saw your daughter—after her death?"

Another silence. "Catherine?"

Catherine was suddenly panicked. "Never mind. Don't answer. It's a crazy question. I'll call you tomorrow and check on Joe." She hung up.

Why had she done it? That question had been wrong on so many levels. It had not only intruded on Eve's privacy, but intimated that she was not stable. Because sane people didn't see spirits.

Or did they?

Catherine wouldn't have gone forward with that question if Eve hadn't made that cryptic comment about sharing something with Gallo that had formed a bond.

Added to what Gallo had said about Eve telling him that she, too, had an experience with seeing Bonnie, it had been too close to miss. So she had plunged into questioning Eve with no gentleness or tact, and Eve had responded defensively. It was perfectly natural.

But what would she have said if Catherine had not backed off like a cat on hot coals? Why had Catherine panicked? Because she had not wanted to offend a friend or because she had not wanted to hear her answer?

She glanced over at Gallo, standing beside the creek. Damn him. He was the core of all the trouble she had been going through. He had disturbed her physically and emotionally, and now he was causing a rift between her and Eve.

No, that wasn't true. How could she blame him for her

own responses? She had told herself she had to deal with him, and this was no way to start. She had to think clearly and coolly and not let her emotions get in the way.

And not get too close to him until she had come to a few decisions. She had wasted enough time waffling back and forth about Gallo. She would either accept the situation as he and Eve were accepting it, or she would come to her own conclusions and act accordingly.

She looked away from him and started to settle down in her sleeping bag. She would lie there and before she faced him again, she could come to a final decision.

Until then, getting any closer to John Gallo would be the worst thing she could do.

CHAPTER 13

"SHE'S CAUGHT UP WITH GALLO." Eve turned to Jane as she hung up the phone. "I *know* it."

Jane frowned. "But she didn't tell you that?"

Eve shook her head. "Not exactly." She was thinking over exactly what Catherine had said. "It was all very vague and ambiguous. I was uneasy from the moment I picked up the call."

"If she's found him, why wouldn't she tell you?"

"How the hell do I know?" She grimaced. "Or maybe I do know. Gallo is . . . unusual. He managed to convince me that black was white in two separate periods of my life. I warned Catherine that he was capable of dazzling anyone." She added with frustration, "But she's tough as nails. I was hoping that she'd be immune to him."

"Maybe she is," Jane said. "You're only guessing, Eve."

"She was questioning me about— She's been talking to him, Jane."

"About what?" Jane asked.

"She asked if I'd—" She moistened her lips. "She said she wondered if I'd thought that Bonnie visited me after her death. In her wildest dreams, she wouldn't have asked that question if she hadn't talked to Gallo. Why would she? There's no more grounded or realistic person on Earth than Catherine."

"Except me." Jane made a face. "And I've made giant strides in accepting the unacceptable. But, then, I've had a long time to come to terms with Bonnie."

"And you still don't feel comfortable with the idea," Eve said. "Well, neither does Catherine. I could tell that she's upset as hell and trying to fight her way through it. But Gallo has her going around in circles."

"What has Gallo got to do with her asking about Bonnie?"

Eve was silent and then said finally. "He's seen Bonnie, too. At least, he told me he had."

"Oh, shit." Jane gazed at her in shock. "And you believed him?"

"I believed him," she said jerkily. "I believed everything he told me. He said she came to him in that cell in Korea when she was still alive. And that she visited him after her death. I fell for everything he told me. That's why I went with him to hunt down Paul Black when Gallo told me that he'd killed Bonnie."

"Why? How could you believe him?"

"Because I was a fool. It all had to be lies. Why would Bonnie come to him if he'd been the one who killed her?" She shook her head. "And now he has Catherine believing his lies." And that put Catherine in greater danger than Eve had dreamed. An enemy within the gates could be deadly. "It has to stop." She turned toward the elevator. "I can't let it go on."

"Where are you going?" Jane hurried to keep up with her. "As if I couldn't guess. Look, you can't go after Catherine. You don't know what kind of situation you'd uncover up there in the woods. Particularly if you think she's been bamboozled by Gallo."

"You think Catherine would hurt me?" Eve shook her head. "Don't be ridiculous. You don't know her, Jane."

"No, I don't. But you said that she wasn't behaving normally. So how well do you know her, Eve?"

"Very well." Eve punched the elevator button. "I just have to see her face-to-face so that I can set her straight. I need you to do me a favor. Joe won't like this when he hears about it. Stall him as long as you can."

"Stall him? He'll be out of this hospital and on your trail the minute he hears that you're not here."

"He's already had his night sedative. All you have to worry about is when he wakes tomorrow. Find a way to keep him here. One day, Jane. That should be all I need to find Catherine and talk to her."

"That sounds simple, but it would be hard as hell. I'd have to lie. I've never lied to Joe." Jane's lips thinned. "And I won't let you go up there alone. You may trust Catherine Ling, but I don't."

"And leave Joe here in this hospital without either one of us? Joe is the reason you came here, Jane. When you first arrived, you asked me what you could do to help me. Well, now I'm telling you. Dammit, Joe is due to be released in the next couple days, and I was trying to think of a way to delay him going after Gallo. This thing with Catherine is going to blow away any chance of that."

"You bet it is."

"Then give me at least a day to get up there and contact Catherine. I'll try to get her back on track."

Jane shook her head.

"Don't you refuse me." Eve's voice was shaking. "You give me that day. I almost lost Joe. I can't prevent him from going after Gallo, but I can keep Catherine on the job to help him."

"That's not all you're doing," Jane said bluntly. "You're going to go after Gallo yourself."

Eve should have known that Jane would guess her intentions. They were too close not to be able to read each other. "Joe said Bonnie told him that we're reaching the end," she said unevenly. "If that's true, then I should be the one to reach it first." She reached out and grasped Jane's arm. "I'm not afraid of Catherine, and I'm not afraid of Gallo. Give me my day, Jane."

"Damn you." Jane's eyes were glittering with moisture. She reached out and hugged Eve close. "One day, Eve. After that, Joe and I will both be on your trail."

Eve brushed Jane's cheek with her lips and let her go. "Thanks, Jane. This means a lot to me."

"I know. Do you think that if I didn't realize you were on the edge, I'd have given in? It's nearly killing me to let you go." Jane watched her get into the elevator. "I hope Bonnie is right. I hope this nightmare is coming to an end."

"So do I," Eve said, as the elevator door closed, shutting her away from Jane. The search for Bonnie had been a nightmare for Jane also, she knew. Jane's strength and courage had caused her to downplay any pain or loneliness that might have resulted from Eve's obsession with finding Bonnie. But those emotions had been there, and Eve had been aware of them.

It's been too long for all of us, Bonnie. Let me bring you home.

"ARE YOU awake?"

Catherine opened her eyes to see Gallo sitting by the fire a few yards away from her. "I am now," she said dryly. "Since it's obvious you want me to be."

He smiled. "Yes, I do. I was lonely. I held off for a little while, but then I yielded to temptation. I knew I wasn't going to sleep, and I wanted company. I never said I wasn't selfish." He crossed his legs Indian style. "Or that I wasn't curious. About an hour and a half ago, you tucked yourself into that sleeping bag immediately after you talked to Eve. It had all the signs of an escape move. But I'd judge that you're not one to hide your head under a blanket."

"I wasn't trying to escape you. If I had, I would have taken off when you gave me the chance. I had some thinking to do."

"And?"

"I did it." She stared him in the eye. "And I decided you were the most outrageously idiotic individual on the face of the Earth, and Eve wasn't far behind you."

His smile faded. "Indeed? I assume you're referring to what I told you about Bonnie. I told you that I didn't expect you to believe me."

"I don't know whether I believe you or not. It would take a hell of a lot more than a tall tale about a red-haired ghost-child skipping merrily through your life to make me give up reality for that kind of fantasy." Her lips tightened. "But it's clear you and Eve have bought into it and won't be argued out of your Bonnie visions."

"Eve told you?"

"Hell no, she danced around it very warily, but it was clear she was talking about the same bond that you were. She sees Bonnie."

"And that makes us both idiots?"

"I told you, that wasn't what I was talking about. You're both idiots because you believed Paul Black when he told you that he knew that you had killed your daughter."

"He was telling the truth."

"You and Eve kept saying that. Because I trust and admire Eve's judgment, I went along with her when she said she was certain. As for you, why should I doubt anything bad about you when you were the enemy?"

"No reason at all."

"Except your blind belief in what Black said has been bothering me lately. It didn't seem right. And the more I thought about it, the more ridiculous it became to me." She shook her head. "I'm no psychiatrist, but I don't think anyone is capable of murdering a child they love unless they're totally mad. You may have had bouts of instability, but you're not crazy, Gallo."

"How do you know?"

"Because I know you. Just as you know me. After these weeks in the woods, I know you very well. Sometimes I feel as if

I can read your mind. I know your slyness, your cleverness, your recklessness; but you've never shown me any hint of cruelty or insanity." She added flatly, "Which means that both you and Eve have to be wrong when you accepted Black's word." She held up her hand as he opened his mouth to speak. "Don't give me that bullshit. I don't care if Black believed what he was saying. So what if he wasn't lying? That doesn't mean he couldn't be wrong." She glared at him. "You and Eve are both so tormented because of your love and guilt about Bonnie that you can't see straight. She's doubted you from the moment you came back into her life. Part of that was my fault. You were number one on my list as Bonnie's killer. You doubted yourself because of the blackouts you were having and the doctors who told you that you were a little bonkers."

"More than a little."

She shrugged. "Whatever. At any rate, you should have thought instead of reacted. Eve was terribly upset about Joe, so she had some excuse. But you should have known you weren't capable of killing Bonnie."

His lips twisted in a one-sided smile. "According to you, Catherine?"

She was suddenly up and kneeling before him. "Dammit, yes. According to me." Her hands closed on his shoulders, and she shook him. "I'm the only one with any sense around here. You were trying to throw yourself off a cliff, and Eve and Joe were going to hunt you down and kill you. Do you know how that would have made them feel when they found out Black was wrong? Guilt and more guilt. And that damn search for Bonnie would have started again." Her breasts were rising and falling with the force of her breathing. "And I would have been right in the middle of all that angst. No way. I've done enough things in my life that earned me my portion of guilt without you bringing me more. Now stop it, and let's clear this up."

His eyes were narrowed on her expression. "You really don't think I did it, do you?"

"At last, a breakthrough." Her hands dropped from his shoulders. "How many times do I have to say it? Black was *wrong.* He may have believed you killed Bonnie, but that doesn't make it true." She sat back on her heels. "Dammit, you'd think that you wanted it to be true."

"God, no." His voice was hoarse. "I've been living in a nightmare."

The pain in his expression was terrible to see. She wanted to reach out and touch him, comfort him. Don't do it. She was already too close to him.

"You deserved it. All you had to do was take the situation apart and look at the separate pieces."

He started to smile, then shook his head. "You know I still don't believe you. I want to. But I'm afraid that I'll find out that I was right, and you're wrong."

"Then you wouldn't be any worse off, would you?"

This time the smile actually came into being. "Oh, I would be worse off. It's a terrible thing to lose hope." He reached out and gently touched her cheek. "But it would be worth it to have a chance to go down the road you're leading me."

She could feel her skin flush beneath his fingers, and her chest tightened. No, she mustn't feel like this. It got in the way.

She moved her head, and his hand dropped away from her face. "Nicc words. Now shouldn't we get down to business? I completely blew it with Eve tonight. I'll be lucky if she doesn't show up here and try to track me down. We need to be gone before that happens."

"And where are we going?"

"If Black didn't kill Bonnie, and you didn't kill Bonnie, then we have to find out who did."

"Logical." He was thinking. She could almost see the wheels turning. "Okay. If Black didn't kill Bonnie and was certain that I did, it was because Queen and Jacobs had told him I had done it. Queen must have even paid Black to shoulder the blame, so that I would search for him all those years. Why?"

"Eve said that she thought that Queen was afraid that if you found out that you'd killed your daughter during one of your blackouts, you'd have a complete breakdown. He wouldn't want you to be put away in a mental institution, where he couldn't control you. Doctors ask too many questions, and you knew too much about his criminal activities." She frowned. "And I accepted that explanation because it all made sense."

"It still makes sense." His lips twisted. "It's difficult to discard it and look in any other direction. Why else would Queen go to all that trouble to make Black a decoy?"

"Unless he killed Bonnie himself."

"And why would he do that? He had no reason. Black might have had revenge as a motive, but Queen was still using me to do his dirty jobs all over the world and had no idea that I was beginning to suspect him."

"I don't know why, dammit." Every question had a roadblock, and her frustration level was climbing. "And we can't even ask the bastard. Black killed Queen."

"Back to square one," Gallo said. Then suddenly an indefinable expression flickered over his face. "Or maybe not. Jacobs."

Her gaze flew to his face. "Queen's assistant?"

He nodded. "You could call him that. Lieutenant Thomas Jacobs. He'd been joined at the hip with Queen at Army Intelligence for years. And he was partner in Queen's various crooked enterprises. He was with Queen from the beginning. He was always there in the background, even in that first meeting when I was sent into North Korea. I never considered him a factor because Queen always dominated."

"But he might know something?"

Gallo nodded. "It's a possibility. Just because he was in the background doesn't mean that Queen didn't trust him. It was a long-standing relationship. Maybe Queen even found Jacobs more valuable because he was the invisible man."

Invisible. Yes, Catherine had not considered Jacobs important when she'd been investigating Nate Queen and trying to trace Gallo. He'd been completely overshadowed by Queen. But now he was standing alone and might be the key. "Where is he? How can we get to him?"

"He was still at INSCOM the last time I talked to Queen weeks ago. But a lot has happened since then. After Black was killed, the ledger that held proof of Queen's and Jacobs's smuggling and drug dealing must have been discovered by the local police. There's no indication in it that it had anything to do with Army Intelligence, but they would have had Eve's statement about that. And the book had to be on Black's body at the time I killed him. If the sheriff followed up on it, then Jacobs has to be in big trouble."

Catherine shook her head. "The sheriff didn't mention any ledger to me when I was on the search for you those first few days. But then we weren't concerned about anything but finding you."

"Yes, I felt very important," Gallo said. "I would have felt still more important if I'd known you'd joined them on the hunt. You were much more interesting."

"Don't bullshit me," she said bluntly. "You didn't care a damn about whether I was after you or not. You were too busy trying to get yourself killed."

"And you've already remarked on that particular idiocy."

"It bears repeating. Why didn't you—" She stopped, and added with exasperation, "If you have this intimate relationship with Bonnie, why didn't she just tell you that you hadn't killed her?"

"I don't know. I was in torment. There were moments when I didn't even believe Bonnie was actually there." He shook his head. "I just knew that I couldn't take my own life."

"Then your daughter is the most unsatisfactory spirit in the universe. What good is she?" She turned away. "And it makes me doubt even more that she actually exists. If you and Eve weren't two of the most intelligent and grounded people I've ever met, I'd be sure of it."

"But you're not sure." He smiled faintly. "And it's bothering the hell out of you."

"I'll get over it." And she'd get over the effect Gallo was

having on her. She just had to block those parts of her mind and body that seemed to be acutely and exquisitely attuned to him. "After I find out what happened to Bonnie and I can put you behind me. Then I'll be able to move on with no looking back." She took out her phone. "Put out the fire while I call the sheriff and see what I can find out about that ledger. Then we'll get on the road and try to track down Jacobs."

He nodded and began to extinguish the flames. "As you command."

For the time being, she thought ruefully. Gallo wasn't going to accept any will but his own for long. She absently watched him work about the camp as she talked to Sheriff Rupert. Lord, Gallo was stunning. In black jeans and shirt he looked lean and yet muscular, and the way he moved . . .

She jerked her attention back to what the sheriff was telling her.

As she hung up, Gallo turned to face her. "Well?"

"The day after Black and Queen were taken to the local morgue, Thomas Jacobs showed up with his Army Intelligence credentials and a story about how Nate Queen was undercover and trying to find a way to trap Black. According to him, Paul Black was supposed to be a suspect in the killing of an Army Intelligence officer."

"But they already had a statement from Eve about Queen's involvement with Black."

"Evidently Jacobs was very plausible, and Sheriff Rupert isn't used to dealing with military and government types. He was even impressed with my credentials."

"It was probably not your credentials that impressed him.

He's a typical good old boy, and he appreciates a beautiful woman when he sees her."

"You should know. Evidently, you became buddies with him and the entire sheriff's office."

"It seemed the thing to do at the time. So did Jacobs get his hands on the ledger?"

"No, the sheriff wasn't that gullible. Though Jacobs tried to tell him that it was evidence and was needed to save military lives. It was in Korea, so Jacobs had a good shot at convincing him of his story. It hadn't been translated."

"Has it been translated yet?"

"No, clearly things move slowly up here." She added, "And Sheriff Rupert was a little suspicious when Jacobs didn't mention claiming Queen's body for burial. It didn't seem to be the proper way to behave when Jacobs was giving him this sad story about Queen's giving his life for his country."

"And he had Eve's statement to compare with Jacobs's story."

Catherine nodded. "Anyway, the sheriff refused to turn over anything to Jacobs since he was implicated in the story that Eve told him. He told Jacobs to have his superior contact him, and he'd cooperate. So Jacobs didn't get the ledger, and everything must have seemed to be going downhill for him. His partner was dead, and he was probably going to be revealed as a crook and his Army career would go down the drain." She picked up her knapsack. "Which means we'd better get on the move. Jacobs has had too long to tie up loose ends and destroy any other evidence against him. We'll be lucky if we're able to locate him."

"We'll locate him." Gallo was already moving down the

trail. "Call your chief Venable as soon as we get to the car and see if he can trace him."

Gallo's tone was as grim as his face. He was in battle mode.

Well, so was she, Catherine thought. It was strange that after being enemies these last weeks, they were walking this path together.

Strange and somehow right.

AN HOUR LATER, SHE HUNG UP from the callback she'd received from Venable and turned to Gallo, who was in the driver's seat. "Jacobs took a leave of absence from the office the day after he returned from Milwaukee. His superiors have been trying to get in touch with him since all hell broke loose about Queen's death. The questions began to fly about Queen's and Jacobs's possible criminal involvement. No luck. Jacobs is not answering his phone, and he's just recently moved out of his apartment." She shook her head. "We may be too late. He could have panicked and decided to go on the run. He's probably flown off to someplace in the South Seas from which he can't be extradited."

"Possibly." Gallo was thinking. "But Jacobs wasn't the type to turn into a beachcomber. It would be too savage for his tastes. He was very urban oriented."

"How do you know? I thought you said he was the invisible man."

"That doesn't mean I didn't make the effort to see him for what he was. He worked closely with Queen. There was always a chance that I'd find a use for him. If he did go on the run, it shouldn't be too hard to track him."

"You don't think he'd go undercover?"

Gallo shook his head. "Maybe. But if he did, then I know what to look for."

"What?"

"A casino. Jacobs is a gambler, an addict. It's one of the reasons that he never left Queen no matter how hot the situation got. He was nervous all the time, but he couldn't let go. He needed the money, and he lost more than he won at the tables."

"There are a lot of casinos in the world."

"Then we'll narrow them down."

"How?"

He shrugged. "First, we'll go to Jacobs's apartment and see if we can find a clue as to where we'd have our best shot. Did you get his address?"

She nodded at the number she'd typed into her phone. "His apartment is in Georgetown."

"Then call and see what's the quickest flight we can get to Washington out of either Milwaukee or Chicago."

She hesitated. "Orders, Gallo?"

"I believe in balance. You were giving me enough orders before we got on the road."

And now he was moving, thinking, functioning with lightning efficiency. Why was she complaining? She should be glad she was going to have to fight for dominance. It would make the possibility of finding Jacobs all the more likely. "Have you forgotten that the police are looking for you? We'd do better to hire a private plane. I have a contact with—"

"No time. I have several sets of false ID that Queen and Jacobs supplied me and a couple I purchased from private sources. I could never be sure when Queen or Jacobs would decide to send one of their hired killers after me, and I might have to go undercover for a while."

"Like Jacobs."

"Exactly like Jacobs."

"You're not afraid that security will recognize you?"

"I'll send you through in front of me. No one is going to look at me when you're around. Like Jacobs, I'll be the invisible man."

"Yeah, sure. But if you're willing to take the risk, it's okay with me." She took out her phone. "I'll bet we'll find our flight out of Chicago. The traffic is much heavier . . .

CATHERINE RECEIVED A CALL from Eve two hours later, when they were heading for Gate 23 at Chicago's O'Hare Airport.

Dammit, she didn't want to face Eve now. Should she ignore it?

Of course not. Eve would not forgive her.

Deal with it.

"Where are you, Eve?" she said when she picked up the phone. "And is Joe with you?"

"I'm on my way to Gallo's place in the hills. I wanted to see you." She paused. "And by the noise I'm hearing in the background, you're not there. An airport?"

"Yes, I knew I blew it when I was talking to you before. I had to get out of there before you descended on us. Joe?"

"He's not with me. I needed a little time to persuade you to forget this idiocy. Jane is trying to give me a day before she tells him."

"She won't be able to do it. You know it as well as I do. Joe is too sharp."

Eve ignored her words. "Us. You said us. You're with Gallo."

"You knew I was, or you wouldn't have come running to save me," she said quietly. "I don't need saving, Eve. He's not going to hurt me." She paused. "And he didn't kill Bonnie."

"For God's sake, he has you believing him." Catherine could hear the despair in her voice. "He did it, Catherine. I know how convincing he can be, but you have to think."

"No, you have to think," Catherine said. "You and Gallo are both so twisted and turned around about how you feel about Bonnie that you're willing to jump at any explanation that sounds halfway reasonable. Only this isn't reasonable. Just because Black believed what he was saying is no sign it was the truth."

"You're the one who is jumping at explanations. What did he do to persuade you?"

"Nothing. Except try to get himself killed. I figured that was unusual behavior and deserving of a little thought."

"What?"

"Never mind. There's no way that I have time or enough valid arguments to make you listen. All I can say is that I know you're on the wrong track. I feel it. You're a great one for believing in instinct. You believed in Gallo when I thought you were a gullible fool for doing it. Now the situation is reversed. All I can ask is that you trust me."

Eve was silent. "I do trust you. But I think you're— Where are you going, Catherine?"

"When you can tell me honestly that you'll help instead of try to stop me, I'll talk to you." She drew a deep breath. "Please. I don't want to do this without you, Eve. I've fought my way through this. I'm doing the right thing."

"Then tell me where you're going."

"Start where I did and work it out for yourself. Good-bye, Eve." She hung up.

Gallo was gazing at her expression. "That was painful for you."

"Of course, it was. She's my friend." Her throat was tight. "All I ever wanted to do was help her, and now she thinks I've betrayed her."

"And that I lured you from the straight path." They had reached the gate, and he turned to face her. "Eve should know better than to think I'd have that kind of power over you. She's usually more clearheaded."

But he did have an alluring charisma, and she had been struggling against it for weeks. She only hoped she'd been telling Eve the truth when she'd told her Gallo hadn't unduly influenced her.

Hope? Dammit, of course she'd been honest with Eve. She had to trust in herself as she always had. Otherwise, she had nothing. "You're Bonnie's father. Evidently you were Eve's Achilles' heel when she was a kid of sixteen. It's probably easy for her to imagine that you might be able to sway me to your way of thinking."

"Achilles' heel? That could have all kind of meanings." He looked away from her, and said haltingly, "If it makes any difference to you, it means a good deal to me that you believe so deeply that you're doing the right thing. In a way, that means you believe in me."

"You act as if that's completely unheard of for anyone to have any trust in you."

"Not completely. But I can remember only a couple of people who trusted me to that extent. Maybe my commanding officer, Ron Capshaw, who was in charge of our mission to Korea. I was just a green kid fresh out of Ranger school but he took me under his wing and told everyone he knew I could do the job. I . . . liked him. He made me feel as if I could do anything if I tried hard enough." His lips tightened. "But we had to split up, and he and Lieutenant Silak were killed, and I was taken prisoner." He shrugged. "Other than Ron, I guess the only other person who trusted me to do the right thing was my uncle Ted when I was a kid. He was the only one who gave a damn about me when I was growing up." He grimaced. "Not that I deserved it even then. I was a real hell-raiser. But sometimes you get more than you're entitled to get." He turned toward the gate agent, who was starting to call the flight. "Like now. Like Catherine Ling fighting the friend she loves to save my ass." He took her elbow. "That's our section being called. Come on, let's get this show on the road."

"Gallo, I'm not doing this for any—"

"I know. I'm not assuming anything that you wouldn't want me to assume. Don't worry, I'm not suffering a major character change." The soberness was suddenly gone, and he was smiling recklessly. "You'll still have to watch me and make sure I don't try to manipulate you to get what I want. I'm still the same hell-raiser I was when I was a kid. I just raise it in different ways . . ."

CHAPTER 14

St. Joseph's Hospital

Milwaukee, Wisconsin

JOE WAS WALKING DOWN THE hospital corridor when Eve got off the elevator at his floor the next morning.

She smiled with an effort. "Busy already? Have you had breakfast yet?"

He shook his head. "They'll bring it soon. I thought I'd take a walk to help increase my stamina."

She wasn't sure how to take that. "I expected Jane to be here."

"She was here when I woke. I sent her down to Administration to start the paperwork going to get me out of here." He met her gaze. "When she said you wouldn't be able to see me until later today. But here you are. What happened, Eve?"

"Nothing to make you leap out of that bed and start worrying."

"I'm not leaping. I'm not that far along yet. But I'm getting there." He steadily met her gaze. "And you've been beside me every waking moment since I've been in this place. I've told you to go back to the hotel any number of times, and you wouldn't go. Now suddenly Jane tells me that you have something to do that will keep you away? It doesn't compute, Eve."

Eve made a face. "And I should have known that Jane's too honest to make you believe that everything was just fine."

"She tried, but she's clear as glass around the people she loves." He smiled. "Like you, Eve."

"That's not so bad." She took his hand. "Except when I want to keep you safe, dammit. Did Jane tell you anything?"

"Only that you were going up to Gallo's property. I figured I'd get everything else out of her on our way there. She said she wouldn't let me go alone."

She shook her head. "No, of course she wouldn't. She didn't like it that I made her stay here and try to stall you until I was sure what was happening up there."

"And what is happening?" Joe's hand tightened on hers. "I'm trying to hold on to my patience, but I'm having a tough time of it. Do you know how much I've hated being stuck in this damn hospital while Catherine was going after Gallo?"

Eve had realized that every day lately. She had been surprised that he had not been more impatient. It was not like Joe. "You've been very good about not complaining until it was time for your release."

"What good would it do? I have to be as strong as possible before I go after Gallo. Has Catherine found him?"

"Yes."

"What aren't you telling me?"

"He's convinced her that he didn't kill Bonnie."

"What?"

"You heard me." She shook her head. "Or maybe she's convinced herself. I can't put it all together. All she'd tell me was that she'd fought to believe what I'd told her was true, but that it didn't work for her."

"So why are you here instead of up there in the woods trying to shake some sense into her?"

"Because I called her when I was on the road, and she wasn't at the property. It sounded like an airport. "

"So you came back here." He added, "To save Jane and face the music."

She nodded. "I was expecting you to be angry."

"Not angry. Impatient, frustrated, confused." He shrugged. "It will take some time for me to muster any anger in connection with you. I came too close to losing you. Which puts everything else definitely in perspective." He suddenly chuckled. "Though being human, I'm sure it will come back to me with full force."

"I'm sure, too." Her lips twisted. "And I come in here, and you're walking the halls and building up stamina. Not very reassuring."

"I can't have you taking me for granted." His tone was absent. "Which airport? Did you hear any flight being called?"

"No, just the Homeland Security bag announcement. And a flight arrival from Miami. "

"What time was it?"

"Three forty in the morning. It had to be either Milwaukee or Chicago. They didn't have time to get from Gallo's property to any other airport. When Catherine called me previously, she told me she was still at the property."

"Have you checked with both airports to see if there was a flight at that time?"

"Not yet. I thought I'd let you do it." She smiled faintly. "It will keep you busy for a little while and give you a little more rest before you take the big plunge. I'm going to try to ration your energy."

He tilted his head. "You're not going to try to stop me?"

"I've bought more time than I thought I'd be able to manage—thanks to Catherine." Her lips tightened. "I can't understand how she could—"

"Yes, you can. Catherine and I were wondering the same thing about you a month ago. Gallo is very convincing." He was frowning. "But Catherine didn't have the same history with Gallo as you did, and she's smart as hell. It's a puzzle. What argument did she use?"

"She said that he didn't do it. She told me to start with that and work back."

"That's all?"

"Something about Gallo trying to take his life."

"Killers sometimes do commit suicide."

"That's not what she meant." She bit her lower lip. "I was so sure, Joe. But all I can think of now was how tormented Gallo was in those days when we were together. I could *feel* how much he loved Bonnie. Was I wrong to believe Paul Black?"

"You said Gallo believed him, too."

"And Catherine said just because Black thought he was telling the truth was no sign it was the truth." Eve shook her head. "I wanted to help Gallo. But I may have pushed him over the edge."

"Stop it," Joe said roughly. "Gallo can take care of himself. And now, evidently Catherine is watching out for him, too. And I've never understood why you've always believed he loved Bonnie."

Because she'd never told him. The relationship between Joe and Gallo had been too strained. But she had to tell him now. "Because . . . Bonnie comes . . . to him, too."

"Shit." Joe muttered a curse. "He could be lying to you."

She had tried to tell herself that lately. "He told me things . . . that song about the horses that she loved so much. I don't think he was lying, Joe."

Joe gazed at her for a moment. "Then what the hell is that supposed to mean?"

"I don't know. But would that mean that Bonnie loved him, too?" She shook her head. "And if that was true, how could she love him if he was the one who killed her? None of it makes sense."

"Why didn't you tell me before?" Joe shook his head. "Never mind. I know why. I was jealous as hell, and you didn't want me to think that even Bonnie was against me." He met her eyes. "Maybe the question should be why are you telling me now?"

"Because you told me that you know Bonnie now, that she brought you back. For years, no matter how we tried to overcome it, she's been between us. But something changed." She whispered, "I don't want to close you out of any part of my life. And she's such a big part, Joe."

He was silent, gazing down at their joined hands. "That's damn obvious. And spreading into all kinds of directions and little nooks. I never thought that she'd take me to John Gallo."

She waited, feeling the tension grip her.

"But you have to hand it to the kid. She's always throwing down a challenge." He looked up and met her eyes. "So I think we have to ride with her."

Relief surged through her. "And Catherine."

"And Catherine." He took the pad and pencil from the table beside him. "She may be wrong. Gallo may be the premier con man of the millennium. But I don't want you hurting for the bastard if there's a mistake. We might as well check it out. I'll call Milwaukee airport. You phone O'Hare. It will help if we can figure out where they're going." He reached for his phone. "And then we'll do what Catherine said and start putting together a scenario of 'what if it wasn't Gallo.' "

JOE WATCHED EVE IN THE hall talking to Jane, and he didn't envy her. They had chosen to keep Jane from going with them when they went after Catherine, and Eve had volunteered to break it to her.

Eve had wanted to protect him from the inevitable explosion. She had been protecting him constantly in big ways and small since he had come out of the coma. Ordinarily, it would have frustrated him, but in this instance, he welcomed it. He needed to think, and no one could reason logically when Jane was upset. She would be hurt as well as angry, and it was terribly hard to hurt someone you loved.

He got to his feet and moved across to the window and looked down at the hospital parking lot.

Okay, Catherine had said to assume Gallo wasn't guilty and figure it out from there.

But he didn't want to assume Gallo wasn't guilty. He was still having problems with the antagonism he felt toward him. Jealousy? Maybe. He had always been possessive of Eve, and he didn't like the idea of any other man in her life, past or present. Or maybe it was the fact that Gallo had endangered Eve since the moment he had come back into her life. Either way, the antagonism was present, and he had to deal with it.

So deal with it. Use intelligence, not emotion. He was an investigator. That was his chosen profession and he did it damn well. This could be the most important case he'd ever been given.

Is it Bonnie? This was a strange twist in the path that he'd been on since he'd come back with her from death's door. Strange or not, he could only do what he could, be what he was. Think. Concentrate. Look over the possibilities and see how the puzzle pieces would fit in different scenarios.

Deal with it.

He was still standing at the window forty-five minutes later when Eve came back into the room.

"Jane wants to see you. I couldn't talk her out of it."

"You shouldn't have tried." He turned to face her. "She has a right to vent her emotions on both of us." He smiled. "Don't worry, she'll be easy on me. She'll only try persuasion. She's been almost as protective of me as you."

"And it's been annoying you." She grimaced. "I can't help it, Joe."

"I know. It will take a little time." He paused. "If it will make you feel better, I'm feeling very strong. Sometimes stronger than I've ever felt before. There are moments when I'm not so good, but then I feel a kind of . . . surge. I can get through this, Eve."

She took step closer and laid her head on his chest. "And you won't take stupid chances?"

He chuckled. "Not too stupid." He took a step back. "Now give me fifteen minutes, then I'll face our tigress, Jane. Let's go over those notes about the flights leaving from O'Hare and Milwaukee. I think I know who Gallo and Catherine are going after. I just want to verify by the destination."

Georgetown, Washington, D.C.

"NOT VERY PREPOSSESSING," Catherine said as she looked up at the small two-story apartment building that looked more like a motel. "When I think of Georgetown, I think foreign diplomats and money."

"That's probably why he wanted an address in Georgetown. Even though he was short of cash most of the time, he needed to put up a front." He was climbing the steps to the second level. "Apartment 26?"

"Yes."

He stopped before the door. "Locked. And probably an alarm shared by the other apartment dwellers." He leaned back against the jamb and crossed his arms across his chest. "Take care of it, Catherine."

"How do you know I can?"

"I watched you on camera when you and Quinn were storming my house in Utah. You were obviously an expert. I was impressed. My alarm system was state-of-the-art. This will be a piece of cake for you."

"You're giving me orders again." She was starting back down the stairs. "And I don't think you're an amateur, Gallo."

"I'm not. But you'll be faster. I'll open the lock by the time you get back. Okay?"

She didn't answer as she hurried down the steps and around the back of the apartment units. She would just as soon deactivate the alarm herself. She was accustomed to working alone, and Gallo was a little too domineering for her taste. His attitude was probably natural since he, too, was used to working alone. They would have to learn to keep pace with each other. She remembered that she'd had no real problem with working with Joe Quinn. But Joe had been her friend, and she'd respected him and felt comfortable with him.

There was no comfort about working with Gallo. She might respect his abilities, but there was a constant awareness that aroused an emotion that was close to antagonism whenever she was with him.

An antagonism caused by that physical disturbance that she couldn't suppress or diminish.

She might not be able to suppress it, but she blocked it when she had a job to do.

Take out the alarms.

Piece of cake as Gallo had said. She was climbing the stairs four minutes later. The door was cracked open, and no Gallo.

She glided silently into the apartment and shut the door.

She was instantly assaulted by darkness and the pungent smell of pepperoni.

"No other alarms in here," Gallo said from across the room. He was going through the drawers of a desk, his LED flashlight piercing the darkness. "Very messy. Jacobs was either a complete slob or he was in a big hurry." He took the Rolodex from the desk and stuffed it into his pocket. "No convenient receipts for airline tickets. I don't see any credit-card receipts either."

Catherine went into the kitchen and opened the refrigerator. "German beer. A California wine." She opened the bag on the second shelf. "And some kind of pasta in marinara sauce. He has international tastes as far as food is concerned."

Gallo was heading for the bedroom. "I'll go through the drawers of the bedside table. You check the bathroom."

The heavy scent of a citrus aftershave coming from a bottle on the sink . . . No toothbrush. A half-used lemon soap left in a green soap dish. Catherine picked up the aftershave and held it up to read the name. "Italian. Naples."

"Nothing here but a pack of prophylactics," Gallo said from the bedroom. "It's nice to know the bastard practices safe sex. We're not finding out much more than that. Anything else?"

"No."

"Then let's get out of here and start going through this Rolodex." He was heading for the front door. "If he traveled out of the country frequently, then he probably had a travel agent. When you're uneasy or afraid, then you tend to go to ground in the place that you feel most comfortable."

"And you can't be comfortable unless you visit a place with some degree of frequency." She closed the front door behind her and followed him toward the steps. “So we check and see where—” She suddenly halted on the top step. “Was this too easy, Gallo?” Her gaze was wandering around the parking lot. “I know we’re both thinking of Jacobs as a second banana to Nate Queen, but it makes me uneasy that we don’t know how he thinks, which way he’ll jump. I don’t like invisible men.”

“I have a general idea how he’ll react.” Gallo looked soberly up at her from the bottom step. “And I’m not underestimating him, Catherine. He’s a cornered rat, and he’s not going to like me going after him. He’s always resented me. He likes everything neat and able to be managed and manipulated, and I stepped outside the box.” He turned and started toward the car. “But I wouldn’t worry too much. I became an expert at killing rats in that Korean prison where Queen and Jacobs sent me.”

“GALLO AND CATHERINE LING just left your apartment,” Nixon said when Jacobs answered the phone. “They weren’t in there for more than thirty minutes. They didn’t carry out any boxes or anything big.”

“But they probably found my Rolodex,” Jacobs said through set teeth. Dammit, he should have grabbed it when he’d left yesterday morning. He’d known he’d have to go on the run soon, but he’d been trying to raise a stake to see him through. When he’d gotten word that his superiors had issued orders for him to be picked up for questioning he’d been thrown into a panic. He’d only grabbed his clothes and spare stash of cash and split. “Why the hell didn’t you go in after it?”

“That’s not what you paid me for,” Nixon said. “I don’t

know anything about alarms. I'm clean with the local police. I don't want anything on my record. I watched. I reported. If you'd given me the go-ahead, I would have taken care of them." He paused. "I'll still do it. I'm right behind them on the freeway. All you have to do is make an electronic transfer into my bank account."

But I don't have the money to make that transfer, Jacobs thought in frustration. His hand clenched on the phone. He and Queen had used Nixon before, and he was the best man for a job like this. He was almost as good as Paul Black had been with none of the bizarre freakiness Black had always exhibited.

He would rid himself of Gallo once and for all. And then he'd have a chance of being safe. He was not afraid of either Army Intelligence or any other law-enforcement body. He'd be able to survive. The world was crooked, and he knew where all the bodies were buried.

But Gallo was different. He'd seen how crazy the bastard could be. He wouldn't stop. He'd keep on until hell froze over, until he had Jacobs in his sights. Those yokel cops had said Black had killed Queen, but it was probably Gallo's doing. Jacobs had told Queen any number of times that it was dangerous trying to manipulate Gallo. Something about him caused a cold knot to form in Jacobs's stomach. He hated being afraid. He hated the arrogant macho bastards who'd tried to beat him down and crush him all his life.

But he'd shown them that it was brains, not brawn, that mattered. He'd plugged along and kept quiet and let them all show off how smart they thought they were. But it was Queen who had been killed. It was Gallo who was on the run.

Except, now, Jacobs was on the run, too.

"Make up your mind," Nixon said. "Do I get the money?"

"I'm thinking about it. I can't decide without studying all the consequences."

"My time is valuable. I can take care of Gallo and the woman tonight and move on to my next job. Yes or no?"

"I should be able to make a decision within the next two days. Just stay close to them." He hung up.

He mustn't let Nixon know he was weak in any way. But Jacobs knew he'd have to find a way to rid himself of Gallo and the woman. He couldn't dangle Nixon for more than the two days for which he'd bargained. He had to move and move—

His phone dinged to signal an arriving e-mail.

It could be the confirmation on his hotel room at the casino. They'd better confirm his reservations. He'd given them enough of his business.

It wasn't the hotel.

> **I warned you, Jacobs. I warned you both. Did you think I'd forgotten? Did you think I wouldn't find out what was going on?**
>
> **You're a dead man.**

No signature. Jacobs didn't need a signature.

SHIT. SHIT. Shit.

His heart was beating so hard, he felt dizzy.

You're a dead man.

He had thought that his luck couldn't get any worse when he'd found out that Gallo and the woman were on his trail.

This was worse. This was deadly.

He felt so scared, he was sick to his stomach.

He had to get control of himself. He could get out of this. He'd made up his mind that he had to disappear anyway. It was just reinforced by that damn e-mail. He would tell Nixon to take care of Gallo, and that bitch, and that would rid himself of one threat. Then he would run and hide and not surface until he thought it was safe.

But to do both of those things, he'd have to have money.

Money was always possible, always just around the next bend in the road. He'd pick a place that had always been special for him.

His luck was due to change. It always did.

And this time he was sure he'd score big enough to set him up for life.

Then he'd have the money to give Nixon.

Then he'd be able to squash Gallo and Catherine Ling as if they were vermin. Then he'd be able to keep that bastard from finding and killing him.

Just as soon as his luck changed.

"WE'RE BEING FOLLOWED," Catherine said quietly. "Three cars back, far left lane."

Gallo nodded. "Gray Mercedes."

"And he knows what he's doing. Slow down. I'm going to try to get his plate number."

Gallo slowed, but it took her three attempts to get the number on the front of the Mercedes. The person tailing them was sliding in and out of traffic like an eel. "Very slick. Jacobs?"

"No, Jacobs wouldn't be doing his own dirty work. Not unless he was forced into it." He glanced at the mirror. "But he would have a large number of lethal personnel to call on to do the job. It wouldn't be anyone from Army Intelligence. Jacobs has blown that cover."

"Another killer like Paul Black?"

"That's my guess. Jacobs set up someone to protect his back. He knew that he'd be on the run." He pulled off the freeway. "And this might not be so bad . . ."

She nodded. "Whoever is following us would probably know where Jacobs is hiding."

He smiled. "Two minds with a single thought."

They did think along the same lines, she thought. It was perfectly natural when they had been trained in the same violent schools of engagement. She had discovered that truth when she had been hunting him through the forests. "Then we need to gather him in and squeeze him for information. Pull over to that Holiday Inn, and let's let him find us."

"If he wants to find us," he murmured. "I might have to go find him."

"We'll see." The gray Mercedes was not coming after them, Catherine noticed. Yes, he was as good as she'd thought. It would have been foolish for him to do anything as obvious as driving into the parking lot. He would come back later, check out their room locations, and perhaps position himself for an attack. "In the meantime, while you check in, I'll try to verify his license plate."

"Probably a rental."

"It will be a start." She got out of the car and glanced at the side mirror. A streak of silver-gray Mercedes shot by the motel entrance. *Come a little closer. We're waiting for you.* "Let's get inside and work on it."

"EDWARD HUMPHREY." Catherine looked up as Gallo came in the adjoining door from his bedroom. "Avis Rental. Residence is in Detroit, Michigan. Venable is contacting the FBI and trying to dig deeper. It's not unusual for a suspect to use the same pseudonym any number of times. There may be a way we can sift it and come up with the right identity."

"Or not." He strolled over to the window and pulled back the drape to look down into the motel parking lot. "It may be better to do a little probing ourselves."

"Is he down there yet?"

"No." He let the drape fall back in place. "But it's still early. He may want to give us time to get settled." He dropped down in the beige easy chair beside the window. "I'll be the one to go for him. Okay?"

"No, it's not okay. How do I know that you'd do a better job than me? We'll discuss it later." She wearily rubbed her temple. "But right now, I'm going to take a shower and change my clothes. I still smell of earth and bark and shrubbery."

"And rotting leaves." He smiled slightly. "What a shame. I've grown to like it."

"Which only proves how weird you are." She got to her feet and moved toward the bathroom. "Call me if you need me."

"Oh, I will. You'll be the first to know."

She inhaled sharply as she looked back over her shoulder. Sensuality. Intense and unexpected. Everything had been pragmatic and commonplace. Yet suddenly there was this searing awareness.

Don't address it. Ignore it.

She quickly closed the bathroom door behind her. Ignore it? Her body was responding the same way it had when she'd watched him wading out of the lake and coming toward her.

She threw off her clothes and stepped into the warm shower. A few minutes later, she was soaping her hair and body. The clean white tile surrounding her was completely different from the primitive lake and forest. No comparison.

Except for the way her breasts were swelling as she thought about Gallo. Except for how her skin felt flushed and silky . . . and ready to touch.

She had thought that she had overcome the sexual magnetism that had so shaken her. She had coolly separated her emotional and physical feelings from logic, instinct, and reasoning. Had she just been fooling herself?

No, she wouldn't accept that she would deceive herself just to get what she wanted. The desire might still be there, but it wasn't what had caused her to embark on this search for Jacobs.

But it could get in the way, dammit.

And Gallo wasn't going to try to tamp it down or walk away from it.

She stepped out of the shower and grabbed a towel from the rack.

That was okay. She'd do whatever she thought was right for her and let Gallo please himself. She was only responsible for her own path. Catherine had never asked anyone for help except Eve. But there had been no question that she would ask Eve to help her find Luke. Her son was Catherine's life, and she'd been willing to sell her soul to find him.

And she hadn't called Luke for the last three days, she realized. It had been toward the end of the hunt, and she'd been completely obsessed with capturing Gallo. Which was another reason why she should distance herself from him. Nothing should keep her concentration from her son. They had not been together for nine years; she owed him all her attention.

She threw on a pair of black pants and white T-shirt and was toweling her hair dry as she opened the door.

Gallo was still lounging in the easy chair, his legs stretched out before him. "Now you smell of lavender. Pleasant, but I miss the—"

"Rotten leaves," she inserted. "I wish I'd never told you about them."

"I'm not. It fascinated me learning about Hu Chang and your Hong Kong connection. I studied your dossier before I met you, but it's the details that create the 3-D image." He added, "I ordered sandwiches and coffee from room service. Would you like anything else?"

She shook her head as she took out her phone. "I'll eat later. I have to call my son."

"It's nearly ten. He won't be asleep?"

"He's a night owl. I don't try to force him into a neat little cubbyhole. He lived a rough life while he was away from me. I'm just grateful he's doing as well as he is." She was dialing as she spoke. "And that he lets me stay in his life."

"Would you like me to give you a little privacy?"

"Why? I'm not ashamed of our relationship. It is what it is. We're working our way through it." She spoke into the phone as Luke picked up. "Hi, how are you doing? Are you reading?"

"No, I was having Kelly teach me about how she does her patterns." He paused. "I don't understand it. I don't think I'm dumb, but she sees things that I don't see."

"You're not alone. Kelly is extraordinary. Her professors say that she's another Einstein. She can start at the beginning of a theory or puzzle and forecast exactly where it's going to go."

"I know all that." Luke's voice was slow, thoughtful. "But she says that if I go back and tell her all about the years that I was away from you, she'll draft a pattern that will help me see things clearly." He added haltingly, "And if I understand it, then I'll be able to forget it."

Catherine had known that Kelly was going to try to help Luke in that way. It was the next best thing to psychological therapy, and Catherine would be eternally grateful if it worked. "Maybe not forget it, but it may help you to let it go. Sometimes, bad things help you to grow, and you wouldn't want to give up the growth. That would mean you'd gone through it for nothing. I don't think Kelly would want you to do that. She's gone through some rough times herself."

"She told me her father was murdered. She saw it."

"And she's trying to learn from it. So maybe she's the right person to talk to you about all of this." She paused. "Unless you want to talk to me. You know I'm here for you, Luke."

"I know."

But he still couldn't talk to her, she thought in pain. No matter how much she loved him, she was part of the problem. She cleared her throat and changed the subject. "How are your studies going?"

"Okay. I finished *Midsummer Night's Dream*. But I didn't care much for it. I've started *Julius Caesar,* and I understand that better."

"Yes, I can see you appreciating *Julius Caesar.*" Ambition and murder and revenge. Luke would comprehend all of those nuances of character from his own experience. "*Midsummer Night's Dream* would have a little too much whimsy for you."

"Maybe I'll go back to it later and read it again if you want me to."

"I don't want you to read it to please me. It doesn't matter."

"I . . . want to . . . please you."

"That's good, I want to please you, too. But let's work on kindness and understanding instead of trying to shape each other's tastes."

"Okay." Another pause. "Are you . . . well?"

"I'm fine. I should be able to get home soon."

"I'd like . . . I know Kelly wants to see you." He added, "Do you want to talk to her, should I go get her?"

"No, don't bother her. Tell her I can't wait to see her and give her my best. I'll let you go now. I just wanted to check in and make sure you were all happy. I love you. Good-bye, Luke."

"Good-bye." He hesitated. "I want you to be happy, too, Catherine." He hung up.

Someday, he would say he loved her. Someday it would happen.

"You said you were working your way through it," Gallo said quietly. "It appears that sometimes it's straight uphill."

"You think that I mind that?" She swallowed hard to rid herself of the tightness of her throat. "We're doing fine. Do you know what he went through? Every day that Luke was held by that son of a bitch, Rakovac, he was told that I was to blame. Every time he was whipped or thrown into a solitary cell, it was all my fault. It's a miracle that he managed to realize that I wasn't to blame. But there have to be residual effects from all that brainwashing. He can't trust me even if he wants to."

"What a bastard," Gallo said grimly. "He's dead, I assume?"

"Yes," she said. "Slow and painful."

"Good, then I won't have to offer to do it for you." He was studying her face. "You had to deal with finding him alone? Your husband?"

"He was murdered the night my son was kidnapped."

"So you had to handle it by yourself. You might have had to do that anyway. He was in his sixties, right?"

"Yes, but I don't know why people keep bringing that up," she said impatiently. "Terry was a good man and great father. That's all that matters."

"If that was all that mattered to you."

"Venable turned me over to him after I was recruited, and Terry taught me everything he knew about being an agent. We were good together."

"As partners or as husband and wife?"

"Both. I wasn't some romantic kid who didn't know what was important. We had a good, solid marriage and had a beautiful child together. I couldn't ask for anything more." She defiantly met his gaze. "So it wasn't anything like what you had with Eve. She said it was crazy and pure sex and nothing else. But in the end, it wasn't about what you were together, it was about the child you had."

"And was that what it was about with you and your husband? Your child, Luke?"

She was silent a moment. "I don't know. We were together for such a short time. Terry wanted a child right away, and that was okay with me. But then, after Luke was born, my son was everything. I guess children change everything."

"Yes."

"You agree with me, but you never knew Bonnie," she said. "I can't believe all that ghost business, you know. You had me going for a little while, but I'm too hardheaded to really think that could happen."

"Hardheaded." He repeated the words reflectively. "What would happen if you'd lost your Luke, and he'd suddenly 'returned' to you? What if he was so real to you that all your doubts were crashing down around you? Would you reject him? Or would you let down the barriers and invite him back into your world?"

She shied away from even thinking about Luke taken from

her in that most final way. Yet she'd had to face that possibility for the entire nine years of Luke's captivity. It was clever of Gallo to bring the comparison with Luke into her rejection of the concept of the spirit Bonnie. "I don't know what I'd do." No, that wasn't honest. "I can't imagine a situation like that, but if it existed, I'd never shut Luke away from me even if it meant being locked up in the booby hatch."

"The defense rests."

"But the situation doesn't exist, and what you and Eve are experiencing could be a hallucinogenic product of the emotional trauma that you've both suffered. Understandable, but with no basis in reality."

"That sounds very slick," Gallo said. "And not at all in keeping with what I've learned about you."

"No, I'm not slick." She wearily shook her head. "The opposite. I'm just trying to fit the pieces of the puzzle together, and I'm coming up short."

"Don't worry about it." He pulled Jacobs's Rolodex out of his jacket pocket. "We'll try to put this puzzle together instead."

She came toward him and watched as he flipped the pages of the Rolodex. "Anything?"

"Nate Queen's address and phone. Several officers' names who probably worked at Army Intelligence." He flipped to the T. "No travel agency. I was hoping to save some time, but no luck. Evidently, he makes his own travel arrangements." He flipped to C. He gave a low whistle. "An entire list of casinos." His finger ran down the list. "Las Vegas, San Juan, Lima, Rio, New Orleans, Mobile, Rome, St. Louis, Monte Carlo . . ." He flipped the page.

"And another entire page. Jacobs evidently traveled the world to satisfy his addiction."

"Too many choices. No indication where he might have gone? No preferences?"

Gallo shook his head, still flipping pages. He reached a list of letters with telephone numbers beside them. "M. S. J. N. It seems that he didn't want to be careless with these particular names." He handed her the Rolodex. "Why don't you give these numbers to Venable and see what he can come up with."

She nodded and started dialing her phone. "No H for Humphrey."

"Surprise. Surprise." There was a knock on the door, and he stood up and moved to answer it. "That should be our food." He checked the security view before opening the door. "I can use that coffee . . ."

Two hours later, Venable called back, and Catherine scribbled down the information.

She hung up and turned to Gallo. "He couldn't trace the S, but they were able to pull up info on the others. Juan Martinez, hit man for the San Juan Mafia, Edward Nixon, no gang association but suspect in three murders in the U.S. and two in London, Randy Jason, former Army Ranger now suspected of two killings for hire in Jacksonville, Florida."

"Martinez is Hispanic?"

She nodded. "And the name Humphrey doesn't sound in the least Hispanic. It would catch attention and be remembered if Martinez didn't look the part. So the gray Mercedes is probably Jason or Nixon."

"Unless Jacobs found another errand boy." Gallo went to

the window again. "Still no Mercedes. Maybe he's not ready to move yet." He turned to face her. "Why don't you try to get some sleep. I'll stand watch."

"We'll take turns. Three hours. Leave the connecting door open." She sat down on the bed. "My internal clock is pretty good. Will you need me to wake you?"

"I believe I can manage." His lips turned up at the corners as he turned out the light and headed toward the door. "I can always use my phone alarm. But if I fall down on the job, by all means shake me."

"And then you'd probably grab me and break my neck." She pulled the sheet over her and closed her eyes. "I'll be careful . . ."

CHAPTER 15

GALLO CROSSED TO THE CONNECTING door and looked at Catherine curled up under the covers like a cat.

She was sleeping hard, having gone to sleep within five minutes of the time that she had pulled the sheet over her two hours ago. Her breathing was light and steady, and her sleep was deep and sound. Yet he'd bet that if she sensed anything that was unexpected, she'd be awake in a heartbeat.

As he would be, Gallo thought. Her CIA training and his years in the Rangers had given them both a military mind-set that would probably remain with them the rest of their lives. Now it was strange thinking of Catherine as a soldier. Her competence was superlative, beyond question; but he could no longer think of her as the hunter who had stalked him through the forest.

He was too aware of her as a woman.

Shit, aware? Understatement.

He had trouble looking at her and not remembering her naked, wet, and shimmering in the sunlight. When she had come out of the water, there had been drops of water on her breasts and nipples, and he had wanted to bend down and lick them, make them taut and ready. Then move between her legs and put his hands—

Hell, he was getting hard just thinking about that moment.

And this moment, too.

She was lying there helpless, asleep, and there was a catlike grace about her. But like a cat, he could imagine her moving beneath him, fierce, sensual, springing forward and taking what she wanted.

As she had wanted to do at the lake. Dammit, she had wanted him as much as he had wanted her.

Stop. Block it as he had done since they had started in search of Jacobs. So what if he wanted her more than any woman he'd wanted in years? Screwing her wouldn't be good for either one of them.

Wouldn't be good? What was he thinking? It would be fantastic.

Maybe in the short term, but she didn't deserve any more complications. God knows, he was too scarred to have a decent relationship with any woman. He had come close to almost destroying Eve years ago.

And Bonnie?

But Catherine had said he hadn't destroyed Bonnie.

He closed his eyes as the pain washed over him. God, he hoped Catherine was right, that he hadn't accepted what she had said because he wanted it to be so. But for that reason alone, he should be thinking of Catherine with gratitude and not as a sexual object.

Not likely. He was too damn selfish, and he wanted her too much.

But he could perhaps put off moving to satisfy that selfishness for a little while.

Keep busy. Find Jacobs.

His lids flipped open, and he turned away from the door and moved toward the window in his room.

Let that Mercedes be there.

He pulled back the drape. No Mercedes in the lot, dammit. Where the hell was the—

But he caught a glimpse of silver out of the corner of his eye.

Around the side of the hotel, in the far parking lot. He took his binoculars out of his suitcase. Be sure.

A shadowy figure at the wheel. Light shirt, dark hair, brawny shoulders. No reason for anyone to be sitting in the parking lot at one in the morning.

Jason or Nixon?

It didn't matter.

He let the drapes fall back, turned, and glided silently toward the door to the hall.

Prey.

CATHERINE WOKE with a start.

Darkness. Silence. Something was wrong.

No Gallo.

She swung her feet to the floor and jumped out of bed.

She ran into his bedroom. She hadn't expected him to be there. But his suitcase was open and on the bed. Binoculars on the table by the window.

She grabbed them and thrust the drapes aside.

"Damn you, Gallo." She lifted the glasses and scanned the parking lot. Nothing.

No, to the far side . . .

She threw the binoculars down, ran back to her room, and slipped on her shoes.

Then she was running out of the room. No time for the elevator. She took the steps two at a time as she ran down to the lobby and out onto the parking lot.

She stopped short.

Gallo and a dark-haired man were wrestling on the ground beside the driver's side of the Mercedes.

As she watched, Gallo flipped him over and climbed astride him. His arm encircled the man's neck. Gallo's face was flushed, his lips pulled back and revealing his teeth. Savage, animalistic anger and something close to bloodlust twisted his features. She remembered he had killed Paul Black with that very hold.

"Gallo," she said through her teeth. "Don't you kill him until we find out what we need to know."

He looked up at her, and, for a moment, she thought he would ignore her. Then he drew a deep breath, and his arm loosened from around the man's neck. "I'm not going to kill him . . . yet." He jerked a knife from the man's grasp. "He nicked me and made me a little upset."

She could see the blood on Gallo's forearm. Nick seemed a

good description for the wound. "He didn't hurt you." She came forward and stood over Gallo and the man. "And if he did, you deserved it, you bastard. You left me without a word." Her gaze shifted to the man who was glaring up at her. "Who is he? Nixon or Jason?"

"Why don't we ask him?" Gallo pressed the edge of knife against the man's throat. "Answers. I want answers. Name?"

"Humphrey."

The knife brought blood. "Name?"

"Nixon."

"Very good. Now, where is Thomas Jacobs?"

"I don't know." He gasped with the pain as the knife bit again. "I tell you, I don't know. He hired me to watch his place and report back to him. He was expecting you to go after him when he heard about Queen's death."

"Report back? And that's all?"

"For the time being. There might have been additional work later. He was going to consider it." His lips curled. "I don't think the son of a bitch could afford me. I wouldn't have even taken the job if I hadn't been having a slow month."

"A 'slow month,'" Catherine repeated. "What constitutes a 'slow month' in the assassination game, Nixon?"

"Where is Jacobs?" Gallo asked again. "One minute."

"He was stalling me. He said he'd decide in two days," Nixon went on quickly, his gaze on the knife. "That probably meant he had to find a way to score before he could pay me. He did it once before when he had me take care of one of the bosses at a casino in Atlantic City. The bastard always thought he could beat the tables. Sometimes he did. Sometimes he didn't. But he was always sure he was going to make the big score."

"That's not enough," Gallo said. "More. Jacobs is going to have to disappear for a while, and it's going to take cash. He'd need money to pay you and to find a place to lie low from the police. Where would he go to get the money?"

"How do I know? He didn't—" He cursed as the blood started to run down his neck as Gallo's knife bit deep. "Maybe New Orleans. He told me once he lost his shirt in Atlantic City and the pit bosses were all crooks. He said that next time, he was going back to New Orleans, where he always won big."

"When did he say that?"

"Six months ago."

"Not when he set you up to do this job?"

"No, he didn't mention anything."

Gallo looked at Catherine. "What do you think?"

"I don't know. I think he's telling the truth."

"I'm not sure." His grasp tightened on the knife.

Nixon gasped. "Let me go. I'll find out for sure and set him up for you. What good is it going to do you to slit my throat?"

"Good point," Catherine said. "Let him make a call and see if Jacobs trusts him enough to tell him what we need to know."

"Pity." Gallo took the knife away and got to his feet. "I was beginning to enjoy myself."

Nixon hurriedly sat up. "You'll let me go if I get you what you want?"

"I didn't say that," Gallo said.

"We don't need him. He's not going to call Jacobs back and tip our hand." She stared Nixon in the eye. "Because he knows we'd be after him and never give up. It wouldn't be good business, would it, Nixon?"

"No." He moistened his lips. "I don't care about Jacobs. Why should I?"

"You shouldn't care. As I said, it's not good business." She backed away from him. "Get in your car and turn the speaker on your phone so that Gallo can hear loud and clear." She turned to Gallo. "I'll take a turn around the parking lot and make sure that we haven't disturbed any of the hotel employees or guests while you keep Nixon company."

"Why should they be disturbed? I was very quiet. He didn't even scream." He opened the driver's door and smiled. "But I agree that I should be the one to babysit him. We've grown so close we're almost like family."

"Family? Maybe the Borgias." She moved away from the car and strolled across the parking lot. She doubted if their encounter with Nixon had attracted attention. It had seemed to go on for a long time, but it had actually taken only a few moments. It was the middle of the night, but there was always the chance that someone had glanced out the window. Or that a motel employee had come out for a cigarette. At any rate, she had to check out possible problems before they erupted to become real problems.

They had to move fast to find Jacobs and certainly didn't need trouble with the police.

She was striding back to the Mercedes ten minutes later. Nixon was just hanging up his cell phone. She glanced at Gallo. "Well?"

"New Orleans. Cadalon Casino," Gallo said. "He was on

his way to the airport. Jacobs promised Nixon that he'd have his blood money by day after tomorrow." He added, "Actually, Nixon handled it very well. He displayed a wonderful mixture of greed and venom. Jacobs didn't suspect a thing."

"You said I could go," Nixon said. "You know where Jacobs is heading. I did everything you asked."

"That's true," Gallo said. "But it was really Catherine who said we'd let you go. I really don't approve of—"

"Let him go," Catherine said. "We don't have time to deal with him."

Gallo shrugged. "Whatever you say." He stepped back and gestured to Nixon. "Run along. Frankly, I'd make time to deal with you, but if we experience any backlash, I may still get my way."

Nixon muttered a curse, but he was frantically starting the car and screeching out of the parking space.

Gallo was gazing regretfully after him. "You know that he'll come after us eventually?"

"But it will take time for him to get over the first intimidation," Catherine said. "You frightened him." She turned away as Nixon peeled out of the parking lot. "I can see why Queen thought you were so valuable when you worked for him as a special agent. He said that there were moments when you were like an ancient Viking with the bloodlust on you. He called you a berserker. You can be—" She stopped, searching for the right word.

"Frightening?" He fell into step with her as she moved toward the glass door. "Did I frighten you, Catherine?"

"No." She opened the door. "But I found it interesting to

watch you. I couldn't decide whether you were bluffing or if you really wanted to kill him."

"I don't bluff. Nixon is scum. Would I have cut his throat?" He smiled recklessly. "You seem to think I'm better than I think I am. So I believe I'll let you wonder."

"You're good with a knife. Is that your weapon of choice?"

"I find it effective. Most people have experience with being cut and fear it. Guns are more impersonal. What about you?"

"Sometimes a knife is necessary, but I prefer being impersonal." She added, "Except when I'm dealing with someone I hate."

"Like Rakovac?"

She nodded. "I would have made him suffer as much as a victim of the Spanish Inquisition if I'd had the time. I wanted to take it slow."

"If you run across a similar situation, let me know. I've learned a lot from personal experience about the methods the Inquisition used in that period. I'll be glad to share." He started up the stairs. "I'll call and make our airline reservations to New Orleans."

He stopped before entering his room. "Nixon should really have been eliminated. You know it as well as I do. It goes against your professionalism and my good judgment. Why?"

Because she hadn't wanted to see Gallo do it. Yes, Nixon was scum and would cause them trouble, but she was holding on to her faith in Gallo by a very tentative grip. She had not been shocked by Gallo's savagery, but it had made her wary.

"Never mind." His gaze was on her face. "I think I know." He shrugged. "I couldn't expect anything else."

"No, you couldn't." She went next door to her own room. "I should be ready to go in ten minutes. But I'm going to call Venable and tell him where we're going and see if he can pave the way for us."

"Good idea. Fifteen minutes then."

But there was a missed call on her phone when she picked up her cell to call Venable.

Eve.

She stiffened, then drew a deep breath.

She pressed the return call. "I just got your call. Did I wake you?"

"No. We're not doing much sleeping right now." Eve was silent. "You said to start with the premise that we were wrong about Gallo being guilty and work from there."

"But can you do that, Eve?"

"I'm trying. Joe says that we should trust you. That wasn't easy for him." She paused. "And either way, it's not easy for me. I trusted Gallo, and it hurt me to think that I'd been a fool. Perhaps that's one of the reasons that I was so stubborn about not changing my mind when you were defending him."

"I can understand that," Catherine said. "And I can't tell you I'm 100 percent sure that I'm right. How can I be when Gallo isn't even sure? But I'm 75 percent sure, and before I'm done, I'm going to know."

"You're going after Thomas Jacobs."

"You bet I am. I see you put two and two together."

"Joe and I decided he would be one of the only people who would know for certain why Queen hired Paul Black to take the blame for Bonnie's killing. And we tracked you to the Chicago airport and found out that there was a flight to the East Coast about the time I talked to you on the phone." She added. "Nonstop to Washington, D.C. Have you contacted Jacobs yet?"

"Not yet. We think he's on a flight to New Orleans. We're going to be right behind him." She hesitated, then asked the question. "What are you going to do, Eve?"

"You mean am I going to notify the police that they can pick up Gallo in New Orleans?" she asked. "No, Joe said I should trust you. Dear God, I want to trust you, Catherine. And I want to trust Gallo." She drew a shaky breath. "Joe left the hospital this morning. I'm going to talk to him now, but I think he's going to agree that we're not going to let the police interfere with what's between us. I imagine we'll see you in New Orleans."

"I'm glad, Eve."

"Don't be too happy. When Joe came out of his coma, he said he thought we were heading toward the end, that Bonnie told him that was happening. But I just don't know." Her voice was uneven. "What I'm feeling is too damn tentative. I'm wobbling back and forth like a weather vane."

"What about Jane? Is she coming?"

"No, she's mad as hell, but I won't let her run the risk."

Catherine could see that Jane would be angry as well as worried to death. "She didn't impress me as someone who would take foolish chances. I agree that the situation may—"

"The situation may be pure hell. I've got a gut feeling that it probably will be. Joe almost lost his life. If we're heading for the end of the search, Jane's not going to be caught up in any of it," Eve said fiercely. "I'll call you when we reach New Orleans." She hung up.

Catherine slowly pressed the disconnect.

"We're heading toward the end. Bonnie told him that was happening."

Bonnie, again.

Catherine seemed to be the only one who was not being affected by that small seven-year-old child who had died those many years ago.

Joe, whom Catherine respected as a friend and professional, was evidently accepting the same bizarre concept as Eve and Gallo. Bonnie, returned from the dead. Bonnie, the ghost, the beloved spirit.

"Catherine?" Gallo had opened the connecting door, his gaze searching her expression. "Are you all right?"

"Yes." She glanced at her watch. "Sorry. I haven't called Venable yet. But I can do it on the way to the airport." She threw her suitcase on the bed and started tossing items of clothing into it. "This won't take me long."

He leaned against the doorjamb. "I asked if you were all right."

She nodded jerkily. "That was Eve on the phone. She said she and Joe would see us in New Orleans."

He went still. "You told her?"

"She said she wasn't going to call the police." She looked up from her packing. "She's going to give us a chance. Though she still has her doubts."

"I can imagine."

Because he still had his own doubts and was fighting desperately to put them aside. Catherine had a few doubts herself, dammit, but she wouldn't give up either faith or determination. If she was the only one driving this show, then so be it.

"Joe is on our side." She fastened the suitcase. "Sort of. Maybe. I guess we take what we can get. When are our airline reservations?"

"In another three hours. I could have gotten a connection through Atlanta a little earlier, but it would have only been arriving an hour before the nonstop."

"An hour isn't going to make a difference." She picked up her suitcase. "Let's go."

BUT IT TURNED OUT TO BE nine hours. The entire Gulf Coast was fogged in, and their Delta flight had a six-hour delay. They didn't arrive in New Orleans until close to noon. It was still damp and foggy when the plane landed at Louis Armstrong New Orleans International, and the forecast was for more heavy fog later in the day.

"Where do we go from here?" Catherine asked as she retrieved her bag. "Where's this casino? A high-rise off Bourbon Street or a riverboat on the river?"

"Neither, it's outside the city. The Cadalon is across the Mississippi and has a very exclusive clientele of jet-setters and high rollers. We'll register at the hotel as man and wife. We'll use the Brookman name I used on the airline ticket." He checked his watch. "It's a little early for play, but in a few hours the casino should be humming. We should wait until after midnight to make a play. Though probably Jacobs is at the tables right now. He's going to be very focused."

"You should know a lot about casinos. You made a great deal of money from them, didn't you?"

He nodded. "I taught myself card counting in prison. It's the most valuable lesson I learned in that rathole."

"It's going to be difficult extricating him from a crowded casino. Have you thought about a plan for taking him?"

"A tentative plan." He smiled as he opened the door for her. "But I'm sure that you have one that's not at all tentative. You were very quiet on the plane."

She shrugged. "Simplicity is best. We find out in what room he's playing. I go in and pretend to greet him. He falls unconscious, and we are very upset. He's obviously ill, and we have to get him to a hospital. We take him away from the casino. End of scene."

"Yes, very simple," Gallo said dryly. "Up to the time that he falls unconscious. That might get a little complicated. One of your friend Hu Chang's magic potions? Hypodermic?"

She nodded. "It will keep him out for at least twenty minutes. That should give us time to get him away from the casino."

Gallo opened the passenger door of the rental car for her. "Unless the casino manager wants to handle his transfer to the hospital himself to prevent liability issues."

"That's why I allowed twenty minutes. Otherwise, we could have Jacobs out of there in seven. I've had Venable send me a dossier on the manager of the casino. I'll study it and see how I can get around him." She looked at him as she got into the car. "Or I'll let you handle it. I'd judge you're very good at manipulating people to suit yourself. I'll do everything else. You get us out of that casino before Jacobs wakes up."

"I'll work on it." He got into the driver's seat and started the car. "Anything else?"

"Yes." She took out a slip of paper from her notebook. "Stop at this address on the way out of town. Neither of us has suitable clothes for that kind of casino. It's a boutique that will supply me with a gown that will make me look as if I belong in a casino frequented by the jet set. I told Venable to arrange for a tux for you, too. It won't be designer, but it will be okay. I'm the one who all the attention will be focused on."

"You don't need a designer gown to garner attention. You walk into a room, and every man will do a double take."

"That is true," she said calmly. "Do you expect me to pretend modesty? That would be foolish. Good looks can be a valuable weapon. They can also be a handicap if you want to fade into the background. Either way, you have to accept what you are and make the most of it."

"I gladly accept what you are," he said softly. "I celebrate it."

Sensuality.

She looked away from him, feeling the familiar rush of heat. How many men had hit on her through the years? Why was Gallo different? She didn't know, but she'd better learn to handle his effect on her.

"You'd better not celebrate anything until we get Jacobs," she said flatly. "And I know you like the way I look. I'd have to be blind if I wasn't aware that I turn you on. But it doesn't mean anything. Looks don't matter."

"Looks don't matter. Age doesn't matter. What does matter, Catherine?"

"Kindness. Love. Fighting for what you believe and the

people you believe in." She paused. "And, again, knowing who you are."

"Admirable," he said quietly. "We're alike on many levels. I'm just a bit more shallow and far more attuned to the physical. I'm afraid I can't get over that particular barrier." He paused. "And I believe you may be having a few problems in that area, too. It's been there since the first time we came together, and you've been trying to ignore it. But it keeps coming back, doesn't it, Catherine?"

"Yes." She wouldn't lie to him. That would be a defeat in itself. "But I'll find a way to not let it get in my way. That's not why we're together."

"No, we're together so that you can help Eve and bring me along for the ride." He was looking straight ahead. "And I'm trying to stop being an ungrateful son of a bitch and forget how you looked in all your rotting-leaves glory. I have to warn you—it's not working too well." He gestured to a street up ahead. "I think that's where the address you gave me should be. Do you want me to wait or go inside with you? I have some calls to make to set up my part of our exit plan."

She felt a little of her tension leaving her. His voice was much more crisp, and it was obviously the end of the intimacy that had caused the tension. She was grateful to ignore anything connected to that intimacy at the moment. Honesty and boldness were fine, but she had to regroup and step back from Gallo. "I'll go in alone." When the car pulled to the curb in front of the elegant stone house, she opened the door. "If they need you to be measured for your tux, I'll give you a call. My fitting shouldn't take long. I'm a standard size and Venable knows my measurements."

"Venable must know a lot about you. How long did you say you've been together?"

"He's been my superior since I was seventeen. He recruited me." She slammed the car door and headed for the front entrance. "And by the time I had Luke, he knew more about me than even my husband did. I was an agent and that's all part of the job."

"If I'd been living with you long enough to have a child, I guarantee that no one would have known you better." He smiled and leaned back in the seat. "And to hell with the job."

Cadalon Casino

2:35 A.M.

"I'M READY." CATHERINE CAME OUT of the bedroom into the sitting room and gazed at him critically. "You look very polished."

"I was aiming at being very James Bond." He tilted his head. "I have to keep up with the competition. But 007 never had a Bond girl like you."

She was totally breathtaking, he thought as his gaze moved from the top of her shining dark hair to the silver heels peeping out of the slit in the dark burgundy strapless gown she wore. The golden skin of her shoulders and upper breasts gleamed under the lights, and he wanted to reach out and touch her, stroke her. Exotic, sexy, and so vibrantly alive she lit up the room.

"I've always thought the Bond girls lacked a certain strength of will." She smiled. "But they usually managed to get things done. Did you locate Jacobs?"

"He's playing blackjack and doing very well. He's excited about it. His cheeks are so flushed, you'd think he had a fever." He opened the door to the hall. Don't touch her. Not the time or the place. "I can stay out of Jacobs's way until after you've taken care of him. But both he and Queen must have read the dossier on you that they gave to me. The photo didn't do you justice, but he'll probably recognize you."

"Then I won't give him time for it to register. I can't let him see me until the last minute."

"He'd have to be distracted not to notice you." The hall was decorated in the same elegant nineteenth-century décor as the rest of the hotel casino. Catherine looked like a splendid peacock strolling past the soft pastels of the wall hangings and faded Aubusson rugs, he thought. "But I'm sure that you'll find a way to do it."

"I'm sure I will, too," she said absently. "Eve just phoned me. I tried to call her earlier, but I got her voice mail. They've canceled all the flights out of the Midwest to New Orleans, so they were on a plane to Atlanta. But they ran across the same problem there. They're waiting for a break in the weather. Damn this fog."

"I thought she might be here by now." He gazed out the window at the thick mist that obscured everything beyond two feet. "It's as thick as any London fog."

"Yes, I hoped it might lift before this." She got into the brass-and-beveled-glass-paneled elevator. "I'm glad that they're not here yet. I told them what we planned, but I don't want Joe and her coming into this mess until we have Jacobs secure. If everything blows up in our faces, I don't want them involved."

"But they are involved, Catherine. One might say more than you." He held up his hand to stop her from speaking. "Since we're almost sure that they won't make it before we're done here, I'm not going to worry about it. Though I have plenty of time to devote to worrying since you haven't left me much else to do until after the finale. Where's your hypodermic? You'd have trouble hiding it in that gown."

"It's under the nail of my right index finger." She glanced down at her gleaming scarlet nails. "It was the most practical place." The elevator doors opened, and they were assaulted by voices, music, glittering mirrors, and sparkling chandeliers.

"The blackjack room is beyond the gold arches to the left. Table three," Gallo said.

"Right." She moved out of the elevator. "Give me a few minutes, then follow me."

He nodded. "I'll let you make your entrance. But don't expect me to miss the performance. I've been looking forward to it."

"I don't know why. I told you it's going to be short and simple."

"Whatever you say." He watched her move across the brilliant foyer toward the blackjack room. He was far from the only person staring at Catherine. Who could help it? She was graceful, stunning, completely confident. She was as different as night and day from the fierce huntress who had stalked him in the woods. He wasn't sure which Catherine fascinated him more, and it was too soon to make a choice. He was certain that he'd be seeing other facets of her that would prove equally interesting.

But for the moment, he'd better follow her and be ready to step in and back her up when she needed him. It was a strange role for him. All his life, he had been a loner, and his missions had definitely been solo. Yet he had accepted Catherine's plan, which had not only put him in tandem with her, but in a semi-passive position.

And he had done it with no resentment and even a touch of amusement.

Strange . . .

CHAPTER 16

CATHERINE PAUSED IN THE DOORWAY, her gaze searching the room.

Table three.

Yes, there he was. She'd had Venable send her a picture of Thomas Jacobs on her phone. He was a small, wiry man in his middle or late fifties dressed in a tux that looked a little too big for him. His thin brown hair was receding to such an extent that he was totally bald in the front. But his cheeks were as flushed as Gallo had told her, and his gray eyes were sparkling with excitement as he gazed at the dealer. He had a stack of chips in front of him, and his expression was totally absorbed.

But he might not stay absorbed if he saw someone glance in her direction. She'd better put the play in motion.

She glided forward, moving to the side to approach Jacobs from the rear.

Be anxious.

Let everyone see her concern.

Okay. Stop short as she pretended to see Jacobs.

She inhaled sharply, her eyes widening with panic.

Now clinch it.

She ran toward Jacobs and touched his shoulder. "No, Thomas, you know you can't do this." Her voice was shaking with emotion. "Why don't you listen? You know what the doctor said about your heart. No excitement. This addiction could be the end—" He was turning to face her, his expression wary. As soon as he saw her, he'd recognize her. She had perhaps thirty seconds. "Do you want to kill yourself?" Her tone was agonized. "I won't let you do it. I know I told you I wouldn't stop you if you were this crazy, but I can't let it happen."

He was looking at her face, and she saw his expression change as he recognized her. He jumped to his feet. "Get away from me."

"You have to listen to me, Thomas." Her hands clasped his shoulders near his throat. "I'm only trying to help you."

"The hell you are." He was trying to push her hands away from his throat. "What are—"

"Just leave here and we'll talk." Her grasp tightened, her nails pressing into his skin. "You don't look— Thomas?" His eyes were glazing. *"Thomas!"*

Jacobs's knees were buckling, he was falling.

She instinctively put out her arms to catch him.

No, be weak, be helpless.

She let him fall to the floor as if he were too heavy for her to hold.

She dropped to her knees beside him. "No!"

Tears.

That was always harder, but they came. She could feel the tears flow down her cheeks. "Thomas . . ." She reached out with a shaking hand to check the pulse in his neck. Strong. Steady. He'd be out no more than the twenty minutes she'd told Gallo.

"Pardon me, Mrs. Brookman." A plump man was pushing his way through the crowd surrounding her. "I'm the casino manager, Anthony Solano. May I help you? Your friend is ill?"

"My brother." Her voice broke. "His heart. The doctor told him to stay away from gambling. He had his last heart attack after he lost at Monte Carlo." She gazed pleadingly up at him. "Can you do something for him?"

"Catherine." Gallo was suddenly beside her, his expression mirroring frustration mixed with concern. "I told you not to come, dammit. He doesn't deserve it. Is he dead?"

"No, but his pulse is so weak . . ."

"I saw him fall and called an ambulance. They should be here any minute." He dropped to his knees and was searching through Jacobs's pockets. He pulled out a prescription bottle and opened it. "This has to be his medication. Put two under his tongue."

She took the pills and did as he told her. Then she sat back on her heels, gazing at Gallo in an agony of despair. "Why would he do this? Why wouldn't he listen?"

"You've been asking that for ten years," Gallo said grimly. "Just because he raised you doesn't mean you have to follow him around and pick up the pieces every time he goes off the rails." He turned to the casino manager. "Do you have a defibrillator on the premises in case we need it, or do we have to wait for the ambulance?"

"No, I'm sure we have one in the first-aid room," Solano said. "I'll send someone to check and bring—"

He was interrupted by the shrill whine of a siren.

"Never mind," Gallo said. "The EMT should have one in the ambulance. I'll go meet them." He jumped to his feet and was gone.

"I'm sorry, Mrs. Brookman." Solano was bending over her. "Your brother was a good customer of my casino. I can't tell you how much I regret this happening. Naturally, we'll do everything we can to help."

"There was nothing you could do. You couldn't stop him." Her lips were trembling. "I don't blame you. He is a sick man in more ways than one. Perhaps after this attack, he'll come to his senses." The tears began to fall again. "If he lives . . ."

"He will live," Solano said as he reached out a hand and gently helped her to her feet. "I feel it. I will personally come with you to the hospital and see that he has everything that he needs."

"You're very kind." She leaned against him, her eyes lowered. Ten minutes. Where the hell was Gallo with the ambulance EMTs? "And I'll be very happy to see you tomorrow morning. Tonight it's better if it's only family with him. You understand?"

"Of course. Whatever you wish is—"

"Stand aside." Gallo was pushing through the crowd, leading the EMTs with their stretcher. "How is he? Has he stirred, Catherine?"

"No. He's too quiet."

Gallo bent over him. "Still breathing." He turned to the EMTs. "Get him in the ambulance and get that defibrillator ready. You may need it." He glanced at Catherine. "Do you want to ride in the ambulance or in the car with me?"

"I want to be with Thomas." She turned to Solano as they took Jacobs out to the ambulance. Keep him close. Don't let him have time to think and change his mind before the ambulance pulled away from the casino. "You've been so very kind. Could you walk to the ambulance with me? I don't want to impose, but I feel—"

"No, it is my pleasure and duty." Solano took her arm, and she leaned against him as they walked through the lobby. "I'll give you my card, and if you need anything tonight at the hospital, just call me. I have many friends in New Orleans, and they'll be happy to help you." He opened the front door for her. "And I will be there for you tomorrow."

"Thank you." She let him help her into the ambulance. She gave him one last look from beneath tear-wet lashes. "If God is merciful, Thomas will live, and I'll be able to tell him what a good friend you were to both of us."

Gallo slammed the doors of the ambulance shut.

Fifteen minutes.

The sirens started wailing as they pulled out of the driveway of the casino.

She smiled at the EMT bending over Jacobs before she leaned back and drew a deep breath.

Done.

The ambulance sirens were cut off three minutes later as the driver pulled to the side of the road.

Gallo opened the doors. "Is he awake yet?"

"We're close." She jumped out of the ambulance. "But he has two minutes left."

"Two minutes. You have it down to a science."

"No, Hu Chang does. He gives me a chart with precise measurements." She watched the EMTs quickly bind Jacobs's wrists before putting him into the backseat of the car. "You should give them a bonus. They did very well, and Solano will probably be out looking for them tomorrow."

"I don't doubt it," he said dryly. "Solano's going to be frustrated as hell that he's not going to get his chance to get you into the sack. You had him practically drooling."

She shrugged. "It was just sleight of hand. If he was paying attention to me, he wasn't paying attention to you and the EMTs." She smiled and waved at the EMTs as she slipped into the passenger seat of the car. "Hurry. Solano may start to process what happened."

"You mean your effect isn't as scientifically perfect as Hu Chang's? I beg to differ." He turned away, and she watched him distribute cash, smiles, and a few words to the EMTs before he walked back toward her. "Yes, a bonus big enough to keep them quiet and out of Solano's sight for the foreseeable future. But I'd already arranged it with them before you made the suggestion."

"I just thought that—" She shrugged. "I haven't worked with anyone in a long time. I've gotten used to running things."

"I noticed." He got into the driver's seat. "But I didn't resent it. I found it very interesting watching you work in a civilized venue. You came across as Cleopatra meets Lara Croft."

"I hope only to you." She began to pin her hair back into a

chignon and reached into the backseat for her black pants, shirt, and boots. She couldn't wait to get out of the gown. "Both of them are wily and strong. It was important that I be helpless and pitiful to disarm Solano."

"And sexy enough to keep his mind on his dick and not on what was happening." He started the car. "Personally, I think your magic potion was better than Hu Chang's."

She heard a muffled groan from the backseat. "Jacobs is beginning to stir."

"He's a minute late."

"No, your watch is probably wrong."

He gazed at her with amusement. "I won't argue with you."

"Where are we taking Jacobs? You said you'd rented a house in the bayous somewhere?"

"Yes, it's about eighty miles from here and very deep in the bayous." He was no longer smiling. "And it will give us the privacy we need to have our discussion. I only hope that he can tell us what we need to know."

"You said that he knew everything that Queen knew. That means he would know who killed Bonnie."

He was silent. "And what if he says it's me?"

"Then we decide if we want to believe him or not." Her lips tightened. "Stop borrowing trouble. There had to be a reason why he hired Nixon to kill you."

"Because he knew I'd probably be on his ass for the rest of his life."

"Or maybe there was another reason. We won't know until he talks to us." She glanced back at Jacobs again. "Let's get moving. He's going to be squealing and cursing as soon as he's conscious enough to realize what we've done. I'd rather be off the road and away from the local police."

IT TOOK THEM OVER TWO HOURS to reach the rental house. The fog had returned and was layering a thick blanket that made driving a nightmare.

"I'd swear we've been driving along this bayou for the last hour," Catherine said. "It seems as if the road is going in circles along this swamp."

"No, the land is in the shape of a hook. The house is in the curve of the hook, and the road continues on from there. It should be right around the next bend. Yes, there it is."

"At last."

The large cedar house was no more than thirty years old but, as Gallo had said, it hovered close to one of the bayous. The surrounding trees were over a century old and draped in Spanish moss that added a touch of ancient decadence.

"What is this place? Where are you taking me?" Jacobs screamed from the backseat. It wasn't the first time. Catherine had profoundly regretted the potion hadn't lasted longer. She had given him another injection about an hour ago, but she hadn't wanted to make it too strong. She didn't want to knock him out for too long. "You can't get away with this." Jacobs started cursing again. "The police are looking for you, Gallo. Do you think that you can just walk into my life and kidnap me?"

"It seems that's what we did," Gallo said. "So I guess the answer is yes." He pulled into the driveway of the house. "Quiet down, Jacobs, you're beginning to annoy me. You don't want to do that. You and Queen have told me for years how unstable I am. You used that for your own benefit, but you were careful to make sure that it was never turned on you."

Jacobs was silent a moment, fuming. "It wasn't my fault. Queen was always the one who ran the show. You can't blame me."

"Oh, I think he can," Catherine said. "Did you step forward and tell anyone when they threw Gallo into that North Korean prison? And when he escaped, did you try to stop Queen from sending him out on suicide missions? No, you were sitting fat and happy, pulling in your share of the profits."

"I'm not talking to you, bitch," Jacobs said venomously. "Queen and I knew you were going to be trouble. Everything was going fine until you started digging."

"Be polite." Gallo got out of the car. "I've never told you exactly what those bastards did to me in that prison, but I'm tempted to show you." He opened the rear door and pulled Jacobs out. "I have a number of questions to ask you. If you answer, you may live."

"We can make a deal." Jacobs moistened his lips. "Let me go. What do you care about me? It was Queen who caused all your problems. Look, I have all kinds of contacts. I know every important drug dealer in the Middle East. You may have money, but I can make you richer."

"We'll talk about it." Gallo pushed him toward the front door. "The key is supposed to be in a lockbox under the fourth windowsill, Catherine." He glanced at her and saw that she hadn't moved. "Catherine?"

Her head was lifted as she gazed out at the fog-shrouded bayou.

"Catherine," he repeated.

She shook her head as if to clear it. "It's . . . eerie here. For a minute I thought—" She turned away and moved quickly toward the house. "Fourth window." She retrieved the key and opened the front door. "Pretty obvious. It's a wonder that the place hasn't been burgled or trashed."

"It's fairly isolated." He pushed Jacobs ahead of him. "I'll take him to a bedroom and secure him. Then we'll let him be alone for a while to anticipate." He added softly, "That was one of the techniques I became very familiar with while I was in prison. It always heightened the pain to have to look forward to it first for a time."

"You won't have to hurt me. I'll tell you anything you want to know," Jacobs said. "But you have to remember, Queen was always the one who called the shots."

"That's hard for me to remember." Gallo was pushing him up the stairs. "Isn't a silent partner just as guilty? The only difference is the lack of guts in execution."

Catherine stood at the bottom of the stairs and watched until they disappeared around the landing.

Gallo was furious. She shivered as she remembered his expression as he had taken Jacobs upstairs. His lips had been set, his eyes glittering and reckless. She had been looking upon the capture and questioning of Jacobs as a job, a project. She had forgotten all that Gallo had suffered at Jacobs's hands. Jacobs might be backpedaling and trying to absolve himself, but he was as guilty as his partner. Considering all that Gallo had suffered, it might be hard for her to defuse that rage.

And did she want to do it? She was beginning to be angry as well. Gallo had not deserved the atrocities he had experienced. Someone should pay.

But the reason they were here wasn't so that Gallo could get his revenge.

She turned away and looked around the living room. Flowered wallpaper, an ornate wood fireplace, and furniture draped in sheets. The house had obviously not been rented in a long time. She went over to the window and gazed out at the bayou.

Fog. Moss draped trees. Shadows.

She tensed. Shadows. Of course, there were shadows. It was foggy as hell out there. Nothing was clear or defined.

"I tied him spread-eagled on that big four-poster bed in the master bedroom." Gallo was coming back down the stairs. "Nothing makes you feel more vulnerable than being in that position. Trust me, I've been there."

"And you'd hate to be vulnerable." Her gaze was still fixed on the bayou. "But now you have a chance to get your own back."

"I thought that was bothering you." He was suddenly standing behind her at the window. "You're afraid of what I'm going to do to him."

"Not afraid. I can understand. When I killed the man who kidnapped my son, I wanted the pain to last forever. But how you feel could get in the way."

"I won't let it. But not because I'm getting soft and mushy about the possibility of making him hurt. I'd relish it. But you're in this with me now, and it's disturbing you. He's right about one thing, he was never a prime player in any of this. If I find he has nothing to do with Bonnie's death, I suppose I can tolerate having him tossed into a federal prison for the rest of his life."

She turned to look at him. "I'm surprised."

"So am I." He paused. "Will it be hard? Hell, yes. I could lose control. Keep an eye on me."

"I will."

He chuckled. "Not if you keep staring out at that bayou." His smile faded. "You've been— What's wrong, Catherine?"

"I don't know." She shivered. "I just feel as if someone was watching me. Someone or something. It's probably nothing. Who could be here? We weren't followed?"

He shook his head. "Not unless they were damn good. They would have had to have been tailing us from the casino. It's not likely."

"Imagination?" She tried to smile. "It's a setting that would spark all kinds of fantasies, isn't it? From vampires to alligators crawling up out of the bayou to devour us. I was even remembering that movie about a vampire who lived in the swamps. Shall we go looking for him?" She looked him up and down. "You look like you belong in a vampire movie." She had changed her clothes, but he had only taken off his jacket and tie and rolled up the sleeves of his white dress shirt. The civilized clothes made the huge bowie knife he had sheathed at his waist appear even more barbaric.

He wasn't returning her smile. "I've seen how true your instincts can be. You're fairly remarkable." He turned and headed for the front door. "I think I'll take a turn around the property and see if I see anything. Why don't you go locate the kitchen and see if you can find any tea or coffee? Maybe something hot will chase away the vampires."

The door closed behind him.

GALLO RETURNED ABOUT THIRTY minutes later. "Catherine."

"Here. The kitchen is down the hall and to the right," she called.

He appeared at the door a minute later. "I didn't see anything or anyone. No vampires, no alligators."

"But could you even see them in this fog? I believe it's getting worse." She handed him a mug. "No tea, no coffee. Only chicken bouillon. I managed to heat it, but the water from the tap looked rusty. I don't know how it's going to taste."

He took a sip. "Not bad."

She wrinkled her nose after she tasted the bouillon. "Liar."

He smiled. "It's hot. The fog was chilly." His smile faded. "Are you ready? We've given Jacobs time to simmer. I think you'll feel better if we get to it."

"You're being very protective." Her lips twisted. "I'm not accustomed to that kind of treatment, Gallo. It's not as if I'm not used to dealing with this kind of situation."

"I can't help it," he said simply. "I know who and what you are. You probably think I'm insulting you. But I keep wanting to . . ." He searched for the word. "Shelter you. Take it however you like."

She was taking it with a strange melting warmth that was like a river warming her, closing out the chill that had been with her since she had arrived at this house. She'd had friends, she'd had Terry, her husband, she'd had Venable, who had looked out for her as much as he could. But they had all accepted her as totally independent and able to care for herself. They had never intruded on that independence because they'd probably been afraid of how she'd respond. They had certainly never tried to shelter her.

Gallo looked at her quizzically. "You're not saying anything. Do you want to spit in my eye?"

She took another sip of bouillon before she reluctantly put the cup down on the sink. "Not at the moment. But I do agree we'd better go up and start questioning Jacobs."

JACOBS'S EYES WERE WIDE OPEN, and he was trying to make sounds behind the tape Gallo had placed over his mouth.

"Hello, Jacobs. You seem to want to talk." Gallo bent over and ripped the tape off Jacobs's mouth.

He yelled, his eyes bulging with rage. "You son of a bitch."

The vulnerability of Jacobs on that monster of a four-poster bed was as obvious as Gallo had said, Catherine thought. His thin arms and legs were tied to each of the four posts, and his chest was rising and falling with the force of his breathing. She had expected him to be frightened, but he was angry, his expression twisted and ugly.

"You didn't have to do this. I told you that we could make a deal. We could be partners. I need another partner now that Queen is dead."

"But I don't want you for a partner," Gallo said. "All I want is information. Give me what I want, and there's a chance you might survive this. Ms. Ling doesn't want to witness any unnecessary unpleasantness. Now it's your turn to prove it is unnecessary."

"I *can't* tell you anything."

"Let's see if that's true. I hope you're wrong, Jacobs."

Jacobs was struggling and pulling at the ropes. "Let me go."

"That's not going to happen. Now let's go step by step with this scenario. First, you and Queen hired Paul Black to take the blame for killing Bonnie. You set it up so that I'd put the pieces together and come out with Black killing her to avenge what I did to him in Pakistan."

"I told you, it was Queen all the way. I just did what he said."

Gallo ignored Jacobs's words. "Second, you told Black that I had killed Bonnie during one of my blackouts." His muscles were suddenly stiff with tension. "That didn't happen, did it?"

Jacobs gaze slid away from him. "How do I know? That's what Queen said."

"And you only know what Queen told you," Catherine said sarcastically. "Amazing."

Jacobs gave her a venomous glance. "That's right."

"But I didn't do it, Jacobs," Gallo said. "Who did kill her? Queen?" He paused. "You?"

"No." Jacobs's eyes widened in alarm. "I didn't touch her. I swear I didn't know anything about it. Queen handled it."

Gallo tensed. "Handled what? Why would Queen kill my daughter?"

"He didn't. Don't be stupid." He moistened his lips. "You did it. We were just protecting you. Queen was afraid that you'd start raving like you did in that hospital in Tokyo if you ended up in a mental hospital. We were just protecting you."

Gallo turned pale. "You're lying."

"He *is* lying." Catherine stepped closer to the bed, her gaze fixed on Jacobs's face. "Why, Jacobs? Why not just blame it on Queen?"

"It was Queen," he said quickly. "You caught me off guard. That was the reason I went with the story that Queen concocted. Queen killed her. It was all his fault."

"I don't think so," Gallo said. "You're too eager to jump from one story to another. It might be Queen. Hell, I don't know who's to blame, but I'm going to find out." He took out his knife and pressed it against Jacobs's left wrist. "Do you know how quickly you can die of blood loss if I cut your wrist? Shall I do it so that we can see?"

"No!" He was staring in panicked fascination at the blade of the knife. "Don't kill me. It wasn't my fault."

"And it wasn't mine either, was it?" Gallo asked harshly. "I didn't do it, did I? Say it."

"Of course not." Jacobs's tone was almost impatient, his gaze on the knife. "It was only the story Queen made up. He shouldn't have even had to tell Black anything. Queen was always getting complicated when simple would have done as well."

Gallo's eyes closed for an instant as the relief surged through him. He hadn't been sure until that moment, Catherine realized. But the very casualness of Jacobs's answer was more convincing than if he'd sworn it on a Bible.

"Okay, now let's talk about Queen," Gallo said. "You said he killed Bonnie. Why?"

"I don't know. Look, I've told you that he killed her. That should be enough."

"It's not enough," Gallo said. "Talk. Tell me what happened."

"I can't do it. I can't tell anyone." Jacobs's voice was harsh with desperation. "Do you think I don't want to tell you? I *can't* do it."

"Then I'll have to get to work," Gallo shifted the knife in his hand. "And I'm a pretty clumsy surgeon, Jacobs."

Jacobs shook his head. "Don't hurt me. None of it is my fault." Tears were running down his cheeks. "He won't let me tell anyone."

"He?" Catherine asked slowly. "Another hired killer like Paul Black? Did Queen hire someone to kill Gallo's daughter?"

Jacobs's jaw clenched. "Don't hurt me."

Gallo leaned forward, his eyes glittering. "Talk, Jacobs. I'm tired of hearing—" He stopped and a shudder went through him. He took a breath, then slowly straightened. "Listen carefully; you're going to talk, or I will hurt you. I'll give you thirty minutes to think about it. Catherine and I will leave you to consider what's your best option. Then we'll be back, and you'll tell me everything I want to know." He turned toward the door. "Thirty minutes."

"I can't do it," Jacobs whispered. "He'll kill me. You may hurt me, but I have a chance to live. I know he'll do it." His lips were suddenly curled with anger. "This is all your fault, Gallo. You may not have killed her, but it's all your fault. You shouldn't hurt me."

"Thirty minutes." He turned back and taped Jacobs's mouth shut again. Then he strode to the door and opened the door for Catherine. "No more. I don't want to hear anything from you until you tell me what I want to know." He shut the door firmly behind them.

Catherine drew a deep breath as she started down the stairs. "I wasn't sure that you were going to stop."

"Neither was I," he said grimly. "I had to stop now or not at all. It was hard as hell."

"But you said it would be easier after he has time to think about what might happen to him."

"That's the plan. He's not a brave man. It should be easy to break him." He frowned. "But I don't know . . ."

"I don't know either." Catherine was remembering Jacobs's terrified expression. "He was afraid."

"And not of me." His lips tightened. "Which would have meant breaking him would have been twice as hard."

"He should have been afraid of you. You were very intimidating."

"Not enough." He had reached the bottom of the stairs. "But I will be when I go back upstairs. He *has* to talk."

"So what do we do now?"

"We sit in that drafty kitchen and have some more of that less-than-pleasant bouillon." He headed for the kitchen. "And we give Jacobs time to become terrified by his own imaginings."

"Who is he afraid of?" she murmured as she followed him. "Was I right? Queen did employ other killers for hire besides Black."

"But what's the motive?" Gallo shook his head. "I'm not

making any more guesses. I've spent years wondering and guessing and trying to make sense of Bonnie's death. I have to know the truth."

"One truth you do know is that you didn't kill her," she said quietly.

"Thank God." He turned on the pan of hot water. "But that doesn't mean I'm entirely free of blame. Not with Queen and Jacobs involved."

"By all means, reserve a little guilt for yourself. You wouldn't want to let yourself entirely off the hook." She sat down in the chair. "Gallo, just because they were part of your life doesn't mean a damn thing."

"It means that sometimes our lives touch each other, and that has a direct effect." He poured a little of the bouillon into her cup. "And you know that's true from your own experience."

She couldn't argue with him. Her life had touched Rakovac's, and it was Luke who had suffered.

His lips twisted. "And the last thing Jacobs said was that it was all my fault."

"Bullshit. You don't know what he meant by that," Catherine said. "He was blaming everyone but himself." She sipped a little of the bouillon. "I hate this waiting. I hate this whole thing. I wanted Jacobs to break down and sing like a bird."

"I won't hurt him unless he doesn't give me a choice, Catherine."

"I know." And it wasn't as if Jacobs was some innocent victim. He had hired Nixon to kill them. And, in spite of protesting his innocence, he had almost certainly been involved in Bonnie's death. The nightmare had gone on too long, and only

Jacobs could cause it to come to an end. "But I don't have to like it. I hate hurting people."

He suddenly smiled. "You'd rather I cut the bastard's throat and get it over with? You're a strange woman, Catherine."

She shrugged. "I'm what life made me. Just like you, Gallo. And you're not so—" Her phone rang, and she glanced at the ID.

"It's Eve." She pressed the button. "Where are you, Eve?"

"About forty-five minutes from you according to the GPS." She paused. "Is everything all right?"

"Do you mean have we found out anything from Jacobs? Not yet." She paused. "Except that he said that Gallo didn't kill Bonnie."

"And you think he's telling the truth? From what you told me, Jacobs is as much of a sleazebag as Queen was."

"I don't think he's lying." Catherine smiled at Gallo across the table. "Jacobs may be a complete sleazebag, but he was telling the truth about that. And he's scared, Eve. He knows who did kill her, and he's scared shitless." She hurried on before Eve could voice the question. "And, no, we don't know who that is. We're following up as fast as we can. We may have something by the time you get here."

"I hope you do." She was silent a moment. "If it's true, I'm happy for Gallo."

"But you're still skeptical. Oh, well, maybe Jacobs will be able to convince you when you get here. I'm tired of being the only positive voice. I've just had a depressing conversation with Gallo about touching people's lives and changing them for the worse. It works the other way too, dammit."

"Yes, it does. And you're proof of it, Catherine. I'll call you when I'm within a few miles of your place." She hung up.

"She's happy that Jacobs cleared you," Catherine said to Gallo as she hung up.

"But skeptical." He added quietly, "I'm glad you're not skeptical. You've been a beacon in the darkness, Catherine. I know I've been a pain in the ass."

"Yes, you have. In more ways than one." She met his eyes. "And you'll owe me when this is done."

"I'll pay you. Anytime. Any way. I'll invent new ways to pay you."

She tore her gaze away. "How much longer do we have to wait down here?"

"Another ten minutes."

She hesitated. "Maybe we should wait for Eve and Joe."

"And maybe we should have everything settled before they get here. I've never encountered Joe Quinn except for those few minutes before Black stabbed him, but he's never had any warm feelings toward me."

"That's an understatement. You can hardly blame him. Eve is his whole world, and he considered you a threat to her."

"I don't blame him. If I'd been in his position, I would have tried to wipe me off the face of the Earth. I'm just saying that there are giant hurdles to overcome, and this may not be the time to do it." He added, "And do you want to have Eve feeling the same way you do about squeezing the information out of Jacobs? I'm the only one who should have to bear responsibility for dealing with the bastard."

No, she didn't want to saddle Eve with anything more than

she was bearing now. But on the other hand, she didn't want Eve arriving and thinking that Jacobs had cleared Gallo because force was used. She wanted Eve to see the situation and judge for herself. Gallo deserved at least that from Eve and Joe. She said, "I'd like to wait, please. They should be here in another forty minutes."

He opened his lips, and she thought he was going to argue with her. Then he closed them again. "Whatever you like. It's your call." He lifted his shoulders in a half shrug. "Who knows? An extra forty minutes of waiting may be the time it takes to make Jacobs more willing to cooperate."

She wasn't at all sure that call she'd made was the right one. It was a delicate situation, and Eve and Joe were as strong-willed as Catherine and Gallo. It could all blow up when they came together.

"And I know why you made it," Gallo said softly. "I believe you may have a protective gene or two yourself, Catherine."

"I do. I'm protective toward my son." She lifted the bouillon to her lips. "You can take care of yourself, Gallo."

CHAPTER 17

"DO YOU WANT ME TO TAKE a turn driving?" Eve asked Joe as she hung up the phone. "This fog is a hell of a strain on the eyes. We're having to creep along."

"I'm fine."

Yes, he was fine, thank God, she thought as she gazed at him. He was still a little pale, and he'd lost at least ten pounds, but other than those two signs of weakness, he was the Joe she had always known. Since he'd left the hospital, he had been quiet, conserving his strength, but that strength was there. And so was his sharpness and incisive decision making. During their frustrating journey, he had managed multiple flight cancellations, rebookings, and dealing with airport and rental-car personnel with far more patience than Eve had.

He shot her a glance and smiled. "It's not my eyes that kept me in that hospital, Eve. And the rest of me is doing just fine, too." His smile faded. "Jacobs said that Gallo hadn't killed Bonnie?"

She nodded. "But if he didn't kill her, who did? Maybe Jacobs or Queen did it themselves?" She rubbed her temple. "I just don't know. Catherine said Jacobs knew who did it and seemed scared to death to tell anyone."

"He'll be more scared when I get my hands on the bastard," Joe said grimly. His foot unconsciously pressed harder on the accelerator, and the car jumped forward.

"Joe."

"Sorry." He lifted the pressure, and the car slowed. "You're right, we don't want to go off the road into the bayou. Hell, I can't even see the side of road in this muck."

"Then just crawl along. I allowed extra time when I told Catherine we'd be there in forty minutes." She glanced out the thick white nothingness beyond the window. Every now and then, she'd catch a glimpse of the twisted branch of a tree jutting out of the bayou, but almost immediately it was gone. "But I wish this fog would go away. It's really eerie."

"You think so?" Joe shook his head. "I was thinking it was kind of . . . comforting."

"You've got to be kidding. Why?"

"I don't know." He thought about it. "Or maybe I do. Before I came out of that coma, it was like this. It was like a soft blanket of fog that I was traveling through. Only it was dark and glowing, not this white mist. But I knew where I was and where I was going, and I wasn't afraid. The fog around me felt warm and it somehow . . ." He searched for words. ". . . filled my heart. I could occasionally see something jutting out of the fog, but nothing was clear. Except you, Eve. " He added simply, "And Bonnie."

Her throat was suddenly tight. "And there's nothing frightening about either one of us." She reached out, and her hand clasped his on the steering wheel. "Because we love you." She laughed shakily. "But I don't believe that this particular fog is warm and comforting. And I'll definitely disagree if you end up by dumping us in the bayou. I don't care for either swamps or bayous. It makes me remember—" She inhaled sharply, her body stiffening.

His gaze flew to her face. "What's wrong?"

"I don't know. I saw something." She turned in the seat, her gaze on the fog-shrouded bayou. "Someone."

"A fisherman?" Joe asked. "Those would be the only people I'd think might be out in weather like this. Was he in a boat?"

"No. Maybe. I only caught a glimpse—" But that glimpse had startled her. "And it wasn't a man. Or I guess it could have been, but I got the impression— Pull over, Joe!" Her gaze was fixed on the bayou just ahead. "Now."

"Why?" He was frowning as he pulled over to the side of the road. "You think there's someone in trouble?"

"No," she whispered. "Not any longer." She hopped out of the car and ran to the edge of the road, her gaze fixed on the billowing mist hovering over the water. "She's not in trouble. That's all over." Her eyes were straining to catch another glimpse of that small figure moving slowly through the fog. No, she had vanished as quickly as she had come.

"It's Bonnie. But why is she here? And why didn't she come closer? This isn't like her. She's acting as if she's—" A ghost, a spirit, a mystery from the mist. Not like her Bonnie. Her daughter had always been so real when she came to her that Eve had felt as if she could reach out and touch her, hug her.

"Bonnie?" Joe had come to stand beside her, his gaze on Eve's face. "Are you sure? We were just talking about her. You could have been thinking about Bonnie and it translated thought into—"

"Imagining that I saw her?" Eve finished. "No, I did see her. That first glimpse could have been imagination, but then I saw her again as we rounded that curve. She was right there before me. I saw her face." She gestured at the bayou. "She was there, Joe. You didn't see her?"

He shook his head. "Not this time, Eve."

She shook her head in frustration. "I tell you, she was *there.*"

"I'm not questioning you about anything concerning Bonnie," he said gently. "I'm far beyond that, Eve. If you say you saw her, then she was here. I'm only saying that I didn't see her. I've no idea how all this works. It's new to me. Maybe she didn't want me to see her this time. Maybe she only wanted you. You saw her for years and years before she ever deigned to pay me a visit."

"But I never saw her like this before. It . . . scared me."

"Why?"

"She wasn't . . . herself." How to explain it to him when she was bewildered, too. "She was always happy when she came to me. I was the one who was anxious and worried and full of guilt.

She'd laugh at me and tease me and tell me that everything was all right with her. That I shouldn't fret so much about finding her and bringing her home."

"And that's a wonderful thing."

"But she wasn't like that when I saw her a few moments ago." She repeated, "She scared me."

Joe put his hand on her arm and pulled her close. "You said that before. Why? What was different?"

"She was sad. Her face was so sad. Bonnie was never sad." She could feel the tears sting her eyes. "Or if she was, she never let me know. Did she hide it, Joe? Did she hide it so that I wouldn't be unhappy?" She swallowed hard. "And what is she doing here, dammit? First, you're talking about that death fog you went through. Then I see Bonnie, and she's not *my* Bonnie. Is she trying to tell me something?"

"If she was, then she'd come right out and say it, wouldn't she?"

"No, she can be enigmatic as hell."

He smiled. "That sounds very human and very special."

"Yes." Bonnie had always been special, and she had remained special even after that monster had taken everything else from her. Her gaze searched the bayou, but she saw nothing but mist. She could *feel* nothing. She turned away. "She's gone." She moved back toward the car. "And you're probably thinking I'm acting as neurotic as hell."

"No." He got into the car and stared thoughtfully out at the bayou. "It's not neurotic to be upset about a change in someone you love. And you love Bonnie with all your heart. The whole thing is very strange. I've just been trying to piece together the puzzle."

"That's like you," she said as she fastened her seat belt. Joe's mind was always delving and striving to make logic out of chaos. And most of the time, he was able to do it. "When you come up with something, let me know."

He started the car. "I'm working on it. Bonnie appeared to you and wanted you to know she was unhappy about something."

"Maybe she's always been unhappy. She's dead, dammit."

"But you have to balance the experience of years against this one episode. That would mean that there was something unusual happening to change that balance." He paused. "Something to do with Gallo?"

"If he didn't kill her, why would she be sad?" She shook her head and smiled with an effort. "Only you would analyze ectoplasm and try to make it rational."

"Would Bonnie like you referring to her as ectoplasm?"

"Yes, she'd probably giggle."

"You said that without even thinking. So it doesn't seem to me that you have to worry about this one case of melancholy."

She nodded, and this time the smile was genuine. "Not as long as I have you to set me straight."

"No problem." He was gazing straight ahead. "But as you said, this is unusual. We should probably be looking out for 'unusual.' "

"Why?" She tilted her head. "I assume you're not just being cryptic?"

He didn't look at her. "No, I'm just remembering what Bonnie told me, that we were coming to the end. Ends aren't always happy, Eve."

She was silent for a long moment. "You've been telling me that for years in one way or another. Sometimes, I resented it. Sometimes, I was grateful. But you've been preparing me for this, haven't you?"

"I've been preparing both of us for it. I knew the first time I met you that we were going to have to be strong to face what life had dealt us. And the end may be the hardest part of all. It's been a long time coming."

"That's what I thought. I tried and tried again, and nothing came of it. I couldn't find Bonnie. I couldn't find the monster who killed her." She whispered, "And I couldn't see why. I thought if there was a God, then He should help me find my little girl. She was so wonderful. Everyone loved her. God must have loved her, too." She turned her head and gazed out at the thick mist flowing by the window. No Bonnie in that mist. She had come and gone. But she was near . . .

"But lately I've wondered if there's a reason that I had to wait. I don't think I was ready. You're right, whatever I have to face, I'll have to be strong enough to take it. Perhaps I had to learn something about myself before I could bring her home. Perhaps I had to learn about you, Joe. I think I learned a lot about both of us when I was waiting for you to wake in ICU."

"And are you ready now?"

"I think so." Her hand reached for his and clasped it tightly. "We'll have to see, won't we? Lord, I hope I'm ready, Joe."

* * *

"THEY'RE COMING." Catherine turned away from the window. "At least, I think they are. I can barely see the headlights in the fog. They should be here in a couple minutes." She leveled a glance at Gallo. "And, no matter what Joe says or does, you're not to respond with any antagonism, do you understand?"

"I understand that you're expecting a lot from me." He got up from the chair and crossed to the window. "I believe you're talking about diplomacy. We both know that's not my forte."

No, it wasn't, and she could already see that familiar trace of recklessness in his face. "I'm not having it, Gallo. Joe was the victim, and you can be patient if he's pissed at you."

"And if I'm not, then you'll go after me yourself. I believe you're proving that you're protective of more people than your son," Gallo said. "But I admit I like it better when it's me you're protecting." He watched Joe and Eve get out of the car. "Do you want me to go and greet them?"

And watch Eve have to handle the confrontation between the two men who had shaped her life? Catherine was already at the front door and throwing it open. "Come in out of this mess," she called. "I wish I could offer you a cup of coffee, Eve. But we're limited to bouillon." She made a face. "Not even good bouillon." She turned to Joe. "You look wonderful." She gave him an appraising glance. "Maybe you've lost a little weight. But I knew you'd make it."

"That's more than I did." Eve gave her a quick hug. "And you've lost a pound or two yourself since I last saw you."

"I kept her on the run," Gallo said from where he stood by the window. "But no more than she did me." His gaze shifted to Eve's face. "Hello, Eve."

She stiffened. "Hello, John."

Joe stepped quickly forward. "Gallo."

Gallo's expression was wary. "Hello, Quinn. Am I going to have problems with you?"

"I'm not sure," Joe said coolly. "You deserve them. You've been getting in my way since the moment you decided to come back into Eve's life."

The two men were like two lions, arching, frozen in place but ready to attack, Catherine thought. She took a step forward, then stopped. They'd have to work it out for themselves sometime. It might as well be now.

But Gallo had seen that movement from the corner of his eye. "Catherine says I have to be diplomatic since I'm the one who has been causing all the trouble. She's about to step in and take me out."

"I'd be glad to save her the trouble." Then Joe glanced at Eve. "But you may not be important enough for me to be bothered with right now, Gallo."

Oh, shit. Catherine saw that flicker of recklessness appear in Gallo's expression again.

He said, "Perhaps I could up the ante, and that would make you think I'm—"

"Stop it." Eve stepped forward between the two men and faced Gallo. "Catherine said that Jacobs knows who killed Bonnie. That's all I care about. If you love Bonnie as much as you say, then that's all that you should care about, too." She paused. "I thought it was you, John. I'm still not certain it's not. Prove it to me."

"Yes, prove it to her, Gallo," Joe said. "I think we need to talk to Jacobs."

"Fine," Catherine said. "We've been waiting for you." She turned toward the stairs. "If you want to ask Jacobs questions, then come upstairs and do it. Maybe you'll have more luck than we did."

Gallo hesitated and gestured toward the stairs. "By all means, I was looking forward to questioning the bastard myself, but I'll forgo the pleasure. Catherine has already pointed out that I need to be kind and diplomatic to guests."

"And you're doing what she wants." Eve was gazing at him searchingly as she started up the stairs. "I find that curious."

"Do you?" He smiled. "But can't you see I'm terrified of your friend Catherine?"

Catherine made a rude sound. "Shut up, Gallo." She turned to Joe. "Jacobs is going to cause us trouble. I hope he'll be more cooperative now that he's had time to think."

"He'll be cooperative," Joe said grimly as he moved past her up the stairs. "Tell me what he's told you so far. No, on second thought, let me start fresh."

"Lord, it's chilly up here." Eve shuddered as they reached the bedroom door. "What are you doing, Catherine? Are you trying to freeze information out of him?"

Catherine frowned. "It wasn't this chilly before." She opened the door. "I don't know why it would—"

"Dear God!" Eve took a step back, her gaze on the bed. "Catherine?"

Catherine's gaze followed Eve's. She went rigid. "No. Eve, no. We didn't— Gallo!"

There was water on the floor around the bed.

Jacobs was still bound, spread-eagled on the bed.

And there was a knife sticking upright in his chest.

"Shit!" Gallo pushed by them and ran to the bed. Jacobs's mouth was still taped, and his eyes were wide open, staring at the ceiling. Gallo checked the pulse in his throat, but they all knew it wasn't necessary. "Dead. But how the hell—"

"The window." The sheer white drapes were blowing from the open window, and Catherine was there in a heartbeat. "We were downstairs. He had to have come in the window."

Dammit, she could see nothing through the heavy fog.

But she could hear something.

The splash of water being moved, the sound of suction in the mud . . .

"He's in the bayou!"

"Heading south." Gallo had already swung his legs over the sill and was climbing hand over hand down the side of house to the roof of the porch.

Gallo might think he was Spider-Man, but she'd make almost as good time going down to the front door and wouldn't risk falling and breaking her neck, Catherine thought. She turned and was running out the room when Joe grabbed her arm and spun her around.

"One question," he said.

"I don't have *time,* Joe."

"You have time for this one." His glance shifted to Jacobs. "This isn't some con you set up to convince us that Gallo was innocent? He didn't get overenthusiastic and stick that knife in Jacobs?"

Her eyes widened. "I wouldn't do that, Joe."

His expression didn't lose its hardness. "I wouldn't think that you would, but I wouldn't think you'd be so dedicated to exonerating Gallo either. I don't know what's going on with you, Catherine."

She tore herself away from him, her eyes blazing. "And you think because he once managed to convince Eve that he was the sun and the moon, that he'd dazzle me so that I'd lie for him? No way, Joe. He didn't kill Jacobs, and neither did I. We were both downstairs waiting for you. Whoever did this must have followed us from the casino." She turned on her heel. "And now I'm going to go into that bayou and try to catch the son of a bitch."

"Go on," Joe said quietly. "Eve and I will be right behind you as soon as I figure out which—"

But she didn't hear the rest because she was already down the stairs and throwing up the front door.

Swirling fog.

Dampness.

And the sudden splash of movement in the bayou.

"Gallo!"

"Here."

He was already in the water.

She took off her boots and socks, left her gun on the bank, and made sure her knife was firmly in its holster on her thigh. Then she jumped off the mossy bank and moved in the direction in which she'd thought she'd heard his voice.

The water was only up to her waist that close to the bank, but she couldn't be sure what was in the water with her. Everything from water moccasins to alligators frequented the bayous. Just be careful and look sharp. She couldn't see anything at any distance, but she would be able to tell if one of those predators was within striking distance.

Hell, she hated being blind in the dense mist. And Gallo would also be blind. They'd be lucky if they didn't attack each other. But she didn't want to call out again and draw possible fire.

Or another wicked knife like the one in Jacobs's chest.

Move slowly, as silently as possible, in the water.

She listened.

She couldn't hear Gallo moving through the water. Not even a whisper of sound.

Where was—

"Catherine."

She jerked with shock. He was right beside her. His white shirt was plastered to his body, and his sheathed bowie knife was shoved into the waist of his black trousers.

His gaze was fixed on the south. "He's heading in that direction. Every now and then, I can hear him brush against something. Or he'll startle a bird, and I'll hear the wings . . ."

Catherine started forward. "What are we waiting for?"

"He's very good. Damn good. We go too fast and lose his sound, and he could circle and come up behind us. There are times I can't hear him at all. The bayou is deeper once you get a distance from the bank. He's probably swimming." He was silent again. "Do you hear that?"

Birds moving from branch to branch.

"He's going southwest now." He started forward. "You circle and see if you can come at him from the west. I'll track him on the direct route."

"West," she repeated as she started out. "You said Jacobs's killer was so good. Yet we heard him plainly from Jacobs's bedroom."

"He was in a hurry. He'd probably just finished knifing Jacobs when we were coming up the stairs. He needed to get in the water and away from the bank."

"And after those first few minutes, he felt safe and could take his time."

"As I said, he's really good. Be careful, Catherine . . ." He disappeared into the mist.

But that mist wasn't as thick, she realized suddenly. Gallo had gone at least four yards before she had lost him to view. Maybe the fog was dispersing.

She went a few more yards, her hopes rising with every step. They had gotten lucky. Yes, the mist was definitely lifting. They'd soon be able to see the bastard who had killed Jacobs.

And the killer would be able to see them.

"THE FOG'S BEGINNING TO LIFT," Joe said, as he and Eve reached the edge of the bayou. "That will help." He grabbed her arm and pulled her toward the car. "We can't help Catherine much in that swamp. Come on, we'll take the car and go along the road bordering the bayou. We didn't see any sign of a car when we drove up to the house, so he must have parked up ahead and around the curve of the bayou. That's where he'll probably be heading."

Eve nodded as she got into the car. "Then why would he jump into—" She answered herself. "A false trail. So that we wouldn't find his car." A bold move, possibly a deadly move. Catherine and John Gallo had followed him into the bayou and were trying to find him while lumbering blindly in the thick fog. Joe said it was lifting, but not enough.

Please, let us have a break in this damn fog.

"I'll go slow. Hell, I *have* to go slow." Joe had already started the car and hit the lights. "You keep an eye out. He could have come back to the bank anywhere along the road."

She nodded, her eyes straining as they tried to pierce the thick layers of fog hovering on the bank. She rolled down the window so that she could better hear anyone moving in the water. Her heart was pounding, and the muscles of her stomach were clenched with fear.

She had a sudden memory of Bonnie's face as she'd seen it earlier. Sadness. Such sadness.

Why? The death of Jacobs?

Or the death of someone else, someone whose death Bonnie knew would hurt Eve? A chill went through her at the thought. Not Joe. Please God, not Joe. You've just given him a new lease on life. Not Catherine, who had hardly started to know the meaning of joy and had a son who needed her. Not Gallo, who had perhaps suffered more than all of them.

If this is the end, shouldn't it be you and me, baby?

"Eve." His eyes were on the road ahead of him, but Joe's voice was soft but clear. "It's going to be all right. We're going to get through this together."

She nodded jerkily. "I know, Joe."

Together. Yes, they'd be together, but maybe not right away.

Eve could not forget the sadness in her daughter's face.

Let it be me, Bonnie.

CATHERINE STOPPED AND STOOD still in the water as she saw the pale fog-shrouded glow of headlights on the road leaving from the direction of the house.

Joe and Eve.

Smart.

They were betting that the man who had killed Jacobs had a car parked somewhere on that road bordering the bayou. It was reasonable that he'd be heading across the bayou in the direction where he'd left it.

She tried to pull up a mental picture of the curve of the road around the bayou. Gallo had said the terrain was shaped like a hook . . .

And Gallo had told her that they should go southwest.

And sent her west.

But the hook of land surrounding the bayou extended to the east. That would be where that car would be parked. Southeast. And Gallo was heading due south.

And would probably soon veer to the southeast.

Damn him.

Anger was seething through her. The son of a bitch was trying to *protect* her. Who the hell did he think he was? She was every bit as competent a professional as he. She should have slapped that damn macho tendency down as soon as it raised its head. Now it was getting in the way of her job.

And could get them both killed.

But not if she could help it.

She turned and headed southeast.

JACOBS'S KILLER WAS DEFINITELY heading southeast toward the hook of land bordering the bayou, Gallo thought.

He could hear him, and, if he got lucky, soon he might be able to see him.

The fog was lifting for a few seconds, hovering, then closing down again. All he'd need would be those few seconds to draw his knife and hurl it.

If he was close enough.

And he would be close enough.

He could feel the excitement and tension searing through him. Another hunt. But this was nothing like the hunt with Catherine. Even in the darkest hours of those days, he'd known that it was different from anything he'd ever experienced. There might have been lethal danger, but it had been coupled by challenge. This hunt was different. No beautiful, sleek, panther who could turn and rend him in the flash of an eye.

This was only prey.

And the sounds of the prey were approaching closer to that far bank.

The fog lifted . . .

Gallo caught a swift glimpse of the shadowy bank, a gnarled cypress tree dipping its roots in the water, Spanish moss hanging from another tree near—

Near a gleam of metal. A car?

He couldn't be sure. The fog had closed in again, dammit.

But that gleam of metal was a little too opportune. The bank had to be the prey's destination.

He began to carefully, silently, swim toward it.

CATHERINE PULLED HERSELF from the water onto the bank. Now that she had a destination, she could move faster over ground. She should be somewhere near the road, and the car would probably not be parked on the road itself but hidden in the shrubbery.

She moved swiftly through the heavy palmettos and shrubbery that bordered the bank. Her sopping-wet clothes were plastered to her body, and the soles of her bare feet were being scratched and bruised with every step.

Pain.

Ignore it. Block everything out. Concentrate on the job.

She had to find Jacobs's killer before he got away.

Find the car. Wait for him to show.

But she had to be careful. She couldn't kill the bastard even though it would be safer.

Eve still needed him. Eve still had to know about her Bonnie—

EVE STRAIGHTENED IN HER SEAT. "I saw someone."

Joe tensed. "Where?"

"He's gone now. I only got a glimpse. This damn fog. Not close. Around that bend. I saw someone climbing out of the water onto the bank."

"Gallo? Catherine?"

She shook her head. "He was thin, wearing a dark blue or black wet suit."

"Around that bend?" Joe pulled to the side of the road. "Then we go the rest of the way on foot. We still have to use the lights and we don't want to scare him off." He got out of the car. "I can do this alone, Eve."

"No, you can't." She jammed her hand in the pocket of her Windbreaker and gripped her .38 revolver. A weapon to protect Joe as Joe had always protected her. Would it do any good? The more time that passed, the greater the cold dread that was icing through her.

She got out of the car and joined him as he strode into the brush bordering the bayou. "You said together, Joe."

HE *HAD* HIM.

A man in a dark wet suit, tall, thin, moving quickly along the bank toward the gleam of metal that Gallo had identified as a vehicle.

Yes.

Gallo unsheathed his knife as he stood up in the shallow water near the bank.

Dammit.

The prey had disappeared as a fresh billow of fog descended.

No, there he was again. He was moving with a lithe jauntiness as if he had all the time in the world.

You don't have any time at all, bastard.

Bring him down permanently or just wound him? Gallo thought as he raised the knife and lined up the target. It would depend on how long he had before the fog settled once—

Oh, my God.

No!

His hand holding the knife fell nervelessly to his side as he stared in horror at the man in the wet suit.

No. No. No.

Not prey at all.

But the man had sighted prey of his own, Gallo realized. His stance had changed, and now he was in stalking mode. He'd drawn a knife from the holster at his waist.

Stalking whom?

Catherine.

Catherine, standing at the edge of the trees. Catherine, setting her own trap for the man in the wet suit, the man who had killed Jacobs, the man who had killed Bonnie.

Dammit, what is wrong with me, Gallo thought in agony. Throw the knife.

* * *

IT WASN'T A NEW VEHICLE, Catherine noticed as she cautiously approached. It was a beat-up blue Chevy truck, and the tires looked worn, almost bald.

No sign of the driver of the truck.

She'd been listening and hadn't heard anyone come out of the bayou.

But she might not have been able to hear him. She didn't have quite as keen perceptions as Gallo. And he had said this creep was good. She trusted Gallo's judgment.

When it didn't concern his damned chauvinistic attitude toward her.

She stopped. She'd been tempted to check out the license plate and the glove box of the truck. Not smart. Better to wait and do all that later. Now she should wait and watch and listen.

Not much watching with this fog, but she could listen.

No sound.

The fog had come in again, and the truck was only a hazy outline before her. But she'd probably have company soon. Just wait and pounce when he came on the bank.

She stiffened. Something was wrong. She felt it. The hair on the back of her neck was tingling.

"THERE'S SOMEONE OVER THERE in the trees." Joe grabbed Eve's arm and pulled her to a halt. His eyes narrowed. "I think it's Catherine." He froze. "Oh, shit."

She could see why he was cursing as she saw the tall man in the wet suit directly behind Catherine. Nothing could be clearer than that he was on the attack.

"I can't get a clear shot," Joe said with frustration as he put his gun down. "He's right behind her. I'll shoot *her,* dammit." He moved to the side. "I'll see if I can get him from another angle. Don't call out and startle him. I don't want to have him move on her before I can get my shot."

If there was enough time.

It was going to be Catherine, Eve realized in agony. Catherine was the one who was going to die. And Eve had to stand there and watch it happen. She couldn't even cry out and warn her.

But Catherine had been with Gallo in the bayou. Why wasn't he there?

Dammit, where was Gallo?

THANK GOD, THAT BASTARD WAS moving slow, Joe thought as he ran quickly through the brush. He just had to hope that nothing would startle him into leaping forward toward Catherine.

But the angle where he was standing now was still bad for an accurate shot, and he couldn't get closer because the bank curved there.

The cypress tree. He should have a chance of a clear shot from there.

He shoved his gun into the waistband of his pants and started to shinny up to the first branch.

Fast.

Faster.

The man in the wet suit was starting to move more quickly toward Catherine.

Joe was drawing his gun as he pulled himself onto the branch.

Clear shot.

But Jacobs's killer was almost on top of her.

Get the shot off.

Out of the corner of his eye he caught a glimpse of another figure standing in the water several yards from the bank.

Gallo.

What the hell?

Forget it. Level and fire, or he'd be too late to save Catherine.

Hell, it could be too late now.

THROW THE KNIFE.

Take him down.

Gallo's hand was frozen on the hilt as he watched the man who had killed Jacobs glide toward Catherine.

Gallo had to move, but he couldn't do it. Not this time. It was as if everything was going in slow motion for him.

He could see Catherine stiffening, and knew that those wonderful instincts with which he'd become so familiar were in play.

She *knew.*

Even as he watched, he saw her whirl and start to drop to the ground as she saw her attacker.

Too late.

He was already on Catherine, a thin dagger gleaming as he raised it.

It was coming down!

She was going to die.

"No!" The agonized cry tore from Gallo's throat.

He threw the knife.

DEAR GOD, HE'S FAST, Catherine thought as she reached for the knife on her thigh.

Fall. Roll. Then stab the bastard in the gut.

But he was over her, his dagger coming down and—

He screamed as a bowie knife pierced the hand holding the knife and came out the other side!

Gallo's bowie knife. She recognized it. And Gallo standing in the water several yards away from the bank.

It gave her enough time to get her own knife out of the thigh holster.

"Dammit, get out of the way, Catherine."

She glanced toward the trees. Joe. Trying to get his shot.

She rolled to the side.

The man in the wet suit was cursing as he turned and ran toward the bayou, bent low, and zigzagging in the underbrush.

A shot.

Missed.

He jumped into the water, reached out, jerked out the knife piercing his hand, and threw it aside. He dove beneath the surface.

Catherine jumped to her feet and was at the bank of the bayou in seconds.

"Gallo, get him!" she called as she slipped off the bank into the water.

Gallo didn't answer, and she couldn't see him. The fog had come down again.

"Catherine, no!" Joe was suddenly standing on the bank beside the cypress tree. "Come back. Don't take a chance. Don't trust him."

Of course, she wasn't going to trust that murderer. He'd just tried to kill her. "It's okay, Joe. Gallo's somewhere out here, too. We'll get the bastard. He's wounded and losing blood." She was starting to swim away from the bank. "Gallo!"

"Catherine, listen to me." Joe's voice was harsh, his fists clenched at his sides. "It's Gallo I'm talking about. I saw his face. He wasn't going to throw that knife. He wasn't going to save you. Gallo didn't care if you lived or died."

Shock went through her. "No, you're wrong, Joe. He did save me. Look, I can't talk." She began swimming faster. "I'll blow my chance of getting that bastard. You'd better jump in the car and patrol the road. He might try to get out of the water as soon as he can. The blood is going to draw alligators."

"Catherine!"

She couldn't see him any longer. She was surrounded by the thick, heavy mist that felt as if it was going to smother her. She suddenly felt very much alone.

But she wasn't alone. There was a murderer out there who had been within an instant of killing her. Was he close? He could be only yards away from her and she wouldn't know it. It would be smart of him to lie in wait and ambush any pursuers. It was probably what she would have done.

Her heart was beating hard, she could feel her pulse jumping in her throat.

She stopped swimming and listened.

She heard something, a displacement of water . . . Where had it come from? Dammit, where was Gallo? She could have used someone to watch her back.

Gallo doesn't care whether you live or die.

She heard the sound again. Closer.

She tensed, her hand reached down and grabbed her knife.

Come and see what's waiting for you, you son of a bitch. I've been on my own all my life. What was I thinking? I don't need any help from Gallo or anyone else.

Come and get me.